The Perfect Mother

A *New York Times* Notable Book of the Year

"It's a premise familiar from some of Hitchcock's best
[...] people, through no fault of
[...]
[...]
[...] —*Seattle Times*

"Written with a [...]
I was eager to find out what [...] dreaded the
worst and I hoped for the best – and I won't tell
you which happens."
—*New York Times*

"The novel reads like a thriller and is brilliant at portraying
the slow, steady disintegration of a seemingly ordinary life
when secrets are unearthed and dark suspicions spread."
—*Baltimore Sun*

"As Cat becomes ever more driven, Leroy gives her daily
life a lurking undertone of menace that adds an element
of psychological mystery…creating delicious
uncertainty about the heroine."
—*Kirkus Reviews*

"This is a gripping medical mystery from an assured
writer who could be the next Minette Walters.
Highly recommended."
—*Library Journal*

"Written with the intense pace of a thriller and the brooding
concealment of a mystery novel… Leroy ultimately plumbs
the complicated depths of motherly instinct to deliver a
novel of great suspense. Did Cat intentionally hurt her
daughter to get attention? The answer will be a hard-won
surprise readers won't soon forget."
—*Minneapolis Star Tribune*

"With wonderfully descriptive writing and psychological
insight, Leroy crafts a mesmerising tale of love and fear."
— www.wordsmitten.com

The Perfect Mother

MARGARET LEROY

MIRA

Published in Great Britain 2010
MIRA Books, Eton House, 18-24 Paradise Road,
Richmond, Surrey, TW9 1SR

THE PERFECT MOTHER © Margaret Leroy 2010

This is the revised text of a work first published as POSTCARDS
FROM BERLIN by Little, Brown and Company in 2003.
© 2003 as POSTCARDS FROM BERLIN by Margaret Leroy

ISBN 978 0 7783 0352 7

59-0310

Printed in Great Britain
by Clays Ltd, St Ives plc

ACKNOWLEDGEMENTS

I am deeply grateful to my wonderful editor, Catherine Burke, for her intelligence, warmth, and commitment to my writing, and to the marvellously dynamic team at MIRA, especially Oliver Rhodes; also to my agent Kathleen Anderson for all her tireless work on my behalf, to my UK agent, Laura Longrigg, for so much empathy and insight, and to Judy Clain, my editor at Little, Brown and Company, New York. Thanks to Lucy Floyd for her perceptive comments on the book. Mick, Becky and Izzie sustained me with their love and encouragement, as always.

I am indebted to the National Children's Bureau, UK, for permission to quote from *Trust Betrayed?*, edited by Jan Horwath and Brian Lawson. Among the other books I read, there were two that I found particularly valuable: *Hurting for Love*, by Herbert A Schreier and Judith A Libow, and *The Pindown Experience and the Protection of Children*, the moving and disturbing report of the Staffordshire Child Care Inquiry conducted by Allan Levy, QC, and Barbara Kahan.

CHAPTER 1

D aisy hears them first: the crunch of feet on the gravel, the resonant clearing of throats outside our living-room window.

She darts to the window, tugs at the curtain.

'They're here,' she says.

She kneels on the sofa, presses her face to the glass. Her warm breath mists the pane.

I turn off the light, so the room is lit by the dancing red of the firelight, and go to stand beside her, pulling the curtain open. My head is close to hers; I smell the musky sweetness of her hair. Sinead hangs back, fiddling with her new velvet choker, an early Christmas present from her mother. She's reached that age when enthusiasms have to be carefully concealed; and anyway hip-hop is really more her thing.

I glance at Richard. He folds his *Times* and turns towards the window. In the shadowed room and the flickering of the firelight, I can't see if he's smiling.

'Look,' says Daisy. 'They've got snowflakes on their eyelashes.'

There are ten of them in the darkness by the steps to our front door. They're bundled in coats and scarves, the everyday colour leached from their clothes and faces by the torchlight. Their breath is thick, there are siftings of snow on their shoulders. They move around and shuffle into position. Nicky is there, in a woollen hat that hides her crisp black hair, with little reindeer dangling from her ears. She looks up at Daisy, grins and blows her a kiss. The earrings shiver.

The others have their eyes down; they're fumbling through their music books with clumsy wet-gloved fingers. There are women I recognise from Daisy's class at school, Kate's mother, Natalie's mother—women I only know by the names of their children—and men from the choir at the church round the corner, and two or three teenage children. The torches they carry suffuse their faces with red: a myriad little torches glimmer in their eyes. Next to Nicky there's a man I don't recognise. He has unruly fair hair, a darkly gleaming leather jacket; I can just make out his heavy eyebrows and the line of his jaw. Above them a nail-paring moon shines briefly through the cloud. Nicky knows what this moon is meant to mean: she's been through Feng Shui and aromatherapy and her current passion is witchcraft—the kind of bland designer witchcraft you can read about in lavish books with pastel velour covers—and she says that the moons have names, and this is the birch moon—the first moon of the year, the moon of beginnings.

The snow began this morning, with a perfect, theatrical sense of timing. In our garden, there's a milky skin of ice on the pond, and the dangling tendrils of forsythia are white knotted strands of wool, and the stone frog fountain has a hat of snow. We played snowballs, Sinead and Daisy and me, staying out far too long, not realising how chilled we were, and when we finally came back into the warmth of the kitchen Daisy's fingers were red and shiny in spite of her gloves, and she cried as the blood came back into them. I told her they hurt because they were getting better, warming up, but it didn't help to know that, she couldn't stop crying. In the cold the foxes are getting bolder, coming close to the house. This afternoon I saw them on the patio, looking in at the French window then shying away, mangy, thin, golden, one with a paw that it couldn't touch to the ground, quite silent yet leaving perfect footprints. Since then more snow has fallen, blotting out the foxes' footprints and our own, so our back garden looks as though no one has ever been there. If you went out there now, you would feel a thing you rarely feel in London, a sense of how high the sky is, of the immensity of the night.

The singers clear their throats and start to sing. Their faces are lifted, eager, their breath like smoke. Singing voices sound different outside, fragile, thinner, half their resonance swallowed up by the air; yet so precise and perfect. I see the ships in my mind's eye: they're like the ships in a toddler's picture book, with rainbow-painted prows and many silken sails, playful, gaudy, cresting the curled waves.

Daisy gives a little sigh and rests her head against me. Sinead comes close, sits on the arm of the sofa. They're both thoroughly irreverent, they have their own salacious parodies of carols, picked up in the playground, yet they're held, stilled, by the song. The room smells of cinnamon and warm wine, of the forest freshness of juniper, of the apple-cake that is cooling in the kitchen, moist and sweet and crusted on top with sugar. I want to hold this moment, to make it last for ever, the scents and the singing and firelight and Daisy's head against me.

There's a long still moment after the end of the song, like a held breath. Then Daisy applauds extravagantly, and I turn on the lights and hurry to the door and open it wide.

There are seven stone steps up to our door. Nicky comes first, bounding up two at a time. She's pink-skinned, eager-eyed.

'Catriona—you look so *good*.'

I kiss her; her face is cold.

'Were we brilliant?' she says.

'You were wonderful.'

She pulls off her hat, shakes out her spiky hair. Wetness

sprays from her, the reindeer earrings dance. She holds out the Christian Aid tin, rattles it hopefully. Daisy puts in our money, with a satisfactory clatter.

The others follow her, noisily talking; they are themselves again, separate, banal, the braid of music that bound them together unwoven. They shrug off their wet heavy clothes; the powdering of snow on their hair is melting already. They stretch out their arms and relish the warmth. The house is suddenly full of noise, of energy.

I bring the saucepan from the kitchen and dole the wine into tumblers. Daisy and Sinead hand the glasses round, carrying them like precious things, holding them right at the top so as not to burn their fingers. I see their heads as they weave their way through the crush: Sinead with hair that's dark and thick like her mother's, pulled back and fastened with a flower scrunchie; and Daisy, blonde like me.

Nicky, passing, whispers in my ear: 'D'you like my new recruit?' She gestures rather obviously towards the man in the leather jacket.

I nod.

'Fergal O'Connor. He's a sweetie—bringing up his little boy on his own. Jamie goes to St Mark's, I think. Remind me to introduce you.'

She moves off to talk to Richard.

I chat for a while to Kate's mother and Natalie's mother. They drink eagerly, cradling the tumblers between their hands to warm them.

Natalie's mother looks greedily round the room.

'Nice house,' she says.

Her teeth are already stained purple by the wine.

I shrug a little. 'Well, we're so lucky to live here.'

'I'll say.' Her fervour isn't quite polite.

They talk about their children: about homework, what a pain, quite honestly you end up having to do it yourself; and the eleven-plus and how ghastly it is, last year some girls were so nervous, they puked up before they went in; and whether eight is really too young for your child to have her first mobile.

These themes are familiar and I only half join in. I look round the room, feeling a warm sense of satisfaction, seeing it with Natalie's mother's eyes, recognising what I have achieved here. Because any woman might look at it now in that greedy appraising way. Yet when Richard and I first came here, and walked between the stone dogs and up the seven steps, and the woman from Foxton's unlocked and ushered us in, I felt such uncertainty. It was empty; it smelt musty, unused, and there were green streaks of damp, and horrible flowered wallpaper. But it still had a kind of grandeur, with its parquet floors and cornices and mantelpieces of marble, suggesting to me a whole way of life that I'd probably gleaned from TV costume drama: men taking a rest from empire building who warm their backs at the fire, port, political conversations. I couldn't begin to imagine that I could feel at home in these imposing spaces. I walked round the edge of this room, my footsteps echoing in the emptiness, and felt flimsy, insubstantial, as though I might float to the ceiling, as though nothing weighed me down. Richard put his arm round me—he did that often then—and I felt his warmth, his weight, his opulent smell of cigars and aftershave, grounding me, making me real. And the estate agent, a pleasant woman, canny about such things, read my hesitation. 'Let me show you something,' she said. She took us through the French windows and into the garden. It was big for a town garden, and secluded, with a round rose bed, badly neglected, just a few tattered rags of roses still clinging to the gangly blood-red stems, and a pond, empty of water, with weeds growing up from the concrete. The starlings in the birch tree were puffed up with the cold, like fruit ready to fall. There were wormcasts in the grass and water lying on the lawn and it all terribly needed tending. But the lovely shapes of it were there—the rosebed and the pond and the way the trees leaned in around the lawn, encircling it with a kind of intimacy. And I saw how it could be, saw the stone frog spewing water from his wide cheerful mouth, saw the lily pads and the old-fashioned roses, palest pink and amber, single flowers not lasting long but scented, clambering up the wall.

From that moment it was easy. We bought it and moved in, and I knew just what to do with it, decorating most of it myself. I seemed to expand to fill the space; it started to feel right for me. And now it is all as it should be, elegant, established, with velvet curtains and tiebacks with tassels and heavy pelmets edged with plum-coloured braid. Our things look right here, in this setting, everything seems to fit: Richard's Chinese vases and his violin, and the two ceramic masks, one white, one black, that we brought back from our honeymoon, and a little painting I did of a poppy, that I thought was maybe good enough to frame and go up on the wall; and on the mantelpiece there's a cardboard Nativity scene, intricate, in rich dark colours, that I bought from Benjamin Pollock's toyshop in Covent Garden. The Nativity scene was my choice, not the girls'; they'd probably have gone for something more contemporary and plastic. But I love traditional things— I'm always hunting them out, in junk shops and on market stalls: things made to old designs, or with a patina of use, a bit of history. Like when I'd decorated Daisy's room, the floors stripped and varnished to a pale honey colour, the ceiling night-sky blue with a stencilling of stars, and I knew there was something missing. It needed something old, loved, a teddy bear to sit in the cane chair, an old bear with bits of fur worn off, like people sometimes keep in trunks in their attics. And I wondered what it would be like to have had a childhood that left such traces—old toys, photos perhaps—things that are worn with use, with loving, to store away then come upon years later and show to your own children, with a little stir of sentiment or mildly embarrassed amusement or nostalgia. In the end I found a bear in a department store: it had old-fashioned curly fur and was dressed in Edwardian clothes, but it smelt of the factory. I bought it anyway. It was the best I could do.

The women are reminiscing about their children's toy

obsessions. Natalie's mother, who has four children, re-members Tamagotchis, these pocket computer animals that you had to feed and care for; the mothers had to look after them while the children were at school. I'm only half listening. Over their shoulders I can see Richard talking to somebody's teenage daughter. He looks too smart for the company in his jacket and tie—he isn't very good at casual dressing. The girl is perhaps eighteen, just a little younger than I was when he met me. She's wearing a sleeveless top despite the snow, showing off her prettily sloping shoulders. Her arms are thin and white and her hair is watered silk and she has a big gleamy smile. I can tell he's charming her; he comes from that privileged class of men who are always charming—perhaps most charming—with strangers. And Richard likes young women; it's what he was drawn to in me, that new gloss. I know I'm not like I was when first we met: I don't have that sheen any more.

Nicky is next to Richard, talking to the man with the unruly hair. She's getting in close—not surprising, really, he's quite attractive. Now that she's taken off her coat, she looks like a picture from a magazine. There's something altogether contemporary about Nicky. She loves biker boots and little tartan skirts, and she works at an adver-tising agency, where, in spite of—or maybe because of—the niceness and easygoingness of Neil, her husband, who is an inventive cook and a devoted parent, she ex-changes erotic e-mails with the creative director. 'You see, we're not like you and Richard,' she says to me sometimes, leaning across the table at the Café Rouge towards me. 'You two are so transparently everything to each other. I mean, it's wonderful if you can be like that—if you've got that kind of marriage—what could be lovelier? But Neil and I aren't like that, especially since the kids. I don't think I'm built to be completely faithful, it's just not in my genes…'

She feels my eyes on her. She turns, speaks to the man again. They come towards me. Kate's mother and Natalie's mother move away.

He smiles at me. His eyes are grey and steady. Nicky puts her hand on my arm.

'Meet Fergal,' she says. 'Our latest recruit. A tenor. Tenors are like gold dust. I love my tenors to bits.'

I smile. He says hello. I remember how much I like Irish voices.

She takes her last bite of apple-cake and licks her sugary fingers. 'Catriona, your cooking is out of this world. I have to have more of this.'

Sinead walks past with a plate. Nicky lunges after her.

My boots have high heels and my eyes are just on a level with his. We look at one another and there's a brief embarrassed pause.

'I liked the carols,' I tell him. Then think how vacuous this sounds.

'Well,' he says, and shrugs a little. 'It's been fun.'

I note the past tense. I rapidly decide that he's not the sort of man who'd like me. I know how I must seem to him, a privileged sheltered woman.

'Nicky's good at arranging things,' I say. 'Making things happen.'

He nods vaguely. He's looking over my shoulder—I've bored him already.

But then I see he is looking at my picture—the painting of poppies that I hung on the wall. It's just behind me.

'Who did the painting?' he says.

'I did.'

'I wondered if it was you,' he says. 'I like it.'

I feel a little embarrassed, but acknowledge to myself that I am quite pleased with this painting. The petals are that dark purple that is almost black, yet there's a gleam on them.

'I don't do much,' I say. 'It just makes a nice break. I can hide away in my attic and the girls know not to disturb me. I suppose it's a bit conceited to put it up on the wall.'

'D'you always do that?' he says.

'Do what?'

'Run yourself down like that?'

'Probably. I guess it's irritating.'

We both smile.

'When you paint, is it always flowers?' he says.

'Always. I can't do people. I'm really limited.'

He looks at me quizzically. His eyes are full of laughter.

'OK, I know I'm doing it again,' I say. 'But it's true. And I can't draw out of my head either. It has to be something I can put on the table in front of me. I can only paint what I see.'

'D'you sell them?' he says.

I nod, flattered he should ask. 'There's a gift shop in town that takes them sometimes.'

He turns to look at it again. 'It's not very cheerful. For a flower. It's kind of ominous. All that shadow around it.'

'Really. How can you read all that into a picture?' But I'm pleased. There's something rather trivial about doing paintings of flowers and selling them in a gift shop alongside scented candles and boxed sets of soap. I like that he can see a kind of darkness in it.

I realise I am happy. My body fluid and easy with the wine, my room hospitable, beautiful, this man with the Irish lilt in his voice approving of my picture; this is easy, this is how things should be.

He's looking at me with those steady grey eyes. There's something in his look that I can't work out: sex, or something else, more obscure, more troubling.

'I know you,' he says suddenly. 'Don't I?'

I laugh politely. 'I don't think so.'

Someone is leaving. The door opens, the cold and the night come in.

'I do,' he says. 'I'm sure I know you. I recognise your face.'

He's staring at me, trying to work it out. It sounds like a come-on, but his look is puzzled, serious. The fear that is never far from me lays its cold hand on my skin.

'Well, I don't know where you could have seen me.' My voice is casual, light. 'Perhaps the school gate at St Mark's? Daisy goes there.' But I know this isn't right, I know I'd have noticed him. 'Nicky says that's where your little boy goes,' I add, trying to drag the conversation away to somewhere safe.

He shakes his head. 'Jamie doesn't start till after Christmas.'

'You'll like it,' I tell him. 'Daisy's eight, she's in year three, she has the nicest teacher…'

But he won't let it rest. 'Where d'you work?' he says.

'I don't.' Then, biting back the urge to apologise for my life, which must sound so passive— 'I mean, not outside the home. I used to work in a nursery school before I got married. But that's ages ago now.'

'It wasn't there. Forget it. It doesn't matter.'

But I'm upset and he knows it. He tries to carry on, he asks what I'm painting now, but the mood is spoilt, it can't be restored or recovered. As soon as he decently can, he leaves me. All evening I feel troubled: even when the singers have gone, calling out their thanks and Christmas wishes, setting off into the snow which is falling more thickly now, casting its nets over everything, under the chill thin light of the moon of beginnings.

We stand there in the suddenly quiet room. It looks banal now. There are cake crumbs on the carpet, and every glass has a purplish, spicy sediment.

'I'll do the washing-up,' says Richard.

Normally I'd say, No, let me, you sit down, but tonight I give in gratefully. Sinead goes to help him.

I turn off the light again, and the firelight plays on

every shiny surface. My living room seems like a room from another time. I stretch out on the sofa. Daisy comes and folds herself into me. Her limbs are loose, heavy, her skin is hot and dry; I feel her tiredness seeping into me.

'Did you enjoy it?' I ask her.

To my surprise, she shakes her head. In the red erratic firelight, her face looks sharper, thinner. Little bright flames glitter in her eyes. Suddenly, without warning, she starts crying.

I hug her. 'It's ever so late,' I tell her. 'You'll be fine in the morning.' She rubs her damp face against me.

I don't want her to go to sleep unhappy. I can never bear it when she's sad—which is silly really, I know that, because children often cry, but I always rush in to smooth things over, want to keep everything perfect. So I try to distract her with shadow shapes, the animal patterns I learnt how to make from a booklet I bought from the toyshop in Covent Garden. I move my hands in the beam of light from the open door to the hall, casting shadows across the wall by the fireplace. I make the seagull, flapping my hands together; and the crab, my fingers hunched, so it sidles along the mantelpiece; and the alligator, snapping at the board games on the bookshelf. Daisy wipes her face and starts to smile.

I make the shape of the weasel; we wait and wait, Daisy holding her breath: this is her favourite. And just when you've stopped expecting it, it comes, the weasel's pounce, down into some poor defenceless thing behind the skirting board.

She lets out a brief thrilled scream, and even I start a little. Yet these animals, these teeth, this predatoriness: these are only the shadows of my hands.

CHAPTER 2

S inead comes into our bedroom in her dressing
gown, her face and hair rumpled with sleep.
'Cat. Dad. Daisy's ill.'

I'm reluctant to leave the easy warmth of bed, and
Richard, still asleep, curving into me. It's one of those
quiet days after Christmas, the turn of the year, when all
the energy seems withdrawn from the world. A little light
leaks round the edges of the curtains. I turn back the
duvet, gently, so as not to wake him, and pull down my
nightdress, which is long and loose, like a T-shirt, the kind

of thing I started to wear when Daisy needed feeding in the night, and then got rather attached to.

I go to Daisy's room. The stars glimmer on her ceiling in the glow from the lamp I leave on all night. I push back the curtain. Thin gilded light falls across the floor, where various soft toys and yesterday's clothes are scattered. Her favourite cuddly sheep, Hannibal, is flung to the foot of her bed. He owes his name to Sinead, who once saw *The Silence of the Lambs* illicitly at a friend's house, having promised they were borrowing *27 Dresses*. Daisy is still in bed, but awake. She has a strained, stretched look on her face, and her eyes are huge, dilated by the dark.

'I feel sick,' she says.

'What a shame, sweetheart.' I put my hand on her forehead, but she feels quite cool. 'Especially today.'

'What day is it?' she says.

A little ill-formed anxiety worms its way into my mind.

'It's the pantomime. Granny and Grandad are taking us.'

'I don't want to go,' she says.

'But you were so looking forward to it.' Inside I'm cursing a little, anticipating Richard's reaction. 'Snow White. It's sure to be fun.'

'I can't,' she says. 'I can't, Mum. I feel sick and my legs hurt.'

Daisy always gets nauseous when she gets ill. They each have their own fingerprint of symptoms. Sinead, when she was younger, would produce dazzling high temperatures, epic fevers, when she'd suddenly sit up straight in bed and pronounce in a clear bright shiny voice, the things she said as random and meaningless as sleep-talk, yet sounding full of significance. Daisy gets sickness and stomach aches. She's been like that from a baby, when she used to get colic in the middle of the night, and I'd walk her up and down the living room with the TV on, watching old black and white films, or in desperation take her into the kitchen, where the soft thick rush of the cooker hood might soothe her at last into sleep.

I go downstairs to make coffee; I'll take a cup to Richard before I tell him. It's a blue icy day, the ground hard and white, a lavish sky; but the fat glittery icicles that hang from the corner of the shed are iridescent, starting to drip. Soon the thaw will set in. It's very still, no traffic noise: the sunk sap of the year. With huge gratitude, I feel the day's first caffeine sliding into my veins.

When I go back upstairs with the coffee, Sinead has drifted off to her bedroom and her iPod.

Richard opens one eye.

'Daisy's ill,' I tell him.

'Christ. That's just what we needed. What's wrong?'

'Some sort of virus. I'm not sure she can come.'

'For goodness' sake, she's only got to sit through a pantomime.'

'She's not well, Richard.'

'They were really looking forward to it.'

'So was she. I mean, she's not doing this deliberately.'

He sits up, sprawls back on the pillow and yawns, disordered by sleep, his face lined by the creases in the pillowslip. He looks older first thing in the morning, and away from the neat symmetries of his work clothes.

'Give her some Calpol,' he says. 'She'll probably be fine.'

'She feels too sick,' I tell him.

'You're so soft with those children.' There's an edge of irritation to his voice.

I feel I should at least try. I get the Calpol from the bathroom cabinet, take it to her room and pour it into the spoon, making a little comedy act of it. Normally she likes to see this, the sticky recalcitrant liquid that won't go where you want it to, that glops and lurches away from you. Now she watches me with a slightly desperate look.

'I can't, Mum. I feel too sick.'

I take the spoon to the bathroom and tip it down the sink. Richard has heard it all.

'Oh, for goodness' sake, let me do it,' he says.

He gets up, pulls on his dressing gown, goes to get the Calpol. But when he sees her pallor, he softens a little.

'Dad, I'm not going to,' she says. 'Please don't make me.'

He ruffles her hair. 'Just try for me, OK, munchkin?'

I watch from the door as she parts her lips a little. She's more willing to try for him; she's always so hungry to please him. He eases the spoon into her mouth. She half swallows the liquid, then noisily retches it up.

He steps smartly back.

'Sorry, sweetheart. Maybe that wasn't such a good idea.'

He wipes her mouth and kisses the top of her head, penitent. He follows me back to the bathroom.

'OK,' he says. 'You stay. It's a damn shame, though,

when they've paid for the tickets and everything. Especially when Mother hasn't been well.'

I think of them: Adrian, his affable father; and Gina, his mother, who favours a country casual look, although they live in chic urbanity in Putney, who reads horticultural magazines and cultivates an esoteric window box, who reminisces at some length about her job as an orthodontist's receptionist. There's something about Gina I find difficult: I feel colourless, passive, beside her. It's not anything she says; she's always nice to me, says, 'You and Richard are so good together.' Sometimes I feel there's a subtext that I'm so much more satisfactory than Sara, Richard's highly assertive first wife. But it's almost as though it's hard to breathe around her, as if she uses up all the air.

'Daisy can write them a letter when she's well,' I say.

'It's not the same,' he says, frowning.

Richard's intense involvement with his parents fascinates me. I know that's how it must be for most people, to have your parents there and on your side, to worry about them and care what they think about you; yet to me this is another country.

Sinead comes down when I'm making breakfast, still in her dressing gown but fully made-up, with her iPod. She takes one earpiece out to talk to me.

'Cat, I really need your opinion. D'you think I look like a transvestite?'

'You look gorgeous.' I put an arm around her.

It's part of my role with her, to be a big sister, a confidante, to be soft when Richard is stern.

'Are you sure my mascara looks all right?' she says. 'I'm worried my left eyelashes look curlier than my right ones.'

'You're a total babe. Look, I've made you some toast.'

'How is she?' she says then.

'I don't think she can come.'

She sits heavily down at the table, a frown like Richard's stitched into her forehead.

'Do I have to go, then?' she says.

She's cross. She's too old to go to the pantomime without her little sister. Daisy was the heart of today's outing, its reason and justification: without her it doesn't make sense.

I put my arm round her. 'Just do it, my love. To please Granny and Grandad.'

'Snow fucking White,' she says. 'Jesus.'

I overlook this. 'You never know, you might enjoy bits of it.'

'Oh, yeah? You know what it'll be like. There'll be a man in drag whose boobs keep falling down and lots of *EastEnders* jokes, and at the end they'll throw Milky Ways at us and we're meant to be, like, *grateful.*'

She puts her earpiece back in without waiting for my response.

They leave at twelve, Sinead now fully dressed in jeans and leather jacket and the Converse trainers she had for Christmas, resigned. I go to Daisy's room. She's sitting up, writing something, and I briefly wonder if Richard was right and I was too soft and I should have made her go. But she still has that stretched look.

She waves her clipboard at me. She's made a list of breeds of cats she likes, in order of preference.

'I still want one,' she says.

'I know.'

'When can we, Mum?'

'One day,' I tell her.

'You always say maybe or one day,' she says. 'I want to really know. I want you to tell me *exactly*.'

I rearrange her pillows so she can lie down, and I read to her for a while, from a book of fairy tales I bought her for Christmas. There's a story about a princess who's meant to marry a prince, but she falls in love with the gardener; and he shows her secret things, the apricots warm on the wall, the clutch of eggs, blue as the sky, that are hidden in the pear tree. I read it softly, willing her to sleep, but she just lies there listening. She's pale, almost translucent, with shadows like bruises under her eyes. Maybe it's my attention that's keeping her awake. Eventually I tell her I'm going to make a coffee.

When I look in on her ten minutes later, she's finally drifted off, arms and legs flung out. There's a randomness to it, as though she was turning over and was suddenly snared by sleep. I put my hand on her forehead and she stirs but doesn't wake. I feel a deep sense of relief, knowing the sleep will heal her.

This is an unexpected gift: an afternoon with nothing to do, with no one needing anything; a gift of time to be slowly unwrapped and relished. I stand there for a moment, listening to the quiet of the house, which seems strange, so soon after Christmas, when these rooms have so recently been full of noise and people; it's almost as though the house is alive and gently breathing. Then I go up to the attic, moving slowly through the silence.

I push open the door. The scents of my studio welcome me: turps, paint, the musty, over-sweet smell of dying flowers. From one of the little arched windows I can see across the roofs towards the park. I lean there for a moment, looking out. There's a velvet bloom of dust on the sill; I rarely clean in here. I can see the tall bare trees and their many colours, pink, apricot, purple, where the buds are forming at the ends of their branches, and the dazzling sky with a slow silent aeroplane lumbering towards Heathrow.

I put on the shirt I always wear up here. Richard doesn't like to see me in it; he hates me in baggy clothes. But I welcome its scruffiness and sexlessness, the way it says Now I am painting—the way it defines me as someone who is engaged in this one thing.

Here is everything I need: thick expensive paper, and 4B pencils that make soft smudgy lines, and acrylic paints, and watercolours with those baroque names that I love—cadmium yellow and prussian blue and crimson alizarin. And there are things I've collected, postcards and pictures torn from magazines, a print I cut from a calendar—a Georgia O'Keeffe painting of an orchid, very sexualised; I laughed when Sinead stared at it and raised one eyebrow and said, 'She might as well have called it,

"Come on in, boys."' And there are pebbles from the beach at Brighton, and bits of wood from the park, and a vase of lilies I brought here when the petals started to fall.

I feel a kind of certainty. There's a clear dark purpose at the heart of me, a seriousness; today I will be able to work well.

I pick up a piece of bark, and see, in the thin golden light, that its soft dull brownness is made of many colours. I take out the pastel crayons and start to draw, using the blues and reds I see there, melding them together. I love this—how you can look intently at the quiet surfaces of things, and see such vividness.

There's a part of my mind that is focused, intent, and part that is floating free. Images drift through my mind, faces: Sinead in her new Christmas make-up, pretty and troubled; Richard, thin-lipped, annoyed with me and with Daisy. They'll be at the pantomime by now. Snow White will be a soap star in a blonde extravagant wig, and the Queen perhaps a man in taffeta and corsets, playing it for laughs. Yet she can be so scary, this Queen, like in the Disney film *Snow White* I saw when I was a child; I remember her shadow, sharp as though cut with a blade, looming and filling the screen. And I see Nicky at the carol-singing, her eager face and her dancing reindeer earrings; and thinking of Nicky I think, too, of Fergal O'Connor. And as I think of him, immediately I'm touching him, putting out my hands and moving them over his face, his head, feeling the precise texture of his skin. He is quite still, watching me. I feel the warmth of him through the palms of my hands. This shocks me, the precision of this picture—when I wasn't sure I even liked him.

I draw on, in the suspended stillness. The drawing takes shape, but I don't know yet if it pleases me. For the moment, I'm not judging it or wondering whether it's any good or whether people will like it, just moving my hand on the page. There's a compulsion to it, as though I don't have a choice. Soon the light will dim; already pools of shadow are collecting in the corners. I draw quickly, with rapid little strokes in many colours, wanting to get it finished before it's dark.

When the doorbell rings, I jump, I'm so lost in my own world, and the crayon makes a random jagged mark across the page. My first impulse is not to go, it's such a long way down. But then it rings again, and I worry that Daisy will wake, requiring drinks and comfort, so I run down the two flights of stairs, through the gathering dark of the house.

It's Monica, our neighbour.

'Sorry to disturb you,' she says.

She's wearing a tracksuit and running shoes: she's off for a jog in the park. Her two red setters are with her, milling around at the foot of the steps. She's bright-eyed and virtuous, and the cold has already brought a flush to her cheeks.

'That's OK,' I tell her. 'I was up in the attic.'

While I've been drawing the world has changed. There are sounds of water and a wet smell, and our breath smokes white in the raw air. As we stand at the door there's a noise from the roof like tearing cloth, and a lump of snow slides off and spatters on the gravel.

'Nice Christmas?'

'Great, thanks,' I say routinely.

Her hair is very short and in the dim light she has an androgynous, classical look: Diana hunting with her dogs, perhaps, or some figure from a Greek frieze that I saw once with Richard in Athens, a taut young runner bringing news of slaughters and defeats.

'These came for you while we were away,' she says.

She thrusts two envelopes at me. I glance down at them: one is for Daisy, with a local postmark, probably a school friend, a child who was away at the end of term and missed the school postbox; the other comes from abroad and I recognise the writing. I have to control an urge to thrust this letter straight back at her.

She watches me. Perhaps she sees some trouble in my face, that she misreads as criticism.

'We've been away,' she says again, a bit apologetic. 'Or I'd have brought them round earlier.'

'No, no. It's fine. They're just Christmas cards anyway.'

'It wasn't our usual postman,' she says.

She's moving from one foot to the other, wired up and keen to be off. The dogs skulk and circle at the foot of the steps, vivid and nervy, damp mouths open.

'Thanks anyway,' I tell her.

'We must have coffee some time,' she says. As we always say.

'I'd like that.'

And she's off, jogging down the steps, pounding across the damp gravel, the dogs streaming out in front of her.

I put Daisy's card on the hall stand; I'll take it to her when she wakes.

I go into the kitchen, sit at the table, hold the other envelope out in front of me. My heart is noisy. It enters my head that this is why Daisy is ill, as though everything is connected, as though this letter brings ill fortune with it, clinging like an unwholesome smell of past things, a smell of mothballs and stale cigarettes and old discarded clothing.

The house has lost its sense of ease; it feels alert, edgy. I hear the little kitchen noises, a drumming like fingertips in the central heating, the breathing of the fridge, and outside the creak and drip of the thaw. I tear at the envelope.

It's a perfectly ordinary card: a Christmas tree, very conventional, with 'Season's Greetings' in gilt letters in German and French and English.

I open it. At the top, an address, printed and underlined. The handwriting is careful, rather childlike.

Trina, darling. 'Someone we know' gave me your address. What a stroke of luck!! The above is where I'm living now. Please PLEASE write.

There's an assumption of intimacy about the way it isn't signed that I resent and certainly don't share. Like the way a lover will say on the phone, 'It's me.'

I look at my hands clasped tight on the table in front

of me. I notice the way the veins stick out, the pale varnish that is beginning to peel, the white skin. I feel that they have nothing to do with me.

I sit there for a while, then I get up and put the card in the paper recycling bin, tucked under yesterday's *Times,* where it can't be seen.

I long for Richard to be here, but they won't be back for hours; it's only four o'clock—they'll still be in the theatre. It's the interval perhaps; they'll be talking politely and eating sugared popcorn. I want Richard to hold me. Suddenly I hate the way we've let our love leak away through a hundred little cracks, like this morning, the irritation, the disagreements over Calpol; and my fantasy about Fergal O'Connor embarrasses and shames me. Stupid to think such things, when I love and need Richard so much. Without him I feel thin, etiolated as though I have no substance. As though I'm a cardboard cutout, a figure in that Nativity scene on the mantelpiece: intricately detailed, looking, in a dim light, almost solid—yet two-dimensional, with no substance, nothing to weigh me down. Only Richard can hold me and make me real.

CHAPTER 3

The house has a fresh January feel, everything swept and gleaming. All the decorations, that some time after Christmas lost their gloss, as though their sheen had actually tarnished over, have been packed away in boxes in the attic. There are daffodils in a blue jug on the kitchen table; they're buds still, green but swelling. Tomorrow they will open, and already you can smell the pollen through the thin green skin. And we have all made resolutions: Sinead to stop biting her nails; Richard to drink wine instead of whisky; Daisy to have a cat—though Sinead protested at this, as she felt it didn't quite qualify as a resolution; and I have resolved to take my painting more seriously. And to that end, today, the first day of term, I am going, all on my own, to an exhibition that I read about in the paper, at the Tate Modern. It is called Insomnia and this is its final week. It is a series of sketches by Louise Bourgeois, done in the night, fantastical—dandelion clocks, and tunnels made of hair, and a cat with a high-heeled shoe in its mouth. And I shall buy a catalogue, like a proper artist, and be inspired, perhaps, and start to draw quite differently: not just flowers, but pictures from my mind.

I am dressed to go straight to the station after dropping Daisy at school. I have a new long denim coat, stylishly shabby, that I chose from an austere expensive shop, with unsmiling scented assistants and very few clothes on the rails: my Christmas present from Richard. It's cunningly shaped, clinging to the body then flaring towards the hem, and almost too long so you'd trip without high-heeled shoes, and it's dyed a smudgey black, like ink, and the fabric feels opulently heavy. Not the sort of thing I'd ever normally wear to the school gate; but today I shall wear it. The thought of my outing gives me a fat happy feeling.

I make toast. Sinead is packing her bag in the hall, cursing under her breath. Yesterday we had the usual end-of-holiday panic: she'd just come back from Sara's, and she suddenly thought of an essay that had to be done, on something complex to do with the growth of fascism in the thirties, and therefore requiring major parental input. Richard was provoked into a rare outburst of irritation with her.

'For God's sake, Sinead. How the hell did this happen? You've had the whole bloody holiday.'

She shrugged, immaculately innocent, with an expression that said this was nothing to do with her.

'I forgot,' she said.

Then Daisy, who's now recovered from her flu though still not eating properly, decided we had to go shopping: there were girls who'd given her Christmas presents and she'd had nothing for them. Even at eight that intricate web of female relationship, of things given and owed, of best friends and outsiders, is beginning to be woven. So we bought some flower hairclips from Claire's Accessories, and found an obliging Internet site so Sinead could finish her essay, and today we are organised: clothes washed, lunchboxes packed, everything as it should be.

It's a windy busy morning. Large pale brown chestnut leaves torn from the tree in Monica's garden litter our lawn. The letterbox keeps rattling as though there are many phantom postmen. When this happens, I jump.

Daisy comes downstairs dressed for school, neat and precise, but her face is white. I put some toast in front of her.

'D'you want honey?'

'I'm not hungry,' she says.

She sits neatly in front of it, her hands in her lap, looking at the toast but not touching it.

'Try and eat something,' I say.

'I don't want anything,' she says.

I can't send her to school with nothing inside her.

'Perhaps a Mars Bar—just this once?' I'm a bit conspiratorial, expecting gratitude.

'I don't want one,' she says.

Sinead leaves to catch her bus, her body misshapen from the weight of the bag she carries on her shoulder. She wears her uniform according to the girls' illicit dress code: her skirt rolled at the waistline so it's far too short, bracelets of peace beads hidden under her cuffs, her socks pushed down and tucked inside her shoes.

I brush Daisy's hair in front of the big mirror that hangs over the fireplace. Her fair hair is thick, lavish, the brush won't go right through it. I've washed it with shampoo that smells of mangoes; a faint fruit scent hangs about her.

'Will you be at home today?' she says.

'No, sweetheart, I'm going to an exhibition.'

'Oh,' she says. Her face collapses a little, as though she is going to cry. I run my hand down her cheek. Her skin is cold.

We go out to the car. The wind sneaks under the collars of our coats. Above the roofs of the houses, dark birds are swirled around like leaves in the millstream of the sky.

There's a sudden ferociousness to the traffic, now term has started. Daisy sits quite silently in the car.

'I wonder what Megan had for Christmas,' I say cheerfully.

She doesn't reply. I look at her in the rear-view mirror; she is crying silently, slow tears edging down her white face.

'Sweetheart, what's the matter?'

'I feel sick,' she says.

'Are you worried about something?'

She shakes her head.

'You'll be fine once you get there. You'll see Abi and Megan, catch up with everything.'

Her tears always bring a lump to my throat, and then a kind of worry that she has such power over me, a feeling that this shouldn't be, that it's weak, ineffectual. I know I'm overprotective, that I find it hard to tolerate my child being unhappy. That I'm not like other women, with their anoraks and certainty. I know this is a flaw in me.

We park down the road from school. I give her a tissue and she wipes her eyes.

'Is my nose red?' she says.

'You look great,' I tell her.

'You didn't answer my question, Mum,' she says.

In the road outside school, there's the usual stand-off, two lines of traffic facing one another. There are parents who persist in dropping their children here, optimism triumphing over experience; they hoot futilely but nobody can move. Children mill round in padded winter coats, some of them newly purchased and a little too large; they're moving fast and anarchically, as though the wildness of the weather is inside them. People have changed over the holiday. One child looks cute in new glasses, another has visibly grown. Natalie's mother, who so liked my house, is pulling at a frenetic puppy. Someone else, hugely pregnant in December, has her immaculate baby in a sling. The baby still has that translucent unfinished look, so you feel if you held his hand to the light, perhaps you would see straight through. The sight pulls at women's eyes and the same expression crosses all their faces, eyes widening, as though this is still a surprise. Crocuses are coming up in the lawn in front of the school; they have the tender colours of paint mixed with too much water, a fragile buttery yellow, and purple, pale as the veins inside a woman's wrist. It's only been a fortnight, and there's so much that is new.

We're holding hands as we walk towards the gate; her hand is tightening in mine. I look down at her. Her face is set, taut.

'D'you want me to wait with you till the bell goes?'

I offer this as a choice, though really I have no choice: her hand is wrapped around mine like a bandage. She nods but doesn't speak.

We stand there together by the gate as the children surge forward. The wind blows my hair in my mouth, but I'm holding Daisy with one hand and her lunchbox with the other, and I can't push it back. My black denim coat, though stylish, is a little too cold for the day. We hear broken-off bits of conversation, blown round us like fallen leaves. Someone is making a complicated arrangement for tonight, involving tea and maths and ballet classes; someone else had fifteen to dinner for Christmas, and honestly it was like a military operation...

Over the heads of the children, I see the back of a man's neck, his leather-jacketed shoulders, his rumpled head. It's Fergal with his little boy. He must have walked straight past me. This makes me uncomfortable. I don't know if he's forgotten me, or simply hasn't seen me. I start to feel unreal with no one to talk to.

And then Nicky is there, her children tugging at her, the ends of her stripy scarf streaming out behind her. Her smile warms me through.

'Wow!' she says. 'So this is the coat. Fabulous! I am *green.*'

'Thanks,' I say.

As always she's rushing, everything on the most feverish of schedules, dropping off the boys before jumping into her car and heading off to her other life at Praxis, the advertising agency. But she sees that Daisy is troubled and she ruffles her hair with her hand.

'Not feeling too good, lambchop?' she says. 'Trust me, you're not the only one. I hate the first day of term. Neil had to positively kick me out of bed.'

She pats Daisy's shoulder; Daisy doesn't turn to her. The boys pull at her, and she's off, her scarf fringes flapping.

The bell rings.

'There we go,' I say, bending to kiss the top of Daisy's head.

She wraps herself around me.

'Come on, sweetheart.'

I try to prise her fingers away from my hand, but they stick like pieces of Elastoplast.

'Mum, I can't do this,' she says. 'Don't make me.'

I cannot disentangle her from me. I know this is ridiculous, but I can't.

People are looking at us with unconcealed curiosity. There are all these warnings in my head, slogans from the war between parents and children. They do try it on… Give them an inch… And I hear Gina at her most dogmatic, pronouncing on the pitfalls of modern parenting: You don't want to go the brown rice and sandals route, you've got to show them who's boss…

'Sweetheart, you'll be fine when you get into class.'

She is crying openly now, shivering with it. She doesn't even seem to hear me.

'Come on, let's go in together.'

I try to move towards the gate, but the whole weight of her body is pressed against me.

'I can't, Mum,' she says again.

Fergal passes, coming out. He looks at me and nods but doesn't smile, recognising my difficulty. Embarrassment washes hotly across my skin.

Something gives way inside me.

'OK. We'll go home,' I tell her.

I bend and hug her, burying my face in the mango smell of her hair. Immediately she stops crying, though she's shivering still. I have a sudden doubt: if only I'd pushed a little harder, I could have got her into class. I feel a pang for the exhibition, for the cat with the high-heeled shoe and the tunnels made of hair. Now I will never see them. But it's done, we can't go back. The front of my new black denim coat is damp where she's been crying against me.

CHAPTER 4

I wake in the night and immediately all the sleepiness falls from me. I hear the night sounds, the clock at St Agatha's emptily striking three, a siren, the staccato bark of a fox as he ranges along the backs of the houses. Beside me, Richard snores softly.

There in the cold darkness, my mind is clear, free of the day's clutter, like a quiet pool. I'm alert, taut: I could run with the fox for miles. In that clarity, I start to add up all the food that Daisy has eaten for the last few days. Yesterday: a packet of crisps and about three spoonfuls of rice with gravy at tea-time. The day before yesterday: two water biscuits and half a packet of crisps. The day before that, I can't quite remember: perhaps it was a piece of apple and half a chocolate crispy cake from a whole batch I made.

I've tried so hard to tempt her, cooked all her favourite things, offered them to her with that warm abundant feeling that fills you when you make good food for your children. Tomato soup from fresh tomatoes, ripe to the point of sweetness, with fennel and herbs for their green flavour, just a few so there wouldn't be lots of leafy bits, and a swirl of cream on top. Fried chicken and noodles, her favourite, and a sponge cake with a lavish filling of strawberry conserve. Daisy helped me, sieving the icing sugar on top, making an intricate pattern of crescents she said she couldn't get right, postponing the moment of eating; then, when I cut her a slice, she crumbled it up and left it. Chocolate crispy cakes, with a slab of organic Green and Black's I found in the delicatessen. I tasted it when I'd melted it: it was velvet on my tongue, its scented richness making me sneeze. Normally Daisy would come and scrape the bowl, greedy and bright-eyed as some small animal, eagerly licking the dark congealing sweetness from the spoon, but she said she wouldn't bother, she needed to finish her drawing. When the cakes were done, still warm, sticky, I put one on a plate for her. She took a bite and left it.

'Sweetheart, don't you like it? Perhaps I used the wrong chocolate.'

'It's fine, Mum,' she said. 'Really. I'll have it later.'

When Sinead came in from school, the house still smelt seductively of chocolate. She came straight to the kitchen, drawn by the smell; her nose and fingers were red with cold. 'Oh, yum,' she said, putting her hand to the plate.

I told her she could only have one, they were for Daisy; that I was sorry, that seemed so mean, but we had to get Daisy well; that I'd make another batch for her.

Daisy looked up from her drawing.

'I don't mind, Sinead,' she said. 'You eat them. I'm not hungry.'

In that moment in the three o'clock dark, I see that all these things I've made are about as much use as nourishment as the offerings of milk or olives that peasants leave by the hearth—to avert catastrophe, perhaps, or please the household spirits. Fear lays cold fingers on my skin.

Guiltily, I whisper in Richard's ear.

'Richard, wake up.'

He mutters something I can't make out, moves suddenly.

'What is it?' There's a splinter of panic in his voice. I've startled him, or intruded into some alarming dream.

He opens his eyes.

I suddenly remember he has an important meeting tomorrow. I feel ashamed.

'I shouldn't have woken you. I'm sorry.'

'It's a bit late for that,' he says. The words are slurred, thick with sleep.

'I've been worrying about Daisy. I was going through everything she'd eaten for the last few days.'

'She's fine,' he says. 'She'll be better soon.'

He inches in closer, moves his hand on my breast. I'm cold, and my nipple is taut against his palm.

'Richard, she's hardly eating anything.'

'Kids can last for ages without much food as long as they're drinking,' he says.

'I'm worried she's going to starve.'

'Darling, don't let's go getting all melodramatic,' he says. There's an edge of exasperation in his voice. 'If you're worried, you'll just have to take her back to the doctor.'

'He wasn't any use before,' I say.

I took her to the GP last week—two weeks into term, and she'd scarcely been to school. He looked at Daisy's ears and tonsils, said everything was fine and she probably had post-viral fatigue and she could go to school but she shouldn't run around. I said, 'She's feeling sick,' and he said nausea isn't anything to worry about, nausea doesn't mean there's anything wrong. I said she wasn't eating. 'She'll eat again in her own good time,' he said. 'Children are tougher than we think, Mrs Lydgate.'

'But what can he do?' I say to Richard. 'She hasn't got an infection or sore throat or anything. She doesn't need antibiotics.'

'You don't know that,' he says.

'And if it's a post-viral thing, you just have to wait for it to get better, don't you?'

'Well, at least it might put your mind at rest,' he says.

'I don't know.'

'Honestly,' he says, 'what on earth is the point of lying here worrying if you refuse to do anything about it?'

'But I know he'll just say, "Come back in a fortnight."'

'Maybe you should ask for her to be referred,' he says.

'To the hospital?' This surprises me.

'Well, if you're worried. You could ask to see a specialist.'

'But I can't just ask the GP to do that.'

'Of course you can. For God's sake, isn't that what we pay our taxes for? It's like you never feel you have a right to anything,' he says, quite affectionately.

I can feel him hard against my thigh; I move my hand down, encircle him. I feel I owe him this, now I've woken him. He's pushing up my nightdress.

'Take this thing off,' he says.

I pull it over my head. I turn the bedside light on; Richard likes to look. He runs his hand down me, eases his finger inside me.

'You're not very wet,' he says.

'Lick your hand. I'll be fine. I'm just a bit tired, that's all.' He moves his wet finger on me.

I'm dragging a net through my mind, trawling for sex, conjuring up images that are more and more extreme, bits of Anaïs Nin, scenes from *Secretary,* things I've read, things I've done, but I can't hold onto them. Like fish in a wide-meshed net they flicker and fade and dive away into darkness. Instead of sex, I'm thinking about this morning, when we'd run out of our usual mineral water, we only had Vittel, not Evian, and Daisy said she couldn't drink it because it tasted like milk. I left her in the house on her own, with strict instructions not to answer the door, drove to the nearest Waitrose through heavy traffic, and bought the kind of Evian she likes best, with a sports cap. It took me forty-five minutes.

I gave her the bottle of water. She took a sip, frowned, pushed the bottle away.

'Sorry, Mum,' she said.

I knelt beside her.

'Daisy, you've got to drink something. You've got to drink halfway down this bottle by lunchtime or I shall call the doctor.'

I put a mark on the bottle. Slowly, through the morning, she drank her way down to the mark.

Richard's cock in my hand is hard and full and his breathing is heavy; and he needs to sleep and he's got that meeting today. I'm not being fair to him, making him wait like this. I lift his hand away from me.

'I don't think I can come tonight,' I say. 'Don't worry.'

I roll over on top of him.

'Well, if you're sure,' he says.

I kneel astride him and he slides into me. He reaches up lazily to touch my breasts. I don't quite like this. Since the months of breastfeeding Daisy, I sometimes don't like to have my breasts touched; the feeling seems to move from irritating to intense with nothing in between, as though there's some short-circuit in me. I don't let this show.

He moves rapidly, comes with a sigh.

I slide off him, turn over, with him tucked into my

back. He sinks rapidly into sleep, his breath warm on my shoulder; I haven't even turned off the light.

I lie there for a while, but sleep feels far from me. The light of the lamp falls on the bedroom walls, which are ragrolled and opulently red; the hatstand and the hat with a plume that I bought in a junk shop cast extravagant shadows. I had a fantasy in mind when I planned and painted this room, as though it were an opera set, perhaps for *La Traviata,* which Richard once took me to see. We have a French cherrywood bed with a scrolled head and feet, the floor is darkly varnished, the red of the walls is rich by lamplight, though rather oppressive by day; and there are heavy curtains patterned with arum lilies, and a poster from an exhibition of designs for the Ballet Russe, that we went to see when Sinead was doing a ballet project. The poster shows a kind of erotic dance, and when I bought it, just glancing at it quickly and knowing I liked it, I thought there were two figures there, entwined in some sexual ritual; though when I got it home and took it out to frame it I saw it was really a solitary figure, neither male nor female, at once muscled and voluptuous, bejewelled and draped in lavish folds of cloth—and the other shape was a scarf red as flame that twisted and curved close, gauzy, without substance, yet moving like the body of a lover.

I get up silently, and take Richard's dressing gown from the foot of the bed and wrap it round me. Mine is silk, and in this weather putting it on just makes you feel colder.

I go down to the kitchen. I make some toast, but the

butter is hard and won't spread. There's some wine left in the bottle we drank with dinner: Richard is keeping to his resolution to drink less whisky in the evening. I pour myself a glass; in the cold, it has no scent, but I feel a sudden easing as it glides into my veins.

The room is untidy, the girls' things scattered around—Sinead's flower scrunchies and copies of *Heat,* and drawings Daisy has done, sketches of injured animals, and her box of magnetic fridge poetry. She hasn't done a new poem for weeks; her pre-Christmas offering is still on the door of the fridge. *'The gold witch crept to the top.'* In the stillness and cold, untidy but with nobody there, the kitchen has the look of a room abandoned in a hurry, by people who've been warned of some disaster or called away. When I see myself in the mirror over the fireplace I realise I haven't washed my hair for a week.

There's a holiday brochure that came in the post, showing villas in Tuscany. I sip the wine and flick through, seeking to lose myself in these fields of sunflowers and cities of blond towers, but worry has its claws in me, it can't be pushed away. With a sudden resolve I take a piece of paper that's lying there and a purple felt-tip of Daisy's. I write 'To Do for Daisy' at the top of the page, then '1. Go to GP. 2. Make a food diary—allergies? 3. Clear out her room—take away all rugs, cuddlies etc. Dust mites? 4. Homeopathy/herbalism—ask Nicky.' Nicky got to know lots of alternative people during her transient passion for aromatherapy; tomorrow I shall ring her. I stick the list up on the fridge, next to Daisy's poem.

I am in control again: there's so much I can do. I tell myself that Richard was right, that I have been over-emotional, that it will soon be over, and Daisy will be well. I picture myself chatting about it with Nicky at the Café Rouge over some nice Pinot Grigio. *Honestly, I was sure that Daisy had something serious—but look at her now...* I gulp down the rest of the wine and feel the fear edge away from me.

On the way back to bed I look in on Daisy. She's sleeping quietly now, the duvet pulled up high and lifting with her breathing. Her room feels warmer than the rest of the house; above her there's a glimmer of stencilled stars. Nothing can harm her here.

I go back to our bedroom and slip in beside Richard, and lie awake and hear the bark of the fox, moving rapidly across the long line of gardens, careless of hedges and fences, as though this whole wide territory were his.

C H A P T E R 5

There's a postcard for me. At first, I don't see it: it's hidden under a letter from Richard's parents, thanking Sinead and Daisy for their thank-you letters. I'm smiling to myself, at these flower-chains of gratitude and obligation that could go on for ever, when my eye falls on the postcard. I pick it up with care, as though it could hurt me. I'm glad that Richard has gone to work already. He doesn't need to know.

There are four pictures. I look at them for a moment, not wanting to turn the card over. They're conventional, touristy scenes. I read the captions. The Reichstag.

Charlottenburg Castle. Kurfürstendamm. Unter den Linden. These places sound familiar, though I don't know how to pronounce them. Charlottenburg Castle is white and opulent under a vast summer sky; Kurfürstendamm and Unter den Linden are shown by night, with lots of neon. The caption says, 'I love Berlin.' The dot of the 'i' in Berlin is a little red heart.

My heart pounds. I turn the card over. I can see the thought that went into this, how it was undoubtedly all planned, composed on a piece of rough paper, then copied out so carefully in this neat, rather childish handwriting.

Darling, I do wish you'd write. It's been so very very long. And I hear you've got a lovely little girl of your own, now. It's honestly no exaggeration to say that I would adore to see her.

And then the address, as before.
Darling. Like a lover. Like somebody who loves.
I have a brief moment of hope, a hope as glittery and enticing as a shard of coloured glass: you could cut yourself on it. Then rage that this comes now—rage at this wretched timing, when Daisy is ill, when I'm so full of this desperate anxiety. I hide the card at the bottom of the bin.

CHAPTER 6

Daisy is a little better. She dresses, eats some toast. When she cleans her teeth, she sounds as though she's going to be sick, but we take some deep breaths together and the worst of the feeling passes. She doesn't cry on the way to school, though she's limping and she says her legs are hurting.

My confidence of last night is still with me: I'm sure I can solve this. I do all the things on my list. I ring the GP and make an appointment for this afternoon after school. I spend the morning cleaning Daisy's room, moving all her cuddly animals out, as you're meant to do if your child has asthma, and taking away her rug in case it's been treated with pesticides, and steam-cleaning the mattress to immolate the dustmites. A sense of virtue opens out in me; I know her room is safe and pure and clean.

At lunchtime I ring Nicky.

'I've got just the guy for you,' she says, when I tell her about Daisy. 'Helmut Wolf. He's a kinaesiologist—you have to hold these little glass bottles and he tests your muscle strength to see if you're allergic. It's weird but it works. He was wonderful with my migraines. Trust me, he can help Daisy.'

I write his number down.

'Neil thinks he's nuts, of course,' she says.

Somehow this makes me less sure about Helmut Wolf, though that's certainly not her intention.

We talk about her boys. Max is doing brilliantly with his reading; his teacher is starting to hint he may be gifted. And Callum came downstairs last night wearing nothing but Nicky's silver sandals and announced he was Postman Pat. Nicky herself is feeling rather smug: she's given up smoking again and is on a detox diet. She says I wouldn't believe the things she can do with a chickpea.

'And how are—things generally?' I say then, using one of those carefully vague phrases we use to hint at that separate, secret part of her—which for now means Simon at Praxis, and the illicit e-mails.

'Fantastic.' Her voice is lowered, with a whisper of risk. 'But, look, I can't talk now.'

We fix a date for a drink at the Café Rouge.

* * *

At three-thirty, I park down the road from the school gate. I open the car door and the rain comes down. I don't have my umbrella. At first I fight against it, turning up my collar, but soon I'm soaked, so I lift up my face and let it fall on me, and it feels surprisingly pleasant, drenching me through. The whole street is musical with water, and outside the church on the corner the daffodils that are just opening around the war memorial are beaten down and ragged from the storm. The church noticeboard is advertising some course they're running till Easter, enticing you in with the promise that you will discover life's meaning. The wet air smells seductively of spring.

I join the group of parents at the gate, their open umbrellas like a flock of bright-winged birds alighting. Toddlers in buggies fight against the transparent rainshields spread across them, angry fists distending the plastic, wailing with red open mouths. Daisy was always like that: she'd fight and fight, she couldn't bear to be shut in. Well, I can understand.

The bell rings, the caretaker opens the gate. Inside, the paving stones are slick with wet.

People around me are talking about their children.

'Yeah, well, we've had them a few times, girls have this long hair and they put their heads together and whisper… My mother used to put malt vinegar on my hair…'

'Ellie was off with a sore throat, and it was really expensive because I had to buy Liam some Lego to bribe him to go into school. It was five pounds, I ask you…'

One of the teachers is leaving already—Mrs Nicholls,

who sometimes takes Daisy for music. She sees me there, half smiles in my direction, comes towards me.

'Mrs Lydgate. I've heard about your troubles with Daisy.' Her face is close to mine, she's speaking in an undertone, as though this is something of which I may be ashamed. 'I did want to say—I really do feel you're doing the right thing in making her come in.'

'I don't know,' I say.

'It's awful if your child's unhappy at school,' she says. 'I had a lot of trouble with my daughter once—she wouldn't go to school. We found it was friendship problems.'

'I really don't think it's that,' I say. 'Daisy's had flu, it's like she can't get over it.'

'I used to send my daughter in with a nice snack for break time. One of those muesli bars, or a packet of raisins. She seemed to find it a comfort. Perhaps you could try that with Daisy.'

'It's a good idea,' I say politely. 'It's just such a problem finding anything that she'll eat.'

'Well, keep up the good work,' she says, and weaves her way out through the mass of parents. I feel uneasy, as though I have been reprimanded, although I'm sure she was only trying to be helpful. The rain collects in my parting and splashes down my face like falling tears.

In front of me the women shift and move. I see Fergal, just ahead of me, the unruly fair hair at the back of his head, the dark wet gleam of his jacket. He has a large umbrella that says Assisted Evolution.

I edge forward. He turns and sees me, eyes widening

with recognition. I admit to myself that this is what I meant to happen. He makes a slight beckoning gesture with his head. With a huge sense of inchoate relief I move in under his umbrella.

'Catriona.' He smiles. I feel that something in me amuses him.

We have to stand close to stay out of the wet. He's chewing gum: I can smell his wet hair and skin. I'm suddenly aware of how pink my face must be, of my hair all plastered down, that I'm wearing my oldest coat and the cuffs are fraying.

'I don't often see you here,' he says.

Maybe, I think, he has been looking for me. I remember that fantasy I had, of moving my hands across his face and his head. My skin is suddenly hot.

'I'm not here very often,' I tell him. 'Daisy's ill.'

'What's wrong?'

'I don't know. Nobody seems to know.'

He's listening, waiting.

'Richard tells me not to worry—he thinks it's just flu—you know, some kind of virus.'

He looks me up and down, taking me in.

'It makes it harder really,' I tell him. 'I know this must sound stupid—but the more he says I mustn't worry, the worse I seem to feel.'

'Poor kid,' he says. 'Poor you.'

He puts his hand on my arm, leaves it there perhaps a second too long. A hunger opens out in me. I would like to peel back my wet sleeve and feel his hand warm on my skin.

We stand there for a moment, watching the children, while the rain beats down like a drumming of many fingers.

'By the way,' he says then, 'I know why I know you.'

'Oh.' I feel that I am falling.

'Aimee Graves,' he says. His tone is easy, as if it's the most natural thing.

He hears my quick intake of breath.

'I'm right, then,' he says. 'I'm sorry—perhaps I shouldn't have talked about it here.'

He turns toward me: he has a frown like a question.

For a moment, I don't answer, I don't know what I think. There are two things at once: this fear that makes my pulse so thin and fast and jagged, and a strange voluptuous sense of relief, of wanting to open myself up to him completely.

'You know her?' I say.

'I met her once,' he says. 'It was a story I was researching.'

'She's alive, then, she's OK?'

'She's OK,' he says.

'So you know all about me,' I say, quite lightly.

'I didn't say that,' he says.

I can see Daisy coming; it's the end of the conversation. Daisy is with Megan, who has her arm around her. She looks so pale, so different from the other girls. She says goodbye to Megan and comes to me. I hug her, she sinks her face into me. Fergal pulls away a little, but holds his umbrella above us.

'OK?' I say, my mouth in her hair.

'Mmm.' She's trembling a little.

I take her bag, as you might with a much younger child. She doesn't protest at this indignity.

'Catriona, if you want to talk some time,' says Fergal. 'I mean, I could explain.'

I nod. He moves off to find Jamie.

The rain is easing up now. There's a gleam of sunlight between the patchy clouds, and a rainbow flung across the sky behind us. I point out the rainbow to Daisy, but she doesn't turn.

We walk back to the car. I feel shaken.

I open the car door for her. 'Look, I brought Hannibal for you. He's missed you,' I tell her.

'Honestly, Mum, he's a *cuddly toy,*' she says. 'And what if somebody sees?'

'Nobody can see,' I tell her.

She tucks him under her arm.

I watch her in the mirror.

'So was it OK today?' I ask her.

'My stomach hurt,' she says. 'I wanted to come home but Mrs Griffiths wouldn't let me. She said, "Well, what should I do? I can't send you home when you're hardly ever here."'

We drive to the doctor's through the white shine of the puddles.

'Did anything interesting happen?' I say.

'We had to do our New Year wishes,' she says.

'So what did you put?'

'I put world peace and a cat. We all put world peace,

and Kieran put, "For my Dad to get his new kidney." Mrs Griffiths said if we put world peace we should put it first, but when we came to Kieran she said, "Well, which do you think is the more important?"'

There's a lump in my throat, but I don't know why. There are so many things to cry for.

CHAPTER 7

I have never seen Dr Carey before; she must be new, or a locum. She's wearing a crisp red jacket with shiny buttons, and she has short elfin hair and upward-tilting eyebrows. She seems earnest, conscientious, pretty in a wholesome schoolgirl way—someone who'd always be top of the class and make lots of neat notes.

She greets Daisy as well as me. She has an open smile. I immediately like her.

We sit by the desk, Daisy in an armchair, clutching Hannibal. It's pleasant in here, for a surgery: the walls are blue, and there are toys on the window sill, and on the doctor's desk a jug of marbled lollipops in cellophane, bright-coloured as balloons.

Dr Carey looks at me expectantly.

'Daisy's been ill for four weeks,' I tell her. 'She went to school today, but that's only the second time this term. It started with flu and she's never really recovered.'

'Oh, dear. How horrid for you,' says Dr Carey to Daisy.

Daisy shrugs, embarrassed.

I breathe out a little; I feel that we are cared for. This doctor is kind, gentle, warm to Daisy. This time at least we will be understood.

'Well, Daisy,' she says, 'we'd better have a look at you.'

Daisy lies on the couch and Dr Carey feels her lymph glands and her stomach.

'Well done,' she says. 'That's excellent. That's absolutely fine.'

Then Daisy stands on the scales and is measured and weighed.

Dr Carey sits back at her desk, gets out a weight chart. A little frown pinches the skin between her eyes. I suddenly imagine how she'll look when she is older, with stern lines round her mouth and glasses on a chain.

'Daisy's really rather underweight,' she says. 'She's on the lowest percentile.'

'I don't know what that means.'

'I'll show you.' She turns the chart towards me, points at it with her pen. 'The average is here,' she says, 'and Daisy's right at the bottom.'

'She must have lost lots of weight since she's been ill,' I tell her. 'She isn't eating—she feels too ill to eat.'

Dr Carey leans towards me. Her immaculate hands are tightly clasped together.

'What does she eat exactly?'

'Today, she had a piece of toast for breakfast and she didn't have any lunch.' I know—I've looked in her lunchbox. 'Yesterday was better. She had a bit of rice and some gravy for tea.'

I want to make it clear I'm not a worrier: that I know that children are tougher than we think, as the other GP told me; that rice and gravy really isn't too terrible.

Still the pinched little frown.

'Just rice?' she says. 'She should be eating meat. She needs her protein.'

'Of course she does. But rice and gravy was better than before.'

'We're fortunate to have a nutritionist working in this practice,' she says. 'I think I should refer you to her for advice about what Daisy should be eating.'

'But I know what she should be eating. Of course I do.' I think of all the books I've bought on bringing up children, books with cheerful covers and energising titles—*Eco Baby*, *Creating Kids Who Can*. 'It's just that she won't, she can't. She feels too sick to eat. She hasn't eaten properly since Christmas.'

She shakes her head a little. I feel this conversation slipping away from me.

She turns to Daisy, looks at her; there's something

she's working out. She fiddles with the wisps of hair that grow in front of her ears.

'Daisy, I wonder if you could tell me a bit about school?' she says then. 'Is it all right? D'you like it?'

'It's OK,' says Daisy.

'Is anything worrying you?'

Daisy shakes her head.

'You're sure?' says Dr Carey. 'Sometimes it's hard to talk about these things.'

Daisy frowns. I see how she'd like to help, to give the answer that Dr Carey wants, but she can't think of anything. She twists her fingers in Hannibal's greying wool. He's dirty; she'll never let me wash him in case he loses his smell. Here in this blue sterile place, I find his greyness embarrassing. I worry that Dr Carey will think that I never wash things properly, that I am messy, sluttish, not a proper mother. Daisy doesn't say anything.

Dr Carey turns to me. 'You know, Mrs Lydgate, I'm wondering whether we should treat all this as psychological.' She says this with a kind of finality, as though it is an achievement.

Panic seizes me.

'But nothing traumatic has happened to Daisy. It started when she had flu.'

'But, you see, she looks so miserable,' she says. 'She looks all pale and hunched up.'

'She's unhappy because she's ill,' I tell her.

Dr Carey ignores this, leans a little towards me. 'Tell me, Mrs Lydgate, is everything all right at home?' Her voice is hushed, confiding: as though she thinks that Daisy won't be able to hear.

'Everything's fine,' I tell her.

'You're living with your husband?'

'Yes.'

'And how do you both get on?'

'We get on fine,' I tell her.

My coat is damp from the rain: I am chilled through.

'You're sure? You don't have awful shouting matches in front of Daisy?'

'No, we don't. We don't have awful shouting matches at all.'

I'm trying not to get angry; I know that if I get angry she won't believe what I say.

'Because if you do,' she says, 'Daisy's sure to react.'

'Really,' I say again, 'we get on fine. It's nothing like that. I just know Daisy's ill.' I take a deep breath, try to keep my voice level. 'I want her to be referred to the hospital.'

There's a pause, as though this is entirely unexpected. She looks unsure; I see how young she is.

'*Please,*' I say. 'She isn't eating, she always feels so tired. I think we should see a paediatrician.'

'All right, then,' she says, but with reluctance, as though she's been constrained.

She's writing in her notes now. 'I'll refer you to Dr McGuire at the General,' she says. 'They'll write to you with the appointment. I'm afraid there's quite a waiting list. In the meantime, we'll get all the blood tests done. You can come in on Thursday and the nurse will take the blood.'

As we go she gives Daisy a lollipop from the jug on her desk.

We walk back to the car, which is parked down the end of the road. There are green fresh smells of spring but the rainbow has faded.

'She was really nice, wasn't she, Mum?' says Daisy.

'I'm glad you liked her.'

'I did,' she says. 'She was kind.'

She starts to unwrap the lollipop; I have to take Hannibal. We stop for a moment because it's hard to do; the paper is firmly stuck to the sugary surface. The lollipop is veined with purple and red, the colour intense as nail varnish. I think of additives but don't say anything.

She rips off the last scrap of cellophane.

'There,' she says with satisfaction.

She takes one careful lick. We walk on for a bit, the lollipop held in front of her, like some precious thing.

'Is it all right if I leave this, Mum?' she says then.

'Of course.'

As we pass the bus stop she drops it in a bin.

CHAPTER 8

Daisy can't sleep; she says she feels too sick. I sit her up, and prop her against the pillows and smooth her hair.

'We'll crack this,' I tell her. 'We'll get you better. I promise. Soon it'll be over.'

I read to her from the fairy-tale book, the story of Rapunzel, who was trapped in a tower by the witch, her mother, and let down her hair to a prince. Sometimes Daisy spits in a tissue.

Sinead comes to the door. She needs me to test her on her homework.

'It's false friends. For crying out loud. How can any word of French be your friend?'

'I'll come when Daisy's asleep,' I tell her.

I read till Daisy's head is drooping, as you might with a very young child. Her eyelids are shut, but flickery, tense; she could so easily wake. Sinead looks round the door again. I put a warning finger to my lips. She mouths melodramatically, 'My vocab, my vocab.' I whisper she'll have to wait. Eventually Daisy's breathing slows and she sinks down into the pillows. I slip off my shoes and creep out like a thief. I sit with Sinead and test her on the words. She isn't very confident, but it's nearly ten, she'll never learn them now. I tell her to go to bed.

Richard has his meeting and he won't be back till late. I pour myself some wine, and try to imagine him there. When I think of it, this world of his that's so mysterious to me, I always see men in suits all sitting round a shiny mahogany table, and heaps of papers in front of them covered in cryptic figures, and the coffee brought in by Francine, his glamorous PA. I met Francine once at a party at Richard's office; she was wearing a rather impressive dress, demure in front, right up to her neck, but almost completely backless.

I take my wine into the living room. It's cold in here tonight: the heating's been off for most of the day, and the house won't seem to warm up. I pull the curtains, shutting out the night, but chill air seeps up through the gaps in the floorboards.

I don't turn on the main light, just the lamps on the little tables on either side of the fireplace. There is darkness in the corners of the room. The masks we brought back from Venice are lit from below, so the lines of the pottery are etched in shadow. I chose them because they charmed me, with their hints of a seductive world of carnival and disguise. But when Daisy was little, and mothers and children were always coming for coffee, I had to take them down; children seem to be often afraid of heads apart from bodies—it's probably something primal—and there were toddlers who'd burst into tears if they saw them. The black one is a little macabre, sinister in an obvious way—it's the fairytale crone, Baba Yaga perhaps, the glossy surface recreating the sagging folds of old flesh—but tonight I see it's the white one that is more frightening: it's simpler, almost featureless, a face that is an absence.

I sip my wine and go back over the conversation with Dr Carey. I don't understand why she wouldn't take Daisy's illness seriously. I must have done something wrong. Should I have cried? Should I have sounded more desperate? Maybe I was too assertive; or not assertive enough? Perhaps there's a code I don't know about, some good-mother way of behaving. I once heard a famous female barrister speaking on the radio. If she was defending a woman accused of murder, she said, she'd urge her to wear a cardigan to court, ideally angora and fluffy, so no one would think her capable of committing a terrible crime. Maybe there's a dress code for taking your child to the doctor that's unknown to me: a frock from Monsoon perhaps, with a pattern like a flowerbed, or a tracksuit and pink lipstick.

There's a clatter from the hall—Richard closing the door behind him, putting his briefcase down. Relief washes through me: I'm always so glad when he's home. He comes in, and I see he's tired; he's somehow less vivid than when he left in the morning, as though the dust of the day has settled on him and blurred him. He's brought me flowers, blue delphiniums, wrapped in white paper, with a bow of rustling ribbon. He's good at choosing things—orchids, silver bracelets; his gifts are always exact.

'Thanks. They're so lovely.' They're an icy pale blue, like a clear winter sky, the flowers frail, like tissue. I hold them to my face; they have the faintest smoky smell.

He kisses my cheek.

'There's pollen on you,' he says. He rubs at my nose with a finger.

'Was the meeting OK?'

He shrugs. 'So so,' he says.

I'm not sure this is true: he looks strained, older.

'D'you want to eat?'

He shakes his head.

'I'll get you a drink,' I tell him.

'Thanks. Scotch would be good. Just tonight.'

I smile. 'It was that bad?'

He shakes his head. 'It was fine. Really.'

He has a still face; he's always hard to read. I don't pursue it, don't know the right questions. There are parts of his life that are opaque to me.

I get him a large glass of Scotch, with ice, the way he

likes it. He doesn't sit, he's restless—as though the uneasy energy that's built up through the day won't leave him. He leans against the mantelpiece, sipping his drink.

In the silence between us I hear Sinead upstairs, the clumping of her slippers and water from the shower running away. I'm worried she will wake Daisy. I've become alert again to all the noises of the house—like when you have a baby and skulk round like a conspirator, and every creak on every stair is marked on a map in your mind.

'We went to the doctor,' I tell him.

'Good,' he says. 'How was it?'

'We saw someone new. A woman. She was rather young, I thought.'

'And was it OK?'

'Sort of. Well, Daisy liked her.'

'Excellent,' he says. 'There. I told you it would be all right.'

'I'm not sure. I wasn't happy really.'

'What is it?' he says, solicitous. 'What's wrong?'

'I told her that Daisy wasn't eating and she said I needed nutritional advice. It felt so patronising. Like she couldn't really hear what I was saying. I keep worrying I handled it all wrong—you know, said the wrong thing or something. D'you think sometimes I don't express myself right—d'you think I'm not assertive enough, perhaps?'

I want him, need him, to say, Of course not, of course you didn't handle it wrong—it's nothing to do with you.

'Darling, you do rather brood on things,' he says.

He's standing just outside the circle of light from the lamp. Half his face is in shadow and I can't see what he's thinking.

'And then she launched into this thing about how it was all psychological,' I tell him.

There's a little pause.

'Well, maybe there's something in that,' he says then.

For a moment I can't speak. The smoky smell of the flowers he's brought clogs up my throat.

'But how can there be?'

'Look, darling,' he says, 'you do worry a lot. Maybe that affects Daisy in some way.'

'I'm worrying because she's ill. How could that make her ill? I don't understand. Is that so bad, to worry?'

'Well, I guess it's not ideal,' he says. 'But with your background, it's maybe not so surprising.'

I hear a sound of splintering in my head. There's a sense of shock between us. He shouldn't have said this, we both know that. But instead of taking it back, he tries to explain.

'You know, all those things you went through. It's bound to affect you…'

He turns a little away from me. I see his face in the mirror, but his reflected image is strange to me, reversed and subtly wrong. The darkness reaches out to me from the corners of the room.

'You're a bit of a perfectionist,' he says. 'We both know that. You want everything to be just right, you can't just go with the flow. That's understandable. It's perhaps one of the effects of…' His voice tails off.

'One of the effects of what?' My voice is small in the stillness.

'Darling,' he says. 'You know I think you're a wonderful mother. No one could care for those girls better than you. But maybe sometimes you try almost too hard.'

His eyes are narrow: for a moment he looks at me as though I am a stranger.

'How can you try too hard?' I say.

'All I mean is—of course it's a worrying situation. But you get worried perhaps a bit more than you need to. And maybe in some ways that makes things worse. Maybe you expect things to go wrong.'

There's a sense of pressure in my chest, like something pushing into me, making it hard to breathe.

'I just don't see how that could make Daisy ill,' I say.

He hears the catch in my voice. He comes to sit beside me.

'Cat,' he says, 'now don't go getting upset.'

He ruffles my hair, as though I am a child. His hand on me soothes me, as he knows it will.

'What about the hospital?' he says.

'We're getting the referral.'

'Well, that's all that matters really,' he says.

'What if she puts it in the letter—that she thinks it's psychological? They won't take Daisy seriously. If they think that, no one'll bother to try and find out what's wrong.'

'Of course she won't put it in the letter,' he says. 'I

mean, these are the experts, aren't they? She'll leave them to make up their own minds. None of this adds up to anything,' he says, and puts his arm around me.

Yet still I feel that something has been broken.

CHAPTER 9

There's a road I won't go down. Poplar Avenue. A harmless name, a name like any other. There's a house in that road, a wide-fronted house set well back from the street. There are rooms in that house with glass-panelled doors, the panels covered over with brown paper. Richard started to drive down Poplar Avenue once, by mistake, when we were coming home from Gina and Adrian's, and a car crash in the one-way system had caused a massive tailback. He turned round when he realised: he knows, I've told him some of it, and he read about it in the papers during the inquiry. But nobody knows all of it, except those of us who were there.

I was thirteen when I went there. My mother couldn't cope with me—or so she told the social worker, as I lurked behind the bead curtain in the squalid kitchen of our tiny flat, that I'd tried to clean up, knowing the social worker was coming, hearing everything. 'I need a break,' said my mother. 'Just for a month or two. To get myself together.'

The social worker said she admired my mother's honesty, and it probably was for the best. She asked if there was anyone I could go to. 'No,' said my mother, 'we only have each other.' The social worker said not to worry, she was pretty sure that there was a place at The Poplars. And I wouldn't even need to change schools, so really it didn't have to be too disruptive.

My mother was drinking three bottles of sherry a day. It had crept up on us gradually, through the years of living in rented flats, or in rooms at the tops of pubs where she worked behind the bar. I knew the story of how we came to be in this predicament—or, at least, the part of it she chose to tell. Her family had been reasonably well-off— her father was a cabinet-maker—but they'd been Plymouth Brethren, very strict and excluding. She'd always chafed against it—the beliefs, the extreme re- strictions. She'd truanted a lot, left school to travel round Europe with an unemployed actor, ten years older than her, who smoked a lot of dope. Her family had rejected her totally—wouldn't see her again. In the Vondel Park in Amsterdam, the man had drifted off. She'd wandered back to London, existed for a while on the edge of some rather bohemian group, people who squatted, who liked to call themselves anarchists, who had artistic pretensions. She wore cheesecloth blouses, worked as a waitress. It was the pinnacle of her life, the time to which she always yearned to return. She was still only nineteen when she met my father. She fell pregnant almost immediately. He went off with somebody else when I was six months old; my mother was just twenty. She never talked about him, except to say that she wasn't going to talk about that bastard. I only knew he'd been part of that arty group, and that his name was Christopher.

It was OK when I was younger. She had standards then, she was quite particular: she talked a lot about manners; she always laid the table properly for tea. We were happy, I think, happy enough, though there was never much money, and often she left me alone in the evenings, even when I was young. I remember how as a little girl I'd sit on the bed and watch her getting ready, perhaps for her evening shift behind the bar, or maybe for a night out on the town with one of her long succession of temporary men. She'd be all sheeny and glossy, with high heels, and a gold chain round her ankle, her skin a sun-kissed brown from her weekly session at the Fake It tanning studio, with the smell that was then so comforting, so familiar, of Marlboros and Avon Lily of the Valley. I'd sit on the bed amid the heaps of her clothes and accessories, her belts and bangles and gloves and floaty scarves. She had a particular passion for gloves, in pastel cotton or silk, with little pearl buttons or ruched wrists. It was eccentric, perhaps, giving her an air of spurious formality, but she liked to hide her hands, which were always rough and reddened from the work she did, all the washing of glasses in the sink at the bar. I'd watch how she'd choose from her glittery sticks of cosmetics, how she'd do her mouth, first drawing the outline with lip-pencil, making her narrow lips a little more generous, then the lipstick, coral bright, eased on straight from the stick. She'd press her lips together to spread the colour out. I thought she was so beautiful. Yet my pleasure in these moments was always shot through with fear, that one day she'd go and leave me and somehow forget to return. Or maybe the fear of abandonment is something I've added since, thinking back, laying my knowledge of what happened later over my memory of those moments, as frost lies over leaves.

There was one man called Marco, whom she met through a Lonely Hearts column in the local paper. He was, or claimed to be, Italian. She always said she liked a man with an accent. He moved in with us; he was smooth, flash, with lots of chest hair and gold jewellery. The flat was clean and tidy while Marco was with us; sometimes I heard my mother singing as she worked. When he left, taking all her savings and even the money from the gas meter, and she realised she'd been conned, that all his protestations of love were just an elaborate charade, something seemed to die in her. That was when she started buying sherry instead of wine. She lost her job. Sometimes she'd be virtually insensible when I came in from school, and I'd have to take off her outer clothes and tuck her up in bed. One day I came home all excited, bursting to tell her I'd won the second-year Art prize: it was one of those moments when life feels full of promise and shiny, like a present just ready and waiting for you to unwrap. But my mother was snoring on the sofa, the front of her blouse hanging open, and there was no one to tell. Sometimes she'd be coherent but maudlin, full of platitudes, weeping and saying again and again how she'd tried to give me a good life but it had all gone wrong, and eating Hellmann's Mayonnaise from the jar with a table-spoon. I started taking money from her purse, to buy food. I spilt nail varnish on her skirt and she hit me with a clothes-hanger. When I got into a stupid fight at school, she turned up drunk and belligerent in the school office, demanding to see the headmistress, and had to be seen off the premises by the caretaker.

That was when the social worker started visiting. The third time she came, she told me to pack and took me out to her car.

The Poplars. It's the smell I remember: disinfectant, cabbage, adolescent sweat. And the texture of it, everything rough, worn, frayed. Lino, and thin blankets, and flabby white bread and corned beef, and having to ask for every sanitary towel. The sofas had the springs sticking through, and when Darren Reames in one of his moods ripped off some of the wallpaper, it stayed like that for months, with a great gaping tear. There weren't enough electric points: you had to unplug the fridge to watch the television, so the milk was usually sour. There was never enough to eat. Once I said I was hungry and Brian Meredith told me not to talk because talking wasted energy.

Brian Meredith ran the place; he'd been in the SAS. He was short, dapper, smart in his red or blue blazers, and pleasant to visiting social workers, who liked his ready handshake and his friendly yellow Labrador stretched out on the floor by his desk. He looked like everyone's favourite uncle—and he knew how to hit without leaving a mark on you. Looking back, I can see why he got away with it: he took the really difficult kids, that nobody else would touch. Girls with shiny, sequiny names—Kylie, Demi, Sigourney—and wrecked lives. Boys who set fires, who used knives. All of them lashing out at the people who tried to help them with what I see now was the terrible rage of those who have nothing to lose: children who couldn't be consoled. Like Darren, who'd set fire to his school and then to his house with his grandfather in it. Or Jason Oakley, who said his dad had interfered with him, who kicked a care worker in the stomach when she was pregnant, so she miscarried: though in the end even Brian Meredith couldn't cope with Jason, and he was sent to Avalon Close, an adolescent psychiatric unit with a grim reputation. Girls like Aimee Graves, whose father had held her head in the loo and flushed it, who came into Care and had seventeen foster placements, Aimee who was so misnamed, for no one loved her. Except me, for a while. Except me.

Brian Meredith solved some big problems for the council. He did what he liked, and his methods were all his own. Two rooms on the second floor. The secret of his success. Pindown. Each room with a bed, a table, a flimsy electric fire, and the glass-panelled door, the glass screened with brown paper. There were no locks, no keys, but saucepans were hung on the outside of the door handle, and someone was always there, the other side of the door. If you misbehaved or ran away, that's where they put you. They took your clothes and shoes: you had to wear your pyjamas. If you wanted to go to the toilet, you had to knock on the door. They sat you at the table to write down the wrong things you'd done. The rules were stuck on the wall, a list with lots of 'no's: no smoking, TV, radio, books; and no communicating out of the window without permission—because you could see the woman who lived in the flat next door, her sitting room was level with your window, you could see right in. You'd watch her dusting, watching television, sitting on the arm of the sofa and having a quiet smoke, and you'd want to bang on your window, to see if she might wave to you. Sometimes you felt she was your only friend.

Most of the staff were young. Some were doing it for experience, they wanted to get on courses and become proper social workers, the kind who sat in offices and went to case conferences, and visited places like The Poplars then drove away in their cars. Some of them just couldn't get anything better. Most of them wanted to help, really. They wore denim and had piercings and said how much they liked the music we listened to and tried to get us to talk about our feelings. You could see when they talked to you, trying to get near you, how they yearned for some kind of revelation—that you would give them the gift of some confidence, a disclosure or confession about your family and what had been done to you, they were longing for your trust, though not knowing what the hell to do with it if you gave it. They were OK, most of them. Only Brian Meredith hit us. But they all used Pindown.

Lesley was the nicest. She arrived soon after me. She was perhaps ten years older than me, twenty-three to my thirteen. Lesley became my key worker. She was different from the others, rather awkward and clumsy, with feet too big for her body, but her eyes were quiet when they rested on you.

Lesley was very conscientious. She took me off for individual sessions. We sat on the square of carpet in the staffroom—the only bit of carpet in the place—and did exercises from a ringbound manual she had, called *Building Self-Esteem*. She drew a self-esteem tree on a big piece of paper with felt tips; there were fruit on the branches, and you had to write something about yourself that you liked in each of the fruit. I remember the dirty cups on the coffee table, and the smell of Jeyes from the corridor where someone had been sick. I couldn't think of much to write in the fruit. She turned a page of her book. 'If I could wave a magic wand, what would you wish for?' she said. 'When you're grown-up and all this is behind you, what would you want to have?' I sat there in the smell of cabbage and disinfectant. 'Close your eyes,' she said. I closed my eyes, and saw it all, clear, vivid. Perhaps it was the tree she'd drawn, triggering something in me. I saw lots of trees, a garden; I saw a house and children and a husband, all these images welling up in me, precise as though I'd drawn them. 'I'd like to have children,' I said. 'I'd like to have a family of my own. And a place to live, just us and nobody else.' I saw, heard it all in my head: a lawn, a lily pool, the splashing of a fountain in the pool, the laughter of children. In a moment of hope that warmed me through, there on the thin frayed carpet: I will have them, I thought, these things.

My mother visited, occasionally, erratically, dressed up, but not for me. Always in a hurry, as though there was somewhere else she needed to be. Like someone at a party, looking over your shoulder for the person they want to talk to, and shifty, as though she was implicated in some guilt by merely being there. Sometimes she brought presents: exuberant cuddly toys, large fluffy rabbits with satin hearts on their chests. I put the toys on the window sill of the room I shared with Aimee. Sometimes my mother was drunk when she came, sentimental, and full of self-pity; saying over and over how she'd done her best for me, done everything she could.

'When can I come home?'

'Soon. Very soon, Trina.' Smoking her Marlboros,

fiddling with her rings. 'I just need to get myself together. You're OK in here, then, are you?'

'I hate it.'

'Oh,' she'd say. 'They seem nice enough.'

Afterwards Lesley would sit on my bed and talk to me.

'How do you feel about your mum, my love? How does it all make you feel?'

I never knew how to answer these questions.

During the week we were meant to go to school. The others mostly didn't; they'd go off to the towpath, where they'd sit on rubber tyres and inhale lighter fuel and throw stones into the water; or to the Glendale Centre, where when they got bored they'd steal things from the shops. I was the only one who went on going to school.

It was a sprawling comprehensive, full of children I envied, with homes to go to and trainers that were regularly replaced. I didn't do well: I was always rather hungry and distracted. I went because of the art: because the art rooms were always open at lunchtime. You could mess about with pens and paints and do whatever you wanted and nobody bothered you. It was quiet, in a way that The Poplars never was—just Capital Radio playing, and a few other girls softly talking, and the drumming of the rain on the mezzanine roof: it always seemed to be raining, that's how it is in my memory, the windows clouded with condensation so no one could see in. And there I discovered this sweet surprising thing—that with a pen or paintbrush in my hand, there was a flow to my life, and I could draw things that pleased me, and the other girls would stop and look as they passed. However tired I was, however hungry, this flow and freedom still happened, till The Poplars faded away, to a smoky blur on the edges of my mind, and I entered a different place, a place of shapes, of colours, viridian and cobalt and burnt sienna, where I felt for a while a secret guarded joy.

There was a teacher called Miss Jenkins who took an interest in me. She had an ex-hippy air—she wore hoops in her ears and liked embroidered cardigans. She never asked me how I felt or wanted to talk about me. She must have known where I came from, but it didn't seem to matter. She showed me things—a book of Impressionist paintings; a postcard of a picture by Pisanello that I adored, of a velvety dark wood studded with birds like jewels; a book of botanical drawings she'd bought at Kew. She gave me pictures to copy, to explore; and suggested materials I could try—fine pens, oil paints, acrylics, and plaster to make a 3-D picture—which they only used in class at A-level. I was privileged, I knew, and at moments like these I felt rich. So I went on going to school, for the quiet hours in the art room and the complicated sweet scent of acrylic paint that I could still smell hours after-wards, and Miss Jenkins whose first name I never knew.

I never got to know the other girls. I kept myself a little apart, not wanting them to find out about me. I saw this as a temporary thing. When things are OK, when this bad bit is over, when I'm back with my mother, I thought—then I will talk to them, make friends, be one of them. Not till then. Aimee at The Poplars was my only friend.

She was wild, Aimee: a sharp, knowing face, hair like fire, tattoos all down her arm. She had a razor-blade sewn into the hem of her jeans. For emergencies, she said. She never went to school.

Aimee got picked on a lot by the staff at The Poplars. They told her she was trouble. She wasn't like me, she wouldn't just go along with things and bide her time. I've always been able to do this—blend into the background, not be conspicuous, not be seen—but Aimee couldn't or wouldn't: there was something in her, some flame that wouldn't be quenched. Brian Meredith hit her more than the others—for nicking stuff and getting into fights and being lippy. She used to call him Megadeath. 'He's got it coming,' she'd say. 'I'll do him over. Just you wait. One day.' Once he kept her for three weeks in Pindown. When she came out she'd ripped all the skin from the sides of her fingernails and sometimes she'd shout in her sleep.

She ran away often. Sometimes she took me with her. She showed me how to do it, how to travel on a train without a ticket by hiding in the toilet, how to steal. We'd plan it all together in the room we shared, the street light leaking through the thin curtains onto the battered candlewick of our bedspreads. Each time it was like falling in love: each time we thought this was the day, the time, the Real Thing. Usually, we'd head for Brighton, where Aimee had heard you could live in a squat and find some people who'd help you. Brighton was our promised land. We knew how it would be. We'd sell jewellery, those little leather thongs with stones on, we'd live on chips, read fortunes: we'd be like the older girls you saw there on the seafront, with their impossible glamour, their ratty ribboned hair and Oxfam coats and thin thin bodies and wide, generous smiles.

We'd pack our bags with a change of clothes and Kit Kats we'd nicked from Woolworths or mini-packs of Frosties, and put on our trainers and go. And maybe we'd get there, and sleep on the beach by the pier, and the police would come and pick us up, and we'd be put in Pindown.

The third time, they let me out after a week of Pindown. I was quiet and sensible and sat at the table and wrote down the wrong things I'd done. But Aimee was kept there for fifteen days, and when she came out she had a chest infection. They'd taken the fuse out of the fire because she'd been stroppy, she said.

I woke that night to see her sitting up in bed, the bedspread pulled up to her chin, her fists all bone, clasping it so tightly. The orange light through the curtains made her skin look sickly.

'I'm going to tell,' she said, through her coughs. 'What it's like here. What he does, that motherfucking bastard.'

'No,' I said. 'You mustn't. You can't.'

'Just watch me,' she said.

Her social worker from the Civic Centre, Jonny Leverett, was a pallid man who wore heavy-metal sweatshirts. The next time he came, he took her out in his Skoda, and they were gone for hours.

'Well?' I said, when she came back.

'I told him,' she said. Tearing at the skin at the sides of

her fingernails. 'They'll have to do something now. They'll have to come and get Megadeath. They'll have to lock him up. Life would be too short for him.'

Two days later there was a case conference in the staff-room. The car park was full of smart cars and Lesley served coffee in the china cups that were kept for visiting professionals. Jonny Leverett came to take Aimee in.

I was watching television when she found me.

'I'm going to Avalon Close,' she said. Defiant still, but her eyes were far too bright.

'You can't be,' I said. 'For Chrissake, they're all nutters in there.'

She shrugged. 'It's got to be better than here.'

She kicked a Pepsi can that was lying on the floor, sent it ricocheting across the room, her flaming red hair flying. But I could see she was frightened: there was shaking at the edges of her smile. I'd never seen her frightened.

'What about Megadeath?'

'They didn't believe me,' she said.

The day she went, she cut her wrists—with the blade she'd kept for emergencies. Lesley told me, when I got back from school. She was all right now, said Lesley, they'd stitched her up in Casualty. Lesley said not to worry too much about her, that Avalon Close would be right for her as she clearly needed help.

I think back to that sometimes. I try not to, but I still do, even now. Because I know there were things I could have done to help her. I could have gone to the police or phoned the Civic Centre and told them Aimee was telling the truth—that someone was lying, but it wasn't her. I didn't have the courage. Only silence seemed safe.

I missed Aimee terribly. What I could bear before, I couldn't bear without her. Sometimes when I'd wake in the night, I'd think for a moment she was there in the other bed beside me; then with a lurch of cold I'd see it was Jade Cochrane, my new roommate—who was sad and mousey and never laughed at all.

My mother came again. She had a dark tan and new jewellery. She brought me an extra-big rabbit, with a satin heart on his chest that said 'Yours 4 Ever'.

'Thanks,' I said.

'I was going to wrap it up,' she said, 'but I didn't have any paper.'

She was excited, skittish, pleased with herself. She smelt of alcohol but I didn't think she was drunk. She looked different. This was it, I knew. At last. The time had come.

'I'm living with Karl now,' she said. 'He comes from Dresden. I always did like a man with a nice accent. Karl's an entrepreneur.' She pronounced this carefully. 'We've got a new flat in Haringey.'

'I can come and live with you, then,' I said.

'Just give me a bit of time,' she said. 'Karl and me have got to get ourselves sorted. We're just getting the flat together.'

Afterwards Lesley sat on my bed, asked how I was feeling. Really, I thought, she doesn't need to bother any more, I won't be here much longer.

'My mum's all right now,' I said. 'She's got this flat with Karl. I'm going to go and live with them. Any day now.'

Lesley put her arm round me. Her voice was gentle, hesitant.

'Catriona, my love, that's not what she's saying to us.'

My mother never came again.

They tried to get me foster parents. They were going to advertise in the *Evening Standard,* they said.

Lesley took the photograph with her smart new Polaroid.

'Smile!' she said. 'Give me a lovely big smile. That's wonderful—you look like Meg Ryan.'

I stood there, smiling my most important smile ever. I tried to make my whole self smiley, the corners of my mouth ached with smiliness.

Lesley showed me the ad. It said, 'Catriona is a bright, pretty teenager with a real artistic talent. Her record of school attendance is excellent. Because of her troubled past, Catriona can be rather demanding at times. Catriona needs firm and consistent parenting.'

I thought about this, lying in bed at night in the orange light of the streetlamps, chilly under the candlewick, missing Aimee. I let myself think, just for a moment, about my foster family, what they might be like: nice food and lots of it, gentleness, and a soft bed with a duvet that tucked in at the back of your neck. And I wondered what it meant to be demanding.

No one was interested; no one even enquired about me. No one wants to adopt a fourteen-year-old girl who can be rather demanding, however bravely she smiles. I told myself I'd never thought it would happen, really, but there was a messy secret shame in admitting that I'd hoped.

I left the day I was sixteen. Two months before my birthday, Kevin from the Leaving Care team came to see me. My mother had been asking about me, he said. She'd moved abroad but she wanted to make contact, and did I want to see her. I said I didn't, really. It was my decision, he said. He sorted out my benefit, found me a flat above a chip shop in Garratt Lane, and a furniture grant from a charity.

My birthday was Lesley's day off, but she came to say goodbye. She held me close for a moment, a quick, hard, awkward hug. It embarrassed me; I wanted her to let go of me. But then, when she'd let go of me, I wished that she'd hold me again.

'I hope you get them,' she said. 'Your wishes, the things you wanted. I'm wishing them for you, too.'

That evening, in my flat in Garratt Lane, I sat at my flimsy new table and such loneliness washed through me, and I briefly longed to be back at The Poplars, just to have people there.

But slowly I put some kind of a life together. I did some temping—I'd learnt to type at school. There were always boyfriends. I guess I was attractive enough: I wore my skirts short and my blonde hair long and did whatever they wanted. I used to worry that my clothes, my skin even, stank of the chip shop, but the men didn't seem to care. I was, I suppose, promiscuous: I needed company in the evenings; I could only sleep through the night with somebody beside me. And if some of them were married—well, I reckoned, that was their responsibility. I never told them about myself and if they asked I made up something, recasting my life as unexceptional. After a month or two they usually drifted off, sensing I guess something in me that would for ever elude them. But from time to time there'd be one who said he loved me, and then I'd stop returning his calls, or say I was washing my hair, and after a while, he'd drift away, however keen he'd been.

Sometimes I thought I'd ring Kevin, and go and find my mother. I'd start to picture a reconciliation: her welcome, her apology, wrapping me in her arms and her scent of Marlboros and lily of the valley. But then I'd think how she'd neglected me and lied to me, and such rage would flare in me, and I knew I wouldn't do it. So the days dragged on: a life of offices, all looking much the same, and vaguely unsatisfactory sex that was paid for with meals at Pizza Express and shots of tequila. It was lonely, but it was better than I was used to.

There are moments when everything changes. I believe that. Moments of destiny, of serendipity. And one hot summer evening much like any other, when I'd just got off the bus in Garratt Lane, I bumped into Miss Jenkins.

'Catriona. What a nice surprise.'

She still had the hoops and the hippy cardigan, and she seemed so pleased to see me. She asked what I was doing. I shrugged a little, told her about the temping, though not the men.

She stood there for a while, her steady eyes on me. There was this school, she said. A nursery school, in Chelsea: private, expensive. Not really the sort of thing she approved of: nursery education ought to be free for everyone. But the headmistress was a friend of hers, they'd been at college together, and she happened to know they had a post going. I reminded her that I only had three GCSEs. She said it didn't matter, it was a nursery assistant post, they needed someone who could help with the art. The reference wasn't a problem, she said, she'd be more than happy to be my referee. I felt cool air against my face; I remember that, a sudden shift in the weather. We neither of us had anything to write on, so I borrowed her biro and scribbled the number on the back of my hand.

CHAPTER 10

The school was in a hushed street off King's Road. There was a cottage, old and rather crooked, at the turn of the road, and a little arched door in the wall. I rang and the door opened: children's noise rushed out into the stillness of the street. Miss Parry, the headmistress, introduced herself; she was tall, gangly, flat-footed as a heron, with vivid bird-like eyes. She took me through the cloakroom, where every peg had a different hand-painted picture—a duck, a tulip, a blue umbrella. This amazed me, the generosity of it, such detail lavished on every child, every name. And we went through the airy playroom, and out into the garden at the back, a story-book garden, a secret between high walls, with a laby-rinth of twisty stone paths and trampled scraps of lawn, and, in the middle, steps down to an old well—now filled in, of course, said Miss Parry—where there grew an old catalpa tree with leaves as wide as hands; and over there by the sandpit, she said, the two mossy stones set into the lawn were Carolingian graves. The whole place was exuberant with children, and messy with the tumbled detritus of their play, plastic animals faded by the sunlight, and the tyres and boxes and blankets they used to make castles and dens; anarchic and disorderly, but the disorder held and contained by the walls of yellow London brick, and the narrow bright beds of hollyhocks and lupins that fringed the edges of the garden.

She showed me round, asked a few obvious questions, then left me in the playroom to see what I'd do. Cast adrift in that sea of children, I did what made me feel safest, and sat in the art corner drawing extravagant pictures, of flamboyant animals with wings and wicked fangs. The children gathered round, adding their own details, colouring in. After a while my self-consciousness fell away. I was surprised to turn and see Miss Parry behind me. She reached out to touch a doleful tiger I'd drawn. 'I think you'll do quite nicely here,' she said.

It wasn't perfect. There was a lot of drudgery, toilets to be cleaned, floors to be swept and swabbed, little plastic bits of things to sort and put back into boxes. And it was physically exhausting, particularly demanding perhaps because it was so unstructured, all these children who tugged at your sleeve with their urgency and demands. The pay was minimal—enough to pay the rent on my flat and to buy a bit of food, though mostly I lived on what I ate at the nursery, the lunches of sausage or stew followed by jelly and bland glossy custard; and just about enough for mascara, and bleach for my long hair, and occasionally a new pair of clingy jeans or a faded knitted top with rainbow beading from one of the second-hand stalls in King's Road market. But mostly I was happy there. I found I had a skill with children, that I could join in their play, enter their worlds: I don't know where it came from, this easy instinctive ability—it seems surprising given the fractured nature of my childhood. But for me there was something so satisfying in the company of these children, with their openness and freshness and unanswerable questions. Where was I before I was born? Are the birds cross? Why do winds in cartoons have faces? Maybe I had some sense that this was what I needed—these years spent eating toad-in-the-hole and playing and reading picture books in a place that was kind and generous, where every child was so precious they had their very own picture next to their peg. It was perhaps a kind of healing for me: a reliving or a recovering of childhood.

Miss Parry believed with a passion in children's innate goodness, and held what I realise now were highly unfashionable ideas about the value of play. Tests and phonics lessons and neat rows of wooden desks were anathema to her. Every week there'd be a staff meeting in her flat above the playroom, when we'd sit on her squashy floral sofas and talk about the children's social and emotional progress: it was gossip, really, in the guise of psychology, singling out children who seemed troubled or reserved, and in the process enjoying the gratifying if dubious pleasures of disapproval. In their passion for the children's welfare, Miss Parry and Mrs Bates, her pink and excitable deputy, did a lot of disapproving: of parents who left their children with nannies too young to know better; of mothers who spent all day at the gym and the hair salon; of fathers who came home too late to kiss their children goodnight. Divorce particularly agitated them: husbands or wives—but especially wives—who abandoned their responsibilities and their beautiful children in pursuit of some cheap and transient sexual thrill. They loved to conclude, their mouths thin and tight, their voices fat with satisfaction, that the children of the affluent can be deprived in a multitude of ways, just as surely as the children of the poor; and at this point Miss Parry and Mrs Bates could grow quite dewy-eyed about the privileges of the poor—who may at least have stay-at-home mothers, and aunts and uncles living cosily round the corner, and granny in the corner by the gas-fire. During these discussions, I said nothing.

I stayed for seven years in that garden of children. I remember winter mornings, with the leaves fallen from the catalpa so the braided branches patterned the clean bright sky, and a crust of ice on the grass round the graves which the sun took a while to reach. All of us stamping our numb feet in our Wellingtons, and feeling even through our gloves the tingling of frost on our fingers; and at orange-juice time the cook, who was hugely fat, with a kind of picture-book rightness to her corpulence, bringing us syrupy mugs of coffee made with boiled milk and sugar, rich with a thick creamy scum, and toast that dripped with melting yellow butter.

And especially I remember summer days, the blossom blowing on the catalpa tree, the smells of exhaust from King's Road blending with the heavy scent of pollen from the dusty lilies in the flowerbeds, the children bare-legged and freckled and their hair warm to the touch. Hot afternoons that unfolded like tumbled bales of cloth, stretching on for aeons, pleasant but exhausting. And then the children would go, and silence would creep back into the place like a cat coming home for his supper. We'd sweep and tidy the garden in the warm and sudden stillness, and I'd feel a deep contentment washing through me.

Sinead came in the summer, when the catalpa was just beginning to flower. She was a three-year-old elf: disorderly Celtic hair, black and thickly curling, her face flushed pink by the heat. Her clothes were expensive but none of them seemed to match. She was troubled—unsmiling, virtually mute, with shadowed eyes.

Sinead's father had talked quite openly, said Miss Parry, leaning forward on her squashy sofa with an excessive eagerness in her bright bird eyes: and she wanted to share it all with us, every detail, in the interests of the child. The mother, it seemed, had a high-powered job in PR. She'd walked out, gone off with a man ten years her junior, a photographer, abandoning her husband and her child. The other staff were gleefully amazed that any woman could walk out on these two people—that delectable little girl, that father. For her father had caught everybody's eye, with his easy elegance, the cut of his shirt, his silk tie, gold cufflinks; and there was also something a little bemused and vulnerable about him, as though for a time he'd lost his way—making him vastly attractive to these women with their hunger to nurture. And then there was his palpable affection for his child.

Sinead was allocated to me, in the face of some competition for she was a perfect subject—an appealing child with emotional problems that were interesting but manageable. She played for hours with Playmobil figures on the steps that led down to the catalpa tree: acting out intricate stories, never speaking. I sat by her, sometimes moving an animal, joining in a little, and she started to let me in, to talk in a hushed monotone, so I could share in these tales of hers, entangled histories that had their genesis in the traditional storybook world of kings and witches and magic, but were far too full of losses and reversals. As the sunlit days spilled one into another, and the hollyhocks flowered then faded in the beds behind the sandpit, she started to sit nearer me; sometimes she hummed a little scrap of song. The plastic figures spread out onto a wall and a pathway; and one or two other children, sensing she might now notice them, appeared, forthright and curious, at the edges of her game. Her stories changed. The princesses became dogmatic and triumphant and accomplished amazing feats of daring; the queens and kings were reconciled, though they lived on opposite shores with between them wastes of ocean; and there began to be comfort in her games, small animals that were soothed to sleep in shoeboxes or under the fallen satiny petals from the catalpa tree. Till one day, when I was for a moment drawn away inside the playroom, I turned to see her careering round the garden with three of the rowdiest boys, waving a stick, noisy, engaged, connected: showing the first signs of that casual exuberance that's so much part of her now. I knew she didn't need me any more.

Mostly the nanny collected Sinead from school; sometimes it was her father. There was a late summer day, a day of thick heat and white sky, when he arrived a little early, and came out into the garden to find her. She rushed to him and leapt into his arms. I saw how he bent his head to her, only half heard what he said, but heard my name.

Sinead came across to me, where I was sweeping by the sandpit. 'My Daddy needs you,' she said. She took me by the hand, led me to him. I felt his gaze on me. I was aware how scruffy I was, bare-legged and my feet bare too because of the sand in my trainers, wearing a short denim sundress I had, that only seemed decent on the very hottest days. I saw how his eyes widened.

'Oh. It's you,' he said.

I smiled, and noticed how I pushed my fringe away from my face with parted fingers—not exactly deliberately, yet knowing that the sunlight would shine through my hair.

'I'm so grateful for everything you've done for Sinead,' he said. His eyes holding me, speculating. 'She thinks the world of you.'

I smiled, shrugged a little, not knowing what to say.

'We could go and have an ice cream, perhaps,' he said. 'You and me and Sinead.'

'I haven't finished clearing up,' I said.

He waited, sitting on one of the little walls with Sinead. Even without looking, I felt his eyes on me.

We went out to the street, to his car. It was big but not ostentatious. Inside it smelled of leather, a rich complicated male smell, like whisky or cigars; the smell excited me, filled me with a sense of astonishment about what was happening to me that was like a sexual high. The engine had a velvet sound and cool air lifted my skirt.

We went to a café in Fulham Road and sat in the window. He bought ice creams, chocolate for Sinead, pistachio for me, served in glittery glasses with silver spoons. I ate hungrily—I was always hungry then— scraping every last sweet drop from the bowl. Richard drank black coffee. Sitting so close, I saw how much older he was than me, his face quite worn, a web of lines at the corners of his eyes.

Sinead finished first. She knelt up on her chair with her back to us, and leaned against the window, looking out into the street.

'Could you have dinner with me?' he said, his voice hushed so she wouldn't overhear.

I laughed a little. 'Today?'

He nodded. He didn't laugh.

'In this dress?' I said, feeling all bare legs and bare shoulders.

'I like the dress,' he said.

We went back to his flat to leave Sinead with the nanny. It was in a cobbled mews where cars like his were parked between tubs of geraniums; inside, there were shiny antique tables and curtains with fringed heavy pelmets and a mantelpiece of pale marble with an over-mantel mirror in a gilded frame. It was polished and perfect, but somehow too quiescent, with the closed-off feel of houses where everything is covered in dust sheets—in spite of Sinead, who moved through these elegant spaces as though she were a trespasser, leaving only small marks of her presence: a toppling pile of picture books, a single butterfly painting stuck to the bathroom door. His ex-wife, I sensed, was a powerful woman: there was a feeling of absence about the place, as though some vital energy had been withdrawn. I saw so clearly then how Sinead had been rendered mute by her going. Yet there were many lovely things there; he showed me botanical drawings, Doulton, African carvings.

'I'm quite acquisitive,' he said, 'as you'll discover.' Talking as men sometimes will, as though it's already decided. 'When I see something beautiful, I want to make it mine.'

On the low table in the window there were three Chinese vases, patterned with birds and mountains and sprigs of blossom, light and lovely; the pictures in a way like children's drawings, simple with flat perspective, yet at the same time somehow old and wise. There was one that was all blue—distant blue hills, and clouds, and cherry trees that grew by a river, and a narrow bridge with three little figures crossing over towards the cherry trees; they were hunched like people who've been on a long hard journey, they had conical hats, one had a parasol. And I thought, I am like them: I am walking across the water towards the blossoming shore.

He took me to a restaurant called Mon Plaisir, with red checked tablecloths and baskets with several different kinds of bread and louche waiters who spoke only minimal English. It was chic but casual: my denim dress felt fine. I took ages to decide what I would eat. This amused him.

'You choose so carefully,' he said.

'I want it to be perfect,' I said. And looked across at him and saw how much he liked that.

We had steak and champagne and he told me about himself, his work, his parents, his childhood at a repressive boarding school. And he told me about Sara, his ex-wife: how it had started going wrong a long way back; how independent she'd been, how she hadn't had time for Sinead; how they'd scarcely ever made love since Sinead was born. This had made him unhappy: sex was pretty crucial to him, he said, his eyes searching mine. In the end he'd moved out of their bed, slept on the futon in the spare room. Looking back, it was the most open he's ever been with me. Perhaps it was easier because we were strangers still, as people in a railway carriage will share astounding confidences. And then—well into my third glass of champagne—I said, 'I need you to know this now,' and I told him about myself: what I had never before told anyone. Told him about my mother, about The Poplars, about Pindown: sensing what kind of person he was, and what he liked in me—that my vulnerability would be acceptable, appealing even, to him. That after Sara, who had never seemed to need him, my neediness might be welcome to him. That I might make him feel he had something to give.

'There's something so hurt in you,' he said. 'I can feel that.' And I thought, Maybe he says that to every woman he wants. Yet really I didn't care, it was certainly true for me.

When the dessert arrived and I eyed his greedily, wondering whether the crème brûlée I'd chosen, though silkily delicious, could really compete with the clafouti with frosted blueberries on his plate, he reached across and fed me some of his portion with his spoon. Watching me, his gaze moving across my mouth and my eyes. It was the nearest he'd come to touching me.

He drove me back to the flat in Garratt Lane. He didn't kiss me.

The next week he invited me out again. He told me he didn't much like the dress I was wearing—it was the only other dress I possessed, ankle-length and lacklustre, from the bargain rail at C & A—and he took me to a hushed boutique off Sloane Square and bought me another. It was in a rather obvious style, strappy, made of silk, but the colour of it was wonderful and subtle, red with a blackish bloom, like mulberries.

The third week we went again to Mon Plaisir.

'Sinead is with her mother tonight,' he said, his eyes holding mine. 'We could have coffee at my flat. Would you like that?'

I nodded, I understood.

We drove there in silence. I wondered how it would be. I worried that he saw something almost virginal in me, something that was an illusion, a kind of innocence—a product perhaps of my diffidence and rounded open face and ignorance of the urbane world he inhabited: that he would therefore be disappointed in me.

He took me into the living room.

'I've bought you something,' he said.

It was a long thin box. I felt unsure: I'd never been out with the kind of man who buys you jewellery. But he'd chosen well, it was easy to be pleased; it was charming, a silver chain with a stone the colour of cornflowers. I had no way of knowing what kind of gem it was. Precious stones were a mystery to me then, like Rolexes or makes of car or expensive bottles of wine.

'It's beautiful,' I said, and made to put it on.

'Wait,' he said. And when I looked at him quizzically, 'I want it to be perfect.' As I'd said in the restaurant, taking care over my choice.

'Come here,' he said. He stood me in front of him, in

front of the over-mantel mirror. I thought he was going finally to kiss me. He put his hands very lightly on my shoulders, turned me to face the mirror, started to ease the straps of my dress down off my shoulders.

'Someone might come in,' I said.

He pushed the front of the dress down over my breasts, doing it very slowly, in this concentrated way, yet scarcely touching me, so I felt only the slight brush against my skin of the warm tips of his fingers.

'No one will come in,' he said.

I saw how my face looked older, more knowing, in the lamplight. I made to help him undo my zip; he moved my hand away.

When he'd taken off all my clothes, he took the pendant and fastened it, still standing behind me, watching us in the mirror. I seemed somehow more naked with the chain around my throat. The metal was cold against my skin, and I felt a quick taut shock of desire. Though I had done so many things, some of them things I now regretted, the men who'd fucked me hastily in cars or riskily in public places or with their wives downstairs, I felt the shock and thrill of it so keenly. I think it was the sense of exposure, him looking at me and taking me in so completely, when we had as yet no sexual connection, when he'd scarcely touched me.

He looked at me for a long time. Then he lifted up my hair and kissed the back of my neck above the clasp, still watching me in the mirror, and pulled me down and made love to me on the rug in front of the fireplace. And it was good, but more ordinary, pleasant but predictable.

CHAPTER **11**

We went to Venice for our honeymoon. His choice; I loved it too. It was so beautiful—like walking through a fairy tale, at once enchanting and confusing, so I never quite knew where we were. It was almost as though the patterning of the streets and alleyways changed—shifted from day to day, from hour to hour; so that what this morning had felt familiar, this afternoon, in a new light—grey, with mist coming in from the lagoon, and sad with the cries of seabirds—started to seem strange. Alone, I'd have been permanently lost, needing a pocketful of pebbles or a ball of white wool to trail behind me, marking out my path. But Richard could invariably find our way, and I let him take over, take charge: liking this, that I could be so dependent, that I didn't have to struggle.

Our hotel room looked out on the Ponte della Libertà. The room was wide, high-ceilinged, as though devised for people much larger than me. There was a bed, vast as adult beds seem to a child, a long mirror, a padded window seat, and out of the window the shimmer and lilt of the water.

Our days fell into a pattern. In the morning we'd wander the city, exploring some mossy basilica of a church, or walking beside the canals, where the little waves lapped at the steps of the crumbling palaces, stuccoed dull pink or purple like rotting fruit. After lunch in some hushed restaurant, we'd go back to our room, and he'd take off my clothes and make love to me on the window seat, so if the curtain moved in the breeze I worried we might be visible from the street. And at night we'd make love in the big bed, and again perhaps at three or four, when the yowling of cats woke us.

As a lover he was sure, quiet, definite: a man who knew his mind, who never spoke, except to say what he wanted. But now that we were married and away from the flat where he'd lived with Sara, I found him less reserved, more adventurous. Or perhaps it was something to do with the staginess of Venice itself, the self-consciousness it inspired, so even the most intimate act seemed to require extravagant props, red ropes or velvet handcuffs, and to be acted out with a certain panache as though for a secret audience. I was very willing, and intrigued, and he never hurt me. But it wasn't quite how I'd imagined marriage. I'd thought this kind of thing was for mistresses, not wives. That marriage was a safer, quieter place—that it wouldn't have quite this urgency, nor all this apparatus of desire.

He liked to buy me things. I wanted a souvenir, so in a little dark shop by the Rialto, where everything smelt of the fishmarket, he bought me the masks that hang now on our wall. But mostly he bought me clothes or jewellery: a filmy dress, pearl earrings, silver chains; and a long fringed scarf of white silk with a pattern like frost on a window. When we made love he liked to see me in the things he'd bought me: the silver chains he twisted round my ankles or wrists when he made love to me in front of the long mirror; and the white silk scarf he sometimes liked to tie around my mouth.

The sex—the memory of it, the anticipation—was always there, so the smell of him seemed to permeate my skin. Yet in some ways we were almost formal still. There were subjects that were closed between us; we never talked again about his marriage to Sara, or my childhood. Mostly we talked about art or classical music. He knew a lot and taught me, and I liked that. Sometimes I looked at him and felt I scarcely knew him. Yet mostly it was happy and we were at ease with one another.

On our last day we had our first and only disagreement, and about something so trivial. We were in a café near St

Mark's, sipping coffee from tiny gold-rimmed cups, when I was aware of him watching a woman at the next table. She had high strappy heels, a dress that was tight and shiny. She was perhaps fifty-five, and plump: she bulged in her glossy clothes. As she got up to go he raised his eyebrows at me, made a disparaging gesture.

'What's wrong?' I said, a little sharply.

'Old women shouldn't dress like tarts,' he said.

'I thought she was just fine,' I said. 'She was enjoying those clothes, enjoying her life.' There was an edge to my voice. 'Why shouldn't she wear what she wants?'

He looked across at me, surprised. Then he patted my arm. 'Darling, why does it matter so much?'

I smiled apologetically, feeling I'd been over-emotional, getting too upset, as women will. 'Well, it doesn't really.' Wanting to seal this crack, to make it all as it was.

But I didn't like what he'd said. I thought, I too will be old one day.

On our way back to the hotel, he must have taken a wrong turn: the street grew narrower, the houses almost meeting overhead. Washing lines were stretched across the street with washing hanging from them, and we could hear what sounded like a Western on someone's television. We came to a dead end, a promontory with water on three sides, and opposite us over the water a tall strange house, each window with a window box, but nothing much grew in them, just a few plants, herbs mostly, straggling, untidy; and there were little plastic windmills stuck in the earth in each window box, like the windmills that children stick in sandcastles, yet they didn't quite have the cheeriness of toys. They were all yellow but in many different shapes, a star, a flower, a sickle-moon, and others less obvious, serrated, sharp, like parts of a great machine. The shadow of the house reached out across the water, and over to where we stood. Where the sun was shut out, the canal looked different. Without all the surface flicker and luminescence, you saw how dirty the water was, how full of mud and rubbish.

He had his arm round my shoulder and he felt my hesitation.

'What's wrong?' he said.

'I don't like it here,' I said.

He seemed amused. He pulled me to him and kissed me lightly, sliding his hand down under the hem of my skirt, easing a finger up the inside of my thigh.

Something made me look up. Over his shoulder I saw a woman right at the top of the house, leaning out to water one of the window boxes. She paused for a moment, looked down at us with a hard, cold, curious stare, then pulled back into the darkness inside the house. A cool wind stirred the windmills, so the whole house seemed alive, and the windmills turned like Catherine wheels, spinning so fast they made new shapes, the serrated circles becoming whole, entire, making a buzzing sound like the whirring of insect wings. I shivered. And then it passed as suddenly as it had come. We found our way back to our room, and he took off my clothes and made love to me, tying my wrists to the bed with the white silk scarf, and I forgot my feeling of unease.

Afterwards, there was music through our window. I went to lean on the window sill, still drugged and high with sex. A man with hair down his back and a rucksack covered in badges was sitting by the canal and playing the flute, and a gondola drifted past, and the underside of the bridge was bright with the fluid dance of reflected light from the water. And I thought, How can these things coexist—the life I used to have: and here, all this silk and shimmer, everything silvered, luminous? How can these things come together in a single life, a single story? And I couldn't reconcile them. It was as though to believe in one world, you had to disbelieve in the other as though those other things—my mother, The Poplars, the cruel room with the door panels covered with brown paper— as though all these things had simply ceased to exist.

I still think back to those moments in our early life together, that moment with the sound of the flute by the Ponte della Libertà; and the first time we made love, when he put the pendant on me, his gaze so hot and complete, my thirst for his touch. Yet now, amid the dai- liness of caring for the children—all the demands, the practical things, the routine pleasant love-making—those moments too have receded: as though they too belong to another life.

CHAPTER 12

We put on our best clothes for the hospital: Daisy has her new red denim jacket, I wear my long black coat. In my bag I have a piece of paper on which I've written a list of Daisy's symptoms. I learnt to do this from a book Nicky once lent me, on how to be assertive with your doctor. It was called *My Body! My Decision!* and had lots of alarming gynaecological drawings. Afterwards Richard will go straight on to his office. He's in his suit, he has his *Financial Times*, he looks substantial, purposeful.

Sinead is getting ready for school as we leave.

'Good luck, Daisy,' she says cheerily. 'And don't forget—if they want to take your organs, you mustn't let them.'

'Sinead, what on earth are you on about?' says Richard.

'They do, though, Dad,' says Daisy. 'They take children's livers and they keep them in jars in garages.'

Both girls are thoroughly pleased with themselves.

We drive there through the thick traffic and the grey day. Daisy is silent now. There's a car park at the hospital, with borders full of those shrubs with dull green leaves that don't respond to the seasons, and we manage to find a space. The receptionist in Outpatients directs us to the clinic. The serious sharp smell in the corridor makes my pulse quicken. Daisy looks unperturbed, but her fingers are wrapped round my hand.

We go through swing doors into the waiting room for the paediatric clinic. There are battered Fisher-Price toys and women's magazines and board books and a GameCube and goldfish. Behind the desk there's a nurse dressed like someone at a playgroup, in a green top and trousers. She has a gentle face.

'You're seeing Dr Taylor,' she says.

'That's not the consultant?'

She shakes her head. 'Dr Taylor is Dr McGuire's registrar.'

She takes Daisy to be measured and weighed; and there is special anaesthetic cream and a big transparent plaster to be put in the crook of Daisy's elbow, in case there are blood tests. When Daisy moves her arm it makes the plaster wrinkle, so it looks like an old woman's skin.

We sit by the goldfish tank and Richard opens his newspaper. A white board lists the doctors who are taking the clinic. Daisy looks yearningly at the GameCube, but it's been monopolised by a lanky boy with exuberant hair like Bart Simpson. A sticker that says he was brave today is fixed to the front of his sweatshirt.

'You could read a book,' I tell her.

She shakes her head. 'They're baby books,' she says.

Two of the children waiting are in wheelchairs, and there's a pale wild girl, with a crooked body and thick glasses. Her father speaks to her in curt commands as he helps her get a drink from the machine. You can tell it's a technique he has perfected over years, the only way to get through. There's something in me, something scared and primitive, that is alarmed by these children, as though their misfortunes and sadnesses could in some way injure my child. I tell myself we're so fortunate that we are not like them—that whatever is wrong with Daisy, soon it will all be over.

The doctors come to their doors to call for their patients. Dr Taylor is a woman in her twenties, in a flowered skirt, with a vague uncertain air. Dr McGuire has the red door; I watch as he comes out. He's thin and fair-haired and cerebral-looking, with his sleeves rolled up to his elbows. He doesn't smile, but he has an acute clever face. I know I want this doctor for my child.

A sense of purpose forms in me. I get up and go to the nurse behind the desk.

'I'm so worried about Daisy,' I tell her. 'She isn't eating

and she's scarcely been to school. Is there any chance we could see the consultant?'

She shakes her head. 'He's all booked up today.'

Tears well in me and I don't swallow them down. 'I mean, I'm sure Dr Taylor is great… It's just…' I can't finish the sentence. A tear spills down my face. It's not exactly deliberate, but I don't try to stop it. I don't like being this pleading, tearful person, but I feel I have no choice. 'I'm really sorry,' I tell her.

Her eyes rest on me, tender with concern.

'Leave it with me,' she says. 'I'll see what I can do.'

I watch as she knocks on the red door and goes in. I sit by Daisy and blink away my tears and we talk about the goldfish, their three-second memories, their frilled and opalescent tails.

The nurse comes out. She's smiling.

'I've fixed it,' she says. 'He'll see you. You may have to wait a little longer though.'

'Thank you.' This is a gift: I want to hug her.

I turn to Richard. 'You don't mind the wait, do you?'

'Of course not, darling,' he says. 'You must do what you think best. Eleven is my absolute limit, though.'

There's a wide French door that leads to an inner court-yard. We can see a play-tunnel and some plastic push-along vehicles, their colours singing out in the dense grey day. Daisy pulls at my hand; she wants to go there.

The toys are inviting, and there's a surface that looks like tarmac but yields to the feet, so you wouldn't get hurt if you fell. We look around for a while, but now she's out here, there's nothing she wants to try. It's starting to rain, the kind of gritty, insistent rain that sneaks in under your collar. It's somehow sad out here, with no-one playing; a sense of desolation washes through me. We wander back inside. Bart Simpson is still intent on the Nintendo, so we skim through *Prima*, searching for pictures of cats. Richard looks at his watch.

But then the red door opens, and Dr McGuire comes out and calls Daisy's name. I take her hand and we go in. I smile and say hello, but he doesn't return my smile. I tell myself this doesn't matter, that this clever unsmiling doctor will help us, will heal Daisy.

There is a sofa for patients; we sit on it, with Daisy in the middle. It's meant, I suppose, to be casual, to put us at our ease, but really it's too low. Dr McGuire sits at his desk, looking down at us. His arms are folded on the desk in front of him.

'So, Daisy, how are you doing?' he says.

She clears her throat. 'All right.'

'Dr Carey tells me you've not been feeling well.'

She nods.

'And how are you today?'

'A bit better,' she says.

'Well, that's good news,' he says.

I don't know whether to speak. But he has to know how things are, or he won't be able to help us.

'It's not quite true. She was feeling very sick last night,' I tell him, my voice high-pitched, insistent.

He raises his hand, as though to silence me.

'Be quiet,' he says. 'You'll get your turn in a minute.'
I feel a quick spurt of rage.

He talks to Daisy about school: whether she's happy,
what are her favourite subjects, whether she has friends.
She replies in hushed monosyllables. None of this seems
to have anything to do with her illness. I think how little
time we have, and there's so much to get through. I worry
I've made a mistake in being so pushy, that we should
have stayed with the vague young woman with the
flowered skirt.

Then at last he asks us for the history of her
symptoms. I take the notes out of my bag. I tell him how
it started with flu and how little she eats, about her
nausea and the pains in her legs and not going into
school. Richard sits there silently, nodding or murmuring agreement, his *Financial Times* beside him on the
sofa. When Dr McGuire responds to what I say, or asks
a question, it's Richard that he looks at. This makes me
feel like I'm not really there.

'Obviously we need to investigate further,' he says
then. 'I want to repeat those blood tests and I'd like to X-ray
her legs and do a barium meal. And we need to get her
digestive symptoms properly under control. I'm going to
prescribe three medicines,' he tells Richard. 'There's one
for stomach acidity and one for nausea and one to
increase lability. And I'd like to see you again in one
month's time. If she isn't better then, maybe we'll have
to approach things rather differently.'

'Thank you,' says Richard. He's starting to get up.

But I don't move. 'Daisy doesn't find medicine very easy to take,' I tell him.

He looks at me then. His gaze is pale and cold. I know just how I must seem to him, as though there is some uneasy empathy between us. That I'm fussy, overprotective, speaking for my daughter, my coat too long and grungey, my voice too shrill.

'She can't keep any kind of medicine down,' I say. 'Not even Calpol.'

'Well,' he says briskly, 'give her a sweet or a biscuit to eat afterwards. All right?'

He half rises. His impatience with me crackles in the air between us.

But I need him to hear. 'I've tried. It doesn't help. The medicine just comes up again.'

'How old is she? Eight?'

I nod.

'Most children can take medicines at eight. I'm sure you'll manage,' he says, and smiles at Richard. He gets up, moves to open the door. 'Right, then,' he says.

We go back to the waiting room.

Richard puts on his coat.

'And now I really must be off,' he says. 'I'll give Francine a ring to say I'm on my way. You're happy to handle the rest on your own?'

'Of course,' I tell him.

'You were brilliant, munchkin.' He kisses Daisy's cheek. She rubs her head against him, basking in the warmth of his approval.

'Feeling happier?' he says to me.

I nod. We can't talk here.

'At least we know it's being properly investigated,' he says. 'I'm sure he'll find out what's wrong. I think we can relax now. You just feel he knows what he's on about, don't you?'

He goes. I hear his footsteps moving briskly down the corridor.

We're taken to the treatment room, where cotton-wool sheep hang from the ceiling, and there are two nurses, one to take the blood and one to be reassuring.

'These are really really good veins,' says the nurse who's taking the blood. 'Daisy, your veins are beautiful.'

Ridiculously, I am proud of her, for having such beautiful veins.

She gets out the sticker that says how brave Daisy's been. Daisy gives me an eloquent look, raising her eyebrows a little, but lets it be stuck on her jacket.

We go to Radiology, where Daisy's legs are X-rayed, and then to the pharmacy where we are given a numbered ticket, like in a children's shoe-shop at the end of the holidays. They ask for Daisy's weight, so they can work out the dose. There's a lot of medicine, some of it with a syringe so you can measure it down to the very last drop. This amazes me—that you could give medicine to a child with such precision. They hand it to us on a polystyrene tray.

'You didn't like him, did you, Mum?' says Daisy, in the car.

'You could tell?'

In the rear view mirror, I see her nod, and the ghost of a smile.

'But I'm sure he's good at his job, and that's what really matters,' I tell her. 'What about you?'

'I liked the sheep mobile. But this sticker is awful.' She pulls it off and screws it into a ball. 'You looked ever so cross,' she says.

When we get home and Daisy is watching television, I put all the medicine bottles out on the kitchen table. I taste the medicines. There's one that's bitter, and one that sticks to your teeth, but the third one isn't too bad, though it has a strange aftertaste, like a stale boiled sweet.

I tell myself this must be possible: eight-year-olds can take medicines; everybody says so. I measure some into a spoon. I get a glass of water and a chocolate flake. From the back of the cupboard I find some aromatherapy oil, a Christmas present from Nicky, and sprinkle it on a tissue.

I go to get Daisy.

'Shall we just do it?'

'OK.' She's resigned.

I sit her at the table.

'The water and the flake are to take the taste away,' I tell her. 'And if you like you can sniff the tissue as you take it, so you won't smell the smell. You do it in your own way. Just in your own time. Perhaps just a tiny sip today, that would be fantastic.'

I sit by the window and flick through the Tuscany brochure, trying to lose myself in those sunflower fields and dazzling skies: trying not to watch her.

She picks up the spoon, looks at it for a moment, raises it to her lips. She takes the tiniest sip. Immediately she starts retching. She rushes to the sink. She's shivering with nausea. I hold her, smooth back her hair.

'We'll leave it for today,' I tell her. 'You did so well.'

She's retching still but nothing's coming up. We go into the living room and I bring her duvet and wrap her up on the sofa. It's *Diagnosis Murder* on the television. There's always something so bleak about these daytime programmes: you think of all the other people who are watching with you, people who are old or lonely, people without purpose. I sit for a while with my arm around her. The nausea shakes her. The medicine has triggered her retching and now it won't be stopped.

Eventually, I go to the kitchen to make myself a coffee. It's only one o'clock, but the light is so low it feels as though dusk is falling. My house is drab in the raw grey light. Outside, water drips from the branches of the birch tree and the lawn is full of wormcasts. We're stagnating here: life is passing us by. I let myself think for a moment of how Daisy's life should be, of the rich familiar rhythms of primary school: choir practice and spelling tests and raw scraped knees from running and skidding in the playground, and noisy rainy lunchtimes, drawing extravagant cats on the backs of spare worksheets with Megan, squabbles and making up—not sitting wrapped in a duvet watching *Diagnosis Murder* and feeling sick. A sense of loss tugs at me.

The medicine bottles are lined up on the table, like a

reproach. The chemical sweetness of the one I tasted is still on my tongue. I wonder what happens now: I don't know how to do this. Perhaps like with a baby—pinching her nose so she has to open her mouth, forcing the spoon in, tipping her head back, holding her while she retches? Is that what I have to do?

I pile the bottles up on the polystyrene tray and shut them away in the cupboard.

CHAPTER 13

When Daisy is sleeping and Sinead is on the Internet—in theory researching a project on the Weimar Republic, though almost certainly on Facebook—I go up to the attic. Richard is still not home: there's no one I can talk to. The night sky through the skylight is black and unforgiving, with spiky stars. I can still see Dr McGuire's acute clever face, as though his eyes are on me. I feel a child's futile rage: I'm repelled by his voice, and his coldness and the way he silenced me.

There are some narcissi that I had in a vase in the

living room. They're fading now, and I've brought one here to draw. Maybe this will calm me. It's waiting on my table. In the dim light you can scarcely see the stem, the flower looks as if it's floating. I shall draw it in pen and ink, just tracing out the form, trying to capture that lightness, that lovely effortless intricacy, the way it moves upwards like breath.

I start to work, but the light isn't good enough really, the overhead light bulb's gone and I'm using just the table lamp; and I'm restless, full of anger, and the drawing goes all wrong. The shape that I draw is lumpen, solid; it sits squat on the page, weighed down and bulbous. I feel disgust with what I've done. I draw a line straight through the drawing, then again and again, all my anger coming out through my hand. I go on like a furious child, crossing out over and over, the feeling moving through me like a charge—my rage that Daisy is ill, that no one seems able to help us, that no one understands.

Then suddenly the mood burns out; it starts to seem strange, excessive. I put down the pen. I look at what I've done, my crossings-out. The lines are like hair being blown, like matted branches or the tendrils of vines. The misdrawn flower is hidden; only hinted at beneath this thick tangled texture of my crossings-out: a ghost-narcissus, a shadow. I find I'm drawing again, the pen moving over the page, adding to my drawing as though my hand is separate from my mind. The lines circle, swirl, the tunnels open out into whirlpools, labyrinths. There is a space in the centre of this shape, in the middle of the vortex. I need to fill in the space: something has to go there. I doodle, playing around, almost at peace now, curious, waiting, the anger all out there in the lines on the page.

I look at what I've drawn. A face, young, bony, scared, with shadow patches round the eyes. A sharp face, like an alien in a cartoon: a thin wild child. I don't know who she is, this child in the heart of the labyrinth.

I look at my picture, and see that it is interesting—the vortex and the child. I draw another child, and another, tiny, in the margins of the picture—but these are complete, not just faces, their bodies twisted, shadowed. I'm doodling really, not trying, letting it happen. The children's arms and legs are slender, sharply angled; their limbs fly around, they are full of movement, of energy, but there is nowhere they can go to, they are trapped, imprisoned, by the lines like tumbled hair or forests. They surprise me, yet they are also familiar: as though I dream these children sometimes, and then forget my dreams.

These are the only people that I have ever drawn.

I sit for a while and look at what I've done. I think of things. The closed door, the saucepans tied to the door-handle that would rattle if you touched it. The smell of scorching dust on the flimsy electric fire. The woman in the flat next door who sat smoking on her sofa. I feel a trace of what I felt then: the pressure on my chest. But this is tolerable; I can bear it now. As though these thin, trapped children have begun to set me free.

I tear the page out of the sketch pad and take it downstairs and stick it up in the kitchen. I want to see if I'll like it in the morning.

Richard comes home at ten. I need to talk about Dr McGuire, but I know this isn't the time; his eyes are smudged with tiredness. He sits down heavily at the kitchen table. I get some ice from the freezer for his whisky, and he notices the picture. He looks at it for a moment, with a kind of concentration I find surprising.

'I didn't think you drew people.'

'No, I don't. Well, I never have before.' The compulsion to be self-deprecating washes through me. 'It's just a little sketch I did—I wanted to try something new.' And, when he says nothing, 'What d'you think? Don't you like it?'

He nods, as though he's giving some assent or recognition.

'It's good,' he says. 'In fact it's very good. It's very well drawn.' He takes a long indulgent sip of whisky; the tension in him starts to ease away. 'But to be honest, darling, it's not my kind of thing. I liked the flowers better.'

CHAPTER 14

'How's Daisy?' says Nicky.

She's ordered a plate of mussels and chips to celebrate the end of her detox diet. The shells of the mussels are shiny and black like her clothes.

'Much the same. We're seeing Helmut on Friday.'

'I'm sure he'll be able to help,' she says. 'He's wacky but it works.'

A rangy waiter lights our candle, a tealight in a tumbler; you can feel the heat of it on your skin if you lean across the table.

'Is Richard being nice?' she says.

'He just keeps saying it'll all be OK. Sometimes I think if he worried more, then I wouldn't have to.'

Shadows move across the poster on the wall behind her; it shows a louche blonde woman who's wrapping herself lasciviously around a bottle of Pernod. Little tea-lights glitter in Nicky's eyes.

'He adores you,' she says irrelevantly.

'We saw Dr McGuire,' I tell her.

'How was it?'

'I didn't like him.'

Nicky considers this, tearing at a mussel with her teeth; her crimson mouth looks briefly predatory.

'Some people I know went to see him,' she says. 'Their son was diabetic. They said he was good—very thorough. I guess he's one of those guys that people either love or hate.'

'Maybe.'

'From what Kim said, I guess he sees himself as a bit of a crusader.'

'God knows. I thought he was foul. He wouldn't listen to me.'

Her face is intense with concern. She puts her hand on my arm.

'You have to be really assertive, Cat. You're just too nice, sometimes.'

I ask about Simon. She leans towards me; her voice is hushed and secret. Things have progressed, she tells me: they made love on her desk after work, while the cleaner was in the corridor. I sense her excitement, shot through with a kind of fear: her pupils are dark and vast when she talks about him.

'What if Neil finds out?'

'He won't,' she says. 'How could he?'

I ought to tell her to stop—I know that's the best friend's role, to issue the warnings—but somehow I can't do it. I wouldn't want to take the shine from her.

She takes a long swig of Cabernet Sauvignon.

'It's the old story, how it happens,' she says. 'I mean, once you've been there, you start to see it everywhere. You have these babies and slob around in tracksuits and you think you're anaesthetised, you just don't get why anyone bothers with sex. Then your youngest starts at nursery and you up your hours at work and buy yourself a lipstick. And you're chatting to some guy about the October spreadsheets, and you're very aware of the way he pushes up his shirt-sleeves, you can't take your eyes off his skin.' She's leaning towards me across the table, her dark hair swinging above the flame of the candle. For a brief, wild moment, I fear she will catch fire. 'And then the libido you thought had gone AWOL for ever sneaks up behind you and hits you over the head… It's danger time for marriage, when your little one starts nursery. Good thing the guys don't know.'

I refill her glass for her. Her lips have left a crimson stain on the rim.

The rangy waiter puts some music on—a singer I know but can't name, a low voice, smoky with sadness. We listen for a while.

'It's different for you and Richard, of course,' she says then, responding perhaps to some hesitancy in me. 'You're just so good together. You're made for each other.'

I shrug a little; I don't know how to respond. Sometimes I wish she wouldn't say these things, about how good my marriage is. It's a superstitious fear, perhaps—as though even to put these thoughts into words might make something start to unravel. Nobody's marriage is perfect.

She puts her hand on my wrist.

'Hell, I've been going on and on. I'm such a selfish pig. When you've got so much to cope with—you know, with Daisy and everything.' She forages in her handbag. 'I've brought you a book,' she says.

She hands it to me. It's called *You Can Heal Your Life* and on the cover it has a rainbow heart.

'The woman who wrote this is a healer,' she says. 'She believes that we create whatever happens to us. By the way we think. I know it sounds mad, but I'm sure she's onto something.'

I leaf through the book. It's full of words like *vibrant* and *abundant*. When I look at it, I feel tired suddenly.

She's watching me. 'I mean, perhaps it won't mean anything to you. But I found it great when I kept on having those migraines, and I did some work on myself— you know, about my dependency issues and stuff—and I think it really helped.'

'I thought it was Helmut who helped.'

She grins. 'Well, maybe a bit of both…'

At the back there's a list of symptoms and their causes.

I look up Nausea. It says nausea is caused by 'Fear. Rejecting an Idea or Experience.' I wonder what Idea or Experience Daisy is rejecting.

'It's sweet of you,' I tell her. I put it in my handbag.

Outside on the pavement, car headlights sweep across us, and there's a sudden smell of spring and a lemon moon that hangs low in the indigo sky. You can see the blotches on the moon, like features on some far-off face whose expression is unguessable.

'Give Daisy a kiss from me,' she says. And goes, all thrilled and shiny, leaving me alone.

CHAPTER 15

The next day Daisy goes to school, walks straight in without crying. Hope surges through me as I watch; just for a moment, I can believe that all our troubles are over.

At half-three I wait anxiously for her. She is pale but smiling. She has a woven friendship bracelet that Megan has given her, and a parents' invitation to a karaoke *Sound of Music* organised by the PSA, and a letter about a sponsored matchbox competition, in aid of a school in Africa, which she thrusts at me. They have to see how many things they can fit into a matchbox—no body parts, medicines or animals allowed—and there will be a prize for the child who has the biggest collection.

'This'll be fun. We'll start tonight,' I tell her.

She shakes her head; she says her stomach hurts. When we get home, she goes to her room and lies in bed watching television.

I take her some toast and a hot-water bottle to hold against her stomach. She's watching a programme on organ donation.

'This looks depressing,' I tell her.

'It's interesting, Mum.' Her face is serious, composed. 'There was a woman whose little girl died of cancer and she had the little girl's cornea donated, and she worried that she might not be able to see when she gets up to Heaven. I worry about that too. But you probably would be able to, wouldn't you?'

'Of course you would,' I say brightly. But I hate this conversation.

In the evening, her stomach ache gets worse.

'There must be something you can do,' she says.

I tell her we'll have to try the medicine again. She acquiesces. I choose a different one, the chalky one that sticks to your teeth. I have some idea that this is meant for stomach pain. She is meant to take two spoonfuls three times a day. I kneel beside her, pour a few drops in the spoon. There is juice and a chocolate flake for afterwards. She takes the tiniest sip and swallows and retches it up. She goes on retching all evening. I sit with her and stroke her back and read from her fairy-tale book. She finally gets to sleep at half past eleven.

Richard is impatient to get to bed: he has a crucial meeting tomorrow.

'Mother phoned,' he says, as he's putting on his pyjamas.

'Is she OK?'

'She's fine,' he says. 'They're both fine. We were talking about Daisy. She thinks Daisy needs to get back her confidence with food.' There's an air of finality to the way he says this, as though it is the answer.

'I don't know what that means,' I say. 'Food makes her feel sick. It isn't to do with her attitude. This isn't in her head, Richard.'

He has a pained look. 'I thought it was at least worth thinking about,' he says.

He buttons up his pyjama jacket. He always seems so much older when he takes off his formal clothes.

'And she said she thinks we've got to get a grip,' he says. 'That staying off school can get to be a habit.'

I'm too tired to be patient.

'Why d'you listen?' I say. 'Why d'you always think she's right about everything?'

'Cat, she's got all those years of experience.'

'That doesn't mean she knows what's wrong with Daisy.'

'She's very concerned,' he says. His face darkens with irritation. 'For Chrissake, she's only trying to help. I'd have thought you'd be *grateful*.'

On Friday we have the appointment with Helmut Wolf. He has a Quaker look, contemplative, white-haired. He has a cluttered consulting room with pictures of Japanese mountains, and shelves that are stacked with bottles of

Chinese herbs. They have a thick green complicated smell, of ferns and disinfectant. He brings out a tray of tiny glass phials of various foods. Daisy has to touch them one at a time with one finger, while he presses on her other arm to test her muscle strength. He says she's allergic to wheat, milk, sucrose, chocolate—and she must give them up, at least for several months. I am appalled. This seems to leave out the only things she'll eat.

But I do as he says; I go to the health-food shop and buy wheat-free flour and rice cakes from a wan and earnest assistant. I tell Richard that I'm trying Daisy on a diet, though I can't bring myself to tell him how much she'll have to give up.

On the first day of the diet, I offer her prawns, carrot sticks, rice cakes, corn spaghetti, chicken and chips, crisps, and some cup-cakes I made with a recipe from the health shop. She eats some crisps and an apple. The second day, she eats a packet of crisps and two small lumps of chicken, and she's so hungry, she lies on the floor and cries. I make her a thick jam sandwich: I know that we can't carry on.

We go to the hospital for the barium meal. We sit in the waiting room and a nurse with a wide white smile and lots of earrings comes to talk to us. There's stuff to drink, she says, which shows up on the X-ray so they can tell if everything's working properly. It's not exactly a McDonald's milkshake.

In the X-ray room, I have to wear a lead apron and promise I am not pregnant. At first they can't get Daisy to drink the barium. The radiologist is impatient, says maybe they'll have to give up. Another nurse comes and talks Daisy through it again, this one too explaining that it's not exactly a McDonald's milkshake. They give her a straw and she sips and starts to retch. But they say she may have swallowed enough to show up on the X-ray. I watch her oesophagus on the screen. Aha, says the radiologist, she has reflux, as though it is all explained. I ask what does that mean and she says it means that stomach acid is coming up into her mouth; and I think how we knew that anyway. I ask what should we do about it, but she tells us to discuss it with the paediatrician.

I read the book that Nicky gave me and try to do what it says. I make up some affirmations and repeat them inside my head. I write them out and keep the paper in the attic. I try to imagine them happening as I write them. In the mornings I speak them into the bathroom mirror, quietly so the girls can't hear: Daisy is well again; Daisy is happy and smiling and energetic and well. I think how strange I look, doing this.

There is a Sunday afternoon when we go to Kew Gardens. It's a perfect day, liquid light pouring down over everything, and I decide the exercise will be just what Daisy needs. Sinead is persuaded to join us. She's reaching the age when family outings can start to seem embarrassing, but she's yearning for an excuse to wear her new ripped jeans. I tell myself that this is a new beginning. For the first time for weeks, I tie up my hair and put on lots of make-up. I will be vibrant and positive, just like Nicky's book.

At Kew, there are few trees yet in leaf, but whole vast lawns of crocuses, white and purple, dazzle in the sun as though they themselves are a source of light; and the orange buds of the crown imperials are fattening and opening out, their imposing shapes like the patterns of damask or Victorian anaglypta, and in the bare brown borders fritillaries hang their heads, their petals softest purple or green as leaves. Moorhens with gangly legs like twigs peck in the golden grass.

Daisy is teasing Sinead about some soap star.

'You *do* fancy him. You *do*. I can *tell*.'

Sinead, riled, gives chase. Daisy runs off across the grass, scattering moorhens, the sunlight stitching yellow threads in her hair. I watch her running and tell myself: Maybe everything's fine, like in my affirmations. I turn to Richard.

'Look!' I mouth.

He nods and smiles; his face is smooth today, as though the sun has eased away some tension in him.

Sinead gives up her attempt to catch Daisy and comes back to join us.

'People think she's so blonde and innocent,' she says, through gasping breaths. 'And really she's *Hitler*.'

By the lake, the big willow tree is colouring up for spring, its fabulous green-gold droop caught in the shining water. Planes roar above us, but the gardens are full of the whistle and shimmer of birdsong. We hunt for tiny things for Daisy's sponsored matchbox; we find a seed-case, an acorn, a feather the size of your thumbnail and pale grey like a pearl.

Richard puts his hand on my arm.

'Darling, are you OK?' he says.

'I'm fine.'

'I've been a bit preoccupied with work,' he says. 'Maybe I haven't always given you quite the support you needed.' He's reaching out to me: this makes me happy. 'You do such a wonderful job,' he says. 'You know I think that, don't you?'

'Yes,' I say.

He puts his arm around me. I feel the thick wool of his jacket against the back of my neck. I am safe, protected.

Daisy wants to go in the glasshouses, to see the plants that eat insects. We pass through the ante-room of desert plants and cacti, and push at a door and enter a different world, smelling of the tropics, wet and oppressive. The air is thick with moisture and Sinead's hair instantly frizzes. The steps are slippery under our feet, and every surface is covered in weed and moss and mould. You feel if you stayed still for too long here, green tendrils might sprout from your skin. There are bromeliads, with leaves sharp-edged as knives, their centres full of water and red-stained as if they've bled, and there are blotchy orchids, ugly and intricate, like deformed faces, and everywhere green earthy smells and the sounds of waterfalls. The girls take off their coats and give them to me to carry, and move on ahead to look at the fat koi carp that ripple in-dolently through the murky pools.

Now, I think, now is the moment: when he's so warm, so open.

'Richard, there's something I need to tell you.'

He hears the shake in my voice, stops walking, turns to me.

'My mother's been writing to me.'

He stares at me. I think for a moment that he will be angry with me.

'Your mother.' His eyes are small and narrowed against the light.

'Yes.'

'Shit. Where is she?'

'In Berlin.'

His face relaxes. 'Well, at least she won't be turning up on our doorstep.' He pats my arm, the way you might comfort a child. 'Poor you. What a total pain. Can't you just tell her to stop?'

'I don't want to write to her. I don't want anything to do with her.'

'OK,' he says. 'You're right, that's probably best.'

I feel a surge of relief. Now it is all out in the open I'm so much less afraid.

We go to the room of carnivorous plants. There's a glass case full of pitcher plants, bulbous and intricate, purple like meat, or pallid and speckled as though they are diseased. There's a sign that says, 'They have no set meal times'. We stand and stare. They have a sinister look.

Behind us a woman says gleefully to her small children, 'These are the ones the security man warned us about. These are the ones he said, "Careful they don't eat you…"'

Sinead has found the sundews, which have shining wet hairs on their leaves. A fly is stuck to one: it's still alive, it's struggling but can't escape.

'That is *gross*,' says Daisy.

Richard gives the girls a little lecture, explaining about the sticky stuff on the sundew, and how the fly is trapped and all the different ways that plants eat insects. He likes to teach them. Sinead has a special expression, sardonic, long-suffering, for when he tries to explain things. Daisy listens for a moment, briefly attentive, then she's off along some inner path of her own.

'Natalie's sister has a friend,' she says, 'and she has some voodoo dolls from when she went on holiday.' Her voice is slightly reverent and hushed. 'And the girl with the voodoo dolls gave Natalie's sister one for wealth and after that their father got ten thousand pounds because he was doing a good job at his work.'

'Wow,' I say. Sinead too is listening, momentarily impressed. She loves this kind of thing; the magazines she reads are full of runes and horoscopes.

'But then Natalie's sister and the girl with the voodoo dolls broke up.' Daisy is solemn as she tells her story. 'And the girl gave Natalie's sister a doll for hate, and next day Natalie's sister broke her ankle.'

'Spooky,' says Sinead.

'You don't want to listen to that kind of nonsense,' says Richard briskly.

Daisy shrugs. 'I wasn't scared,' she says.

Downstairs there are aquariums. We see black catfish that move through the water like shadows or absences, and a grey spangled piranha, and tiny platys with ripply rainbow tails. Daisy climbs up on the railing. The flickery lights from the tank are in her eyes.

'They're so gorgeous—the rainbow ones, the platys,' I say. 'All their colours.'

Richard turns to me. His face is close to mine, the smell of the aftershave that I gave him for Christmas, musky, rich, is all round me. I curve in towards him.

'I love it when you get excited about things,' he says. He pushes his hand through my hair. 'You look so pretty this afternoon,' and he kisses me with considerable seriousness, right there by the aquarium in front of several people.

On the way out we buy ice creams from the kiosk— traditional creamy ones in cones, with no E-numbers.

'This is delicious,' says Daisy, taking a first lick.

We wander past the crocus lawn again with our ices, drinking in the lavishness of the flowers.

Sinead and I have nearly finished, but Daisy has a lot of ice cream left.

'Get a move on, Daisy, or it's going to melt,' says Richard.

A large drip lands on her foot. She holds the ice cream well out in front of her. I wrap a tissue round the cone.

'Actually, Mum, d'you mind if I leave this?' she says.

'No, of course not, sweetheart.'

I take the ice cream and drop it in the nearest bin. I glance at Daisy; her face is white as wax.

We sit quietly in the car going home.

'Well, that was a nice outing, wasn't it?' The brightness in my voice sounds forced, even to me.

No one says anything.

'Mum, Daisy's retching,' says Sinead then.

Dread washes through me. I turn to Daisy, reach back to stroke her knee.

'Maybe the ice cream wasn't such a clever idea,' I say.

My optimism of earlier seems pointless, stupid, worse than stupid, as though with my transient, febrile cheerfulness, like the girl with the voodoo dolls, I have provoked ill fortune.

CHAPTER **16**

nother postcard comes. It's Checkpoint Charlie, taken in summer; the sky is wide and clear. There's a kind of cabin that's been preserved, presumably for tourists, a notice that says 'U.S. Army Checkpoint', a large framed picture of a soldier—Russian, I think, in khaki uniform—stuck up in the street. You can tell from people's clothes that the photo was taken recently: a woman in jeans and a vest top ambles along the pavement, a man in combat trousers is walking across the road. Beside the hoarding that says 'You are

leaving the American sector', there's now a traffic light
and a shop selling sunglasses.

She's written her address and telephone number at the
top.

Darling, Just in case you lost my address!! I know you
must be so busy, with your little girl and everything.
And how old is she now, I wonder, your little one.

Hope you like the picture and that all is going
well! Perhaps you could lift the phone? My number
is as above. Just whenever you can, my darling, in
one of those spare moments! Well, I'm sure you
don't have many of those! But I'd be so happy to
hear from you. This comes with all my love.

CHAPTER 17

Daisy and I sit by the pile of board books in the clinic. Daisy is afraid.

'What will he say about the medicines, Mum? Will he tell me off?'

'Of course he won't. You really tried to take them.'

But now we're here, waiting to see him, I wish we'd tried again.

It's clear but cold. Through the glass doors the playground is full of light, so the colours of the plastic toys look pallid, faded. There's no one on the GameCube, but Daisy isn't interested today.

The nurse with the gentle face is weighing a teenage girl, saying how much weight she's put on, and how fantastic this is. Everyone glows—the nurse, the girl, the mother. I feel so envious of them.

'I wish Dad would come,' says Daisy.

'Me, too.'

Richard is meant to be joining us, coming from a meeting somewhere in Surrey. I look at my watch; our appointment is in two minutes. The clinic door bangs back and we look up, full of hope. It's a woman with a frayed face who's pushing a child in a buggy.

And then Dr McGuire comes to his door and Daisy's name is called and we have to go in.

Some X-rays are displayed with the light behind them.

'I think those are your legs,' I say to Daisy.

'Come and have a look,' says Dr McGuire. She goes to stand beside him. Half of his face is bright and half in shadow; his hair is whitened, his profile sharp in the light. He names the bones for her. Daisy smiles, enjoying this.

'There's no arthritis. Your legs are fine,' he says. He points to another X-ray. 'And this one is the barium meal,' he says. 'Now, this shows how your stomach contents come back up the oesophagus. What it doesn't tell us, though, is why that should be happening.'

He switches off the light behind the X-rays.

She comes to sit beside me on the sofa; he's in an upright chair at his desk. Behind him there's the window, and you can see out over the hospital, the faceless windows of the wards, their bedheads and floral curtains, and the stains of damp on the concrete.

'So, Daisy, how are you now?'

'All right,' she says.

This time I know I mustn't interrupt.

'Now, I sent you home with some medicines,' he says. 'How did you get on with those?'

She turns to me. I can feel her leg shaking a little against me. She doesn't say anything. I put my arm around her.

I wish Richard were here; I long for him to be here, to handle this for us.

'I'm afraid she didn't manage to take them,' I tell him.

'Most children of eight can take medicines,' he says.

'But I think it's part of her illness,' I say. 'It's because she feels so sick.'

'She managed to swallow the barium,' he says.

'Yes, in the end. Though they were about to give up. But barium's easier, isn't it? It kind of coats your throat, it doesn't have a bitter taste…'

He's writing in her folder. He doesn't look at me.

The door bursts open and Richard comes in. Relief washes through me.

'Sorry I'm late.' His face is flushed and his voice is loud; he's been rushing and breathing heavily. 'I got stuck in this massive tailback. It's one of those days when the system seizes up.'

'Don't worry, Mr Lydgate,' says Dr McGuire. 'I'm grateful to you for making the effort. Too many fathers simply wouldn't bother.'

Richard sits beside us. I sense his warmth, his solidity; the opulent smell of his aftershave wraps round me. I'm so glad he is here.

'Now, what have I missed?' he says.

He's brisk but genial; he's brought a kind of urgency, a sense of the busy adult world, in with him. Briefly, I feel an envy I rarely feel: I long for a proper job, for an office like Richard's, for those crisp tailored suits that people wear for meetings, and a glamorous PA to keep you organised, and phones all ringing at once, and being taken seriously.

Dr McGuire explains about the X-rays. Richard stretches out his legs and reaches an arm along the back of the sofa.

'And we also have the results of your blood tests, Daisy,' says Dr McGuire. 'And the good news is that everything is absolutely normal. Except the test for allergy. And that is a bit on the high side, but I'm sure it's nothing to worry about.'

I ask if it shows what she's allergic to.

He shakes his head. 'It doesn't test for particular foods—we can't do that unfortunately.'

'Perhaps we should try one of those diets,' I say. 'When you leave out different things.' I don't tell him about the diet we've tried: I can too vividly imagine what he'd think of Helmut Wolf.

He shrugs. 'Those diets can be very tedious,' he says. 'Children generally know what's good for them. We have to trust our children.'

Warring ideas mill around in my mind. What if Helmut

Wolf was right? Yet the diet was so difficult. But if she's so allergic, perhaps we should try it again? I don't know who to believe now.

There's a little silence. I hear a baby crying the other side of the door—a strange, disturbing cry, too rhythmic, not quite natural. I think how all these tests have been done, yet we're no further on.

'So what happens now?' I say. 'We still don't know what's wrong.'

'That's what we need to talk about,' he says. 'Whether we ought to be taking a different route. But for now she really must take her medicines.'

'But she can't…'

He holds his hand up, silencing me: that gesture that I hate.

'I know your position on this, Mrs Lydgate,' he says. 'You've made that abundantly clear. In fact I'm sure she can take them. But it's so important to have the right attitude. Sometimes parents can convey a kind of uncertainty to a child, and children pick up on that. Children are very sensitive to what their parents are thinking. Daisy, you'll promise me you'll take your medicine, won't you?'

She nods, eager to please.

'And now, Daisy,' he says, 'would you mind leaving us for a moment? I'd like to speak to your mum and dad on their own.'

I take her hand and we go back to the waiting room. I find her a worn copy of The Worst Witch, that she loved when she was younger. She opens it at random.

'Is he going to talk about the medicine, Mum?'

'Don't worry, sweetheart, it's not your fault,' I tell her.

In the consulting room, Richard and Dr McGuire are talking amiably together, about the M25, and how the government really will have to get to grips with our antediluvian transport system. As I sit, they stop smiling.

'Right then,' says Dr McGuire. He leans back in his chair, his fingertips touched together. A new seriousness darkens his face. 'Do you have anything else you want to tell me?'

I shake my head.

He doesn't respond; he's waiting.

'Not really,' I say. 'No. Nothing else.'

The silence between us is tense, charged. I know what he's expecting, what he's wanting. She's being bullied at school… There was this paedophile… To be honest, my husband and I do have our difficulties, Doctor… But there's nothing to say. The silence stretches on, constraining me.

'Well, I don't think it's psychological, if that's what you mean,' I tell him.

'I think it is,' he says.

I feel a hot spurt of fury. 'How can it be? She's got lots of friends, and no one's died or anything. There's nothing to bring this on.'

'Children see things differently,' he says. 'Something that seems unimportant to an adult can seem major to a child.'

'But there isn't anything. It started when she got flu. And she was always such a happy child.'

'She's also a child who's quite old enough to speak for herself,' he says. His pale eyes flick across my face. 'And somehow you won't let her. When she tries to tell me something, you keep on interrupting.'

Richard doesn't protest. Why doesn't he intervene, defend me? I turn to him, but I can't read his expression; he's looking at Dr McGuire.

'Daisy was nervous about coming,' I say. 'I could feel her shaking. Because she hadn't taken the medicine. Sometimes you have to speak for your child. It's an intimidating situation for a child.'

'Intimidating?' he says. 'I really think that's overstating the case. In my experience, most children don't find it remotely alarming to come here. They know about hospitals, they watch *Casualty*. Today's children are very sophisticated, Mrs Lydgate.'

I shake my head. 'I just can't accept that her illness has a psychological cause.'

He leans towards me, his face sharp, intense.

'I'm very struck by the fact that you seem so reluctant to consider that Daisy's problem might have a psychological explanation. This convinces me that this is something we have to look at,' he says.

I'm reaching around for things to defend ourselves with, to defend Daisy.

'But we're a perfectly normal family. Her older sister's never had anything wrong. She's scarcely ever had a day off school.'

'She has an older sister?' He looks at the notes,

frowns. 'According to what we have here, Daisy is your first child.'

'Catriona means Sinead,' says Richard. 'My daughter by my first wife.'

'Ah,' says Dr McGuire. 'I understand.'

His eyes glitter. He makes a note in the file.

'This happened before,' I tell him. 'It happened at the surgery. Daisy was hardly eating, and the doctor said it was because she was unhappy, and wouldn't have done any tests at all if I hadn't insisted.' I'm trying to explain, but anger sharpens my voice. I know how he sees me, a harridan, a shrill, insistent woman. 'If people decide she's ill because she's worried about something, they stop trying to find what's wrong, and that panics me.'

'But you see,' he says, 'you seem so sure about this, and you get so cross when I suggest it's psychological, and that makes me think it is.'

There's an image in my head—vivid, exact. I walk across the floor to him, see him flinch away from me, hear the crack of my fist on his face.

Richard senses this perhaps. He puts his hand on my arm.

'Darling, don't get too upset. Dr McGuire's just trying to cover all the bases. I mean, don't you think we ought to give every suggestion serious consideration? For Daisy's sake,' he says.

My throat is tight: I can't speak.

'The fact is, this illness of Daisy's is really very perplexing,' says Richard. 'He doesn't mean she's making it up.' He turns to Dr McGuire. 'You don't mean that, do you?' he says.

'Not at all,' says Dr McGuire.

'Do you have any theory?' says Richard. 'Anything in mind that might be causing Daisy's illness?'

'Obviously we need to investigate properly.' He's looking at Richard again. 'I'm fortunate to work very closely with an excellent psychiatrist. I'm sure you'll find her extremely approachable—'

Panic rises in me like nausea.

'No.' My voice is too loud for the room. 'I just don't see that it's right. I don't see that it's necessary.'

'You see?' He's speaking quite mildly, as though to a recalcitrant child. 'You're doing it again. You're interrupting.'

CHAPTER 18

It's mufti day at Sinead's school, in aid of science textbooks, and she has a flower scrunchie in her hair. But her forehead is creased in a frown as she packs her bag.

'What's wrong?'

'I've got a French test,' she says.

'You'll be all right,' I tell her. 'I know you will. French is your thing.'

'No, I won't. It's Miss Premenstrual Johns.'

'But you're brilliant at French, Sinead.'

She pushes a hand through her dark abundant hair. Her brown eyes harden as she looks at me.

'I wanted you to test me on my verbs,' she says. 'But you were so stressed last night—I thought you'd be cross if I asked.'

Penitence washes through me.

'I'm sorry, my love. I'm always so busy with Daisy.'

'Yes, you are,' she says. There's a splinter of bitterness in her voice that's new to me.

She opens the door and cold air rushes in. Her face is set. She goes without saying goodbye.

Daisy is dressed for school. She looks fragile, shrunken, inside the formal clothes, and there are pastel-pencil smudges round her eyes. She hasn't eaten anything.

I pack her bag for her.

'You have to take in your matchbox today, remember? For the sponsorship thing. They're collecting them in. You don't want to miss that, do you?'

'I don't care.'

'But you worked so hard on it.'

Ridiculously, this matters terribly to me—that she is part of this charming quixotic project, just like the other children.

The matchbox is on the dresser. I open it up for her, to see where all the things we have collected nestle together; the paperclip, the broken-off lead from a pencil, the sunflower seed, the feather, grey as a pearl, that we found on the grass at Kew; this tiny box of clustered treasures.

'Look. Doesn't that look wonderful?'

'I don't care,' she says again.

There's a vase of yellow tulips on the table, their colour rich as butter. They're starting to ease apart, to sag a little; a single petal has fallen. I pick it up—it's firm, cool, soft as vellum. I tuck it on top and close the matchbox up. She shrugs and turns away.

We go out to the car. There's wind and a white sky and white blossom blowing. We drive slowly to school through the cold pale day. The traffic is heavy, the drivers have tense, set faces; a man in a lorry leans out, his face contorted with rage, and swears at another driver who won't give him room.

Daisy is silent, but her unhappiness is like a physical presence, pressing down on me, as though it's my own feeling.

'Maybe you'll feel better once you're there, and you see Megan and hand in your matchbox and everything.' My voice is bright, brittle.

She says nothing.

I look warily in the rear-view mirror. I see that she is crying.

'Sweetheart, you'll be all right.'

'Why does this have to happen to me?' she says.

'Sometimes bad things happen to people, they just do. It's not for any reason.'

We get out at school and I hand her her bag. We walk slowly towards the gate; we have to stop sometimes because she feels so sick. A woman with a double buggy comes up too close behind us, pushing through; we wait on the edge of the pavement to let her past. She has flat laced shoes and a knitted jacket with pictures of animals on, and I hate her; I feel such rage with her pushiness and her sensible cheerful clothes. I feel such rage with everything.

'D'you want me to stay with you till the bell goes?'

Daisy nods.

I lean against the railing outside school. She has her back to the gate; she presses her face into me. I watch the children go in, shiny and vivid, with all their gear and lunchboxes; and the hurried urgent women, making arrangements, weaving the rich complex web of their children's everyday lives out of tea-time visits and Spanish Club and choir practice. We're separate from all this, Daisy and me, cut off; we stand there, still and cold, behind our wall of glass.

Fergal comes, with Jamie. He looks as though he's been rushing—he hasn't shaved; he's wearing his leather jacket. He turns to me and smiles. I nod and try to smile but my mouth is tight and dry.

'I can't do this,' says Daisy.

The bell goes. There's a flurry at the gate, a sudden urgency, the late ones rushing in, hair and school bags flying. Suddenly I breathe out: I can't do this either; I don't know what possessed me, why it seemed so necessary to put her through all this. I bend down, put my arms around her.

'Let's go home.'

There's a huge sense of relief in giving in; then, stitched into the relief, a slender thread of regret, a feeling that I have failed: that we got this close, that she is dressed and here at the gate, that maybe I should have pushed a little harder.

'We'll crack this,' I tell her, as we drive home through the traffic that's thinning now school has started. 'We'll solve it. We'll get there. I promise.'

I think how often I have told her this. She doesn't say anything.

At home, she goes upstairs to change into her pyjamas, and I unpack her school bag and throw her lunch away. I take the matchbox out of her bag and put it back on the dresser. There seems no sense in keeping it—the seed and the paperclip and the feather have no meaning apart from the purpose for which they were collected—but I feel a thin scratch of psychic pain at the thought of just discarding them. I open up the box. The petal has the faintest flower scent, but it's freckled with brown already.

I take Daisy a hot-water bottle and a drink of water. She's sitting up in bed watching television. Her room is tidy because she doesn't play any more, all her Lego and plastic animals still neatly in their boxes. It looks dull in the harsh April light, that seeks out all the dust and the flaws in things.

'Mum, I want...' She swallows. 'Mum, give me...' There's a kind of fog in her face.

'What is it, Daisy?'

'I put him down here,' she says. Her eyes are clouded. 'I know I did... Mum, I can't remember what he's called.'

A thin clear shaft of fear goes through me.

'You mean Hannibal?'

'Hannibal,' she says. 'Oh. I couldn't remember.' She's troubled. 'Sometimes I can't remember the words for things.'

I turn from her, looking round the room, looking for Hannibal: hiding my fear from her, pushing it away.

Hannibal has fallen under the bed.

'There. I've got him. I bet he was lonely down there.' My words, cheerful, unreal, seem to hang in the air between us.

I turn on her television and leave her.

The kitchen is messy with the remains of breakfast. I sit at the table and leave it all as it is. Dread washes through me, like some bitter fluid; it's in my mouth, I can taste it on my tongue. Things come into my head: BSE, cancer, leukaemia, terrible things. When I was at nursery school, one of the helpers, a woman in her forties, had a brain tumour. She became rather quiet and fiddled too much with her glasses and had several minor car accidents and once or twice she fainted; by the time they found the tumour, there was nothing they could do. I try to remember if she used to forget things. And BSE—what are the early symptoms of BSE? Everything seems to start with depression, withdrawal, a difficulty in thinking, an ill-formed sense of something being profoundly wrong. My pulse skitters off and my stomach turns to water. This is one of the worst times; as I sit in my bleak kitchen in the hard spring light, all the dribbles of spilt milk and crescents of burnt toast on the table, and outside the spring wind and the silver birch holding the white of the sky in the nets of its branches: when I start to think the very worst things, and there's no help anywhere.

I find that I am praying. Mouthing the words like a child in school assembly. Or maybe not praying exactly—certainly not asking reverently or politely—but arguing with God, demanding, railing. Do something: help us. If you do by chance exist, which I very much doubt, why won't you help us? What about that thing it says in the Bible? If you ask for bread you will not be given a stone. I'm asking, God. Just now I could do with some bread.

I'm whispering the words into the stillness of the kitchen. But my voice is swallowed up by the silence as though I never spoke.

The ring of the phone makes me jump. It enters my mind that it must be the school secretary: I haven't rung her yet to say that Daisy is off again. I don't know why she's bothering me, when she surely must know what's wrong. I almost don't answer it.

'Catriona?'

A man's voice. It's familiar, but I can't place it. I feel a slight warmth of comfort, without knowing why.

'Yes?'

'It's Fergal.'

I don't say anything.

'From the school gate. Remember? We met at your carol-singing party?'

'I know who you are.'

It sounds a bit abrupt: I worry he'll think he's upset me.

There's silence for a moment, as if he's working something out.

'I've wanted to say this for ages,' he says, 'but I'm sorry if I alarmed you with all that stuff about The Poplars.'

There's such warmth in his voice; I want to wrap it round me like a blanket.

'That's OK,' I tell him. 'It was just a bit of a shock.'

'When I saw you at the gate today, I thought I might ring.'

'That's sweet of you.'

Another silence. I can sense his uncertainty.

'Are you OK?' he says then. 'You don't sound OK to me.'

'No, I'm not.'

His warmth loosens something inside me. There's a sob in my voice.

'It's Daisy?' he says.

'I'm so scared.' I find that I am crying. I don't know if he can hear it over the phone. 'She's started forgetting things. What does that mean—forgetting? I keep thinking such terrible things.'

'Of course you do,' he says. 'Anyone would. That doesn't mean you're right about those things.'

His voice is level, soothing; and he takes me to a safer, gentler place. Somehow, talking to him, I start to feel that maybe I've been hysterical—I even imagine, for a glimmer of a moment, that one day we will be through this, through to the other side—that this will all be something that has happened, part of our history.

Immediately I am stronger, clearer, seeing a way forward. 'I know what we need to do really,' I tell him.

'This doctor we've been seeing—he's just no help at all. I guess we need to see someone different. I need to go back to our GP and ask for another referral.'

'That sounds good,' he says.

'I'm being pathetic. It's just a bad day. I mean, most sick kids get well in the end, don't they?'

'Of course they do.'

'I'm not like this usually. I'm sorry.'

'Don't be,' he says. 'Look, I mean what I said—about coming round. You could bring Daisy if she wants to come: Jamie's got the world's biggest collection of Zelda games.'

'She'd love that.'

It's the end of the conversation, but I'd like to keep him there for a moment, fending off the fear.

'Well, look, take care,' he says, and ends the call.

Afterwards I sit in the silence for a moment, thinking how things used to be—how they might be again.

There's a photo on the mantelpiece: Daisy at four, in muddy yellow wellingtons. I took it at the farm park. We had a season ticket, and we often spent afternoons there in the lazy easy year before she started school. There were geese on a pond, and goats and fabulous peacocks. Daisy loved the goats. I found them rather alarming, with their hard insistent heads and the agitations that would ripple like a sudden wind through the group of them and the way they chewed your clothes. But she'd always want to pet them, to rake her fingers through the coarse hair of their coats; and she'd laugh when they pushed at her with their lean bony flanks or when she fed them and they nibbled her fingers. Once we saw two kids that had just been born, shaky with newness but avidly sucking at their mother, the placenta spilled in the straw, glossy and marbled with colour, inkily blue and magenta, lavish and shocking. There was a smell of birth, a hot rich smell of mingled hay and blood, both intimate and strange. Daisy went as close as she could, watching, intent, wide-eyed. That's how she was then—always, from very little, fearless, curious: wanting to reach out to the world, to dig her fingers in. At two she'd climb to the top of the climbing frame and let go with both hands and stand there flushed and laughing, so I'd constantly have to be biting back the instinctive words of warning. And if she ran off, you'd always have to go after her, she'd never come back on her own.

One day, when she was three, Adrian and Gina took us for a picnic tea in the New Forest. There was a broad expanse of grass, like a great wide cloth thrown down, stretching almost as far as you could see. Animals grazed there, cows with blotched coats, and horses. It was one of the last days of summer, the sun low in the sky, laying golden light across the land. Gina had brought an elaborate picnic, with a checked cloth and different kinds of salad all neatly sliced and segregated in various plastic containers; I as usual had contributed the pudding, a tarte tatin I'd made. Adrian, who didn't much like picnics, had some white Burgundy in a cooler, to compensate for the afternoon's irritations, all the twigs and insects. We ate and drank, and sat around in the sunlight, talking vaguely, flicking through the papers. Sinead sprawled on the grass, intent on some teen ghost story; Daisy, in red dungarees, worked her way determinedly through a packet of ginger biscuits. Then, as if in response to some irrefutable inner prompting, she licked the crumbs from her fingers, and got up and started to run. Her long hair streamed behind her. I watched her, small and blonde and intrepid, moving across the grass between the slow laconic cows, the red of her dungarees singing out, and the brightness of her hair.

I stood, rather reluctantly, warm with Adrian's wine. 'I guess I should go after her.'

Gina looked up from her *Sunday Telegraph*. 'Don't worry, Catriona, they always come back,' she said.

'Daisy doesn't. She just keeps on going.'

'No, dear, really, you don't need to worry,' she said. 'Little children never run far from their mothers. I read it in Penelope Leach.' She took off her glasses and polished them on her cardigan. 'Richard always came back,' she added contentedly.

Richard, hearing his name, put down the *Business News*. 'Just relax, darling.' He yawned. 'I'm sure she'll be fine.'

'I guess so.' But I didn't sit.

'Any time now,' said Gina. 'Just you see. She'll turn round any moment.'

We watched, but Daisy kept on going, diminishing in the distance, a little red dot with flying yellow hair.

'I think I should get her,' I said.

I walked, at first, so as not to look overprotective—

thinking how Gina might turn to Richard with a slight knowing smile. But Daisy was moving rapidly, running straight into the sun. I called but she ran on, not hearing, not aware of me, or choosing not to hear. I wasn't gaining on her. I started to run. But the grass, that had looked so beguilingly smooth, was rough and uneven to run on, and the light was dazzling, meaningless dark shapes skimming across my sight. I ran faster; I was becoming short of breath, my chest was tight from running. I had a sharp urgent fear that I would never catch her, that I'd lose her there in the sunlight, that she'd disappear in the brightness and go away from me.

And then suddenly I was almost on top of her. She heard me, put on a spurt of speed, let out a gleeful shriek. I flung myself at her, the momentum of my running carrying me forward so both of us toppled and fell. I remember how warm and solid she felt, and her smell of ginger biscuits and sun-warmed skin, and the sound of her breathy laughter. I'd like to be there again, everything restored.

CHAPTER 19

I t's Dr Carey again, in her crisp red jacket. But today
she isn't smiling.

'I haven't brought Daisy,' I tell her. 'I thought it
might be easier to talk without her here.'

'Absolutely,' she says. 'So how are things?'

'She's just the same,' I tell her. 'We went to see Dr
McGuire.'

'Yes,' she says. 'I have a letter from him.'

I know what I will say: I have rehearsed this.

'I felt he didn't listen. I'm really not at all happy with
what he's doing,' I tell her.

Her eyes are on me. This doesn't seem to surprise her.

There's a thick hot smell in the surgery, as though the smell of an earlier patient, someone unwashed and anguished, has lingered on in here. A slice of sunlight falls across the floor.

'I rather gathered you had a difficult time,' she says. She takes a typewritten sheet from Daisy's notes and smoothes it with her fingers. I can tell that she's read it already. 'Is Daisy taking her medicine now?' she says.

'She can't, it makes her sick.'

'I think he's worried she isn't taking her medicine,' she says. 'Most children of eight can take medicines.' There's certainty in her voice. 'If you're firm. You need to give them a reward, like a sweet or a biscuit.'

'That doesn't work,' I tell her.

There's an edge to my voice, perhaps. A slight frown creases the skin between her eyes. She's looking at the letter.

'I need to tell you what it says in here,' she says. 'I'm afraid he does mention…' She hesitates. 'He does say that he thought you were quite demanding.'

I hate that word: it triggers a brief wild rage. I'm the girl in the ad, who could be rather demanding: the girl that nobody wanted, although she smiled and smiled.

'That's utterly unfair.'

She gives me a wary look, from under her eyelashes. She's flushed as though she's nervous.

'And that you wouldn't let Daisy speak for herself.'

'She was really scared. She was trembling. Of course I would speak for her.'

She shakes her head a little. 'Children of eight are perfectly capable of speaking for themselves.'

It's happening again: the consultation is slipping away from me.

'But doesn't he say anything else—you know, about the illness?'

She's wearing a low-cut T-shirt under the jacket. There are weird red blotches on her neck and chest.

'I was coming to that,' she says.

She clears her throat, an abrupt sharp sound, as though she's making a speech.

'Tell me, Mrs Lydgate, have you ever heard of Münchausen Syndrome by Proxy?'

'Kind of.' Magazines articles skimmed through come back to me. 'You mean, like Beverley Allitt—that nurse who killed those children?'

She moves her mouth a little, as though she's trying to smile.

'Well, it's nothing like that usually,' she says. 'It's usually in the family.'

'Like when people poison their children?'

'There are some terribly disturbed mothers who do behave like that,' she says. 'It's a very strange condition. But there are also mothers who perhaps exaggerate their child's illness, or do odd things like putting blood in the child's urine sample—so the children end up having lots of unnecessary investigations.' She's straightening

Daisy's notes between her hands, as though this is important, to have them exactly aligned with the edge of the desk. 'Sometimes today we call it fabricated illness.'

I shrug. 'I've never heard of fabricated illness,' I tell her. I don't know why she's saying all these things—when time is short and we haven't started talking about Daisy.

Her throat moves as she swallows. 'Dr McGuire says that Münchausen Syndrome by Proxy is one diagnosis that he's considering here.'

For a moment the words don't make any sense: as though she's speaking in a different language. A kind of mirthless laughter starts to move through me.

'This can't be true.'

She shakes her head. 'I'm serious, Mrs Lydgate. This is about you and Daisy.'

I'm in a looking-glass world: this is all so crazy, so bizarre. But I feel how my pulse is skittering in my wrist.

'He thinks I'm like that? He thinks I'm making it up?'

She moves her head; it might be yes or no. The blushing deepens on her throat, the blotches red as paeonies.

'It's just one of the things they're considering,' she says. She's looking down at the letter, not meeting my eye.

'But why on earth would I do that? Why would I make it up, or hurt her, or do any of those things?'

'I guess he's got to cover all the bases. He's got to consider everything,' she says. She's careful, cautious, moving a word at a time. 'When the illness is quite confusing, and the child doesn't seem to be responding to treatment.'

I lean towards her. 'But what do you think?' I'm pleading, trying to reach her. 'You don't believe him, do you?'

She hesitates. Some anxiety or uncertainty flickers across her face. I sense the conflict in her, that there's part of her that wants to stay on my side.

'He *is* a very respected physician,' she says, 'but, to be honest, I do think this is a rather strange suggestion. From everything I've read, we tend to find mothers who do these things will be people who've had very disturbed childhoods—really quite damaged people.' She smiles at me, a warm inclusive smile, a smile that says how very undamaged we are, Dr Carey and me: how very undisturbed our childhoods have plainly been. 'Nothing like what we're dealing with here.'

I'm worried she will hear the thud of my heart.

'As you know,' she goes on, 'I do think that there may well be a psychological element to Daisy's illness. But that's a different thing.'

The nurse in the treatment room next door is saying goodbye to someone. Her voice is vivid, cheerful, it resonates in the corridor. From the waiting room I hear a child shouting. It amazes me that all these ordinary things are still happening.

'But I don't understand,' I tell her. 'Why do they do it? The women you were talking about, who make their children have all these investigations?'

She considers. 'It's thought to be attention-seeking behaviour. For some people, being a mother of a sick child makes them feel needed and admired. As a society, we tend to view mothers of sick children as rather heroic and special.'

I think of the school gate—Daisy crying; me, frantic and somehow ashamed, peeling her fingers from my wrist like sticking plasters.

'I don't feel special,' I tell her.

She shrugs a little. 'That's how it's generally understood.'

I'm trying to find a way through the maze in my mind.

'What happens to these women? What happens to their children?'

The blotches are dark on her throat.

'Well, in extreme cases the children have to be taken into Care. In extreme cases. To be protected from their mothers.'

This is all so stupid, laughable, nothing to do with me. But the inside of my mouth has turned to blotting paper.

She pushes back the cuff of her jacket, and looks at her watch rather pointedly. The consultation is nearly over, and still I haven't said what I need to say.

'This isn't what I came for,' I tell her. 'I came to ask to be referred to somebody—you know, a specialist. Someone who will be able to work out what's wrong.'

She shakes her head a little. 'I just don't think that's how we should go about things,' she says. 'I really think that for now we'd do best to go along with what's been recommended. We don't want to keep chopping and changing. All he's asking is for you to see a psychiatrist— just to check some of this out.'

'But I don't want to see this psychiatrist—I want to stop all this right now. It's mad and it won't help Daisy.'

'Mrs Lydgate, I don't think you understand,' she says. 'I'm trying to help you here.' She leans towards me across the desk. Her breath smells of spearmint and her teeth are very white. 'And my advice would be that you should go along with this. You see, if you don't co-operate, it'll only make him more certain he's onto something. It's up to you, of course. No one can make you do it, not at this stage. But I really think you should.'

'What d'you mean—not at this stage? Is there a stage when they *can* make me?'

She ignores this.

'Listen,' she says. 'Just go and see the psychiatrist—and I'm sure this will all blow over. Dr McGuire will have his assessment and that'll reassure him. And hopefully it will help us find out what's really going on with Daisy.'

She folds up the letter, pressing on the creases so it's really neat; she's going to tuck it back in Daisy's folder. The consultation is over.

'Could I see that?'

She hesitates.

I have some vague sense that patients have rights—that there's a charter or something.

'I think I have the right to read the letter, don't I? To see my daughter's notes?'

She raises an eyebrow: she wasn't expecting this.

'Well, yes, you do,' she says.

It surprises me how readily she acquiesces.

She hands it across to me. I unfold it. There are two pages stapled together.

'Not here,' she says. She looks again at her watch. 'D'you mind? I'm running out of time. Could I ask you to read it in Reception?'

'Of course.'

'Just give it to Sheryl at the desk when you've finished.'

'Yes. Thank you.'

I go out to the waiting room, holding the letter with care, as though it could hurt my hand.

There are only two people waiting: a bleary huddled woman, coughing over a copy of *Hello*, and a mother with a baby in a sling. The mother is preoccupied with the baby, pressing her lips to his head. I know how that feels, the sensuous simplicity of it, the tender heat of a baby's hairless head. I envy her. There are two receptionists: one in a blue cardigan who's hunting around in the filing cabinet, the other on the phone.

I sit down and reach for a magazine and open it, to shield the letter from view.

It starts with a paragraph about the results of the tests on Daisy. I skim through this, not really understanding.

On the next page the tone of the letter changes.

After I had explained the results to the parents, I broached the possibility that their daughter's illness might have a psychological cause, and suggested that this possibility should be further investigated. The mother immediately became extremely hostile and aggressive, and adamantly refused to consider this possibility. This reaction concerned me a great deal, and in view of this concern, I would suggest that Münchausen Syndrome by Proxy or fabricated illness should be part of the differential diagnosis.

This mother does in several respects fit the stereotype that is described in cases of MSBP. She presents, as these mothers usually do, as very nurturing and concerned, and is also somewhat overprotective—for instance, not allowing her daughter to speak for herself, in a way that is quite inappropriate with an eight-year-old child. She is very demanding of medical staff, and appears excessively knowledgeable about and preoccupied with her daughter's illness—flourishing a sheaf of detailed notes on the girl's symptoms during the conversation—but has nonetheless failed to comply with the recommended treatment.

In view of these concerns, as well as the shifting and elusive nature of Daisy's illness, I am referring the family to child psychiatry for an in-depth assessment. In the meantime, I have suggested that Daisy continue with the prescribed medication, though I am not over-optimistic about the mother's willingness to comply.

Tears start in my eyes.

I glance round the waiting room. The other patients are lost in their worlds, the mother murmuring to the baby, the coughing woman intent on her magazine. One receptionist has her back turned, the other is still on the phone, talking in her brisk Glaswegian accent, explaining something to somebody down the line, who keeps on interrupting; her head is turned away. I fold the letter and tuck it in my pocket and walk briskly through the door.

CHAPTER 20

He comes straight to me where I'm sitting on the sofa, under the masks from Venice. He's home quite early tonight; it's his string quartet rehearsal. He kisses the top of my head, then moves a little away. He's leaning against the window sill, looking at me. Behind him, there's an operatic sunset, a wash of apricot light, and the new leaves of the birch are precise against the florid sky.

'What's the matter?' he says. 'Is something wrong? What's happened?'

I put my glass of wine on the side table, moving slowly, carefully: it could so easily spill.

'I went to see Dr Carey.' I can't breathe; there's a constriction in my chest. 'She showed me this letter… She says one of the things they're considering, to explain Daisy's illness…it's called Münchausen by Proxy.' The awkward words are like solid things in my mouth; it's hard to spit them out.

He raises an eyebrow.

'Dr Carey says it's when mothers make their children's symptoms worse, or exaggerate them, or invent their children's illnesses. Like it's the mother who's actually causing the illness…'

I put out my hand to pick up my glass but I can't, my hand is shaking.

His eyes are narrow, watching me.

'What are we going to do, Richard? Should we make a complaint? D'you know how to do that? D'you think we should do that? Isn't there a committee or something we could go to?'

'Darling, hang on a minute,' he says. 'Let's just try and sort this out.' He's leaning back against the window sill. He's dark with the light behind him, his face in shadow; I can't see his expression. 'I don't suppose for a moment we need to do anything drastic. It's probably just that some medical student's out to impress the consultant— had this bright idea. Coming up with something really obscure.'

I shake my head. 'No, it was him—it was Dr McGuire.'

He frowns a little. 'Anyway, didn't you say it was just one of the things they were considering?'

'Yes.'

'Well, then. Maybe it's something they always consider with sick children. I mean, they've got to be on the alert—there are some very weird people out there.'

'No,' I say, 'it's not like that. It's not something they always think of. It's about me. There's this letter about me. About how aggressive I am.'

He thinks about this. 'To be fair to Dr McGuire,' he says, 'you did get rather upset. I mean, I'm just trying to see both sides of the picture. I know he was tactless—but you did rather lose your cool.'

'Anyone would, he was foul.' There's a splinter of rage in my voice.

He shrugs, moving his hand a little, as though his point is made.

I was going to show him the letter. It's there in the hall, in the pocket of my jacket. I had some kind of inchoate notion that he could copy it before we took it back to the surgery, and we could take the copy to show someone. There are surely people who will help you—advisors, advocates, local councillors—people to advise you if you want to make a complaint; there must be—I'm sure I've read about these things. All I have to do is to get up and go to the hall and take the letter from my pocket. But my body is slow and heavy, as though my limbs are drenched.

'What did Dr Carey make of all this?' he says.

'She said she thought it was a wrong diagnosis. But she

seemed to think we ought to go along with what he was suggesting, or he'd just be even more convinced he's right. That's like blackmail, isn't it?'

'Blackmail?'

Why can't he see?

'It's like a trap,' I tell him. 'So if you say he's wrong and won't do what he wants, it only proves he's right, so either way you lose.'

'Darling, you make it sound like some kind of battle,' he says. 'I mean, I know you're very opposed to the psychological approach. But what if there's something in it? They must have seen so many of these cases. And lots of illnesses are thought to be psychosomatic, aren't they?'

'Not Daisy's illness. It started with flu, for God's sake. She's a happy child. I'd know if she wasn't—I'd just *know* if something was wrong. And look at us. I mean, we're happy, aren't we? We're a happy family…'

He doesn't instantly reply. There's a little silence between us. There's a rushing sound in my ears: the chill movement of air, the windmills turning.

But then he smiles. 'Of course we are,' he says. 'Of course. Well, that goes without saying.'

'I mean, what am I doing wrong exactly?' The injustice of it all seizes me. 'I try to find food she'll eat, I take her to the doctor, I try to get her to take the medicines but she can't. I'm always hunting around for people we can go to, people who might help… What's wrong with that exactly? What do they expect?'

'Darling, I had wanted to say…' He's turned away

from me, profiled darkly against the apricot sky. 'Well, maybe now's not quite the time to raise this. And it's your thing—I don't like to interfere. But some of the people you've taken Daisy to have been rather iffy.'

'Helmut Wolf, you mean? But Nicky said he was good.'

He shrugs. 'Exactly,' he says.

Sinead is walking around upstairs; there's a blare of ferocious hip-hop, and the bang of the bathroom door.

'Richard.' My voice is a whisper; I don't want her to hear. 'They want us to see a psychiatrist. You and me.'

He nods. 'OK. But I'll need a bit of warning so I can schedule it in.'

'But I don't think we should go. I don't see why you're just accepting it like that. This is all wrong, Richard. Daisy needs someone to make her well—she doesn't need a *psychiatrist*.'

'Sweetheart, I know what you think. But I guess they're just asking—is there anything going on in the home that could be adding to the problem? And that's a perfectly valid question: you know, if one stands back a little, gets some kind of distance. Sometimes it helps to stand a little outside things.'

The tears that I've been holding back start spilling down my face.

At last he comes and sits on the sofa beside me and puts his arm around me. I cling to him, his warmth, the rich smell of his aftershave, wanting to hide in him.

He strokes my wet face. 'You're shaking,' he says. 'You seem so frightened. There's nothing to be frightened of.'

'Richard, it's serious,' I say through my tears. I wipe my eyes. 'These are really serious things they're saying. It's a really serious allegation.'

'Only if we let it be,' he says.

He's ready for his rehearsal, but he's a little reluctant.

'Will you be all right?' he says. 'Maybe I should give it a miss this once.'

'Don't worry, I'll be fine.'

He gets his violin and goes to say goodbye to Daisy, the violin case in his hand. She's propped up in bed, her hot-water bottle clutched to her stomach.

'Dad, play me something,' she says.

'Daisy, Dad has to go now,' I tell her.

'No, that's OK,' he says. He takes out his violin.

'Play *"The Long and Winding Road"*,' she says.

This always impresses her so much—not the dazzling ripples of notes in the pieces he practises for his string quartet, but that he can call up any tune she chooses. He plays and she watches raptly; it's the wide-eyed wondering look she'd have for a magician, who conjures rabbits and pigeons out of swirls of magneta silk. The tension in her face begins to ease away.

When he's finished she reaches out and plucks a string with her finger. He kisses the top of her head.

We go downstairs.

'She doesn't seem too bad,' he says as he puts on his jacket.

'I don't know,' I say.

He touches my shoulder. 'Cat, are you sure I shouldn't stay? You look quite shaky,' he says.

'Really, I'll be OK.'

Daisy settles more quickly tonight. I stay for a while and watch her sleeping. Her face is soft, easy, now she's asleep, and the light from her lamp in its terracotta shade makes her skin look warmer, healthier. A strand of hair, dark blonde like wet sand, has fallen over her face. Her hair needs washing, but she hates to have it washed, and I haven't the heart to do it when it's not important. One arm is flung out on top of the duvet, as if she were reaching out to somebody just as she fell asleep. The braided friendship bracelet of tatty wool is still wrapped round her wrist. I feel a surge of love for her so strong: I believe for a moment that it could make her well, that it's like an amulet or a witch's circle of fire, to drive away whatever is harming her. I kiss her quietly so as not to wake her.

Sinead is watching *House* in her room. There are urgent voices, and monitors going off.

I take the rest of the bottle of wine and my glass and go up to the attic. I didn't turn on the lights: there's still a little brightness in the sky. The pictures I've been drawing are there on the table. More children. They're trapped or imprisoned or seeking to find their way through twisty labyrinths, and some of them have chains on their hands and feet. I look at them for a moment. I don't know if they're any good—though Sinead assures me that Mr Phillips, her adored art teacher, would like them: he likes weird stuff, she says. There's a paradox in these pictures, the images themselves, the sense of limitation and constriction, and the freedom and flow with which they seem to emerge from my pen. But I know that won't happen tonight. It's not even worth trying tonight; I know I couldn't draw.

I turn off the light and lean on the window sill, looking out. I can see down into Monica's garden, where in the shadowed places under the apple trees the darkness is dense and absolute as ink. I hear the sound of foxes, screeching at one another, the noise they make when they fight. When first we came here and I heard their screeching, I rushed out into the garden, not knowing what had happened, afraid I might find some maimed or slaughtered creature.

I feel the wine loosening me. I drink and think about things. I remember Daisy's story about the voodoo dolls, the girl who got given a doll for bad luck and broke her ankle. I wonder if someone has cursed us. Is that possible? Can such things be? I think about the letters from Berlin, about my mother: who knows where I live, who wants me to visit her. I see I am afraid of her—as though she has some occult power over us, as though her knowledge of me and of Daisy could harm us. I don't want us to be there in her mind—even if now, as she claims, she wishes us well: I fear she could harm us just by thinking about us. As if all this has happened because of her. And I think about the letter from Dr McGuire, that's downstairs in the pocket of my jacket. I feel his hostility reaching out to me from the letter, as if his words could hurt me. Words, phrases, graze me—that I am demanding and overprotective and hostile and aggressive.

The apricot fades from the sky and the shadows lengthen and night comes into my room. I'm wandering through the maze in my mind, the paths that don't take you anywhere. Dead ends, confusions, curses. Outside, the trees are a deeper darkness against the sky and there are spiky stars and a thin fine moon.

The alcohol eases into my veins, making everything simple. I feel a sudden certainty.

I go downstairs, quickly, purposefully, although my steps are unsteady. I get some matches from the kitchen, and a big glass ashtray that we never use. There's that sound in my ears again, the windmills caught in the wind. I take Dr McGuire's letter from my jacket pocket, and go back to the top of the house.

I don't turn on the light. I glance at the letter but it's too dark by the light of the moon to read the words. I strike a match, and hold the match to the page; the paper flares. I drop it in the ashtray so as not to burn my fingers, the brief heat searing my skin. It happens so quickly: the transient fierce brightness, rapidly extinguished, the last few scraps of paper edged with beads of flame. Then the final sparks go out, but the sudden dark is full of the scent of burning.

There in the darkness, my certainty seeps away.

I take the ashtray downstairs—carefully, with my hand across it, so the ashy scraps of paper won't blow everywhere. I go to the kitchen and wash the ashtray out in the sink. I see myself reflected in the window—my eyes are narrowed with the dark, my face is relaxed from the drink and somehow wary; for a moment my face reminds me of my mother's. I rinse all the smudges of ash from the sink, so no one could ever guess what I have done, as though this is a crime I have committed.

CHAPTER 21

I take Daisy some toast to eat in bed. She's sitting up watching television, with Hannibal tucked in the crook of her arm. She's only just woken; she has a bewildered look. Her blue eyes follow me as I put out her school clothes on her chair, and her face crumples a little, but she doesn't say anything. Today I am determined to get her into school.

I drink my coffee in the kitchen. Outside, there's a sepia water-laden light and a pearl of rain at the end of each twig of the lilac and tense white buds on the pear tree. Through the half-open window I hear the shiny song of a blackbird.

Sinead is cramming felt tips into her pencil case and trying to make space in her bag for her Weimar Republic project, which she's covered in red paper. She smells of some hair styling product, a sugary chemical smell. She's frowning.

'What if it's mufti again?' she says. 'I'd die.'

'It won't be mufti,' I tell her. 'They'd have sent a letter home if it was mufti.'

'It's a Friday, it could be. Maybe it is, and they didn't tell me.'

'Sinead, it won't be. Trust me.'

She goes off, looking doubtful.

Eventually I hear Daisy coming downstairs. She's dressed for school. She holds onto the bannister, and puts both feet together on each step, moving cautiously, seriously, as though her shoes are heavy, as though a line has been drawn around her that she must move within.

'My legs are all stiff,' she says. 'They feel funny. My kneecaps feel funny.'

'You're my brave girl.'

I give her a hug as she gets to the bottom of the steps. She resists a little.

'Megan will be so pleased to see you,' I tell her.

She shakes her head. Her eyes mist over as she pulls away from me. 'Sometimes I wish I had someone else's life,' she says.

I brush her hair; her eyes are wet and full. I keep up a

stream of bright chatter, trying not to leave her any space to say how ill she feels. Her hair is tangled because she's been off sick for two days and I haven't brushed it: I always forget to do it when she stays in bed, though it's probably the kind of thing that sensible ordinary women do routinely. I've brushed out the tangles and I'm holding a clump of hair in one hand and a scrunchie in the other, poised to fix her ponytail, when the phone goes. I curse whoever it is in my head and fix the hair in a hasty lopsided clump and hurry to the phone, unable to let it ring—though it's probably just someone wanting to sell me a kitchen.

'Could I speak to Mrs Lydgate?'

'Yes. Speaking.' My voice is curt: I'm looking for the sales pitch.

'Ah. Good morning, Mrs Lydgate. It's the surgery here.' I place her then, the brisk Glaswegian accent. 'I'm sorry to bother you. Dr Carey tells me she gave you a letter to read in Reception yesterday—a letter from the hospital.'

She stops there, waiting, requiring something of me.

'Yes, that's right.'

'The letter seems to have gone missing, Mrs Lydgate.'

'Oh.'

'Are you quite sure you handed it back?'

'Absolutely.'

'We were just wondering if you had perhaps taken it by mistake.' Her voice is silky.

'No.' I try to remember, to think up something plausible. 'I gave it to the other receptionist—the one with the blue cardigan.'

'Carolyn? Well, I've asked her, of course. She says she's sure you didn't.'

'No, I did, really. Maybe it got put back in the wrong folder.'

'We'll have another look,' she says. 'But perhaps you could also have a look at home. We can easily get a duplicate, of course. It's just that Dr Carey is very keen to find out what happened to the original.'

'I gave it back,' I tell her.

'Right, then, Mrs Lydgate.'

There's a knowingness to her voice. I can tell she suspects me.

Daisy is sitting on the sofa, hunched over, her head in her hands, the way an old person might sit.

'Shall we do your hair again?'

She shakes her head dully.

'I can't be bothered,' she says.

We put on our coats and I take her hand and we go out to the car through the brownish light. It's raining more heavily now. There are smells of petrol fumes and wet lilac.

'You're shaking, Mum,' she says. 'Why are you shaking?'

'I'm all right,' I tell her.

The traffic is heavy and sluggish, everything slowed by the rain. At the gate, she wants me to stay with her till the bell rings, but then goes in without protest. I wait there for a moment once she's left me, my eyes holding onto her as she walks in, poised and careful, through the gate.

The bookshop is in the shopping centre. There's a fountain lined with turquoise tiles and smelling faintly of chlorine, and jazzed-up Vivaldi over the sound system, and cheerful shops selling flimsy exuberant clothes to teenage girls. Last time I came here it was to do the Christmas shopping. I spent hours hunting for perfect things, presents for the girls' stockings, beaded bags and Viennese truffles and tiny soaps smelling of flowers. It seems so long ago now, that world of pleasant ordinariness—when I thought myself unfortunate if the queue was slow in the Body Shop and I got a parking ticket.

Inside the bookshop it's warm and bright and hushed, with the thick, slightly scorched smell of new carpet. I wander round the shelves with a rather deliberate nonchalance. There are few people here: some women with protesting children in buggies, one or two older people in taupe mackintoshes. The medical section is near the back. It seems well stocked; students from the hospital must come here. There's no one else in this part of the shop except an elderly man in a jacket the colour of mud, who's looking at military history. The other side of the bookshelf, a man I can't see is talking into his mobile. 'Of course I love you. Why would I say it if I didn't?' A private voice, but irritable. 'Well, there you are, then…'

The books are mostly weighty-looking, substantial. I read through the titles on the spines, finding that half of

them are words I don't understand. It seems there's
nothing here that will help me; perhaps I was stupid to
come. I'm just about to go when my eye falls on a book
called *Trust Betrayed*. It's a grey paperback. I pull it out;
the subtitle takes up half the cover: *Münchausen
Syndrome By Proxy, Inter-agency Child Protection and
Partnership with Families*. I open it. It's obviously written
for professionals, but the print is quite big and it doesn't
look too technical and it seems like a book that I could
understand.

I come to a list of Manifestations of MSBP—the sorts
of things they say these mothers do. This is shocking,
strange to read in this bright, bland, pleasant place. 'Star-
vation or interfering with parenteral nutrition or with-
drawing stomach contents through a naso-gastric tube.
Administration of salt solutions, laxatives, diuretics,
sedative drugs, warfarin or anti-epileptic drugs. Altering
blood-pressure charts, temperature charts or interfering
with urine testing…'

I can hear the music from outside in the mall. The man
the other side of the bookshelf is still talking into his
mobile. 'We're not having the tone of voice argument
again, are we?' I glance back over my shoulder, like a thief.
The frail old man is immersed in a copy of *Stalingrad*.

I turn to the back of the book and start flicking through.
Bullet points catch my eye. '*Table 5. Confirming the diagnosis*. Check on personal, family and social details
with relatives, the GP and social services. The perpetra-
tor is often an inveterate liar…'

The conversation with the receptionist comes into my mind. I realise I am sweating. I leaf back through the book.

'*Table 3. Clues to the diagnosis of MSBP.* The mother is unusually knowledgeable about medical problems and treatments. Treatment is ineffective…' My pulse is skittering in my wrist. I try to work out what it means to be 'unusually knowledgeable'.

I turn back a bit further, and the book falls open at '*Table 2. Features commonly found in perpetrators.*' So this is what I'm meant to be like, I think. 'Usually the birth mother is the child's exclusive carer.' That's not so unusual, either. 'Previous paramedical training.' That's OK, I don't have any paramedical training. 'Previous contact with a psychiatrist.' I think of my sessions with Lesley at The Poplars: the thin carpet, the smell of disinfectant, the self-esteem tree with the fruit that I couldn't fill in. I don't think that qualifies. I'm beginning to breathe a little more easily: so far, this isn't too terrible. Then, at the end of the list: 'In local authority care during childhood (children's home and foster care).'

The rushing in my ears is like a roar. I close the book abruptly, as though it could hurt me.

There's a hand on my arm: the man in the mud-coloured jacket.

'Excuse me, but are you all right?'

He smells pleasantly of cigars and his eyes are mild.

'I'm OK. Thank you.'

'I could get you a glass of water,' he says.

'Please don't worry.'

'I thought you were going to faint for a moment there,' he says.

'It's probably just the flu,' I tell him.

'It's nasty, that flu,' he says. 'I take echinacea myself. You ought to try it.'

'Thank you. Yes, I will.'

'Well, if you're sure you're all right…'

He goes off to the desk, with *Stalingrad* under his arm.

I take the book. I half expect someone to stop me, to ask why it is I want to buy this book. I go towards the cash desk through the children's section. It's soothing here, all the little bears and dazzling colours, the gorgeous multiplicity of things. I choose a book for Daisy, something from the mythology shelf: a book of Celtic folk tales, with a white stag in a blue mist on the cover. At the cash desk I put the folk tale book on top. The assistant treats me as though I am perfectly ordinary, but my face is hot as I pay. I leave the bookshop hurriedly, with a rush of relief.

But when I get home with my bag of books, this stupid thing happens: I can't get my key in the lock. The tag of metal that falls down over the keyhole has fallen sideways and got stuck into the door jamb, and it's blocking half the keyhole and can't be moved. I try to push it up but I can't do it; to look at it, you'd think it would be easy, but somehow it's got wedged. It's ridiculous. I'm standing there with the key in my hand and I can't get into my house. I feel conspicuous, up at the top of the steps, the thin rain falling on me, unable to open my door. If someone was passing on the pavement, they'd think I was breaking in.

I push yet again at the tag with my finger. Nothing happens. I hit it with the key, and it finally swings round and I can undo the lock, but I've broken the skin on my hand. There's just a single drop of glossy blood, richly red as the vermilion in my paintbox. It hurts a lot for such a little cut.

Richard is home earlier than he's been for weeks, early enough that we'll be able to eat together. He's brought me flowers—purple arum lilies, sculptured and exquisite. They are to cheer me up, he says, because I was upset. I think how thoughtful this is.

Daisy hears and comes downstairs, her stilted walk, one careful step at a time.

He hugs her.

'How's life, munchkin?' he says.

'My stomach hurts,' she says.

'You poor old thing,' he says.

'Dad, can we *do* something?' she says.

I think he'll tell her he's tired, that he needs to read his paper. But he says, 'Of course,' and they go to look through the stack of board games in the living room. We have Monopoly, Cluedo, a game with jumping frogs—most of them presents from Gina and Adrian; Gina likes to say how very valuable it is to have family time together away from the television. We used to play these games in the evenings sometimes, but we haven't done it for ages and I don't know when we stopped. Sinead has so much homework now, and Richard works so late. Something slides away from you, and for a while you don't even notice its absence.

They choose the Cluedo and open up the box on the living-room floor. I heap some cushions for Daisy to sit on, and make her a hot-water bottle.

'Mum, you could play.'

I shake my head; I have to cook the dinner. But Sinead is persuaded to join them, pleased to have an excuse to postpone her cross-section of the Aosta Valley.

Daisy tips out the weapons, and the little grey figures on their coloured bases. She wants to be Miss Scarlett.

Sinead is reading the book of instructions. 'They even have birth dates,' she says. 'Wow, these people are *old*.'

Daisy shoots Sinead with the tiny silver dagger. Sinead dies extravagantly. Richard starts to deal.

'Do that cool thing where you shuffle them,' says Daisy.

He shuffles them with panache; she watches with admiration.

I go to the kitchen, but still half watching through the open door. Daisy is intent, leaning a little forward. When Sinead suggests it was Reverend Green and Miss Scarlett in the broom cupboard, Daisy is outraged. 'You're so *immature*, Sinead. You've got to play it *properly*.'

But Richard is playing seriously, just as Daisy wants. I love to see this. It's how he used to be when the girls were younger—untangling puppets, gallantly losing at cricket, entering into their world. I wonder if something has changed in him, after what I told him yesterday, and at last he sees how much we need him here.

'I want to win,' says Daisy. 'I really want to win.'

He ruffles her hair; his face is softer, tender.

I breathe out a little. *Trust Betrayed* is still in its carrier bag, hidden in the make-up drawer in my bedroom. I need so urgently to talk about it with him: for him to see the danger we are in. But I'm sure now he will listen.

There's a sudden silence: Richard is about to make an accusation. I go to the door to see.

'It was Professor Plum in the library with the candle-stick,' he says. He's relishing the moment; his voice has an edge of melodrama.

Daisy holds her breath; her eyes gleam in her white face.

'If you're wrong you're out, Dad,' says Sinead.

Richard looks in the envelope that holds the answer. He says nothing for a moment, his face a caricature of regret.

'Oops,' he says. 'Well, at least I was close.'

Daisy laughs, her fat happy laugh that you hardly ever hear now. I wait for a moment, listening. I love him for making her happy.

'Now I can win,' she says.

After the meal, we wash up while the girls are watching *Holby City* in Sinead's room.

'There's something I need to talk about,' I tell him.

The flowers he brought are in a vase on the table, their stamens dark and powdery as soot. I focus on them, clear my throat; I know what I will say.

'There's something I want to talk about, too,' he tells me.

'Oh.'

He's washing a casserole in the sink, wearing the rubber gloves he always uses to keep his skin smooth for violin-playing. Now he turns towards me; he hasn't finished the washing-up, but he's peeling off the gloves.

'Darling, I've been thinking. I mean, I know how tough it is for you. With Daisy at home so much, and having to care for her and everything.'

'I'm all right.'

He shakes his head a little. 'Well, I hope so. You seemed quite overwrought yesterday. I've been wondering if you could do with a bit of help,' he says.

'You mean like going to a therapist or something?' This irritates me, yet I know he's only being caring. 'It's sweet of you, but really, I'm OK.'

'I didn't mean that exactly. I meant help in the home.'

'What's wrong with our home? I thought I was coping fine. It still looks OK, doesn't it?'

'Of course,' he says. 'You always run the house beautifully. That isn't quite what I meant.'

'Really, it isn't necessary,'

'I'm not so sure,' he says again. 'Anyway, I rang an au pair agency today. It seems an ideal solution.'

I put down the saucepan I'm drying.

'No. I don't want an au pair.'

'It really doesn't cost a lot,' he says. 'And there might be spin-offs—it might help Sinead with her languages.'

'And where were you planning this person would live, exactly?'

He isn't looking at me; he turns a little away. 'There's masses of space in the attic.'

'*No.*' A sudden hot anger flares in me. '*No.* The attic's *my* place. She couldn't live there. Richard, I don't want this.'

He sighs. 'This always happens. Whenever I try to help, you just get so emotional.'

I sit down heavily at the table. I rub my face with my hands.

'No, Richard. I couldn't share the house like that. I *couldn't*. I don't know how people do it. I'd hate to have some other woman here all the time. *Hate* it.'

'There's really no shame in having help,' he says. 'Most people have someone living in—a nanny or au pair or someone. They couldn't manage without it. Even your mate Nicky has an au pair.'

'Nicky's different from me.'

'Sure,' he says. 'Well, thank goodness. I'd rather have you.' He's smiling, trying to be mollifying. 'But all the same—I've never quite understood why you haven't wanted those things.'

I think of the years I spent living with strangers—everything worn, tattered, smelling of other people, scuffed and shiny with the pressure of other people's bodies, of never having a place to be my secret separate self. And then of the joy of having this house that belongs to me, lived in by those I love, held and protected by its steep tiled roof and stone dogs and thick hedges, where every wall in every room is washed in a colour I've chosen. I couldn't have a stranger here—to look, to judge, to know about me, to be there even in my most intimate moments, with Richard, with my children. Surely he knows this. Surely.

'Was that why you came home early?' I say. 'To ask me this?'

He puts his hand on my shoulder. There's a stale rubbery smell to his skin, from the washing-up gloves. The smell is briefly, sharply, repellent. I turn my face away.

'Cat, do something for me. Promise you'll at least think about it. I really believe it could make things easier for you.'

I don't understand why he's being so insistent.

I shake my head.

'I don't want to be watched all the time,' I tell him.

The words fall like little stones into the space between us.

CHAPTER 22

On Saturday, there's another postcard.

I'm making our morning coffee when the postman rings. There's a music magazine for Richard that won't go through the letterbox, and a heap of catalogues, bills and offers of cheap insurance. The postcard is sandwiched between the Boden catalogue and the telephone bill. It shows a marble statue of a woman who's reading a book and wearing voluminous clothes. The caption says it is the personification of History on the plinth of Schiller's monument in the Gendarmenmarkt.

I turn it over.

Darling, Well, it's spring time here and the pink oleanders are out at the café in the Tiergarten. You'd love this city in the spring, Trina, I know you would, you always were very artistic! Berlin is changing so fast now, it's a different city, my darling, not what you'd expect. They say the guidebooks are all out of date now!

Don't leave it too long to get in touch, my darling, my health is not what it was. Much love, as ever.

Her writing evokes her. I see her vividly for a moment, smell her smell of Marlboros and lily of the valley, hear the faint jangle of her gilded bracelets.

I read it through again. 'You always were very artistic.' That fills me with a sour anger. What right has she to claim to know what I'm like, to know anything about me? I put the card in the recycling bin.

I take Richard his coffee and the *Financial Times*. Sinead is up and dressed already, in jeans and a cut-off top that says in sparkly letters, 'Never judge a girl by her T-shirt'. She's going out with a gang of friends, to ice-skate at Queensway and eat Dim Sum and buy stickers and notepaper with cartoon animals on from the shops in Chinatown.

'Cat, is my lipliner OK?'

'Of course it is. You look gorgeous.'

'I don't. I look really rank today.'

I put my arm round her. 'Nonsense. You look like a supermodel. See you have some breakfast before you go.'

'What is it about breakfast? Daisy never eats breakfast.'

'That has nothing to do with anything,' I tell her.

Richard is still asleep, his face pressed into the pillow. The air is thick and sour, used up with our breathing. I part the curtains a little. This morning our red-walled room oppresses me, with its darkly varnished floor, its heavy curtains patterned with lilies; in the cool morning light it seems stagey and overdone. I have a sudden impulse to redecorate it, to paint it white and green and fill it with light.

I put the coffee down, but I don't wake him.

When I go back to the kitchen, Sinead is perched on the table, eating a KitKat. I'm about to protest that this isn't exactly what I meant by breakfast, when I see she has the postcard in her hand.

'D'you mind if I take this, Cat? For my Weimar Republic project?'

My heart thuds. I don't know what to say.

Anxiety darkens her face. She's trying to read me.

'I mean—not if you want to keep it. But I thought you didn't want it, Cat. You'd put it in the bin.'

I take a deep breath, keep my voice easy, level. 'Of course you can have it.'

She's holding it out between finger and thumb in front of her. I think for a moment that she will turn it over. My pulse skitters off: I don't want to have to explain.

But then the caption catches her eye.

'The personification of history. Teachers love all that stuff. It's, like, *symbolic*.'

She finishes the KitKat and licks her fingers lavishly. As she goes out through the hall she puts the postcard in her school bag.

Richard and Daisy both spend the morning in bed. Richard has his newspaper, Daisy has a new video game and some colouring-in from school. She's started on an RE worksheet, a *Where's Wally?*-style picture with lots of Biblical figures. It says, 'Jesus is lost in Jerusalem. Can you find him?'

I go up to the attic. There's a frame I have bought, on impulse passing an art shop: simple, of stained black wood. I choose one of my pictures, selecting it almost at random. There are three children, imprisoned behind bars; they have distorted faces and large shadowed eyes. The bars are made from a woven texture of spiky lines like briars. At the edge of the picture, the lines are delicate, evanescing into nothing, but they're solid, immutable, in the centre, where the children are. I slip the picture into the frame. Immediately it looks different. The thought enters my mind that this is a good drawing, perhaps the best I have done. I take it downstairs and nail it to the wall in the drawing room, beside the flower painting.

The phone rings and I worry automatically that it's Sinead, that she's stranded at a bus-stop somewhere, or she's broken her ankle skating.

'Catriona, darling.' Gina's resonant voice. She sounds

more nasal over the phone. 'Nothing special,' she says. 'I'm just ringing for a chat. How are things?'

'OK.'

'And how's my little Daisy?'

'She's much the same. Still quite poorly.'

'Oh, dear,' says Gina. She sounds rather hurt, as though we have let her down. 'I was really hoping she'd be better by now.'

'Well, we all were. It just goes on and on.'

'Is she eating any better?'

'Not really. It's quite a struggle.'

'You ought to give her a nice English breakfast before she goes to school,' she says. 'Bacon and eggs. You really should try it. You don't want to listen to all that nonsense about cholesterol. I'm a very great fan of bacon and eggs.'

'I don't think she'd eat it.'

'You don't know that unless you try, Catriona,' she says.

I feel a surge of irritation. I want to let her know how bad things are, to make her understand.

'She still retches a lot,' I tell her. 'And sometimes she forgets things. That frightens me.'

'Everyone forgets things sometimes, Catriona,' she says.

'Yes. But not like this. She says she can't remember the words for things. Really familiar things. Like the names she's given her cuddlies.'

Gina is brisk. 'It sounds like she knows just how to wind her mother up.'

I've had enough.

'I'll get Richard for you,' I tell her.

For lunch I cook spaghetti. I make this often now—it's one of the few things Daisy will sometimes eat. I make a sauce of tomatoes and onions and peppers, and sieve it thoroughly, so there won't be bits in it. I leave out the garlic, but it still smells good, a Tuscan smell of basil and warm olive oil.

Richard comes down. He's showered, his hair is damp. He looks into the saucepan, raises his eyebrows.

'Spaghetti again? Pushing the envelope, are we?'

'It's Daisy's favourite. I'll cook you something else.'

'No, no, that's fine,' he says.

I call Daisy. She's wearing some new Marks & Spencer dungarees, that I chose because they wouldn't press on her stomach. I went for the six-year-old size, but they still look baggy on her. I tell myself that Marks & Spencer sizes are always generous.

It feels too quiet, sitting down to lunch without Sinead. I always miss her when she's away, out with her friends or staying over at Sara's. Today, I'm very aware how we depend on her—to be a little sardonic, to shift the mood.

I put out a small portion of lunch for Daisy.

'That looks delicious,' she says. But she doesn't pick up her cutlery.

'Shall I cut up your spaghetti?'

'That's babyish,' she says.

'There's no one but us to see. Why not if it makes it easier?'

She shrugs. 'OK,' she says.

I cut it up into very small pieces.

She spends a long time attempting to get exactly the right bit of food on her fork: the spaghetti keeps falling off. I try not to watch.

Finally she puts the fork in her mouth. She chews very slowly, puts the fork down again.

'Mum, d'you mind if I leave this?' she says. 'I'm not that hungry right now.'

'Just try,' I tell her. 'Just one more bite.'

I can feel how Richard is watching me. In the pale washed light that floods the kitchen, the pupils of his eyes are contracted, just little specks of dark. He doesn't say anything.

'*Please*, sweetheart.' Her wrist that rests on the edge of the table is so thin, sparrow thin. There's pleading in my voice. I know that this is pointless, that nothing will make her eat, but I can't stop myself. 'I know it's an effort, but you've got to eat something.'

'I can't,' she says.

'Let's think of something else then. What about jelly? I could make you some jelly. Could you eat that, d'you think?'

'I don't know,' she says.

I hate the way he's looking at me, that hardened narrow look. There's anger in my head, a brief searing rage. I want to shout at him—You bloody deal with it, then. See if it's all so fucking easy, what I have to do.

Suddenly I can't bear to stay in the house. I leave my meal, push back my chair.

'Let's go out,' I say to Daisy. My voice is bright, brittle. 'You and me. While Dad does his music practice. I'll make some jelly and then we'll walk to the petshop. You could manage that, couldn't you? And if I put the jelly in the freezer it'll be exactly ready when we get back. Shall we do that?'

'Could we look at the kittens?'

'Of course we could.'

We walk there slowly through the paintbox dazzle of spring. The scents from people's gardens brush against us. There's a magnolia with flowers like gentle, pale hands, cupped to hold something precious. Horses and riders from the riding school in the park go past us, indolently slow, in the middle of the road, holding up the traffic. The horses' luxuriant tails are golden, they glisten in the light. The sun is warm on our skin.

The pet shop is in the main road. On the pavement outside there are baskets heaped up with huge knuckle bones for dogs, red and raw and savage. Daisy likes to look at these. Inside, the shop has a smell of warm straw, shot through with something hot and wild, like the smells of zoos or circuses.

There is a grey African parrot; it has a cruel beak, but the colour of its feathers is soft as smoke. It whistles its jungle whistle and splashes drinking-water out at us as we pass. And there's an adder in a glass tank, its glossy coils heaped up against the glass; its discarded skin lies beside it like creased translucent paper.

'D'you think it hurts snakes when they shed their skins?' says Daisy.

I think how it might feel, that sleek new slippery skin. 'Maybe they're glad to,' I tell her.

We come to the cage of kittens. They have short dark velvet fur. Daisy is entranced. One of them comes up to her and presses against the cage.

'That kitten really likes me,' she says.

The kitten pushes its paws through the bars. Daisy laughs. It's her old laugh: breathy, with a catch in it. For a moment we are happy.

We've come just to look round, but we've spent so long here I feel we have to buy something, so we choose a book about how to look after your cat. The boy at the till has a filthy cold; he coughs into his hands and wipes his nose on a piece of used tissue. This alarms me: I've become so afraid of the simplest things, of other people's colds and viruses, anything Daisy might catch. My credit card won't go through at first, and he blows on it to try and make it work. Later, when we get home, I shall wipe it with Milton bleach.

On the way back, she slows. She's walking in that careful way, with small deliberate steps.

'Are your legs hurting?'

'Yes.'

'We'll just walk very slowly, then.'

Her hand is loose in mine. I see that she is limping. The afternoon starts to feel tired, oppressive, in spite of the loveliness of the soft spring light.

'When can I have my kitten, Mum?'

'We'll think about it.'

'You always say that,' she says.

'We need to get you well first. Before we take on looking after a kitten.'

She's cross. She tries to kick a can on the pavement, but the movement hurts her, she flinches. She's suddenly near to tears.

'If God loves you so much, why does he give you all these illnesses?' she says.

'I don't know, sweetheart. Nobody knows.' I put my arm round her but she shrugs it off.

When we get home, she lies on the sofa, white and drained. I feel so guilty: I shouldn't have taken her out, shouldn't have tried to behave as though everything was normal. Richard is practising his violin. It's music I don't recognise. It might be Bach, it's often Bach, but I have no way of telling; there's so much knowledge he has that I don't share. The music is pure and stern and feels like a reproach, reminding me austerely of how little I know.

I take the jelly out of the freezer. There's a crusted rim of white ice-crystals round the edge of the bowl. I spoon out some from the middle, where it isn't icy, and go to give it to Daisy; but she says it's too cold, she leaves it in the bowl.

I dream I am back at The Poplars again. I can see it, sense it, so vividly in the dream. I am sitting on the sofa with broken springs, waiting for something, smelling the overcooked cabbage and Jeyes fluid. And in the dream I feel as I did then—constricted, as though a heavy weight is pressing on my chest.

I wake from the dream and feel the dark around me, hear Richard's breathing and the thin chime of St Agatha's—four o'clock; but the sense of pressure in my chest won't leave me.

I lie there for what feels like a long time. I hear the birds begin, the dull low sound of a rook, then many smaller birds, their spiky glittery songs. I ease myself out of bed; light is splintering round the edges of the curtains. I go quietly downstairs.

The kitchen is bleak in the cold morning light and it smells of last night's dinner, but through the window the sky is a colour that cannot be described or painted, a dark lavish colour, depth on depth of blue, with a narrow moon, still a crescent, and a delicate stitching of stars.

I unlock the door, go out into the garden. The paving slabs are gritty under my bare feet. I step across the patio and down onto the lawn. The air is like blue gauze, like a sheen of smoke over everything, and the shadow is black under the pear tree. There are no flower scents, all the flowers are closed up, the daffodils drained of colour, the tight buds of the pear blossom pale and grey; there's just the smell of wet grass, wet earth, and the whole garden shivers with birdsong.

The grass is chilly with dew; the cold tightens my skin. I stand there for a long time. It's all blue and cold and beautiful and has nothing to do with people, nothing to do with me: I am a stranger in my own garden. In some unguessable way, this soothes me.

When I go back inside, my feet are completely wet, as though I have walked through water, leaving perfect prints on the kitchen tiles. The blue air is inside me, like something I've drunk in, and my heartbeat is slow and gentle and I know what I will do.

CHAPTER 23

He's shorter than I remember, and he's wearing jeans and a loose white shirt with the sleeves rolled up, and he has a sandwich on a plate in his hand. His grey eyes widen as he sees me standing there on his doorstep.

'I'm sorry,' I say.

He shakes his head. 'It's lovely to see you,' he says.

Jamie's school bag and Bob the Builder lunchbox are flung down on the wooden floor of the hall. From the front room, I can hear *Neighbours*, and know that Sinead and Daisy too will be watching now. He steps aside to usher me in.

'You didn't bring Daisy.'

'No.' I don't tell him the reason—that I didn't tell the girls I was coming here, that I didn't want Richard to know. Maybe he guesses this: he doesn't press it.

'You could go into the back,' he says. 'I was just taking this to Jamie.' He indicates the sandwich.

The back room is uncluttered, almost bare: white walls, stripped floors, a table, chairs and a sofa, and a bookcase that is full of books about globalisation and climate change. I wonder briefly how different I would be if I lived in a room like this one, a simple room with white light pouring in. There are photographs on the walls—big black and white pictures of Jamie at a playground; a picture of Fergal with a woman who presumably must be his ex-wife—svelte and dark, her head close to his, in a garden somewhere; Fergal in a flak jacket in front of a burnt-out house that's stark against a summer-blue sky.

'I like the room,' I say as he comes in.

'I didn't do it myself,' he says. 'It was like this when I bought it. But it seemed just right for me. I like to travel light—I'm not very domestic really.'

I point to the photograph. 'You've done some interesting things.'

'I used to be into all this gung-ho stuff,' he says. 'But not since Jamie came to live with me. It wasn't possible any more. Though to be honest, I didn't want to anyway.'

'I think that having children can make you more afraid.'

'Yes,' he says.

We stand there for a moment, not knowing what to do.

'Why don't you sit down?' he says.

I sit on the sofa. He looks down at me with eyes that are grey and steady, and my body feels big and ungainly, and I don't know why I've come.

'I'll get you a drink,' he says. 'Would you like that?'

'Yes. Thank you.'

He goes to the kitchen, comes back with two glasses, and a bottle of wine from the fridge, with a sweat of cold on it.

'It's rather rough,' he says as he hands me my glass, his fingers brushing mine. 'If I'd known you were coming, I'd have got something better.'

I drink gratefully. 'It's good,' I tell him.

He's standing there looking down at me with his glass in his hand. I sense his awkwardness. He's very direct, but he isn't smooth like Richard. He's no good at glossing over the gaps in conversations; he isn't the kind of man who'd open doors for you or slickly end up at your elbow on the outside of the pavement. The silence stretches on, and I'm desperate to break it.

'It's a weird feeling. That you know so much about me.' And immediately I wish I hadn't said that: it's too close, too confessional. Heat washes over my skin.

His eyes don't leave me.

'Well, I don't, of course,' he says. 'I saw a photo of you, that was all. When I was doing a piece on The Poplars, during the inquiry.'

'But that was years ago.'

'Yes.' He's very serious, his steady gaze on me. 'It was one of my first pieces. It got to me, the whole story, the way you were silenced.'

'I still don't see how you could recognise me.'

'There were these photos: you and some of the other kids in this big empty room—it looked so bleak some-how—and one that was just you, smiling for England,' he says.

I remember the photo that Lesley took, for the adver-tisement in the *Evening Standard*.

'I can't have been more than fourteen,' I say.

'No,' he says, 'but your smile was just the same.'

I feel myself flush again. I turn away a little.

'And Aimee?' I say. 'You told me you met her?'

He nods. 'She's got a little boy. She works in a dry-cleaner's in Peckham.'

'And she's really OK?'

'I only met her once. She was keen to talk,' he says.

'Maybe I should go and see her,' I say, uncertainly. 'It's just so hard to imagine.'

'I don't know,' he says. 'Well, that's up to you—I mean, I can give you her number.'

I sense that he wants to dissuade me. And he's right, maybe. I think of how it would be if I went to see her now: how everything that joined us once has gone.

'What did you say about me? Was she angry with me?'

'Angry? Why would she be?'

'I thought she might be.'

He shakes his head. 'She said you were the clever one, she always thought you'd make it.'

I wonder what that means, to make it—and whether it's true of me.

He turns from me, opens a window onto the back garden. It's a nondescript garden: a motorbike, a climbing frame, a patch of grass worn down from football games; a prunus with pink extravagant blossom and dark leaves the colour of scorched paper. Warm air comes into the room, with a smell of the changing earth.

'That isn't the only reason I came,' I say. 'There's something else—I needed to talk to somebody.'

'Daisy?'

My heart has started to pound. 'Something's happened...' The words clog up my throat.

'Catriona, what is it?' he says. There's a sudden urgency in his voice, responding perhaps to the fear in mine. 'What are they saying?'

Suddenly, in this simple bright room, the whole thing seems preposterous; I scarcely believe it myself. I think he'll shrug it off—or say, like Richard, You're exaggerating, it'll all blow over... I take a deep breath.

'They think it's my fault—that I'm making her ill.'

'They're saying *what*?'

'That it's my fault, that it's this syndrome.'

His face changes. He's sharp, alert. He stares at me. 'Münchausen's?'

I nod.

'Jesus.'

'I love her so much. How could I possibly hurt her?'

He makes a brief little gesture, waving my protestation aside.

'I don't believe this,' he says.

'I've seen the letter.'

'Jesus,' he says again.

He's silent for a moment. He pulls up a dining chair, sits down in front of me, his eyes never leaving me.

'Catriona, this is a criminal allegation,' he says. His voice has changed; he's so quiet, serious. 'When a doctor says this, he isn't talking medicine any more, he's talking crime. You need a lawyer. Now.'

This shakes me.

'How can I possibly get a lawyer?'

'I could find you someone,' he says.

'But Richard would never agree. Richard thinks we should just go along with what they're saying—not make a fuss. That we shouldn't rock the boat, that they all know what they're doing. He'd be appalled if I suggested seeing a lawyer.'

'Go on your own, then,' he says.

'How can I? I'm totally dependent. I've no money of my own, no training. I've got three GCSEs—I mean, I have nothing that's just mine…'

My voice is small. I feel a kind of shame at this recital of my deficiencies—that I am so dependent, like a child.

'At the very least,' he says, 'you must get another

doctor.' He's talking fast and his urgency frightens me. 'You have an absolute right to a second opinion. If they really believe this, they could take Daisy away. They don't have to be certain.'

'I don't know anyone to go to.' I think how feeble he must think me—that to everything he suggests I say that I can't do it. 'I've asked my GP—she couldn't suggest anyone.'

'That's crap,' he says. 'Listen. There's a woman I know who's on the Health Authority—a local councillor, Thelma. She knows lots of medics. I'll get you a name.'

'But how can I do that, if Richard doesn't want to?'

'You've got to make him see.'

I shake my head a little, thinking of Richard. There's silence between us for a moment. The lazy easy sounds of spring evenings float in through the window—children calling in the wide back gardens, the leisurely clatter of horses being ridden down the road.

'Why doesn't he understand?' I'm talking half to myself now. 'Why does he seem to believe what these doctors are saying?'

'How should I know?' He's looking out at the garden, looking away from me. 'I'm possibly the very last person you should talk to about Richard.'

It's because of the warmth behind his words, perhaps, but tears of self-pity start to well up in me. I swallow them down.

'I feel so helpless,' I tell him.

'Yes. I know. But you're not.'

He comes and sits beside me on the sofa. He puts out a hand and briefly touches my wrist. I look at his hand on mine. I see how worn his fingernails are, and the tracery of blue veins inside his wrists. 'I think you're also strong.'

I shake my head. 'I don't feel it.'

'Aimee told me a lot,' he says. 'About what you all went through. If you can come through that, you can come through anything.'

We're too close. I don't look at him.

'I don't think it works like that,' I tell him. 'I don't think awful things make you stronger.'

'But you've made it through,' he says. 'When I look at you, I see this poised woman with this perfect house, this perfect lifestyle—but someone who knows about the other side too. Someone who's survived... Catriona, you've got to fight this.'

'But how can I? How can I if Richard won't? Because everything I do will be held against me. They're watching me now—just watching to see if I put a foot wrong, if I give them any little clue. I know they're watching me. And Dr McGuire—I feel he hates me. I can't fight him.'

'I don't think you have a choice,' he says.

'But the way he looks at me—it's like I appall him somehow...'

'No,' he says. He gets up abruptly. 'It's nothing to do with that.'

He's looking out of the window, his back to me.

'There was a case up at the hospital,' he says. 'Several years ago now. Dr McGuire was involved. Nice couple, Mum had been a nurse, stable ordinary family. I heard about it—Thelma had a contact on the paediatric ward. First kid died of a cot death. Terrible thing, everyone was very sympathetic, big funeral, lots of white flowers. Mum had another baby. Second kid died, just like the first. Tragic coincidence. A year or two later, Mum had a third child—had a monitor to check on the baby's breathing, loved him to bits, everyone was very happy for her. But the baby wasn't thriving and the GP was worried, made a fuss—and, rather against Dr McGuire's wishes, mother and baby were admitted to a covert surveillance unit in Birmingham. They got her on video, trying to suffocate the baby.' He's staring into the garden. 'They're pretty bloody wary up there now,' he says.

I sit there, thinking about all this. I don't know what to say.

'I don't know if that helps at all,' he says then.

'Yes. Maybe.'

We're silent for a moment. I feel his eyes on me.

From the front room I hear the music at the end of *Neighbours*.

'I've got to go,' I tell him.

'Yes,' he says. 'But I'd like you to come again. You could show me some of your drawings. I'd like that.'

'Yes. I will.'

I get up. Our eyes are just on a level.

'You don't believe it,' I say. 'That it *is* my fault. Everyone else seems to suspect me, but you don't.'

'For goodness' sake,' he says.

I go into the hall. He follows me. We're standing there and neither of us has opened the door.

I turn towards him. I'm going to say thanks for the drink and for listening to me. We're looking at each other: we can't look away.

'Catriona.' The way he says it, it's as if he touches me, like warm fingertips sliding across my skin. 'I've wanted so much to see you. There are things I've wanted to say to you. That I probably shouldn't anyway, but I wanted to. And now I can't,' he says.

My skin is hot.

'That's the very last thing you need,' he says, 'the stuff I was going to say.'

I shake my head a little.

He looks at me like a question, and reaches out and puts his arms around me. He holds me lightly for a moment, carefully, as though I am fragile. I rest my head on his shoulder. Then I turn and go without looking at him.

CHAPTER 24

Nicky rings, wanting to know how Daisy is and whether I'm going to the *Sound of Music* karaoke. She asks what we thought of Helmut Wolf's diet. I confess, rather ashamed, that we've tried but we've had to give up. She says, Well, maybe it wasn't right for Daisy; she has someone else to recommend, a cranial osteopath with amazing healing hands. I feel a surge of hope—as I always do when someone is suggested. I write his name in my address book.

Every night I wake and lie there for hours, hearing Richard's breathing and the bark of the fox, my worries

growing in the night, feeding on darkness and sleepless-
ness. I make endless lists in my mind, conjure up new and
intricate theories, things to try. I wonder whether Daisy
is allergic to household chemicals: I buy ecological
washing-up liquid and clean the kitchen with bicarbonate
of soda. In the dentist's waiting room I read a magazine
article about housedust mites and how our bedding is
full of their toxic excrement: I send off for a dustmite-
proof cover for Daisy's duvet and mattress. I order a
weekly delivery of organic vegetables. They have lots of
leaves and the carrots still have their feathering of green,
and they come in a string bag and leave rich trails of soil.
When I cut into the carrots they give out a sweet scent
that fills me with a warm earth-motherly feeling, as
though I am a country housewife presiding over an Aga
and hens and hollyhocks. Richard and Sinead and I all
enjoy the vegetables. Daisy eats just the potatoes.

I worry too about Sinead, worry that she is neglected:
she's more closed up, more silent, chewing the sides of
her fingernails. I try to make time for her. Her school will
be doing *The Tempest* for their summer production, and
she so longs to be Ariel; we choose a speech together, for
the audition. And in Art they're doing city streets, and she
wants to photograph a car that someone has abandoned
round the corner, and a hole that's been dug in the
pavement where pipes are exposed.

'Come with me, Cat,' she says. 'It's embarrassing.'

The car is a grey Mondeo. Someone has put a brick
through the back window, and the windscreen is cracked

all over, as though it is crusted with frost. Sinead takes lots of photographs.

When we go to the hole in the pavement, a woman comes out of her house.

'Excuse me, but are you complaining about the hole?' She's very clean, with crisp grey curls.

'No, sorry,' I tell her. 'It's for a school art project.'

'Oh.' She looks dejected. 'I complained about it, you know, I rang the council, but they said, "It's not our hole." EDF dug it and they smelt gas, so they rang the gas people, and the gas men made a little camp and sat in it drinking tea… It's dangerous—the mothers can't get past it with their buggies.'

Sinead is assiduously photographing, ignoring the woman.

'Sorry,' I say, 'we're just looking for an interesting picture.'

'You think it's artistic? I'm disappointed in you.' She waves, goes back to her house.

When the photographs are developed, Richard shows Sinead how to manipulate them on the computer, playing around with the colours. He's very patient with her, and the results are lovely. The lines in the cracked glass are like a spider's ordered threads or a patterning of veins. We all admire these patterns. Sinead glows, a little surprised, as though this rarely happens, to have so much attention.

We make an appointment with Nicky's cranial osteopath. He's bearded and intense, and he has a consulting room with framed charts of the body showing the meridians, and on his desk a little plastic skeleton. There's a dual carriageway outside; when a lorry roars past, the skeleton shakes. He asks for Daisy's birth details, and announces that she has stomach trouble because she was born by Ventouse extraction. He lays her down on his couch and moves his hands on her head. Afterwards some of the tension has eased out of her face, and she says she feels less sick—but in the morning, when she wakes, she's pale and ill again.

In Waterstones, I look at a book of spells, the one that Nicky uses. The magic seems harmless enough—it's all about candles and scented oils and wishing people well. Maybe I should become a witch, like Nicky. There's a spell for healing. You make a circlet of ivy and a pentangle from ribbon, and you write the name of the person you want to heal on a piece of scented paper, and burn a green candle and think of them being healthy. I would like to try this. I don't exactly believe in it, but I would like to try. The only thing that stops me from buying the book is the fear of Richard finding it, and the thought of the look on his face.

I do a drawing that I'm especially pleased with. It's a child, alone, with around her a lavish texture of lines that circle and swirl to the margins of the page. The child reaches out of the picture; her hands are huge and angular, you can see the lines on her palms. When I've finished it and look at it, I see how ambiguous it is, this gesture that she's making—reaching out to someone, or pushing someone away. There's part of me that would like to show the drawing to Fergal, just as he suggested, but when I think of this I feel a kind of fear.

Spring comes to our garden. There are lilacs, and flimsy purple irises round the pond, and a single waterlily, its petals thick and perfect as though it is fashioned from wax, and a blue smoke of rosemary flowers in the herb bed. But everything is neglected; I never seem to get out there any more. The daffodils need tying up, their leaves are brown and broken, and there are weeds in the rose bed.

One afternoon when Daisy is off school I wrap her up in her fleece—she always seems so cold—and we go into the garden. There's a smell of wet earth and lilac. She sits on the patio step, her arms wrapped round herself. Her hair is dull, tangled.

I pull up the couch grass under the rose bushes; it's tough—it hurts your hands. She's watching me.

'There was this man who was cutting his hedge,' she says, 'and he found a gold ring.'

'Wow. Is that really true, d'you think, or just a story?'

'It's true. I saw it on *Antiques Roadshow*.'

There are tiny rust-coloured spiders on the paving slabs. She pokes at one with a stick. If you crush them they leave a reddish smear, like dried blood. 'It was really really old,' she says. 'It came from the Anglo-Saxons. His wife thought it was a ring from a Christmas cracker.'

'Imagine that,' I say. 'Imagine just poking around in your hedge and finding a beautiful thing.' I'm trying to pull up a dock, but its tap root is deep; it hurts my hands as I pull. 'Some people have all the luck,' I say, thoughtlessly.

Daisy looks at me. She is so pale, so serious.

'Why can't I be lucky?' she says.

I wish I hadn't said what I said. I sit back on my heels; I struggle with this, not knowing what to say.

'Maybe luck kind of comes in cycles,' I tell her. 'I mean, you've had a horrid time this year, but maybe soon you'll have good times again with lots of luck.'

'I don't need lots of luck,' she says. 'I just want to wake up in my bed and feel fine.'

One day when I go down to make my morning coffee, Richard hands me a letter. There's a wariness about him. He looks me up and down.

I take it. It's from the hospital.

An appointment has been made for you to discuss Daisy's illness with Dr Jane Watson, Consultant Child Psychiatrist. This appointment is for Mr and Mrs Lydgate only, without Daisy. All patients are given individual appointment times so please arrive in good time. If you arrive late it may not be possible for the clinician to see you. On arrival, please report to the receptionist in Outpatients, who will direct you to the clinic.

He turns back to the mirror, smoothing out his tie.

'I've had a look in my diary,' he says. 'I've got something in for the morning, but I'll get Francine to sort it out. It's such a help to have a really efficient PA.'

'You mean—we're just going to go along with it?'

'Well, what else do you suggest?' It's his work voice—cool, brisk, as though he's chairing a meeting.

'But, Richard—what if they find out about me, about my childhood?'

'I don't for a moment suppose they'll bother with that—I mean, that's all in the past.'

'But surely you see.' I wonder if I should have shown him the book I bought. But it's never seemed the right moment. 'They think that if you have that sort of child-hood it means you must be disturbed. That you can't be a good parent.'

'You worry so much,' he says, routinely. He slips on his jacket. I notice that he's wearing a different aftershave. It has a rather thick aromatic smell, like a cold cure.

'They mustn't know,' I say. 'They must never ever find out.'

'OK,' he says. 'If that's what you really want.'

He goes. He doesn't kiss me.

CHAPTER 25

It's a bare grey room: thinly upholstered armchairs arranged with studied casualness, a clock on the wall with a loud metallic tick, a desk with a few framed photographs. In the corner there's a rubber plant, so glossy and symmetrical it seems to be made of plastic, although in fact it is real. There's nothing on the table in the space between the chairs except a box of tissues. The air is thick and warm.

She is quietly dressed, in a sweater and skirt. She has elegant pale legs and high boots made of snakeskin.

'I'm Jane Watson.' She's shaking hands with both of

us; her hand is cool and firm. 'Thank you for coming in. Are you happy if we use Christian names?'

'Sure,' says Richard.

Her hair is blonde and neatly tied, and she's wearing a sandalwood scent, and she has a vivid, practised smile that doesn't reach her eyes. We sit, and she crosses her long pale legs. Her skirt is short; it eases up her thigh.

'I like to tape my sessions with clients,' she says. 'Are you happy with that?'

'Sure,' says Richard again. He's affable, relaxed; he seems at ease here.

The clinic is in an annexe at the edge of the hospital site. The windows are thick; you can only hear the faintest sound of traffic—the outside world seems very far away.

She turns on her cassette player and leans back in her chair; her elbows are on the arms of the chair, the finger-tips just touching. The whole room smells of her scent.

'We're here to talk about you and Daisy,' she says. Her voice is sleek as Vaseline. 'To try and find out whether there are any psychological issues here, that might be making her ill.'

'I really don't think there are,' I say immediately, then wish I hadn't spoken. Be careful, be careful, says something inside me. I take a slow deep breath. I say to her what I said to Dr McGuire. That Daisy's happy at school. That there haven't been any big changes in our lives. That no one's died or anything…

She looks at me appraisingly. Her eyes are green as

ferns. She has a quiet casual beauty, the sort of beauty that makes a man think, Only I have seen this.

'But you see, children do react differently to adults,' she says. 'Children can be very sensitive to atmospheres, for instance.'

'Could you explain that for us, Jane?' says Richard. I'm aware of the warmth in his voice.

'Well, if perhaps there's tension in the home,' she says. 'Maybe quite subtle tensions in the family. Sometimes children pick up on atmospheres and somatise their feelings—that means, they turn them into physical symptoms. To take a common example—today's children are very aware of the possibility of divorce.'

'But we get on fine,' I tell her.

She doesn't respond. My protestation hangs in the air between us, glaring and conspicuous. I feel my face go hot.

'Perhaps you could tell me who is in the family,' she says. 'I believe there are the two of you and Daisy, and also your daughter, Richard, by your first marriage?'

Richard nods.

'In one of our later sessions,' says Jane Watson, 'I may want to see you together, the whole family.'

'I'd rather not, really,' I tell her. 'I'd rather not put Daisy under any more stress.'

'So you would agree that Daisy is under stress at the moment—for whatever reason?'

I feel a hot red flicker of rage. 'Only because she's ill.'

The anger is there in my voice. Richard glances at me.

'Yes. Well, of course, that's what we're here to try

and understand,' Jane Watson says in her soothing Vaseline voice.

She settles back in her chair and uncrosses her legs, the narrow pale thighs sliding over one another. Out of the corner of my eye, I see how Richard watches.

'Perhaps we could go back to the beginning, when you became pregnant with Daisy,' she says. 'Perhaps you could tell me how you felt when you found you were pregnant?'

'I was thrilled,' I tell her.

Her green eyes rest on me.

'It's strange when you say that,' she says, her voice so emollient, so understanding, 'because what I notice is that you don't sound thrilled, you sound a little unsure.'

The tick of the clock is loud, intrusive, as though it's right inside me. I can't work out what to say.

'Well—it's a long time ago now,' I say. 'But really, I was very happy. I wanted to be pregnant more than anything.'

'And Richard, what about you?' she says.

'We were both delighted,' he says. 'Though, quite honestly, Jane, I guess I'm not much good at showing things like that. I'm just your average emotionally impaired male. You know—I need to retire to my cave from time to time.'

A brief smile flickers across Jane Watson's face: she likes this. But then she turns to me again.

'And so, Catriona, did you feed her yourself?'

The coyness of this surprises me.

'Breast-feeding, you mean? Yes. I loved it.'

'Can you tell me what you loved especially? What was so special for you?'

'Being so needed,' I tell her.

Her look is acute, intense. I know that she is filing this away.

'It's very special for you to feel needed?' she says gently.

I nod, but have a sudden doubt, a fear that I have said something rash, dangerous.

'And of course later that would have changed,' she says, 'as Daisy grew up. As she became more independent, and went to school. And perhaps you found that she didn't need you then in quite the same way…'

'Of course. Well, I enjoyed that part of it too.' I hear the shake in my voice.

'Now, a baby's arrival always means big changes in the family,' she says. 'How did that affect you, would you say? I mean, there will always be losses as well as gains.'

'I wasn't aware of any losses,' I tell her.

'There's such an expectation today that parenthood will be a fulfilling experience,' she says. 'It makes it difficult to acknowledge that there were things that were hard.'

I try to think of something. I see Daisy and me on our afternoons at the farm park, Daisy in a knitted hat that she had, petting the goats and laughing at their insistence, her face glowing, healthy, everything sunlit, tulip-coloured. A feeling like grief tugs at me.

'Darling,' says Richard. He reaches across and rests his hand on mine. It slips into my mind that this gesture is really aimed at her, to show how empathic he is. 'You were quite tearful in the days after Daisy was born. Don't you remember?'

'But everyone's like that.' There's an edge to my voice.

I move my hand from under his. 'That's perfectly normal—it doesn't mean anything.'

'I think Richard is trying to help you here, Catriona,' says Jane Watson.

'But I mean—the baby blues,' I say. 'Everyone has that. It's just a hormone thing. I adored her right from the beginning.'

'Perhaps I could give you a little feedback here,' she says. 'Because when you spoke to Richard then, I saw you move away from him a little. And now you've got your arms crossed in front of you, as though you're defending yourself from something, or protecting yourself. I'm wondering what you feel you need to protect yourself from.'

I uncross my arms. Be careful, be careful, says the voice in my head. 'I just think my reaction was perfectly normal,' I tell her.

'It may very well have been,' she says. 'I don't deny that. What I do see is how you react when Richard reaches out to you. Sometimes it's very hard for us to accept help.'

I don't know what to say to this. There's nothing I can say.

'Perhaps you could tell me about your childcare arrangements when Daisy was little. Now—what work were you doing before you had Daisy?'

'I worked in a nursery school.'

'And after Daisy was born?'

'I've never gone back to work.'

'It can be very demanding,' she says. 'Spending all day with a small child. Children can be very demanding.'

'I always enjoyed it,' I tell her. 'I didn't want to work. I never considered going back, to be honest. I thought I was just incredibly lucky.'

'Lucky?' She looks at me quizzically.

'It was what I'd always wanted.'

I see myself on the carpet at The Poplars, the smell of disinfectant all around me, and Lesley sitting there with her self-esteem tree drawn out in coloured felt tip, asking what I would choose if I could wave a magic wand. I remember the picture as I saw it in my head: the lawn, the lily pond, the laughter of children. And how when I met Richard, when we came to the house with the seven stone steps and the green front door—and then, when Daisy was born—I knew the answer to her question. I thought, This. This is what I would choose, what I have always wanted.

'Daisy wasn't demanding at all,' I tell Jane Watson. 'She was just always good fun. I like being with children— I think they're often more interesting than adults. You know, the things they come out with: I love that.'

'Sometimes,' she says, 'we can hide our feelings from ourselves. And it's perfectly normal to envy people whose lives are different from our own.'

'But I really don't think I felt that. I never wanted to be a power-suited career woman.' I realise too late that Jane Watson doubtless has a wardrobe full of pristine tailoring. 'I was happy with my life.'

'And Richard? What about you?' she says. 'How did you feel about this—Catriona staying at home? I find that some men today can quite resent it.' A half-smile curves her lips, softening what she's saying. 'That they want their wives to be out in the workplace bringing in lots of money.'

'It was fine,' he says. And then, as though aware this sounds rather lukewarm, 'Catriona was always a wonderful mother.'

'OK. Well, let's move on a bit. I'd like you both to tell me a little about your childhoods and family backgrounds.' She says this as though it is the easiest thing in the world. 'It's always important, I think, to have a look at the past and see how it may have shaped us.'

I try to keep my face still, but I can feel the sweat on me.

'Richard, perhaps you could go first,' she says.

'It was mostly OK,' he says. 'Though I hated boarding school. I went when I was eight. A ghastly place—some of the staff were sadists. I mean, trust me, that's no exaggeration.'

Her face seems to open when she looks at him. 'I know the kind of thing,' she says.

'I was homesick as hell at first,' he says. 'But you get used to it.'

'And your parents are still alive?'

He nods. 'They're in their seventies now—but yes, still going strong.'

'And, Catriona? What was your childhood like?'

'OK. An ordinary childhood. Nothing remarkable.'

I feel unreal suddenly, my body long and thin and etiolated. As though I am too tall for the room, as though I could reach to the ceiling: but so flimsy, fragile, a cardboard cut-out body, easily blown away.

'My mother was on her own. My father left when I was a baby—I never knew him.'

She has the look of a hunter, eager and alert.

'So you must have been aware, growing up, of being in a rather unusual family, of feeling different, perhaps of missing out?'

'I suppose so. Though it was what I was used to.'

The palms of my hands are wet.

'And your mother—how often do you see her now?' she says.

I clear my throat.

'My mother is dead,' I tell her.

Out of the corner of my eye, I see Richard turn towards me. I will him not to say anything.

Jane Watson leaves a small respectful silence.

'And how long ago did she die, Catriona?' she says then, serious, gentle.

'Oh, quite a few years now. It was a heart attack. She never saw Daisy.'

I'm walking on ice, listening out for splintering.

'That must be a deep source of sadness for you.'

I nod. Richard says nothing.

There's another pause, acknowledging my grief. These silences chill me.

Richard clears his throat, and my heart pounds. I am so afraid he will speak. But he says nothing.

She leans back in her chair.

'Well, I think we should maybe leave it there for today.'

Relief washes through me. I cover my mouth with my hand, afraid it will show in my face.

She turns off her voice recorder. 'Now, what I'd like you to do for next week is to maybe talk together about your childhoods. To see how what happened then may have affected you as parents. I always find that a valuable exercise. In our parenting, so often we do as we are done to.'

We walk out through the waiting room, where there are faded armchairs and copies of *Hello*. I can still smell her perfume and it catches at my throat.

'She seems good,' says Richard as we get into the car.

I'm in the driving seat as I'm dropping him off at the station. But I don't start up the car.

'Yes, I thought you liked her.'

'A clever woman, I thought,' he says.

'I didn't think that was what impressed you about her.'

'She's quite attractive, of course,' he says. 'But I did think she was pretty much on the ball.'

'But what use can any of this possibly be to Daisy?'

'They know what they're doing. They handle this kind of thing all the time.' He frowns. 'You should have been straight with her,' he says. 'About your mother.'

'No, Richard. No.' I'm appalled. I grasp his sleeve. 'I don't want her to know. She mustn't ever know.'

He shrugs. 'Well, if that's what you want,' he says, as he said before. 'But I'm really not happy with it.'

'I don't trust her.'

He shrugs. 'No. Well, you never trust women, of course.'

We drive to the station in silence.

CHAPTER 26

There's something on my patio, something that shouldn't be there. I'm in the kitchen, waiting for the kettle to boil when Sinead has left for school, looking out into the garden where the paeony buds are fattening, ready to flower, when I see it. At first, with a slight sense of surprise, of something being out of place, I think it is a forgotten thing, abandoned or flung down, an item of clothing or cuddly toy that one of the girls has left there. I go to the window, hear my quick inbreath. It's a fox, dead, in a pool of blackish blood, lying there quite precisely in the middle of my patio; and it enters my mind that there's a deliberateness to the placing of it, as though it has been put there, as though it has some profound and disturbing significance. I push the thought away.

I take the washing-up gloves and a rubbish sack and go out to the garden. There's a smell of rottenness, rich and meaty and foul. The fox is quite small—smaller than the foxes I usually see in the garden—just a cub really. There's a trail of blood that leads back round the side of the house: it was knocked over by a car perhaps and slunk round here to die, looking for a hidden dark place, but only reaching this far. Its face is contorted by its death throes, the mouth pulled back from the teeth, and its legs are stuck out stiffly as though it keeled over where it stood and died before it fell.

I put on the washing-up gloves, holding my breath as I approach so I won't breathe in the smell. Even with the gloves on I don't pick it up directly, I hold it through the plastic of the rubbish bag. The body is rigid as wood. When I've manoeuvred it into place, I tie up the bag and put it in the dustbin. You can still smell it, but faintly, and the dustmen come tomorrow. I get some Cif and scrub away the blood; it leaves a paler bleached mark there in the middle of the patio. I throw away the rubber gloves and the scrubbing brush and go inside and wash and wash my hands. It leaves me with a troubled feeling; as though it's a malevolent act, something that has been done to me.

There's a knock at the door. I wipe my hands and go to open it, expecting the postman; or Nicky, on her way back from school, perhaps; or even Monica from next door, to fix up that coffee we're always going to have.

It's Dr Carey. She's wearing a decorous little jacket with buttons bright as coins.

'I just thought I'd drop in on spec,' she says. 'I was visiting in Ferndale Road, and I thought I could fit in a quick visit and see how things were going.'

She's studiedly casual and friendly, as though this is the most natural thing, for her to call on me.

I stand aside to let her in. 'You'll be able to see Daisy, she didn't make it into school today.'

'Right,' she says.

I take her into the living room. It's fresh in the morning light that falls through the wide windows, and there are irises on the mantelpiece, in the Chinese vase.

She looks round appraisingly, eyes widening.

'It's a lovely house,' she says.

I can tell this room and its elegance have impressed her: as though my tasselled tie-backs and pelmets edged with plum-coloured braid have somehow strengthened my case. I despise her for this, but I'm also grateful for it.

'Well, we're lucky to live here,' I say.

Her eyes skim over everything, come to rest on my drawing on the wall, the one I've just put up: the children who peer between bars that are woven from a texture of spiky lines like briars.

'Who's the artist?' she says.

'I am,' I tell her. It's some unexamined impulse, to show there are things I can do, wanting to say, Look, I can draw, I have another life, there's a bit of an artist in me, I'm not just a demanding hostile overprotective mother.

'I wondered,' she said.

She has her head on one side, looking at the picture.

'It's very dark,' she says. Though whether she means the colour or the subject, I don't know.

'I paint all sorts of things,' I tell her. 'Gardens mostly. Flowers.'

'Really, it's quite sinister in a way,' she says. 'The children look so scared. What's the meaning of it, would you say?'

'The meaning?'

'You know—what do you think you were trying to say?'

'I don't really think about it like that.' I'm struggling to find the right words. 'I mean, I don't plan it. The picture just comes to me kind of complete, in my head.'

'Oh,' she says. 'I see.' She looks as though she wants to say more, as though she's trying to formulate a question that evades her. She shakes her head a little. 'To be honest,' she says, 'art isn't really my thing.'

She looks at the picture for a moment longer. I start to feel uncomfortable.

'Let me get Daisy for you.'

She turns to me. 'Let's not disturb her,' she says. 'If there isn't any change. Really, it was you I wanted to see. Just to find out how things were going… You went to see Dr Watson?'

I nod.

'And how did you get on?'

'Fine,' I say. 'She seemed pleasant.'

'She's very approachable, isn't she?'

'Yes,' I say.

'She's extremely well respected in child psychiatry circles,' she says. 'She has some inpatient beds at the Jennifer Norton Unit. That's a psychiatric unit for children—you might have heard of it?'

'No, I haven't,' I tell her.

'It's very well regarded,' she says. 'Dr Watson has done some notable work with anorexics there.'

'Right.'

'So, Mr. Lydgate came as well?' she says.

'Yes,' I tell her. 'Yes, he was happy to come.'

I sense that she wants to talk about our marriage, like when I first took Daisy to see her, but she doesn't know how to start or what to say. Here, on my own territory, the balance has shifted a little: I see how uncertain she is. It's different from the surgery, as though the normal rules of courtesy operate here.

'I don't think I've ever met Mr Lydgate,' she says.

'Well, he isn't often ill.'

She nods and waits. She wants me to say more. We sit for a moment in an awkward silence.

'Oh,' she says then. 'By the way. That letter from Dr McGuire.'

'The receptionist rang me,' I say.

'You managed to read it, did you?'

'Yes,' I say.

'We didn't ever find it,' she says. 'Never mind. We got another copy from Dr McGuire's secretary.'

She picks up her black bag and goes towards the door. There's a vague dissatisfaction about her, as though she hasn't got what she came for.

Outside, at the top of the steps, she turns towards me. I wonder if she can smell the stench of decay from the dustbin. Her face looks harder, older in the brightness of the light.

'It's crucial for you to be straight with me, Mrs Lydgate,' she says. Her eyes are narrowed against the sun and I can't read her expression. 'You see, I really can't help you and Daisy unless you're straight with me…'

She turns and goes before I can reply.

C H A P T E R 27

I see, driving there through the grey afternoon, how lavish all the borders are, after so much rain and sun, how even the tidiest gardens look overgrown.

I stand on his doorstep and ring the bell and the grey warm air wraps round me. There's a musky, intimate smell, where the hawthorn has been rained on. I'm suddenly afraid: there's part of me that hopes there'll be no answer. I'm turning round to go when he opens the door.

He's wearing one of those baggy shirts, and his hair is unruly, as though he's just run his hands through it. He looks at me; he doesn't smile. He doesn't seem surprised.

I suddenly feel I have no right to be here. 'I'm sorry—are you busy?'

'I'm writing a rather worthy piece on the politics of coffee.'

'I won't come in, then…'

'Of course you'll come in,' he says, standing aside to let me through. 'Trust me, I can handle this kind of interruption.'

I follow him through to the back room. On this clouded afternoon, it seems more ordinary and smaller than before.

I go to the window. Jamie and a friend of his are somer-saulting on the climbing frame. Everything's further on since last I came here. There's a ragged mist of thistle-down on the lawn, and in the borders under the prunus a tangle of docks and bluebells; the flowers are a soft faded blue, as though they've been soaked in water.

'It all needs cutting back,' he says. 'There are things in that lawn that really shouldn't be there.'

'I like it as it is.'

He smiles at me and pushes up his shirt-sleeves. I'm very aware of his skin, of the fine fair hairs on his arms.

'This is great timing,' he says, as though my presence here is the most natural thing. 'I was going to give you a ring—I've got that name for you.'

'The doctor?'

He nods. 'A gastro-enterologist who specialises in children. You'll have to get your GP to refer you.' He rifles through a heap of papers on top of the bookcase. 'Here.'

He's written the name on an envelope, someone from Great Ormond Street. I put it in my bag.

'I'm really grateful,' I tell him.

'It seemed the least I could do.'

'Thank you.'

'We'll have some wine,' he says.

I notice that he doesn't ask if I want it, as though we already have our rituals, the ways we usually do things. As though he knows what I want.

He goes to the kitchen, brings a bottle and glasses. As he hands me mine our fingers touch around the cool bowl of the glass.

There's a little silence. I don't know where we go from here. With relief I remember the picture.

'I brought a drawing, like you said.' I take it out of my bag. I glance at it for a moment, the child with the angular hands who's reaching out of the picture. I'm not sure now why I wanted him to see it; it seems raw, unfinished. I feel a kind of shame, that I could presume to imagine that anyone would like it. But it's too late to turn back now. 'This is the kind of thing I'm doing now. I guess they're rather weird.'

He takes it, smoothing out the creases at the corners. I watch his hands moving across my picture.

'It's very different to what you did before.'

Perhaps he doesn't like it, the way he liked the flower. I glance away from him, looking along the bookshelves, nervously reading off the titles of the books. I feel opened up, exposed. He holds my picture in front of him and looks at it. This seems to take an age.

'It's very powerful,' he says.

Powerful. No one ever called my drawing that before. In spite of everything, I feel a surge of pleasure.

He props it up on his mantelpiece. It's oddly intimate, to see my drawing there, surrounded by his things.

'Now we can see it properly,' he says.

He's right: it looks different there. I see it now as someone else might see it, see how acute the child's face is, how urgent and alive.

'Can I keep it?' he says.

I'm surprised. 'Yes. Yes, of course. I've done lots of them.'

'There's someone I know,' he says, 'who has a gallery. I'd like to show it to him.'

There's a brief astonishing thrill—like the glitter of a fish I once saw in a summer river, leaping right out of the water and into the sun. But then the old familiar doubts crowd in.

'But he wouldn't be interested, surely? I mean, I've never had any training—I just did a bit of drawing at school…'

He's looking at me, his head on one side, a little smile at my self-deprecation playing across his face. I bite back all the things I was going to say. I let myself smile too.

'I'd love you to,' I tell him.

'I'll give him your number, then—is that OK?'

'Of course. You take me so seriously.'

'Yes,' he says.

We sit for a while in silence. The children shout in the garden. Light from the window falls across his body: his strong pale arms, the curve of his hand round the glass.

'What's happening with the doctors?' he says then.

'We're seeing the psychiatrist.'

He frowns. 'You decided to go?'

'I couldn't see a way out.'

His face is serious now. He shakes his head.

'I hate it,' I tell him. 'I feel she's always judging me.'

'I'm sure she is,' he says.

'I feel so trapped. That for Daisy's sake we have to do as we're told. That if I protest, it'll only make things worse for her…' I see how his mouth turns down when I say this. I wish I had his certainty: that I weren't so afraid. 'Everything seems so simple to you,' I say, a little accusingly.

'That's probably true,' he says. 'I'm sorry.'

'Richard thinks she's good. He just won't listen to me.' I sense Fergal's eyes on my face, but I don't look at him. I'm talking on, thinking about Richard, talking to myself really.

'I thought I really knew him. I mean, I've always felt our marriage was so strong…' My voice is very low. 'A bit traditional, rather old-fashioned perhaps. But that it all worked fine.'

'Yes,' says Fergal quietly.

'I just don't get it—why he never listens.'

There's a kind of clarity here, in this still room, as though I can see further than before.

'Maybe…' My voice fades. 'Maybe I don't understand him as well as I thought I did. Maybe there are things I don't know about him…'

Fear moves across my mind like smoke from a hidden

fire, making new shapes that I don't want to look at. He senses this perhaps; for a while he doesn't say anything, just fills up my glass. He waits for me to say more. I shake my head a little. Outside the boys are quiet for a moment. Birdsong spirals down from the warm wide sky.

'Tell me how Daisy is,' says Fergal then.

'She's just the same.' I see her in my mind as she was when I left her, thin and still and unhappy. 'You know— sometimes I have these mad thoughts. That someone's cursed us—that someone's got it in for us. Such things aren't possible, are they?'

I think he may laugh at me. But he's quite serious, thinking about this. 'No. But I can see how you might think that.'

'I mean, I can really understand…like people a long time ago, when they had a miscarriage or their cow died, and they thought it was a curse. Crazy thinking, really.'

He's quiet for a moment, considering this.

'If someone was cursing you,' he says then, 'who might it be?'

And, when I hesitate, 'Catriona, I didn't mean to upset you—you really don't have to answer.'

But I've answered it already, here in the silence, smelling her nicotine and lily of the valley, hearing the jangle of her gilded bracelets.

He reaches out and touches me, his hand just brushing the bare skin of my arm.

'You look so sad,' he says. 'I shouldn't have asked.'

His touch confuses me.

I pick up my bag. 'I think I ought to go.'

'You don't have to,' he says.

'I'm keeping you from your work…'

'Believe me, I can cope with that,' he says.

I get up anyway.

He follows me to the hall. We're standing close together; the hall is narrow. His eyes are on my face, his gaze pulls at me. I'm looking anywhere but at him. If I look at him, I think, something will happen, something irrevocable.

'Catriona.'

I lift my eyes to his. He reaches out and takes my hand and raises it to his mouth. Very slowly, he kisses the palm of my hand. I hear myself gasp: the sensation shakes me; all the nerve-endings in my body are in the skin of my hand. His eyes are on me—his look has an absolute seriousness. And as he looks he kisses the tips of my fingers, pressing my fingers against and into his half-opened mouth. The quick thin heat runs through me. Just for a moment, I forget everything.

There's nothing to be said now. I go without saying goodbye.

In the car driving home past the blue disordered gardens, I feel the sensations of making love to him, his mouth pressed into mine, the thrill as he eases into me, as though this is something I remember. It has a vividness beyond what can be imagined, as though it has happened already.

Another postcard comes. It's a picture from before the Wall came down. The Wall is in the foreground. It's covered with graffiti—trolls and exuberant monsters and spotted cartoon snakes, in pinks and yellows. And there are lots of slogans in German that I don't understand, apart from 'Soldarität', and, in little white letters on the dark rim at the top, 'God loves you'. Behind the wall, there's a wide desolate space, a no-man's-land of mud and earth and tarmac, with very tall lamps like in a sports arena. In the distance, against the cloudy sky, there are tenements like grey boxes.

Under her phone number she's written an e-mail address, and ringed it in purple pen.

So how are you, my darling? Every time the phone goes, I think it might be you. Well, I'm sure one day it will be!

You'll see I've gone on e-mail now. Quite keeping up with the times. Do you have e-mail, darling? Well, I'm sure you do. I must say, I'm really quite a convert. It's the easiest thing in the world to send someone a line!

I chose the picture for your little girl. I hope she likes the animals! Thinking of you, as ever.

The picture would be perfect for Sinead's cities project, but I bury it at the bottom of the bin.

CHAPTER 29

There's a sudden massing of clouds as tall as towers; then, just as we get to the clinic, the rain begins, spattering on the gravel in the car park. I have an umbrella. Richard runs ahead and waits for me in the entrance. His hair is wet, sleeked down. He pushes it back from his forehead with his hand. Raindrops fall from it.

We wait in the bland waiting room, among the copies of *Hello*, and I watch Jane Watson's door, and feel the beat of my heart. Exactly on time, she opens her door and ushers us into her room. Today her hair is loose, just grazing her shoulders. She takes our coats and hangs them on her door, on top of a smart black trenchcoat that is presumably hers. We talk about the weather—is it climate change that is causing these heavy storms? As she moves her hair swings out, and her sandalwood smell brushes against me.

We sit down and she switches on her voice recorder.

'So—how are things?' she says.

I tell her how Daisy has been.

She nods and murmurs something sympathetic.

She talks to Richard, for a while, about Sinead and Sara. It sounds, she suggests, as though they've worked out an excellent modus vivendi; it's an achievement, not everybody can manage this. I sit quietly while they talk, feeling a sense of reprieve.

But then she turns towards me, her face serious, intent.

'I've been thinking about our session last week,' she says. She leans back in her chair, in that pose she likes, her elbows on the arms of the chair, her fingertips lightly touching. 'We talked about your mother's death, Catriona, and I realised I was left feeling quite unsure how that affected you…'

She leaves a little space, for me to fill.

'It's a while ago now,' I tell her.

'Of course,' she says. 'But the loss of your mother is always a huge event in anyone's life. Perhaps one way in would be for you to tell me what your mother was like when you were a child, how you remember her.'

I hesitate. It's such an obvious question, but I have nothing to say.

'I know this will be painful for you, Catriona.' Her voice is silkily empathic. 'That when we talk about somebody we've lost, in a sense we're reliving that loss.'

I try to shrug, as if this is nothing to me. My back is rigid, set.

'It's not that. It's just that there's nothing special to say.'

I realise I am sweating. I wonder if she can see the spike of my pulse in my wrist.

'What kind of a woman was your mother?' she says.

'She was…quite pretty.' I flail around. 'She was always very suntanned. She liked jewellery…'

There's silence for a moment; this isn't what she wants.

'D'you see anything of her in yourself? Are there ways in which you feel you're like her?' she says.

'No. Not at all,' I tell her. Too readily, too quickly.

She has a rather deliberate puzzled expression, an expression that's asking us to help her understand.

'Richard, perhaps I could ask you what you think,' she says. 'Whether you'd say there are ways in which Catriona reminds you of her mother?'

'Well, I've never met her,' he says.

The present tense panics me.

Her green eyes flick across our faces.

'Perhaps you have some memories of her that you could share?' she says to me.

Images of my mother crowd my mind. Putting on her make-up, all the glittery coloured sticks, putting on her bangles and gloves and going out for the evening and leaving me alone. Drunk, her speech slurred, weeping about her life and how it had all turned out, dark mascara streaking her face, eating mayonnaise from the jar with a spoon. Coming to The Poplars, bringing me the rabbit with the stitched-on heart. Just give me a bit of time. Karl and me have got to get ourselves sorted…

'She—always worked.'

Jane Watson nods encouragingly.

'What did she do?'

'She was a waitress.' I keep my voice quite level.

'Tell me some more,' she says. 'Just any memories. Anything that comes into your head.'

But nothing comes, nothing that's safe. I feel a flicker of panic. I dredge down into my mind, trying to find something, anything, that will satisfy her.

There's a sharp brittle sound as Richard clears his throat. He turns to me, and relief washes through me. Thank God, I think, he's going to rescue me.

He reaches out and puts his hand on mine.

'Darling, don't you think we should be a little more open?' he says.

I stare at him.

He turns towards Jane Watson and takes his hand away.

'The fact is, Jane, there are things we haven't told you,' he says. His tone is friendly, conversational. 'Catriona had a very difficult childhood, more difficult than we've said. Didn't you, darling?'

My heart thuds.

I glance at Jane Watson. She's sitting very still, as though there's some rare wild animal she's worried she'll frighten off. There are shiny spots of colour in her cheeks.

'Don't you think we should talk about that?' he says to me.

I hear the sudden blare and jingle of an ice-cream van from the road outside—an ordinary sound, as though nothing has changed, as though things are just as they were. Jane Watson nods very slightly.

'Isn't that for me to decide?' I say. But I know this isn't true, that now I don't have a choice.

Jane Watson leans forward. 'You seem very angry with Richard, Catriona,' she says. Her voice so tender, careful. 'Yet to me it seems that he's trying to help you here— trying to make things more open, more trusting, between us. And all my instincts tell me there's something here we need to open up.'

'It's my life,' I say, pointlessly. 'It's up to me what I say about it.'

'Of course,' she says. 'Of course, in the end it's your choice. But you do have a sick child, Catriona. We mustn't let ourselves lose sight of why we're here.' And, when I don't respond, 'Richard, perhaps you could help Catriona out here, just fill me in a little on what happened.'

'Catriona's mother couldn't care for her,' he says.

Jane nods almost imperceptibly. 'Yes,' she says, quietly, encouragingly.

'Catriona was put in a children's home when she was thirteen. I mean, surely we should talk about that, darling?' he says to me.

I look at him. He's smiling slightly, a smile that's an echo of hers, and his hair is flattened against his head by the rain. For a strange dizzying moment, he's someone I don't know.

'Catriona, I know this is very difficult for you,' says Jane Watson.

I can't speak.

'I just want to say how grateful I am to Richard,' she goes on. 'For opening all this up. You see, one thing that's puzzled me, Catriona, is why you're so opposed to the idea of looking at psychological reasons for Daisy's illness.'

She leaves a little pause. I hear the slow tick of the clock. I'm aware of Richard beside me nodding slightly.

'And I think I understand much better now,' she says. 'That maybe to do that would mean opening up deep sources of unhappiness for you—looking at things that are very hard to look at…'

Richard nods again.

'But sometimes that's just what we need to do,' she goes on. 'To open up those scars, to look at the painful things… Catriona, I'd like you to tell me a little about what happened?'

The damage is done now, everything ripped away.

'My mother was an alcoholic. When I was thirteen, she couldn't cope any more, and she put me in a home.'

'And where was that, Catriona?'

'It's called The Poplars.' My voice is dull, reluctant.

'Ah,' she says. 'The Poplars.' A flicker of recognition crosses her face. She read about it, perhaps, when the

Pindown inquiry was in the news. 'I'm wondering what that experience was like for you…' She's taking it all so slowly, peeling away the layers, like a child with a precious parcel she's delicately unwrapping. 'You must have felt very lost and lonely, and perhaps very angry with your mother who had virtually abandoned you…'

Rage flares in me. What right has she to tell me how I felt? What does she know about those things—the sour milk, the torn wallpaper; never having anything that is your own? Jane Watson's never run away with just some stolen Frosties in her rucksack, or hidden in the toilet on the train, or slept under the pier on Brighton beach. Jane Watson's never had anything to run from.

'It was all so long ago.' I keep my voice flat. 'The trouble is, people can make all sorts of assumptions. If they feel you've had that kind of childhood. I mean, I'm just a perfectly normal person now.'

She shakes her head a little.

'You've had some terrible things happen to you, things that must fill you with rage. I mean, I sense a lot of anger in you, Catriona,' she says. 'But it seems so important to you to say it doesn't matter, that it wasn't significant.'

'Perhaps that's how I cope.'

'Well, maybe it's one way. Or one way of *trying* to cope.'

'I just don't see why any of this is relevant. I don't see what it has to do with Daisy.'

'Thank you, Catriona,' she says. 'I'm so very grateful to you for keeping us on track. Because you're absolutely right, we need to see what all this means for

Daisy. And, you see, I think there *are* ways in which all this could relate to Daisy's illness. I think, when you've had the kind of terrible experience you've had—when you've been so unloved—then there's a very needy child inside you. And if there *is* that part of you that still feels uncared-for—however loving your relationships in adult life,' she says, with a quick, warm glance in Richard's direction, 'then the caring that doctors provide can seem very special. It gets to be, even, something you might seek out—because it satisfies that needy child inside.'

I think of Daisy: the hours of retching, the pains that lock her limbs. There's a white glare of rage in my head: I'm dazzled, I can't see.

'I went to the doctor because my daughter was ill.'

The rage is in my voice. Both of them lean forward. There's the same look of concern in both their faces.

Richard puts his hand on my arm.

'Catriona, Jane is only trying to help,' he says. 'To help all of us—you and me and Daisy.'

Jane nods, leaves one of her delicate pauses.

'Well, maybe we've come to the end of what we can usefully do today,' she says. 'You've both worked very hard. Thank you so much.'

I pick up my handbag. She's watching me.

'You look so tired, Catriona,' she says.

I nod, but I don't want her sympathy.

'I know you will have found this a difficult session,' she says.

'It's nothing to do with that.' I try to control the anger that still surges through me. 'I'm tired all the time. Having a sick child is tiring.'

'Of course,' she says. 'I understand.'

She gets up, brings us our coats.

'The trouble is, she's such a perfectionist, aren't you, Cat?' says Richard, helping me into my coat.

I shrug. 'Maybe.'

'Well, I can see that,' says Jane. She's smiling, casual, as though this is just a bit of small talk, a normal conversation.

'She's ever so hard on herself really,' he says. 'Everything has to be just right. You do try to do everything yourself, don't you?'

'You need to learn to delegate,' says Jane.

'Exactly. But she won't,' says Richard. 'I did talk—a while back—about getting someone to live in—just to help out through this bit, while Daisy's ill. I mean, I rang the au pair co-ordinator—I was prepared to organise it. She didn't want it, did you, darling? Didn't want to have anyone else in the house with you.'

'I didn't feel I needed it.' I wish he hadn't raised this.

'That seems like quite an inviting prospect, surely,' says Jane Watson, 'an au pair to help out.'

'It's just not necessary. My neighbour's always happy to babysit. We manage fine,' I tell her.

Her leaf-green eyes rest on me for just a little too long.

'Well, thanks so much for coming in,' she says again. 'I'd like to see you both once more, if you're happy with that. I'm planning for that to be our last session together.'

'Sure,' says Richard.

As we go out he holds the door for me—this man I thought I knew and loved, who has become a stranger.

I get into the driving seat but I don't put on my seat belt. He doesn't look at me.

'Why the fuck did you tell her about me?'

'Just calm down,' he says.

It's raining still. I hear the hissing sound the rain makes on the gravel.

'I can't believe you did that,' I say. 'Just can't believe it.'

'For God's sake,' he says. 'Can't this at least wait till tonight?'

'No,' I say. 'It bloody can't.'

He turns to me.

'She needed to know, Catriona,' he says. His voice is level, reasonable. But his face so close to me seems too big, gross even, and there's contempt in the downward curve of his mouth.

'Why the hell do you think you can trust her? She's not on our side, Richard.'

'It's not a question of sides,' he says. 'You get so paranoid.'

'I hate it when you say that.'

'Catriona, these people think they can help,' he says. 'I mean, these are the top medics—Jane Watson is a consultant. They know what they're doing.'

'Just because she's some bloody consultant doesn't mean she's right.'

'She's very sharp,' he says. 'She knows her stuff.'

'I don't trust her,' I say. 'I think she's just looking for evidence.'

'Look,' he says, 'I know you don't like her. We've been into all that. OK, I do think she's attractive. For God's sake, men are like that. It doesn't mean a thing.'

'It isn't that,' I say. 'She's slippery as hell, Richard. I mean, why can't you see that? That's what these people are like. Why on earth should I trust her? I've known too many people who claim to be there to help you who do such terrible things.'

He has a particular expression—a little disdainful, saying that life is simple and obvious and I just don't get it. 'That's not most people's experience, Catriona. Do we really need to spell this out? I mean, let's face it, your childhood was a little exceptional. Like Jane said, it's bound to leave its mark.'

Rage seizes me by the throat. 'You bastard.'

We stare at one another. I see the shock in his eyes. Our faces are too close for so much anger. The air in the car feels frail, hot, glimmery—as though something is burning.

Over his shoulder I see Jane Watson go past, just a few yards away across the car park. She's wearing a black rainhat, and the chic trenchcoat from her consulting-room door, and she's walking easily through the storm in her elegant snakeskin boots, as though she is inviolate. I hear the hissing and spitting of the rain.

I start up the car. I drive off too fast for safety, not looking at him.

CHAPTER **30**

I peel the apples and cut them into crescents. They're Russets, smelling of orchards, of golden bee-rich afternoons. My fingers are wet with juice.

Daisy puts down her pencil and watches.

'I used to like tarte tatin,' she says. 'Didn't I, Mum?'

'You did.'

I cut a tiny crescent of apple and put it on a plate in front of her. She doesn't touch it. I see that on the first page of her new notebook she's drawn a cat with a top hat and a walking stick. Since she's been ill, her drawing seems somehow static, the same pictures over and over, all these cartoon animals.

'I love the cat,' I tell her.

'Megan likes my cats, but Abi doesn't,' says Daisy. 'Abi says they're stupid.'

'Can Abi draw cats?'

'Not really,' says Daisy.

'Well, then. Maybe she's jealous.'

Daisy considers this, trailing a finger through the pale siftings of flour on the table, where I've rolled out the pastry.

'Abi's got this crazy scheme,' she says. 'She's practising hopping in case she twists her ankle.'

I smile in spite of myself, in spite of what happened this morning. The last piece of apple skin peels off in a perfect spiral, shiny as metal.

Just for a moment, I'm almost content, pushing the fear away from me. Here in my apple-scented kitchen, with my knife and my rolling pin, I have magicked up a temporary safety, like Nicky with her ribbons and pentangles, weaving a spell of protection; as though only these things are real, the warmth and the smells of cooking and the blue-glazed vase of lilacs on the table and Daisy beside me drawing cartoon cats.

'*And* she has silly sandwiches,' says Daisy. 'She has lettuce and ham and Philadelphia and jam, and a bit of mayonnaise, in little patches. Gross, or what?'

It's exactly Sinead's intonation.

'Gross, definitely.'

'It makes me feel sick,' says Daisy. 'Lunchtimes at school make me feel sick.'

'Daisy, is there ever a time when you don't feel sick?'

She shakes her head.

'I even feel sick in my dreams.'

There's a hot smell from the oven and the windows are steaming up. I open the window. The sky is a livid purple and the air is hollow and echoey with birdsong. Soon it will rain again.

Daisy stands beside me as I stir the sugar. It sparkles, melts to a translucent syrup, darkens to yellow-gold. A rich scent of caramel wraps itself around us.

'Were you allowed caramel when you were little?' says Daisy. 'Or wasn't it invented then?'

'It was invented, I didn't have many sweets though.'

'Your mother wasn't very nice to you.'

'No, she wasn't really.'

I've told the girls a little about it—how when I was thirteen she didn't want me to live with her any more. Once I heard Daisy say to Megan, I only have one granny, and Megan saying, Everyone has two grannies, and Daisy saying, They don't, they don't *all* have two…

Now, she says, 'She should have been nicer, Mum. I'm going to be very nice to *my* children.'

We watch as the sugar deepens to a lavish acorn-brown.

'Why do things change when you heat them?' says Daisy.

'I don't know, sweetheart. Isn't that awful? There are so many things I don't know. I should have listened better at school. D'you want to put in the butter?'

'OK.'

It sputters noisily, frothing, as she stirs it in.

I pour the caramel sauce on the apples and cut out a circle of pastry and tuck it down round the apples and put the pan in the oven, the heat brushing my skin. When it's cooked and I turn it out, tenderly, meticulously, the apples will be golden-pink and glossy.

There's a whispering outside the window, the first raindrops falling. Thunder growls in the distance.

'We might see lightning,' I say.

'I know all about that. It's electricity,' says Daisy. 'We did electricity at school. You have to use a light bulb and lots of wires. I liked electricity.'

'Maybe you should be a scientist when you grow up.'

'I want to be a vet,' she says. 'Or have a pet shop.'

It's such a heavy storm it demands attention; there's a thrill to it. We stand at the window and watch.

'Sinead will be *drowned*,' says Daisy.

I look at my watch; she really should be home by now. We try to remember whether she took her raincoat.

The rain turns to hail, big hailstones that bounce exuberantly on the patio and knock all the thistledown off the dandelions in the lawn and rip the blossom off the pear tree so there's a white sleet of petals. Behind us hailstones rattle down the chimney and burst out onto the hearth; they have an oily coating of soot; they leave black smears where they fall. I go to get newspaper to protect the floor, but in the time it takes to spread it the storm has eased, just gentle rain falling onto the wreck of the garden, the leaves of the birches lush, wet, holding their darkness to them, the lawn covered in drifts of snowy petals and the bedraggled skirts of the dandelions.

Daisy goes upstairs to play on her PlayStation. I wash up, tidy the kitchen. Still Sinead doesn't come. I ring her mobile, but I get put through to voicemail. I tell myself she's with friends or she's gone shopping, but the usual visions are there in my head—accidents, abductions—as though there's a film reel that switches on automatically if she's twenty minutes late. Since Daisy's been ill, everything feels so fragile.

At the sound of the front door opening, I feel such relief I could cry. I go to the hall. She's soaked, her hair is sleek and glossy as seaweed, as though she's been hauled from the sea. The washed cool air comes in with her.

'Sinead. Thank goodness.'

I put my arms lightly round her. Her hair smells like a sweet canned drink, from the styling foam she uses.

'What happened?' I ask her.

She shrugs.

'I went to McDonald's with Kerry,' she says.

'Why didn't you ring?'

'I thought you wouldn't notice.'

'I've been really worried.'

She peels off her soaked denim jacket and lets it fall to the floor. I don't say anything. She goes through into the living room, collapses on the sofa in front of the television, arms and legs flung out. I see how long her legs are, how her shirt looks suddenly too small. She's grown, she's almost a woman, and I hadn't realized; I was looking the other way.

I want to do something for her.

'D'you want something to eat?'

She shakes her head without looking at me.

'There's tarte tatin. It's nearly ready.'

'I went to McDonald's,' she says. 'I just told you.'

She flicks through the channels, finds some quiz show. Her skirt below where her jacket came is wet; it clings to her legs.

'Sinead, you ought to change. You're soaked, you'll get a cold. I'll run you a bath.'

She doesn't move. Drips run down her parting.

'I didn't get it,' she says. 'Thanks for asking.'

For a moment, I don't understand.

'The part. I didn't get it,' she says again.

'Oh, sweetheart, I'm so sorry. *The Tempest*. I forgot.'

'You do that,' she says.

'I'm sorry. We've had a horrible day. I've been worried about Daisy.'

She pulls a face. 'Yeah, well. So what's new?'

She turns back to the television.

The tarte tatin tastes good but I can't eat it. My throat is clogged up with the things I need to say.

'Richard—I've been thinking. About what happened with Jane Watson.'

He looks at me warily.

'Daisy is all that matters,' I tell him. 'Somehow we have to get focused on Daisy again.'

'I thought that was exactly what I was trying to do.'

His voice is a little too loud. I go to close the door. Sinead is watching TV in her room and Daisy should be sleeping, but I want to be sure they can't hear.

His eyes are on me.

'Listen,' I tell him. 'This is where we go from here. We'll ask to see another doctor. I think we have the right to that. Everyone has the right to a second opinion. I've got a name—a doctor at Great Ormond Street. And we have to get a lawyer.'

He looks intently at me. I can see the red flecks in his eyes.

'Who have you been talking to?' he says.

I flush. 'I haven't been talking to anyone.' I can't quite look at him.

'Well, this idea of yours, wherever it comes from—it simply doesn't make sense,' he says. 'Getting a lawyer is exactly the wrong way to go about this. I thought we'd already agreed that. It's so confrontational.'

'You don't understand. Today changes everything. What you did.'

'Look,' he says. 'I know what you think about what I did. Would it be too much to ask for you to just stop going on about it?'

'They'll think I'm guilty, after what you said. People make assumptions about the kind of person you are.'

'Not necessarily,' he says. His voice is hard and dry. 'That depends on the person.'

'They'll think I'm disturbed. They'll think all this proves them right. Don't you see? They'll think I'm some terribly damaged person who's damaging her child.'

He says nothing.

'Richard. Sometimes I feel…' My voice is small, shaky. 'Sometimes I feel that even you don't trust me.'

It's suddenly so quiet. From outside I hear the drip of water falling from the gutter onto the lid of a dustbin. It's far too loud in the sudden silence, as though it's here in the room.

Then he shakes his head.

'How could you possibly think that? Of course I trust you,' he says. 'All that stuff's nonsense, of course. The Münchausen thing. Somebody's hare-brained scheme, some student with a theory. But this idea that maybe there are psychological elements to what's happening— that's a quite different proposition. And I do think maybe there's something in that. As you know.'

'You just don't get it, do you?'

'What don't I get?'

I take a deep breath. 'That we could lose Daisy.'

'Oh, come *on*,' he says. 'That's just crazy talk.'

'Richard, they could take her into Care. They do that. It happens.' A door bangs upstairs; there are footsteps. I know I should stop but I can't. 'I don't understand why you won't see—'

'What I see,' he says, 'is that people try to help you

and you just won't let them.' His voice is sharp with exasperation. 'You just create issue after issue… Like Jane says, you're always so angry, you've got a lot of anger in you—'

'I don't give a fuck what Jane says.'

'She's the expert, Catriona.'

'She doesn't know the first thing about me.'

He says nothing. He shrugs a little. I wish he would get angry, shout at me. Anything but this cold withdrawal, the raising of his eyebrows, the hardening of his eyes.

'Just because you fancy her.' I'm almost shouting now. I know this is pointless, juvenile, but I can't stop. 'Is that why you did what you did—because you wanted to please her?'

'For God's sake,' he says.

'Well, it's true, isn't it?'

'What's that got to do with anything?' he says. 'I know exactly why you don't like her.'

'Which is?'

'Because she's right.'

'She's *right*?'

He gets up, moves to the window. There's an uneasy yellow glare of light in the garden: the storm will start again soon. He has his back to me now; he's looking out at the garden and blotting out the light.

'Well, you *are* damaged, of course,' he says. 'By what happened.' His voice is quite matter-of-fact—as if he's commenting on my clothes. 'I mean, I've always known that. I've made allowances.'

Anger tightens my throat.

'Richard, how can we possibly carry on if you say these things, if that's how you see me?'

And immediately I wish I hadn't said that, as though just saying these words makes something seem real, possible; perhaps I have opened a door that cannot again be shut.

He turns and looks at me with narrowed eyes.

'Well, if that's how you feel,' he says.

The door swings back: it's Daisy, in her frog pyjamas. Her hair is curled against her head where she's been lying, and her eyes are huge and shadowed, dilated with the dark.

'It's so noisy,' she says. She looks at us sternly. 'I can't possibly get to sleep with all that noise.'

I go to put my arms around her.

'Come back to bed,' I tell her. 'I'll come and sit with you while you go to sleep.'

I take her upstairs.

'My chest hurts,' she says as she gets into bed. She spits stomach acid into a tissue. I prop her up with three pillows behind her. She turns away from me and I stroke her back, pushing aside the soft mass of her hair, so my fingers don't snag in it. I keep doing this for what seems like a very long time.

It's raining again, lashing against the glass the other side of the blind. I can hear a little torrent gushing down the wall of the house, where the gutter is blocked, perhaps, splashing onto the rubbish sacks in the alley. In this drenching rain our house feels less substantial. I worry that the rain will get in, will find some hole or crack, some space between the tiles. The roof needs mending, we know that, the building society said as much when we moved here, but it costs a lot and we've kept on putting it off. I see how wrong we were, how terribly misguided: we should have had it mended while there was time. I see it in my mind, the place where the rain gets in, in the darkness of the roof space, at first just a drip, then a tiny stream of water, steadily encroaching, easing its way between joist and plank, making its smells, its stains. It's happening now, it's happening at this moment, rotting timber, softening plaster, damp fingers reaching out and down and silently weakening what once was solid and strong. How could any house withstand such force of rain?

Daisy's shoulders sink, the shape of her body under the duvet softens, eases down, her breathing deepens. I'm so impatient to go back to Richard, to make everything all right; but I force myself to wait a while, till she's securely asleep, then I slip off my shoes and creep out of her room.

As I close her door, very quietly, I see Richard on the stairs that lead up to the attic. Under his arm he has the airbed that the girls use on holiday. It has a pattern of palm trees, Sinead chose it in a shop on the beach at Tirenia; the last time we used it was in a Tuscan swimming pool. The footpump is in his hand.

I stare at him. 'What are you doing?'

'Isn't it obvious what I'm doing?' His cold, still voice.

I remember what happened with Sara, what he told me

at dinner at Mon Plaisir, when we were falling in love—how he moved out of their bed and they never had sex again. Panic seizes me.

'You can't sleep up there. Richard. *Please.*' My voice is shrill, the words all tumbling out. 'We've got to sort this out—we won't get anywhere if we just go on quarrelling. That doesn't solve anything.'

'I wasn't the one who started this,' he says.

'We've got to talk. We've got to understand one another.'

He shrugs. 'Wouldn't you say it's a little bit late for that?'

There's the click of a latch behind me. I turn, bite back the things I was going to say. Sinead is at her door. She looks from one to the other of us. She looks smaller, younger, in her dressing gown; she's trying to look hard and cold, but there's a child's fear in her face. I want to tell her, Don't worry, it'll all be OK, it's just a bad patch, sweetheart, we'll sort this out… But my mouth won't move.

We all stand there silently for a moment. Then she goes back into her room and bangs her door behind her.

CHAPTER 31

All that week we treat each other with formal, unsmiling politeness. But at night I always wake at three, sensing at once from the heaviness in my body and the furred thickness of the dark that it is still very early, and I lie there for hours, alone in the wide empty bed, hearing the birds start to sing, first some rook or jackdaw, then the growing and mingling of all their metallic songs, and the hourly chime of St Agatha's.

On Thursday evening I'm meeting Nicky at the Café Rouge. It's a still hot evening; it's hard to breathe, as though the air is all worn out or used up. I'm early and she isn't there. I sit in the window, looking out onto the pavement. People's shadows fall in front of them as they pass; I try to guess what people are like from their shadows.

Eventually, she comes—so sorry to be late, yet she has a vacant, distracted look, as though part of her is somewhere else entirely. I ask about Simon, but knowing what she'll say, because the shine has gone from her. It's only little things, she says. He's kind of evasive, saying how busy he is; and, at this after-work party, he spent a long time talking to this woman who had rather tarty shoes and a very appealing cleavage. But then, why shouldn't he? Perhaps she's being paranoid…

I nod, sipping my wine. I notice how her hair needs washing, how everything about her seems to droop. As if she trails a kind of sadness around like a scent of dying flowers.

'He's a strange guy really,' she says. 'You know that thing that happens—that the better you get to know a person, the weirder they start to seem?'

'I know what you mean,' I tell her.

There's jazz over the sound system, Ella Fitzgerald, that voice like a skein of silk. We listen for a moment.

'And you, Cat?' she says. 'How's it going?'

I shrug; I don't say anything.

'Hey.' She leans towards me across the table, as if she's only just seen me properly. 'Something's happened, hasn't it? Daisy? Richard?'

'Richard,' I tell her, but a little reluctantly.

'Oh, Cat. Want to talk about it?'

'I don't know.' It's as though to talk about it would be to make it real, something you couldn't turn back from. 'Sorry.'

She looks at me warily. 'It's probably just a bad patch,' she says. 'Everyone has bad patches. It must be so tough with Daisy ill and everything.'

She waits for a moment, watching me, to see if I want to say more. I shake my head a little.

'Cat, any time you want to talk… Well, you know that.'

'Thanks,' I say.

She fills my glass to the brim. By the way, she says, she'd been meaning to tell me—someone at Praxis knows this totally brilliant homeopath. Would I like his number? I take it down, but only because it would seem impolite to refuse.

We eat toasted chicken sandwiches, and listen to Ella Fitzgerald singing 'Into Each Life Some Rain Must Fall,' but somehow it's hard to keep the conversation going, and at ten she says she's sorry but she feels so terribly tired and she really ought to get home.

The lights are off in the house, Richard must be in bed already. I think that maybe tonight I'll stay up for a while, try lying down really late to see if that helps me sleep through. I'll sit downstairs and watch *Newsnight* and some predictable thriller, and only go to bed when I'm almost falling asleep.

But when I go into the kitchen to get a drink of water, a hot smell of whisky hits me. I turn on the light.

He's slumped at the table. In front of him there is a nearly empty bottle of Glenfiddich.

'Richard. What the hell are you doing?'

He looks up slowly, as though his head is heavy.

'Would you mind terribly turning off the light?' he says. His speech is careful, slurred.

For a moment I don't do anything.

'Turn the fucking light off.'

I do as he says, but I switch on the light in the cooker hood.

'Richard, for God's sake. What's happened? Are the girls OK? Is Daisy asleep?'

He looks at me with his eyes half open; in the thin light, his eyelids look swollen as though he's suffered some injury.

'It's always,' he says carefully, 'the girls. The bloody girls. What about me? Do I count any more? Do I? Or is it just the bloody girls?'

I sit at the table beside him.

'Of course.' I put my hand on his. 'Of course you count. It's just that it's all such a strain, with Daisy ill and everything…'

He ignores me.

'There's something I want to know. Do I have a place in your fucking universe, Catriona? Do I mean anything?'

'You know you do. Don't be an idiot.' It's the way I might speak to a child—light, encouraging. 'You know that. Don't be silly.'

'Do I count at all?' he says again. The words are difficult, amorphous things he struggles to master. 'Some-times I wonder. Whether I count at all.'

'Richard, you've drunk too much. Come to bed now.'

He shakes his head, too many times.

'I don't know that I do,' he says. 'I don't know that I do count.'

'Richard—you're only saying these things because you're drunk…' I touch his hand to soften what I'm saying.

He slowly lifts his head; he's looking at me, the gleam of the cooker-hood light reflecting in his eyes. 'Some-times…' he says. 'Sometimes I wonder what happened to that girl. The girl I saw in the garden under the…the… You know, that tree thing,' he says.

'You mean the catalpa tree?'

He nods, but his face is dreamy, unfocused. 'The girl under the tree. The girl with the sun in her hair. Whatever happened to her?'

'Richard, you need to sleep.'

He pours more whisky: some of it misses the glass. I just let this happen.

'I liked you like that,' he says. 'That beautiful girl. I want to know what fucking happened. Where she fucking went…' His voice fades.

'Everyone changes,' I tell him, reaching for soothing platitudes to calm him. 'That's life. People change, move on. Of course I'm different than when I was twenty-three.'

But he's in his own world, seeing his own vision. I have no sense that he hears a word I say.

He drinks more whisky. I wonder how on earth I am going to get him to bed. Perhaps I could just leave him here, in the hope that he will sober up and go upstairs eventually. But I don't want the girls to see him like this.

He puts down the glass, with too much noise, and reaches his hand to my face.

'You know, you're beautiful,' he says. 'You're very beautiful.' He's looking at me as though he's only just really seen me. He runs his hand down the hair at the side of my face with a kind of residual tenderness. 'Still beautiful. But you're not like you used to be. You're not that girl any more…' He leans towards me as though he is sharing a secret, something dark and private. His eyes are clouded, troubled. 'I shouldn't be telling you this, Catriona, you must realise that. But sometimes I don't bloody know what I want…' There's a weird incongruence between the banality of this and the intimate intensity of the way he says it. 'Sometimes I just don't fucking know what I want.'

'Never mind,' I say.

'That girl,' he says. 'The girl with the sun in her hair.' Separating out the syllables, as though he's speaking a language he's only just learnt. 'I want to know what fucking happened.'

There's a sound in his voice like a sob. Someone different looks out of his eyes, someone with such a sense of deprivation. I hate this—hate the easy tears that alcohol induces. He makes me think of my mother.

'Richard, people change. That's how it is. Just come to bed now.'

There's impatience in my voice, perhaps; at last he seems to hear me.

'Bed,' he says. 'That is a very good idea. What good ideas you have, Catriona.'

He reaches out and starts to unbutton my shirt with one hand, pushing his hand straight inside my bra, clutching blindly at me like a boy.

I take his hand between both of mine.

'Let's go upstairs,' I tell him.

He follows me, stumbling a little on the steps, grabbing at the bannister. I close the bedroom door behind us with a quick rush of relief.

He comes across to me as I'm pulling the curtains, and starts to take off my clothes. He's impatient, there's heat in his eyes, his fingers are clumsy, eager. Undressing one another in the middle of the room feels daring, strange. Not like the way we usually make love, in bed under the duvet, by the forgiving light of the bedside lamp. More like when we were first together, when it was all shot through with a sense of danger, when he used to dominate me, and want to deck me out in bangles and silver chains. Maybe he feels this too; he's holding my wrists together behind my back. I feel a flicker of the old excitement.

'I'd like to…' he starts to say. 'Cat, what I'd really like…'

And then he seems to give up, to slump. He collapses onto the bed, pulls me beside him. He still has his shirt on. He rolls on top of me, slides straight into me—he's very heavy; he presses down on me; his muscles are too relaxed. The whisky on his breath is all over my face.

He thrusts a few times.

'Fuck,' he says.

I feel his erection soften.

'You've just drunk too much,' I tell him. 'Let's go to sleep now.'

He rolls off me. He lies with his back to me and is instantly asleep.

I pull the duvet up over him and go to check on Daisy.

Next morning, he is full of apologies. He's binned the rest of the whisky, he promises he'll never have it in the house again. He's afraid he was thoroughly pathetic, and he hopes I'll just forget it. I tell him, Never mind, you just got a bit emotional—I mean, we're both so stressed, with everything that's happening… He uses a lot of mouthwash before he goes to work.

When I go up to the attic, I find that he has put the airbed away and the sheets he used are in the laundry basket. I feel a profound relief, thinking that maybe things will be all right now, that his drunkenness has in some obscure way healed the rift between us.

CHAPTER 32

She's wearing a trouser suit. She looks harder, older, today—definite, as though there is a black line drawn all round her. Next to her I am messy and unsure.

She leans back in her chair. She has a folder on her knee.

'Thank you both for coming in,' she says.

It's our last session, I tell myself. I only have to get through an hour.

'Now, since I saw you last, I've been discussing Daisy's case with Dr McGuire, and I want to share our conclusions with you,' she says. I notice that she doesn't turn on her voice recorder. 'I'm going to, as it were, set out my stall—then you can come back to me.'

Richard nods.

I wonder why she feels the need of this elaborate preamble.

Her green eyes move across our faces.

'We believe,' she says, 'and, as I say, we've talked this through together as a team…we believe that some time out from the family would be useful for Daisy…' I open my mouth; she silences me with her hand. 'That that would enable us to comprehend more fully just what is happening here.'

'I don't understand,' I tell her.

'What we're talking about here is a spell for Daisy as an inpatient, for assessment,' she says.

I feel a warm surge of relief, that Daisy's illness at last will be properly investigated.

'OK. Well, good. I think she needs that.' My mind is racing ahead, making lists and plans. Sinead can go to Sara's; Daisy will need new pyjamas, she wouldn't want to appear in public in her animal ones; and we'll both have to get slippers, they insist on slippers in hospital, I remember that from when Daisy was born; and we'll need some drawing paper and all her fairy-tale books… 'And I could stay with her, couldn't I? They let you stay with your child now, don't they?'

'That's true on a medical paediatric ward,' she says. 'But, you see, that isn't quite what we're talking about here.'

'I don't understand.'

'As you know,' says Jane Watson, her voice as sleek as silk, 'we do have concerns about Daisy and just what is going on and why she isn't responding to treatment. So it would be more a case of following up on the psychological side of things, and seeing just what happened to Daisy's illness when she's away from the family.'

For a moment I can't process this—it doesn't seem to make sense. But Richard is murmuring agreement beside me.

'Now, as you may know,' she says, 'I have some beds at an inpatient unit for children and young people. The Jennifer Norton Unit. It's quite an easy journey from where you are. And that's where I'd like to admit her.'

I recognise the name. For a moment I can't remember where I heard it, then I think of Dr Carey's uninvited visit. But I can't recall what she said, remember just the smell of fox and my feeling of unease.

'But surely that's psychiatric.'

She gives me a little frown. 'It's a unit where we have the space and time to look at psychological problems,' she says smoothly. 'It's time out from the family, time out from some of the pressures in these young people's lives.'

Fear is rising in me. 'And I could stay with her?'

'I'm afraid we don't have the facilities for that,' she says. 'And in a way it would defeat the purpose of the assessment. Which, as I say, is about time out from the young person's normal environment. But you'd of course be able to visit weekly.'

'*Weekly?* She's only eight, for Chrissake.'

Richard puts his hand on my wrist. I move my arm away.

'And how long would this be for, exactly?' I say.

'Obviously there's a settling-in process,' she says smoothly. She's looking at Richard, enlisting his support. 'We need to get to know her, and she needs to get to know us.'

Richard nods. 'Of course,' he says. His voice bland and reasonable, keeping everything calm.

'And we would certainly need some weeks to do a full assessment.'

'Weeks? But she's ill,' I say. 'What would happen about her illness—who would look after her?'

She smiles at me, that shiny practised smile that doesn't reach her eyes.

'I really don't think you need to worry,' she says. 'As I say, we've got a very good staff ratio. And you don't need to worry about her school work either. At the Jennifer Norton we're fortunate to have two full-time teachers and an occupational therapy department—you can rest assured she won't get behind. So, any more questions about what I've said so far?'

But Richard is shaking his head, and I cannot speak.

'Let me tell you a little more about the unit.' She's moving forward carefully, as though examining every word she says. 'We do have quite a mixture of children. We have some girls with anorexia, for instance. Obviously these are all children with troubles of one sort or another, and where it's been decided that for whatever

reason a period away from their families would be bene-
ficial. But, as I say, the staff ratio is excellent—virtually
one to one.'

'But this is ridiculous—Daisy doesn't have psychiatric problems.'

'Maybe not as such,' says Jane Watson. 'But if there
are, as we think, issues in the family that need to be ad-
dressed, this will help us to get a handle on that.'

She waits for my response.

'And if we refuse?' I say.

Richard leans towards me.

'Cat, we need to talk all this through properly,' he says.
The turn of phrase is hers. I feel a brief wild rage with
him, that he's taking on her language.

'I want Jane to answer my question. What if we say no?'

'Well,' she says, 'I'm very much hoping that that won't
happen. I'm very much hoping that you'll recognise the
necessity for this.' She smiles briefly at Richard. 'You've
been so very co-operative so far, in coming to sessions
and working with me here…'

'But if we don't want this, if we don't let her go?' I say
again.

Richard lets out a small exasperated sigh.

Jane Watson clears her throat.

'We do feel this is very important.' Her voice is hard,
clear. Now there's none of that tentativeness that invites
you to confide. 'It's Daisy's future and health we're
talking about here. And—just in the hypothetical situation that you did have objections—to be frank, we would

need at that point to take some legal powers, because we do feel that it's crucially important to have Daisy thoroughly assessed.'

I realise I am shaking. I clasp my hands tight together so she won't be able to see. I feel the walls press in.

'You mean a Care Order?'

'It's something we could do.' She turns to me—she's talking just to me now. 'And I have to say—I mean, I don't want to dwell on this—but if it came to that, we would have good grounds for a Care Order in Daisy's case, if that's the only way for the assessment to be done. Though to have to go through the courts would greatly increase the stress on Daisy, as I'm sure you recognise.'

Richard glances at me and away again. 'Jane, I really don't think you need worry. Like I said, we'll talk it through at home.'

Her face softens. She nods. 'Well, obviously it's far far better for all concerned if we're agreed on how to move forward… Now, you will I'm sure want to look round the unit before Daisy is admitted—just to put your minds at rest. You'll find it's a very friendly place and the dormitories are quite small and really very cheerful. In the meantime, I'll reserve her a bed.'

'When would you want her to start?' says Richard.

'I'll have to check out the bed situation,' she says. 'But I think I do have a place coming up, probably at the end of the week—normally we'd have to wait for very much longer.' She's brisk now, leaving no space for disagreement. 'As I'm sure you'll appreciate there's tremendous demand for beds in the Jennifer Norton. Right, then.' She snaps the folder shut. 'I'll try and get the letter confirming everything in the post as soon as possible. I'm confident we can all agree on this.'

She stands. We get up too.

'Look, I'll find you our leaflet. And you can look at the map and reassure yourselves that it's very easy to get to…'

She rifles around in an in-tray on her desk. Her hair falls over her face.

'Here we are,' she says.

It's like the publicity for a holiday play-scheme, with lots of paintbox colours and photos of smiling children.

She brings it over, stands close to us, next to Richard. I smell her sandalwood scent. She turns to the map on the back, points to the place with one discreetly manicured fingernail. I just catch sight of the road name for a moment, then she tips the leaflet slightly away from me. I tell myself I must have read it wrong.

'There's been a unit on the site for quite some years,' she says. 'It's named after a psychiatrist who was superintendent there for a while. She lectured on our course when I was a student—a rather wonderful woman. She died suddenly in her forties.' Her face is briefly poignant. 'A stroke, so terribly sad—and they renamed the unit in her memory.' She hands the leaflet to Richard. 'Before the name was changed they called it Avalon Close,' she says.

She's showing Richard the easiest places to park, but her voice is thin, remote from me, as though she's speaking from very far away.

In the car on the way to the station I can scarcely speak. But Richard seems perfectly at ease. He takes out his diary, starts flicking through.

'What are you doing?'

'I guess we should fix up a time to go and look at this place,' he says.

'Richard, I'm not going to let her go there.'

A motorbike pulls out sharply in front of me. I only just see it in time. I swerve violently.

'For Chrissake,' he says. 'Calm down, or you'll get us both killed.'

'Daisy is *not* going there.'

He sighs. 'I wish you'd stop acting like this is some major tragedy,' he says.

'Richard, she's only eight.'

'Oh, come on,' he says. 'Loads of kids go to boarding school at eight. I did.'

'You hated it.'

He shrugs. 'It was fine. It didn't do me any harm.'

'That's not the line you usually take. Anyway, you weren't ill.'

'For God's sake,' he says. 'This whole bloody place is geared up for children who are ill.'

'No. Not ill like Daisy.' The car is full of the thick cough-sweet smell of his aftershave: it makes it hard to breathe. 'Richard, there are girls with anorexia there—very disturbed girls, and they've probably got kids who cut themselves—a lot of those girls do. I used to know girls who did… Daisy can't even manage *school*.'

'I just don't get it,' he says. 'You worry yourself sick about Daisy, and then when they offer you help you won't take it. I mean, this has been dragging on for months, and you take her to see all these weird mates of Nicky's and we don't seem to be getting anywhere. Somebody's got to find out what's going on.'

'Richard, she is not going there. I'm not going to let this happen.'

I pull up outside the station. He puts his diary away, clicks his briefcase shut with a sharp little sound like the breaking of a bone. But he doesn't get out of the car.

He turns to me. 'Well, what do you propose to do exactly?' There's a kind of controlled rage in his voice.

'There is another way. We could get a lawyer. We could fight.'

He shakes his head slowly—as though I exhaust him, as though I am someone he is very weary of.

'*Please*,' he says. 'Not all that again. What on earth is the point of wrecking our relationship with the very people who are trying to help us?'

He gets out of the car; he isn't looking at me.

'There's a dinner after work tonight.' He's speaking to the dashboard. 'A leaving do. I shouldn't wait up—I could be really late.'

C H A P T E R **33**

I sit beside Daisy and stroke her back. She's white, retching. These evenings make me so desperate, because I cannot help her. The nausea exhausts her, but she can't get to sleep. I read to her from the book of Celtic tales. I don't hear a word I read.

At last her eyelids flicker extravagantly and close. I stay beside her for a while, waiting till she's deeply asleep to put her pillows flat. All I can hear is her breathing, and the faintest sound from Sinead's television, some frenetic soap she's watching, and in the distance a siren, blaring then abruptly cut off. I sit there in the middle of the silence, trying to trace out a path, to find a way through. I could ask for Daisy to see another doctor—but she'd need to be referred by Dr Carey. I could go to a solicitor on my own—but I have no money that is mine. If Richard is happy for Daisy to go to this place, and the doctors will use the law if I try to prevent it, do I have any power to stop it happening? I wish I knew about these things. I'm like a child, so ignorant of the world. And I spell out what they have on me—the lost letter, the lies I have told, my secret history, my wish to be alone in the house with my child: everything on my charge sheet. Despair washes through me. Every turn I take, it seems the way is closed to me.

Daisy is sleeping deeply now. I ease her onto her pillows; she scarcely stirs. I stand and my shadow looms across her and halfway to the ceiling, huge, stretched out, the shadow of my hair like a fall of black water against the blue of the wall. And I think, for a moment, my darkness falling across her: but what if they are right— these people who suspect me? What if, as Jane Watson seemed to be saying, I am the environment from which Daisy needs to be removed? I've striven to be the perfect mother, wanting to create a perfect childhood for my child, a safe, encircled place of tenderness and picnics, a childhood that would be so different from mine. Yet something has gone wrong. Maybe I am not like other people. Maybe, as Richard says, I try too hard, am too protective; or perhaps there is some knowledge other people have that is denied me—some mothering art that I don't understand. And all these experts look at me and see this—the profound unnamed thing that is missing in me. Or there is perhaps something subtly, secretly wrong with me—bad thoughts, bad blood, the passing on of some psychological taint. A blight, a contagion, handed down in the genes. And so I must surrender to them and let her go to this place, which to me is the worst thing. For I was shut away, and now it is going to happen to my child.

I have the dream again—the one where I am back at The Poplars, waiting on the broken sofa, smelling the disinfectant and the stale vegetable smell. I wake, or surface a little, at least, into some state between sleep and waking, still with the feeling that I had in the dream, a feeling of being trapped by some great soft heavy weight that presses into me, so I can't move, can't even call or cry. Instinctively, I reach out to Richard, but the bed beside me is empty. I hear St Agatha's striking one o'clock. I turn on the bedside lamp to try and dispel the feeling, and the light falls on the red of the walls, the stiff heavy folds of the curtains, the solitary dancer—but all these things are less real to me than the dream.

I close my eyes and sink back into sleep, and I am again in the room I shared with Aimee. Now, it's night in the dream. The edge of the washed-out candlewick bedspread has ridden up over the sheet, it's crisp against my face, smelling of detergent, and the light from the street lamp filters through the curtains with their patterning of leaves, and falls across my bed and Aimee's bed and the restless heap of her body under the bedclothes. She's wide awake; light glints in her open eyes. As I watch, she throws her covers back. She stands, rips off her nightshirt; the orange glow falls across her rangy urgent body and her pale arms with their intricate tattoos. There's so little flesh on her, I can see the bones through the skin. There's darkness under her shoulder blades and in the hollows in the small of her back; leaf shadows dapple the white planes of her body. She pulls on her knickers, her sweat-shirt, the jeans that have a razor sewn into the hem; she pushes her feet in her trainers, runs her hands through her flame-red hair, in a vain attempt to sort it. From under the bed she pulls out the school bag she never uses because she doesn't go to school. She flings a few things in: a couple of T-shirts, the Tommy Hilfiger rip-off that she nicked from the Northcote Road market—I was with her, I had to keep the stall-holder talking while she did it—and some greying underwear, KitKats she's nicked from Woolworths and stashed behind her chest of drawers, a bit of change, cigarettes, a lighter some man gave her, a crumpled dog-eared photo of her mother. She knows I am awake: she turns to me. I see her milk skin, her acute features, the way her flaming hair falls over her face. It's as if she wants to tell me something, but the dream is soundless, I don't know what she says. She's happy, I think, full of hope: her eyes are laughing, eager. She sits down on the bed and ties the laces of her trainers. She's sharp, alert, relentless: ready to run.

CHAPTER 34

It's a clear bright morning, light splashing around as I push back the bedroom curtains, and the sky is blue and vast and full of promise. I go downstairs; I am all purpose.

Richard is standing in front of the mirror, smoothing his tie.

'You must have been very late last night,' I say to his reflection, keeping my voice quite level, behaving absolutely normally, as though this is a perfectly ordinary day. 'I didn't even hear you get into bed.'

His face, the wrong way round, looks subtly different.

'It was a leaving do,' he says. 'I told you.'

He's defensive, as though I have accused him of something; but really I'm not thinking about him, I just don't want him here.

'I went to bed early,' I tell him. 'It wasn't a problem.'

He seems relieved, as though he expected a scene.

'We went to a restaurant,' he says. 'Lebanese.'

'Was it good?'

'Very good,' he says. 'It's one of Francine's discoveries. She's really into ethnic food.'

'Right,' I say. I wonder briefly if she wore her backless dress. 'I'm glad it was a good evening,' I tell him.

It's how we are together now—formal, polite, restrained.

He picks up his bag, opens the door. Noise from the road surges in; there's a dustbin lorry outside, holding up the traffic.

'OK, then,' he says. He doesn't kiss me.

I take Daisy some toast. She scarcely looks at me; she's lying on her pillows, watching a weather forecast. I kiss the top of her head, breathe in her smell of mangoes and warm skin.

'I thought we'd give school a miss today,' I tell her.

'I couldn't manage it anyway, Mum,' she says. 'I can't do my work when I feel sick.'

I go back to the kitchen to make coffee. Sinead is in front of the mirror, doing something complex with her hair, involving several scrunchies. She has her weekend case with her: it's half-term tomorrow, and Sara will pick her up from school.

'Cat,' she says, her head on one side, wheedling.

'Yes?'

'Is Daisy going to school?'

'No.'

'Well, you wouldn't take me in, would you?' She puts in the final scrunchie and looks at herself appraisingly in the mirror. 'I'm so-o-o late, and we've got a maths test. *And* I've got my bags.'

'I can't, Sinead, I'm sorry. Not today.'

'Oh,' she says. She's surprised—I usually do what she asks. She waits a moment, hoping I'll change my mind, then shrugs, puts on her jacket. 'OK. Is everything all right?'

'Yes. Why?'

'Your voice sounds kind of weird.' She hauls her bags up, one over each shoulder. 'Bye, then.'

I reach out and wrap my arms around her; it's awkward, because of the bags. She hugs me back briefly, colouring a little.

'I hope today goes really really well,' I tell her.

'Cat, don't overdo it,' she says. 'It's only an algebra test. I'm not, like, having major surgery.'

She slips away from me.

Once the door closes behind her, I go straight to her room, feeling strangely weightless, as if gravity doesn't pull on me. I rifle around on her desk, through all the rainbow clutter—pages about popstars, a scrumpled Julius Caesar essay, Korean notepaper, astrological supplements. The Weimar Republic project is hidden inside a copy of *Heat*; the postcard showing the Schiller monument has been stuck to the cover with Prittstick. I ease up one corner of the postcard. I can see all the digits of the number except one. I try to lift it off the page, but it's comprehensively stuck, I have to tear it. A bit of paper is still stuck down, obscuring the number; it flakes off when I scratch at it.

I use the phone in the living room, shutting the door so Daisy won't be able to hear. I put the postcard down on the phone table, where there's a vase of paeonies. I sit there for a moment, tracing a path with my finger through the fallen paeony petals. I feel quite cool as I dial, but I see that my hand is shaking. It seems to ring for ages. I hear the thud of my heart and the sound of the phone at the other end of the line.

She gives the number in German, but I know her voice the way I know my own.

'It's me.' It's hard to form the words: my mouth is stiff and dry. 'It's Catriona. I'm ringing from London.'

There's a pause.

'Who is this?' she says.

'Catriona.'

'Catriona?' Her voice is tight with suspicion.

'It's *me*,' I say again. 'I want to come and see you like you said.'

'Oh,' she says. 'Oh. *Trina*. Oh, I'm sorry, darling—it's just that I wasn't expecting this. Darling, that's wonderful.' The words tumbling out now. 'You don't sound like you used to—well, of course you wouldn't, how silly of me, you'll be much bigger now. I don't know what to say. It's just so sudden. And when were you thinking of?'

'I want to come today.'

Another little silence, like an intake of breath.

'Today?'

I sense her hesitation and feel a quick flicker of anger: that she's pleaded with me to visit her, and now I've said I'm coming, and suddenly it's all too much and yet again she's pushing me away.

'Yes. Today. It has to be today.'

Another pause.

'That will be wonderful, darling,' she says then. 'Wonderful.'

'It'll probably be late afternoon. I don't know when exactly. I've got to book the flight. You'll just have to expect us when you see us.'

'*Us*, darling?'

'I'm bringing my little girl. Daisy.'

'Daisy,' she repeats. 'How wonderful to see her. Tell me, how old is Daisy?'

'She's eight.'

'How lovely. Eight. It's such a lovely age. And you'll be staying over?'

'If we may.'

'Karl's away,' she says. 'A business trip. So that's really very convenient. Sometimes you feel that things are just meant to happen.' As though her moment of reluctance had never been. 'The only thing is, darling, there are just two bedrooms…'

'D'you have a sofa? Daisy could sleep on a sofa.'

'Well, if you're sure,' she says. 'I'll make her nice and

comfortable. Don't you worry, Trina, I'll get something sorted. You've got my address, have you, darling? You got my postcards?'

'Yes.'

'Now, listen carefully, darling. You need to get the bus to Charlottenburg. They might try to tell you Zoo—but Zoo station isn't very nice, darling, there are lots of drug pushers there. Go to Charlottenburg, and take the S-Bahn to Hackescher Markt—and then you take the tram up Prenzlauer Allee…'

I write it down.

'We live on the fifth floor,' she says. 'The name is Mueller. You have to ring the bell and there's an intercom thing.'

'Don't worry. We'll manage.'

'Now, the airport's very busy, Trina. Keep an eye on your bags. You can't trust anyone nowadays.'

'We'll be all right.'

'And, Trina, look, where I live, it used to be the East, of course, but you mustn't let that worry you. We're really coming up in the world here now. It's not at all like you'd think. This afternoon, then?'

'Yes. This afternoon.'

I put down the phone. My whole body is trembling.

I fetch my credit card and go on the computer. I've never done this before: Richard's always made our travel arrangements and I've never flown without him. But it's all so easy. There are still seats on the afternoon flight to Berlin. It lands at Tegel Airport. I can check in online, and I'll have to pick up our boarding passes once we get to Heathrow.

I get the Yellow Pages and look for a taxi firm. There's a name I recognise, from when we last went to Tuscany. I ring; this too is easy. I have an hour and a half before the taxi comes.

I have a sense of triumph: I am high, pure, clear; I can do anything. I pack my hand luggage first: credit card, money, passports. I take some phone numbers—Nicky, Fergal. Then I find a bag, start flinging things in. I don't know what to expect, how hot it will be or whether it might rain. I just throw in whatever comes to hand—two skirts of mine, not bothering to fold them, some T-shirts of Daisy's from the tumble-dryer; and I put on a brown silk dress I have that works for any occasion.

And then I can't postpone it any longer—the thing that I am dreading. I go to Daisy's bedroom.

She's slumped in her bed. *Jeremy Kyle* is on, but she's playing with her Nintendo. I take her cut-off jeans and a polo shirt from her wardrobe and put them out on her bed. Her eyes are on me, dull, a little suspicious. Suddenly I can't believe what I'm doing: it seems delinquent, wild.

'Why am I getting dressed?' she says.

'Because you and I are going on a trip.'

She frowns. 'What sort of a trip?' She's wary. I know she thinks this is cheery adult-speak for something un-pleasant—a doctor, clinic, blood test.

'Not what you think. We're going to the airport.'

At once she sits upright. Her eyes are wide.

'We're going to fly to Berlin,' I tell her. 'D'you think you can manage that?'

Her eyes hold me; her whole face gleams.

'Berlin,' she says. The word is like a sweet she's rolling round her mouth.

For a moment I think that she will accept it and I won't have to explain. But then a shadow moves across her face.

'Why are we going now?' she says. 'Is it because I'm ill?'

'Kind of. Dr McGuire and Dr Watson want you to go into a hospital.'

'To stay?' she says.

I nod. 'It's a place for children with psychological problems.'

'I'm not making it up, Mum,' she says.

'Of course you're not. But anyway I don't think that place is right for you. I don't want you to go there.'

She looks at me, accusingly. 'So are we running away?'

'No. We're going to see your grandmother.'

A stern frown creases her forehead.

'But she was horrid to you. You keep on telling me.'

'Yes. But people change. Maybe we'll find we get on better now. And she really wants to see you. I rang her just now and she said how very much she wants to see you.'

There's light in her face: this pleases her. 'Really?'

'Really.'

'D'you think she'd like it if I wore my red denim jacket?'

'I'm sure she would,' I tell her.

Her school bag is on the floor by her bed. I tip everything out of it.

'You can take this bag to keep with you on the plane, for Hannibal and some books. D'you want to pack it yourself?'

She nods, gets out of bed. She starts to choose books from her bookshelves, her book of Celtic tales, two books about cats. The bag will be heavy, but I just let her take them; I can carry it for her. Hannibal goes in the top.

And then she turns to me; her face is dark with worry.

'But what about Sinead?'

'Sinead will be at Sara's.'

She zips up her bag. 'I wish Sinead was coming,' she says. 'And Dad. I wish they were coming with us. It won't be fun without them.'

Guilt washes through me.

'I know, sweetheart. But if we're going to go, we have to go today.'

'Dad and Sinead will miss us, won't they?'

'Yes, they probably will.'

She looks at me for a moment, an intent, questioning look. Then she shrugs a little.

'OK,' she says. 'Well, don't just stand there, Mum. I'm going to get dressed.'

When the taxi comes, we're waiting in the hall. The driver is a woman, scrubbed and genial.

'You're certainly travelling light,' she says as she carries our bags to the car. 'I wish they were all like you, I must say. So where are you going?'

'Berlin.'

'Oh. Berlin.' Suddenly, she is serious. 'My cousin was there in the forces, before the Wall came down. It freaked him out, he said. If you went to the East in the train, they locked you in.'

'Yes, I'd heard that,' I tell her.

She checks we have fastened our seat belts.

'It must have been so weird,' she says. 'Before the Wall came down.'

'Yes,' I say. 'It must have been.'

'It's the families I feel sorry for,' she says. 'All the parents and children. All those poor people who lived there, who couldn't visit their families.'

'Yes,' I say. 'That must have been hard for people.'

She starts up the engine.

Daisy loves the glamour of airports: the glittery shops selling suntan oil and sarongs that are patterned with pictures of tropical islands, the computer screens with their lists of resonant destinations. We wander round the shops, and I buy her a Pokémon magazine, and we go to a café and toy with some tough chocolate croissants. People look at us benignly—anxious mother and pale fragile child. They don't know about us.

As we go through passport control I am seized by a sudden fear, that I am being watched or followed, that somebody will stop us, that this man will not let us through. I see it all so vividly—how he takes our passports away while the other passengers stare at us, quite openly and curious, for now we are not like them, we have crossed to the other side. How he leads us off to a small bleak room, and asks me questions to which there are no good answers. But none of this happens; he grins at Daisy, says how he likes her jacket, waves us cheerily through.

Daisy has a window seat. As the plane taxies we watch the film about what to do in emergencies. Daisy is conscientious, and pulls out the card of instructions from the net pocket in front of her.

'Look,' she says, waving it at me, gleeful. 'They made a mistake here, Mum.' She's pleased with herself: she loves to come across misprints in anything official. 'It says that if there's a person with a child, they need to fix their oxygen mask before they fix the child's.'

'That's what they always say.'

'No, Mum. You should see to the child first,' she says sternly.

'But the mother has to look after both of them, and if the mother can't breathe she isn't much use to her child.'

This doesn't satisfy her. 'I think she should help the child.'

The plane speeds down the runway. She watches through the window, relishing the thrill of take-off, as I used to do. I remember the very first time I flew, when Richard and I went to Venice for our honeymoon, and how he loved my ignorance and my delight in everything; and, when he saw how charmed I was by the in-flight meal with all its cups and packets, how he smiled and pulled me to him and pressed his mouth to my hair.

The light through the window glosses over Daisy's pallor; her eyes shine with pleasure. She looks for a moment like a healthy child. I peer across her as the land opens out beneath us, the patterning of fields, green and brown and bleached-blond, the scribble of wood and hedge. The plane tilts and banks. Daisy grins, unafraid.

We cross the bright white line at the edge of the land, and the sea is spread below us, placid and gleaming. The waves near the shore are white and still, as though sketched with chalk by a child; or as they might have been drawn on some faded sepia map, fabulous with dragons, at the rim of the charted world. Through the window of the plane it is all blue and silver, and suddenly my heart is light, as though we are set free.

C H A P T E R 35

Tegel Airport seems quiet after Heathrow. An official takes our passports and studies our faces to see if we match our photographs. I try to breathe and look at ease. But then he waves us through.

We buy a travel card and take the bus to Charlottenburg Station, just as my mother told me. We are tired now; we stare silently out of the window at the cobbled side streets, the canal, the hoardings; at Charlottenburg Castle, pale and splendid, that I recognise from one of my mother's postcards. Daisy is intrigued by the foreignness of everything: the street names and the hoardings, the German posters for *Hannah Montana*.

At the station we take a train with red and yellow carriages, which seems to have come straight out of an old spy movie. Through the window we glimpse vast city vistas, building sites and distant opulent buildings and the shining glass on massive office blocks, all the glamour and frenzy of the city. Alongside the track there are graffitied walls and flats with sun-awnings, and from a balcony at the top of a block of flats someone has hung a sheet that says 'Fuck Capitalist Overkill' in shaky black letters.

At Hackescher Markt we find the tram stop out of the back of the station. It's hot, waiting here. The sky is white, hazy, and it's hushed for a city, only a handful of other people waiting. The tramlines sing at the approach of the tram.

Our carriage is almost empty. Behind us a man with a ponytail and guitar, who has guessed or overheard our Englishness, announces, 'Ladies, I play some things for you.' He sings Bob Dylan, *Shelter from the Storm,* his voice reedy, mournful. The tram swings round and starts to climb, and he comes down the carriage and asks for money for the music, though with the air of one who has few expectations. I give him a handful of coins—perhaps because we are strangers, feeling a need to be generous, to placate.

We chunter up the hill, up Prenzlauer Allee. I'm unsure exactly where the Wall used to be, but it's easy to tell we are now in what once was the East. There is an air of neglect, a lot of boarded-up buildings. We pass what looks like a public park with many tall trees and darkness under the trees, where nothing has been tended: the brick-work is crumbling in the perimeter wall; the intricate iron gates are red with rust. The sense of hopefulness I felt in the plane has all seeped away from me.

When Knaackstrasse shows on the indicator at the front of the tram, we get up at once, long before the stop, as you do when you are travelling to a place you do not know. And we step out, and the tram pulls away up the straight line of the street into the glimmery white distance. It is completely quiet. Daisy grips my hand.

We cross the road, walk down a side street. The road is cobbled, and the pavements are broken and uneven, and tawny flowers with a musty smell grow up through the gaps in the paving stones. The blocks of flats here are five stories high. They have metal shutters across the ground floor windows, and all have been floridly written over with rainbow graffiti as high as the reach of a hand. You can tell these buildings were splendid once. Some of the façades have been done up with fresh stucco the colour of clotted cream. But there are many buildings where the stucco has peeled off entirely, as though the façade has been flayed. These buildings have an injured look, the brickwork worn and soot-blackened. You cannot believe that people live in such ruins. Above us, a little girl steps out onto the balcony of one of the ruined blocks. She is wearing a long dress, perhaps a party dress, rose pink, sprigged, and she has her hair elaborately piled up. She leans on the railing next to a bleached wicker birdcage with no bird inside; she is still and serious, looking down into the street. She and Daisy are instantly aware of one another: they stare with open curiosity. Daisy turns to me, gives me a quick complicit smile. We look up again, and the little girl has gone, as though we dreamt her.

We pass a patch of waste ground where there are very tall trees, far too tall for the city, as though they've been left to grow wild, like trees in a forest—chestnuts, and planes with blotched bark, and limes that litter the streets with the pale question-marks of their seed-cases. Small dun-coloured birds scatter in front of us, casual, light as leaves, and the pavement is dappled with sunlight yellow as butter. There are no cars on the road, and hardly any people. A blind girl in a short gold dress walks past us, her male companion guiding her, his hand on her arm. She has a festive look; they are going, I think, to some celebration; her eyes, which are like slits, scarcely opened, are elaborately painted with shiny make-up. Ahead of us a young man crosses the street, walking through a slice of yellow light, holding a bunch of gaudy sunflowers wrapped in green tissue paper.

I'm so convinced she won't be waiting for us that I'm planning what to do when we ring her bell and there's no answer—where will we stay, what will we do, adrift in this strange city?

Daisy is tired now, pulling at me. 'Is it much further, Mum?'

'Not much further,' I tell her.

She trudges on. She says her feet have blisters.

We come to a square where the ground floors of some of the flats have been turned into cafés and bars. On the corner a sign says Café Esposito. A young man with silver bracelets is sitting there under the lime trees. As we pass a woman with a clear bright fall of blonde hair comes up and greets him, and he stands and kisses her, running his hand down her side, resting his hand on her hipbone: they have the melded gestures of long-time lovers. I want so much to be that woman, so casual, so at ease. Here in the still hot afternoon street, nearing my mother's door, my fear is a taste in my mouth, a chill on my skin. My steps are slow, our bag is very heavy. Daisy tugs at my arm.

The block where my mother lives looks out on a children's playground. The door is faded as though salt winds have blown on it and graffitied with many colours. Daisy points to where someone has drawn a smiley sun, its chin resting on top of the intercom panel.

'Hello?'

'It's me.'

'Trina, darling. I'm on the fifth floor. Come right up.' Her voice crackles over the intercom. 'There's a light switch but it's on a timer. It won't last very long.'

I push at the door.

It's dark in the hall, just a square of sunlight falling through the glass in the door at the back. We glimpse a courtyard, where there are bicycles and a rusting fire escape and a wall that has that peeled decrepit look and is covered with plastic sheeting, and a hydrangea bush with milk-white flowers. We find the light switch and start to climb. My body is heavy, as though my limbs are drenched.

Just as she said, the lights go out before we get there.

'Shit.'

'Don't worry, Mum,' says Daisy. 'You can feel your way in the dark.'

Above us, a door opens and there's a line of light down the stairs. You have to put your head right back to see up to the door. I hear her voice.

'Not much further now.'

Her shadow falls across us as we climb the last few stairs.

'Trina, my darling.'

I try to smile, but my mouth feels stiff and strange.

'So you made it,' she says.

'Yes.' My voice is shaking a little. We don't know whether to touch each other. The air between us feels shimmery and thin.

'You're looking well,' she says.

'Thanks, I am really. And you… Are you OK?'

'Not so bad today, darling. Mustn't complain…'

But her appearance shakes me. She's dressed as she always dressed—capri pants, high-heeled sandals, lots of jewellery—but her skin is thin and worn, stretched over the bone, and her eyes are hooded with shadow. I see how the years have washed over her and started to wear her away.

'So this must be Daisy,' she says. She bends to her. 'Goodness, how pretty you are. Your mum and dad are going to have trouble with you. You'll only have to flutter your lashes and it'll be raining men… And look at this hair.' She reaches out and takes a strand of Daisy's yellow hair between her finger and thumb, lifts it and lets it fall so it catches the light. Her hand with its many glistening rings is trembling. 'She's got your hair, Trina.'

'Yes.'

'Well, why are we standing here?' she says. 'Come on in.'

There's an entrance lobby, then a sitting room with windows looking down into the street. The room is cluttered, full of heavy old furniture—a dark varnished dresser with painted flowers, a sofa with red velour cushions, a lamp with a beaded shade. Daisy walks round the room, touching the lamp, the cushions, with the tips of her fingers, as though these things are hers.

In the window there's a table with carved clawed feet and upright chairs. I sit with my mother at the table, breathe in her smell of nicotine and lily of the valley. I realise I'd had some shiny tentative hope that things would be different between us, that everything would be changed or reconciled. And now I'm finally here with her, and we're being so careful and polite with one another, yet I feel the insect-crawl of all the old resentments across my skin.

She pulls a carrier bag towards her.

'Look, I got you something, darling,' she says to Daisy. 'Just a little present. I was going to wrap it, but I didn't have any paper…'

It's a jointed bear with denim paws and a solemn face and a gauzy blue-green bow. I think of the presents my

mother brought me at The Poplars, the rabbits with
stitched-on satin hearts that she always intended to wrap.
I feel a brief cold repulsion. But Daisy knows nothing of
this. She smiles and hugs the bear.

'He's dead cute,' she says. 'Thank you.'

She has an easy confidence here; she knows how to
behave.

I start to say, 'Really, you shouldn't…'

But my mother misunderstands. 'There, your mum's
feeling all left out now,' she says to Daisy. 'We don't
want your mum to feel left out, do we? I ought to give
your mum something, shouldn't I? So, Trina, what would
you like? Would you like some money? I'd love to give
you money.'

'No, no. Of course not.'

'I'd love to, really, darling,' she says. 'I'm not so badly
off now, you know. Things have changed, things have
turned around…'

It's as if she refuses to hear me.

'I could write you a cheque,' she says. 'Everyone needs
money. Some money of your own.'

'No, really…'

She lights a cigarette. Her hand is shaking a little; the
flame trembles. She takes a deep inbreath; smoke catches
at her throat. She starts to cough, a gasping, choking
cough that's like a violent struggle, that threatens to over-
whelm her. Daisy edges away, alarmed. I sit beside my
mother, not knowing how to help her.

At last the cough subsides. She wipes her face with a tissue.

'So was it a good journey?' she says then, as though the cough never happened.

'Yes.'

'You flew into Tegel?'

'Yes.'

I'm very aware of her deliberate, thought-out politeness, that is so like my own. There are certain questions that always have to be asked.

'Now, really, I'm forgetting,' she says. 'You must be hungry. After your journey.'

She has food for us, sausage and bread and sauerkraut. There is flowered crockery in the china cabinet. She lays the table fastidiously, just as she always did—back in the days when we still managed some kind of life together. I eat greedily, realising I am famished. Daisy has some bread.

'Eat up, my darling,' says my mother to Daisy, tipping a piece of sausage onto her plate. 'You need your food, a growing girl like you…'

She's too insistent. Daisy turns to me.

'Daisy's been ill,' I tell my mother. 'That's why she can't eat more.'

'Oh, dear,' says my mother. There are mannerisms I've forgotten, like the way she frowns when everything seems too much for her, the sharp little vertical lines that are etched between her eyes. 'What seems to be the matter?'

'No one can give us an answer.'

'Poor Daisy,' she says. 'A pretty thing like you shouldn't ever be ill.'

For dessert she brings in a cake in a box of expensive white card.

'Now look at this, Daisy. Sachertorte. You'll love it.'

She unfolds the box around the cake. It's magnificent: it has glossy chocolate icing and marzipan flowers.

'There,' she says. There's an air of triumph about her: this is a moment she has waited for. Her eyes have a febrile brightness. She cuts into the cake, her many bracelets rattling on her wrist.

A shadow seems to pass over her.

'Oh, dear,' she says. 'It's still a tiny bit frozen in the middle.'

She stands there with the cake knife in her hand. Her face has collapsed, her eyes are full of tears. I see that this sachertorte has some profound significance, as though she'd intended that it should be the answer, the reparation: that it could heal everything. A brief rage flares in me—that she abandons me for years, then seeks to be loved and forgiven because of some trivial gesture, some cake she's bought.

'Never mind,' I tell her, the way you might speak to a child. 'We'll eat the outside now and we'll have the middle tomorrow. I'll cut it if you like.' I take the knife from her.

Even the outside of the cake is brittle and cold, its sweetness muted.

There are smudges under Daisy's eyes, her head is heavy, she's almost asleep at the table. I tell her it's bedtime.

My mother looks across at her, the lines in her forehead deepening, as though it's all a mystery. And I realise then that she can't see Daisy's exhaustion, can't see the most obvious signals. That she looks at people and somehow cannot read them, can't see the things that the rest of us so effortlessly interpret—the arched brow of contempt, the smile that doesn't reach the eyes—can't even read the tiredness in a child.

'She could sleep on the sofa, you thought?'

My mother gets the duvet.

I unpack Daisy's pyjamas and she changes in my mother's bedroom, where there are chairs heaped up with velvet scarves and filmy, complicated blouses, and, on the dressing-table, gloves in silk or cotton, pale apricot and lavender, with ruched wrists. I remember how she always wore them because she hated her hands. I tell Daisy not to clean her teeth, in the hope that she won't start retching, and she curls up on the sofa under the quilt, with the bear and Hannibal precisely placed beside her, and to my relief is instantly asleep. My mother turns off the overhead light. The lamp with its shade of beads casts broken fantastic shadows. We take the plates to the kitchen.

'Now, Trina, what do you say to a little drink?' says my mother. There's a gleam in her dull eyes: a schoolgirl look, unnerving on her worn face.

'Are you sure you should?'

'Darling, I know I had a problem,' she says. Brisk and impatient, a bit cross with me. 'But that's all in the past.

I've done the Twelve Steps. I know my limits now. Anyway, I got a nice Moselle in specially.' She goes to the fridge. 'It would be a sin to let it go to waste. Get me some glasses, would you, darling?'

I take two glasses from the cabinet in the living room. The heat has gone from the day; the blue cool air from outside brushes my face like a hand as I pass the window. I look down into the street. The sky is deepening above the lime trees, and the bars are opening, waiters spreading tables out on the rough cobbled pavement. The Café Esposito is filling up with young people in student casual clothes, combat trousers and T-shirts; their easy talk and laughter float in through the window. And there are musicians—a guitarist, and a singer with a tambourine that he slaps against his thigh. The singer has a pleasant tenor voice; he sings Simon and Garfunkel in heavily accented English.

My mother fills our glasses to the brim. When she bends her head, I see how sparse her hair is, the skin of the scalp showing, pink and somehow vulnerable.

We sit by the open window, drinking quietly, suspended in this waiting summer stillness, hearing the laughter of strangers and the singing from the street.

CHAPTER 37

My mother clears her throat.

'She's such a pretty one, your little girl… You were like that, Trina, the spitting image. Well, you're still looking good, darling.' She touches the silk of my sleeve. 'This is beautiful,' she says. 'I can see you've done really well for yourself.'

I shrug a little. I don't know what to say.

'Don't be modest,' she says. 'I'm so happy for you, Trina. I so wanted you to do better than me. And you've certainly done that, haven't you? That's such a comfort to me… What does he do, your husband?'

'He's in insurance—something in the city.'

'Ooh,' she says. 'Something in the city. Very nice. And is he good to you? Is he kind?'

'Yes,' I tell her. 'Yes, he's been good to me.' I'm not sure how married I am any more, but I don't say that to her.

'And what about your painting?' she says. 'Are you still doing your painting?'

'Now and then. I've sold some pictures to a craft shop.'

'How lovely,' she says. 'I always knew you'd do well. You get it from your father, of course. That arty streak. You take after your father…'

'You never used to talk about him much.'

'No,' she says. 'No, perhaps I didn't. Well, to be honest, I tried to forget all about him.' Slowly, she lights her cigarette, the flame from the lighter flickering uncertainly in her eyes. 'I've been thinking about him a bit, these past weeks, though. Thinking back over things.' She blows out smoke. The air around her is thick; her face is veiled. 'He was a total sod to me,' she says. 'He treated me very badly. But when there's all that water under the bridge… I mean, it's different for you, Trina, you've got your whole life ahead of you…'

'Tell me about him.'

'You'd have liked his painting,' she says. 'Great big canvases, very colourful. I didn't really understand them, to be honest. Nudes, mostly, but he seemed to think it was all very spiritual… He went off with one of his models in the end—when you were just a baby.' Her voice has an edge of anger. 'Well, how could I compete with that,

I ask you? I was stuck in this poky flat in Battersea, looking after you, and there she was in his studio, taking off her clothes.'

I nod, I murmur something—so she will carry on.

'I was head over heels to start with, mind,' she says. 'That was me then. Always in love, all these dreams. It seems so strange to me now… He was a great romantic, was Christopher. He saw me sitting on a bus. Did I ever tell you? That was how we met. I was just sitting there, and the bus had started to move, and he ran and caught the bus and came and sat beside me. He told me I was the loveliest woman he'd ever seen…' There's pleasure for a moment in her wrecked face. 'Well, I suppose I probably did have a certain something, if I'm honest. I used to get a nice tan, and I liked to wear these cute little skirts. Though I say it myself, I probably looked the part. I've always tried to look after myself,' she says. 'Well, you know that… The trouble is, I've just never had any confidence. Do you have any confidence, Trina?'

'I don't know. Not much, probably.'

She takes a long slow sip of wine, looking out over the city. 'He was the best man I ever had, really, your father,' she says quietly.

This amazes me.

'You used to sound so angry with him.'

'Well, I was, of course.'

'Why wouldn't you ever talk about him properly? I used to long for you to talk about him.'

'Did you, darling?'

Outside, the sky is deepening, and there are white fairy lights at the cafés, caught like luminous little fish in the shadowy nets of the trees. The music floats in through the open window. The song has changed; it's older, wilder, in some unknown language, with many high notes so the singer's voice sounds like the voice of a woman: a lament, a song of infinite yearning, Slavic, perhaps, or Yiddish, I don't know how to tell.

'He was out of my league, if I'm honest,' she says, after a while. 'He had such nice manners. Classy.' She inhales deeply. 'Though I have to say he could have chosen better when he left. A right little tramp, she was,' she says, with satisfaction. 'And definitely on the podgy side. Well, she was there, I suppose, conveniently to hand, so to speak.'

'What did he look like, my father?'

'I used to have a photograph,' she says. 'I kept it all these years but when I moved in with Karl I threw it away. Didn't I ever show you?'

I shake my head. I have a sensation of loss so bitter it's like a taste on my tongue.

'Tell me,' I say.

She shrugs a little. 'Tall, good-looking, everything you'd want. Strong-looking, though appearances can be deceptive. His health really wasn't all that good when I met him. Trouble with this and that… But a big bull of a man—you wouldn't know it to look at him.'

I start to ask what kind of trouble, but she doesn't seem to hear, she's wandering off along some track of her own.

'You look back, and you think how it might have been

different,' she says. 'Well, you can't help thinking these things. That if this man or that man had stayed with you, it might all have worked out… I expect you think I'm hopeless, don't you, Trina? That I've got dreadful taste in men—that my life's been a bit of a failure…'

I don't say anything.

'That's what you think, though, isn't it? I know what you're thinking, Trina. You might as well come out with it.'

And then all the hidden anger flares in me.

'Why did you do it?' My voice is harsh, loud. 'Why did you send me to that place?'

'I wasn't doing you any good,' she says. 'I knew I wasn't coping. It was all beyond me…'

'But we could have managed. We could have got by… Nothing could have been worse than that place. Nothing.'

It's as if she's flinching, pulling back into herself, as though she's scared I'll hit her; but she doesn't turn away.

'I thought I couldn't look after you,' she says. 'I thought you'd have a better life. I knew I wasn't getting it together… Trina, it was hard for me too. It was a hard life.'

The anger surges through me, threatens to sweep me away.

'You should never have let it happen. It was wrong, what you did.'

'But that Brian Meredith. He was nice enough, wasn't he? He was very well turned-out.'

'He was abusive. He was a cruel man.'

'He was always very nice to me,' she says. A bit hurt, as though it's mean of me to question her opinion.

'He hit us round the head. He knew how to hit you so there wouldn't be a mark on you. If you did something wrong—just the stupidest little thing—you got shut in this room for weeks, you thought you'd lose your mind.'

'Those are terrible things to say, Catriona,' she says. As though it's the saying that's terrible, not the fact that these things happened.

'That's how it was. That's where you sent me.'

'I didn't know,' she says. 'How was I to know? Why didn't you tell me?'

This enrages me. 'You never know anything. "It wasn't me. I wasn't there. I didn't know." That's your cop-out. So nothing is ever your fault.' Suddenly I can't sit still: I get up, pace the floor. 'You never loved me.' My voice is shrill, the voice of a child. It echoes in the big room. 'Not like a mother should.'

I want her to deny this, to still the echoes: Of course I love you, of course I do. She doesn't say anything.

She's looking away from me, staring down into the street.

'Perhaps there was something missing in me,' she says then. Slowly, feeling her way towards the words. 'I never quite felt that thing you were supposed to feel—you know, when I had you. I mean, don't get me wrong, I was fond of you, of course; and I was proud of you because you were so cute, and people would say, "What a pretty little thing," "What a pretty baby…" But those feelings you're meant to get, when your baby's put in your arms…' She shakes her head. 'Maybe there's something wrong with me,' she says. 'If you could do it again, you might want to do it differently…'

'You stopped visiting,' I say. 'You couldn't even be bothered to visit me.'

'I knew you were angry with me,' she says. 'I guess I gave up really. I thought you wouldn't want to see me. Well, you didn't, did you? Be honest, Trina. Not the way I was then… And by the time I got myself together, it was all too late.' Her voice thickens; the coughing starts again. 'Story of my life,' she says, through the cough. 'I've never been lucky.'

The cough is her enemy: it has her in its grip now. She shakes with it; I can tell it hurts her. This frightens me—I fear that it will choke her. I get her some water, my anger all spent suddenly. I sit beside her.

Eventually it stops. She wipes her mouth and looks across at me.

'I'm ill,' she says.

'Yes.'

'Cancer. Too many fags.' She sounds quite matter-of-fact, but her face is troubled, darkened. 'Nobody knows…'

'Not even Karl?'

She shakes her head. 'I didn't want to worry him. He's got a lot on his mind. I said I had a little problem with my lungs.'

I think how she and I tell lies routinely, how we believe that we are kept safe by these lies.

'You ought to tell him. You can't go through this on your own.'

She shrugs.

'But, darling, you know, he's younger than me. He wouldn't want to be hitched to a sick old woman. People don't always stick by you when you're ill… I can tell you because you're family.' She taps her cigarette on the edge of the ashtray. A little ash drifts down. 'Things are as they are,' she says. 'There's nothing you can do.'

We're very still, we just drink for a while, sitting there by the window. The rich smells of the summer city—pollen, exhaust, decay—drift round us like a profound nostalgia. I look down into the street. At the Café Esposito the tables are all full now. A girl is laughing, flinging back her hair, and lovers kiss under the lime trees, but the singer with the tambourine has gone.

'I don't pull down the blinds,' she says. 'Not since they told me—you know, about the illness. I never pull down the blinds. I like to see out of the window—to see as far as I can.'

There's a look of such loss in her face.

I get up and go and put my arms around her shoulders. She feels frail, sparrow-boned, like a child or someone very old. And I know, as I touch her, her absolute weakness and helplessness: that something in her has died already; that she has given up. This knowledge shocks me. That all this time, for all these years, I have felt her to have such a hold over me, to have such power to shape and devastate me—and here she is in my arms, this tiny shrunken woman.

She rests her head against me for a moment.

'Well,' she says.

She raises her hand and puts it over mine. Awkwardly, as though it's a gesture she doesn't quite know how to do.

On the sofa, Daisy stirs. The beading hanging from the lamp casts broken patterns across her, lines of shadow stitching. We watch as she turns over, flings one arm out on top of the eiderdown.

'Daisy,' says my mother. 'It's such a pretty name… I've always liked flower names. I wanted to give you a flower name, you know—I was going to call you Lily. But Christopher didn't like it—he wanted to call you Catherine. That's how we came up with Catriona. I wasn't having Catherine. I thought it was rather plain.' She pats my hand. 'Not nearly special enough—not for my baby.'

CHAPTER 38

I wake to the hollow chiming of a distant church clock and the high sweet sound of swifts and the awareness, unnerving at first, in the confusion of half-wakefulness, that I am far from home. I put on my dressing gown and go quietly into the living room. My mother is there already, in a thin robe with a tatty boa collar. She puts her finger to her lips: Daisy is still asleep, the duvet rising gently with her even breath. We go to the kitchen and make coffee, not saying much. I feel awkward with my mother again, easily irritated, last night's intimacies blotted away by the white illusionless morning light. I drink my coffee quickly and dress and go out to find a cashpoint, relieved to leave the flat for a while.

The street seems half asleep still. In front of the Café Esposito, the furniture is all stacked up, and the waiter is tipping water from a bucket and brushing it over the pavement, so the flags shine in the bleached light. A smell of disinfectant catches at my throat. I glance down a side street, where there's a patch of waste ground, and beyond it the blank windowless end wall of a block of tenements. The wall is all blue-painted and right in the middle someone has written Ende, high up, in immaculate white brush-strokes. A little movement of air shivers the leaves of the lime trees.

On the corner there's a snack bar called Japan-Imbiss, which has a narrow window crammed with advertisements for Lucky Lights, and next to it a bank with a cashpoint. The bank is shut still. I go to the cashpoint, put in my Visa card, select my language, tap in my PIN number, trying to work out how much money I need. But the wrong display comes up: it doesn't seem to recognise my card. Maybe I can't use my card abroad after all, yet I'm sure this is possible; I know I've used it in Italy. There's someone behind me; I hear the rustle of the plastic bag they're holding, and how they move from foot to foot. The presence of this unseen waiting person makes me nervous, yet if I turned and tried to explain they wouldn't understand me. I wonder how many goes you get before the machine eats your card. I take the card out of the slot and start all over again. The same display comes up. I take the card and put it in my bag. Suddenly, London is real to me again: our drawing room, the vase of paeonies on the table by the telephone…and the postcard—where did I leave the postcard? I see it in my mind—the picture of the monument, the woman in white marble—and on the back my mother's address and phone number. I see myself about to dial, putting it down by the phone where I could see the number. Then after the call, rushing around to pack, calling the taxi, speaking to Daisy, feverish, a little high—it's all a blur now. I can't remember where I put the postcard.

I turn, walk past the woman who's waiting there with a plastic bag of vegetables, whose rustling made me nervous. I tell myself, Everything's fine, it's just a problem with the credit card. Later, when the bank is open, I will get everything sorted. The cashier will smile, will explain to me in careful precise English exactly what has happened. It's just some kind of mistake. I tell myself this over and over. Nothing has happened, it's just a computer error. Everything will be fine. But when I get back to the flats where my mother lives and push against the door handle, I find my hands are slippery with sweat.

Daisy spends the morning on the sofa, watching television. She feels sick, she says. She is tired, her eyes stained with shadow. I help my mother tidy the kitchen, though there's scarcely enough to do to occupy two people. Daisy's illness frustrates my mother.

'I thought we could go out,' she says. 'I thought we could go to the Tiergarten. We could have a chocolate muffin at the Café am Neuen See.' Her German is careful, ponderous. 'We could take a boat on the lake. A little rowing boat. Daisy would like that…'

She's somehow unable to cope with this change in her plans. She tries to talk to me about England, about my life and all the things I have done, but there's a fog in my mind and I can't talk easily. In the end we sit and drink more coffee and watch the television with Daisy. It's a dubbed comedy, set in some English country house, which bizarrely stars Ricki Lake who mostly appears in full hunting rig.

Lunch, which we eat early, is much like yesterday's supper; bread and sausage, and the now fully thawed sachertorte. Daisy eats some bread. After lunch she says she wants to get up.

My mother and I take the plates to the kitchen and my mother stacks them in the bowl. Through the narrow window beside the sink you can see down into the courtyard, the worn grey wall, the hydrangeas. It all looks shabby, neglected, in the harsh noon light. The hydrangeas are nearly over, some of the flowerets brown and crumpled like paper. It's the empty time, when everything feels flat and meaningless: the sun has gone in, the vitality has all seeped out of the day. A wave of despair washes through me. I wonder what on earth I thought I'd find, in coming here.

I hear Daisy go to the bathroom. She's left the door half open. She must be trying to clean her teeth—I hear her start to retch.

My mother turns to me, eyes widening.

'That's Daisy?'

'Yes.'

'Poor little scrap.' She shakes her head. She puts on hand cream and then her rubber gloves, and runs water into the washing-up bowl. I find a tea towel in the drawer of the dresser. 'That takes me back. Christopher used to do that,' she says. 'That weird dry retching.'

'Like Daisy?'

She nods. 'Christopher had a lot of health problems, you see, darling. Like I said, you wouldn't have thought it to look at him. But he used to get so ill sometimes and nobody knew what it was. The doctor didn't know what to make of it—well, he said it was probably stress.'

'My father.'

'Yes. Of course, darling. Your father.'

'You never told me.'

'Didn't I? Well, I guess it never seemed important.' But she turns to me then. Her eyes are wide, as though something has surprised her. 'But it might be, mightn't it? D'you think it might be important?'

'Yes.'

'Maybe it's in the blood. That happens with illnesses, doesn't it? Things get passed on, down the generations.'

'Yes, that happens.' I feel excitement prickle along my skin. I put the tea towel down. 'Tell me about it. Anything you can remember.'

'There's not that much to say, really. There was this diet he tried…'

'Tell me.'

'I can't remember exactly, darling. He got it out of a book. I had to use this funny flour—he couldn't have wheat, you see. It was quite a pain to be honest. I bet she didn't do it, the little tramp he went off with,' she adds with satisfaction. 'I shouldn't think she bothered for a moment…'

I feel a surge of rage with her, with the way she's always sidetracked by her own concerns. 'Please try and remember. Please.'

'I'm trying, darling. Now don't go getting all cross with me,' she says. 'I'm doing my best. It's all so long ago now.'

The sound of the intercom buzzer makes me start. I swear under my breath, can't bear this interruption.

'Leave that. Please,' I tell her.

'But of course I can't just leave it, darling.' She peels off her rubber gloves. 'I don't know who it is….' She goes to lift the receiver.

She speaks in halting German, turning to face me as she talks. Her eyes are wide, alarmed, fixed on my face as though she's signalling something.

'Yes,' she says then, switching to English. 'They are. Well, you'd better come up. We're on the fifth floor. There's a light switch by the door—it's on a timer.'

She puts down the receiver, comes to me. The little lines deepen between her eyes.

'Trina.' She's speaking in an urgent whisper. 'It's the police.'

'Oh, my God.'

'They wanted to know if you and Daisy were here.'

'No. No.'

'They want to see you and Daisy.'

'No. And you let them in.'

She flinches from my anger.

'Well, what could I do? They were going to come up anyway. Trina, are you in some kind of trouble, darling?'

'Yes.'

My mother is frightened. Her hands move in front of her face, fluttering like birds.

My heart is pounding in my chest. I shout for Daisy.

'Get your jacket on. We've got to go.'

She appears at the bedroom door.

'We can't go, Mum. We've only just got here…'

'*Just do it.*'

A shadow darts across her face. I'm rarely cross with her. She goes rapidly back to the bedroom.

I turn to my mother. 'There's a fire escape, isn't there?' My mind is racing. I will grab Daisy and go, find a way out of the back of the flats. We will run, hide. 'I'm sure I saw a fire escape. Where's the door? Show me.'

'It's on the landing,' says my mother. 'But, Trina, you can't go that way…'

I rush out onto the landing. A blind fierce panic seizes me: I will take my child and flee. The fire escape is behind some stacked boxes. I slip behind the boxes, push at the door. It's locked; I can't move it.

My mother follows me, helpless. 'Trina, they're coming now…'

A desperate rage fills me. I beat my fists on the door.

'Trina, they'll hear you…'

My hands hurt, and the wild mood leaves me. I hear their feet on the stairs. I follow my mother back into her flat. Despair overwhelms me. I see with a sudden terrible clarity just what I have done in running away with Daisy, in coming here: that I have confirmed their worst suspicions about me.

Daisy has her jacket on. She looks at me warily, nervous of my mood.

'Daisy.' I kneel down, wrap my arms around her. 'There are people coming. They're from the police. They want to speak to us.'

'Mum, why are you squeezing me like that? I can't breathe.'

'I think it's to do with that hospital—the one I told you about.'

'Oh,' she says. Her face is clouded, all this is unreal to her.

If they arrest me, I don't want her to see.

'Sweetheart, why don't you go and brush your hair. See if you can find the butterfly hairclip—it's in the bag somewhere…'

She goes to my mother's bedroom.

'Listen,' I tell my mother. 'I want to change my mind. About the money.'

At first, she doesn't know what I mean. She stares at me.

They are here. There are heavy footsteps, voices, on the landing, then someone bangs on the door. My mother turns; I grab her arm.

'No, please don't. Not yet. Leave them.'

'Trina, what can I do? I don't want my door kicked in.'

'The money,' I say again. 'The money you wanted to give me. I'm going to need it now.'

'Oh. Why didn't you say so?' She's looking anxiously at the door, but she gets her cheque book from the dresser. 'Just a moment,' she shouts towards the door. She writes a cheque, hands it to me. I stare, I'm amazed by how much it is.

'Thank you.'

'I was going to leave it to you,' she says. 'If, you know, anything happened... Trina, look, I'm going to open that door.'

There are two of them, a man and a woman, in brown and khaki uniforms. They walk straight in. They seem too big, too urgent, for the room. The man immediately places himself in front of the window, as though he thinks I might fling myself through. They ask in exact, evenly accented English for Daisy and Catriona Lydgate.

'I'm Catriona Lydgate,' I tell them.

It's hard to breathe, as though the room is filling up with water.

'We need to see Daisy Lydgate,' says the woman. 'Daisy is here?'

'Of course she's here. She's my daughter.'

'We need to see her, please. We have to send Daisy back to England. She has been made a ward of court. We have copies of the documents if you wish to see them. I need to see her now.'

I call her. She comes from the bedroom. I put my arm around her, afraid they will immediately take her from me.

'You are Daisy Lydgate?' she says.

Daisy nods. She looks much younger suddenly.

'Your police in England have asked me to find you,' she says. 'They want you to be in a special hospital in England.'

Daisy nods but doesn't speak. I feel how she presses into me.

They say they will take her to the airport and put her on the flight and that a social worker will meet her at Heathrow.

'I'm going with her,' I tell them.

They say they can take me to the airport along with Daisy, but first I should check if I can transfer my ticket. I am obsequiously grateful, though I know it's just that they want me out of the country.

My mother's telephone is in her bedroom. I ring the airport; it's arranged. And then I find Fergal's number, in my wallet. I can't work out what time it will be in England, whether he'll be picking Jamie up from school. It's his answering machine. I leave a message, tell him what has happened, and that we are coming back to England, and that I will need a solicitor.

I start to pack. They tell me to hurry. There's a crazy part of me that yearns to shout at them, to scream out that I am not a child abductor, that I am simply a mother trying to do her best for her child, that all this is so cruelly unjust. But I don't say these things, I just get on with the packing, sorting everything, putting Daisy's things in her hand luggage, so we won't have to reorganise it all at Heathrow.

The man and the woman sit at my mother's table. She offers them coffee but they refuse it. My mother is anxious, placating, her hands fluttering. She tries to make small talk, tries to tell them about Daisy, how happy she has been to see her grandchild at last. Do they have children? If they do they will surely understand… Mostly they ignore her.

I put our bags together in the hallway. The policeman pushes at the door.

My mother comes towards us.

'I need to say goodbye to my daughter,' she tells the policeman.

To my surprise, he shrugs.

She turns to me. We stand there for a moment. Awkward, not knowing whether to put our arms around each other.

'We never got to the Tiergarten, then,' says my mother.

'No, I'm sorry,' I say.

'Daisy would have loved it,' she says. 'A muffin and a rowing boat on the lake. We'll do it next time?'

'Yes. Of course we will.'

'And we'll go to the KaDeWe, where your teddy bear came from, Daisy. Everyone has to go to the KaDeWe. The toys are wonderful there: it's got a worldwide reputation.' Pride briefly fattens her voice. 'They had an animated display, when I went to buy your teddy bear. A cat that played the violin and a monkey on the drums. And we'll have some cake in the wintergarden and look out over the city.'

'That sounds lovely,' I say.

'We'll do it when you come again. We'll do it next time.'

'Yes,' I tell her. 'Next time.'

'There's so much to see here,' she says. 'You wouldn't believe how much.' She spreads it out before us like a magic carpet, this fantasy city. Her face seems briefly younger, more alive. 'This woman I know said she took her little boy to the Märkisches Museum, and in the garden at the back they found a family of bears. Just imagine that, Daisy. A family of bears.'

Daisy's eyes gleam.

'Real brown bears?' she says.

'Real bears,' says my mother. 'A family of bears. We'll go there when you come again. We'll go and see the bears.'

'Can we, Mum? Say we can.'

'Yes, of course,' I tell her.

There's a little silence. The policeman clears his throat.

'Well, then,' says my mother. She's run out of things to say, to keep us there. The tentative light goes out in her. It's as though she shrinks, withdraws into herself.

'I'm sorry that we had to leave like this,' I tell her.

She shrugs a little. 'Story of my life,' she says. 'I never was very lucky.'

She moves her hands apart, palms outwards, as though to show how empty they are.

'Don't think too badly of me, darling,' she says.

Daisy holds up her face and my mother kisses her cheek. I see again how the warmth that she can't quite manage with me comes easily with Daisy.

'Now, see you get yourself well, Daisy,' she says. 'Do that for me, won't you?'

Daisy says she will.

My mother straightens up. 'Well, no point in hanging about,' she says.

I put my hands on her shoulders. She pats my arms. We hold each other briefly. I smell her scent of Marlboros and lily of the valley.

'All right then,' she says.

The policeman opens the door. I pick up our bags and my mother follows us out onto the landing and presses the timer switch.

'You'd better be quick,' she says. 'You'll find the light won't last.'

On the plane, they give us seats together. Daisy seems exhausted: she slumps sideways into me, so I feel her warm weight against me. Soon after take-off she falls asleep. There are thunderstorms over Hanover and a lot of turbulence. The pilot warns us about this, says he's flying ten thousand feet lower to try and avoid the turbulence, but the plane still shudders and lurches and some of the passengers catch each other's eyes and raise an eyebrow and smile with a determined, bright bravado. But Daisy sleeps through everything, in the crook of my arm.

CHAPTER 39

She's waiting at passport control; I see her straight away. She must have seen a photograph—she's coming straight to us; she knows who we are. She's in her fifties, rather severe, with neat grey academic hair. She shakes hands, introduces herself. She says that she is from the Child Protection Unit, she has a copy of the order in her hand.

'So this must be Daisy?'

I nod.

She bends and says hello to Daisy.

Now it's really happening, I feel a kind of heavy hopelessness, everything weighing down on me, so I can scarcely move.

I kiss Daisy, bury my face in her hair.

'It won't be for long,' I tell her.

The woman takes her hand. Daisy's face is stiff, set. I see the struggle in her—how near to tears she is, and how afraid of crying in this public place.

'She'll be well looked-after,' says the woman brightly.

'When can I ring?'

'I should leave it till nine,' she says. 'Give her a little while to settle in.'

Daisy's eyes move from me to the woman and back again, widening. Suddenly, it's real to her. Her face crumples. She starts to sob, noisily. She snatches her hand away from the woman; she clings to me, she wraps herself around me. I can feel her whole body trembling.

'It's best if we just get on with this,' says the woman. She takes Daisy's hand again and pulls her away.

I watch as they go. Daisy's shoulders are shaking. I'm worried because the woman is letting Daisy carry the bag and it's too heavy for her. Perhaps I should go after them and tell her. I wait till they get to the corner, to see if Daisy will turn, but the woman is pulling at her and they don't stop walking. I stand there, staring after her. Long after they've gone from sight, the sound of her crying tears at me.

I take a taxi home. The driver is friendly, but I can't talk. The journey takes an age. The things I see seem remote, unreal, the streets, the lines of traffic, as though there's a wall of glass between me and the rest of the world.

We drive along the road by the park, and I start to think about Richard. I see us in the drawing room, Richard leaning against the mantelpiece, looking at me with that uncomprehending look, me trying to explain. Picturing him, I rummage around in my mind for my love for him, but somehow I can't find it. I work out what to say. I will tell him that I'm sorry if I frightened him. That maybe I acted in haste, but I felt I didn't have a choice. That I felt cornered, helpless. But that now I am quite determined to fight this diagnosis all the way, and I have found a solicitor, and, if he is still opposed, I shall instruct her myself, with my mother's money…

But when I get home, his car isn't there. It must have been raining: the tracks in the gravel where his car is normally parked are filled with water. There are no lights on in the house.

I pay the taxi driver and go to unlock the door. I half expect a smell of whisky to hit me, to find Richard sitting in darkness at the kitchen table, drunk and full of talk—half hope for this, because it might make it easier.

'Richard!'

There's no reply. I am so geared up for this confrontation, its absence unnerves me.

The little red light on the answering machine is flashing in the hall. I press Play. Nicky's voice. 'Hi, Cat. Just checking everything's OK. Ring me! Lots of love.'

Next, after the beep, a quick high-pitched cough. 'This

is Lauren Burns from Social Services for Catriona and Richard Lydgate.' Her voice is brisk and sibilant: it resonates in the emptiness of the hall. 'Just a reminder that the case conference on Daisy is tomorrow morning—at ten-thirty at the Infirmary, in the conference suite. I very much hope you'll both be able to make it.' I stop the machine for a moment and write the details down.

Then Gina. 'My dears, I was just wondering how things were. I trust you're over the worst with Daisy. Anyway—give me a ring.'

And at last the message I'm looking for. 'This is Meera Williams from Braisby and Jones, for Catriona. Listen, Catriona—I'm going to give you my home phone number. You can ring me any time this evening…'

Before I take off my jacket, I ring.

'Meera speaking.'

'This is Catriona.'

'Catriona. Excellent,' she says. There's warmth in her voice. 'Now, Fergal said a bit about what's been happening.'

I tell her about the case conference.

'Goodness. They were quick off the mark,' she says. 'I think I should come with you. How would it be if we meet up first, so you can fill me in?'

We agree to meet at nine-thirty next morning, in the hospital entrance.

And then there's nothing more to do. I take off my jacket and leave it where it falls. I have an unnerving sense of not quite being at home here, that if I called out, the voice of someone strange to me might reply. I don't go upstairs: I can't bear to pass Daisy's door, to see all the things that will make me feel her absence still more vividly. The scene at the airport plays out again and again in my head—her face collapsing, the sound of her crying, the woman pulling her away. Wanting her is a physical thing, like a constant ache or hunger. I can still smell the scent of her hair.

I go into the living room. It's been tidied since I left. The paeonies that I'd kept there though they were dripping petals have all been cleared away. In the evening light, the room has a tenuous quality, as though it might dissolve, or blend into something else entirely. Like a room in a dream, where you're wandering through some vast house, looking for some indeterminate thing you think you've lost or forgotten, moving through many interconnecting rooms, not knowing how big this place is or what its boundaries are or who it belongs to; whether it is yours, why you are there at all. The white mask gleams in the remnants of the light; the black one seems to draw back into the shadow, so you can't quite make out whether there's a face there. I see exactly why Daisy's friends used to find them so frightening.

I'm far too anxious to rest here. I wander through to the kitchen. Things have been put away, but not in their usual places. It takes me a while to find the coffee, which is not in the cupboard where I always keep it. I wait for the kettle to boil, resting my hands on the sill. Outside, the garden is just as it was when we went, in all its summer sprawl and lavishness: the amber roses opening, the flowers loosening, easing apart, and the poppies bright as carnival in the herbaceous border. You can just make out the shape of the stone frog through the blue of the irises. Somehow this surprises me, that all is as it was: I realise I expected everything to be further on, some things over and dying, new things opening out, as though we'd been away for many days. Long braided shadows reach across the grass, and the sky is the colour of cornflowers. A fox moves out from the pool of black under the birch tree. He's still for a moment, poised, his sharp sad face angled towards me in the window: staring at the house then turning away, as if he can't find what he's looking for, and sidling off into the intricate dark at the back of the border.

There is no reason to stay. My bag, still packed, is in the hall. I don't know if I'll need it but I take it anyway. I pick up the bag and my jacket and go out to my car.

He answers the doorbell at once, as though he is expecting me.

The words tumble out. 'Richard isn't at home and Daisy's in the unit and I didn't know where to go…'

He reaches out and puts his arms round me. I rest my head on his shoulder.

He takes me through to the back room. Jazz is playing and through the open window you can smell the rich night scents of the gardens.

'Did you speak to Meera?' he says, before I've sat down.

'Yes. She seemed good. Thank you. There's a case conference tomorrow.'

'And Daisy? Have you rung to see how Daisy is?'

'Not yet.'

'Ring them now,' he says.

'They said not to ring till nine.'

'I think you should do it now.'

He brings me the phone.

A woman answers. I explain who I am. She seems surprised I've rung.

'Oh. I'll get someone,' she says.

A man comes to the phone—he says he is Terence, a charge nurse. His voice is soft, deliberate. He is Daisy's key worker, he says. I try to imagine him, this soft-voiced Terence, this stranger, who is now my daughter's main care-giver—try not to immediately hate him. He answers all my questions with a rather exaggerated patience. Yes, Daisy is asleep now. No, she was a bit too tired to eat anything. Well, she seemed OK, perhaps a bit subdued, but I must appreciate that children do take a while to settle. I say to tell her I'm thinking about her all the time.

'There's nothing more you can do,' says Fergal. 'Not for today.'

'No.' I lean back on the sofa, slip off my shoes. I am exhausted but restless.

He brings me wine and sits in the chair opposite me.

'So tell me,' he says.

I tell him the story of what has happened. About my mother, and what I learned about my father. About the police, about Daisy being taken away. He listens, doesn't say much. Sometimes he nods a little.

When I've finished we sit in silence for a moment.

'You look different,' he says.

'Is that good, I wonder?'

He smiles, but doesn't reply.

It's getting darker: outside, a yellow moon is rising over the gardens. The moon has a pattern on it; you can see why, when you were a child, you half believed there was a face there. It's soothing, sitting there in the quiet darkening room. I feel that I can breathe now.

He turns on a table-lamp. In its amber light I notice things about him—the line of his jaw, accentuated by shadow, his rather square hands and bitten fingernails. When he looks at me, his eyes lingering on me, I feel that I am being told a secret.

The wine slides warmly into my veins.

'I feel as though I've been away for years,' I tell him. 'When I got back to the house, it was strange—as though I hadn't been there for ages. Almost as though it wasn't mine any more…'

I yawn. A great weariness overwhelms me.

He's looking at his hands.

'You can stay if you like,' he says. 'You don't have to go back there and be on your own.'

I don't know what to say.

'I mean, whatever you want,' he says.

I look away from him. I'm scared to sleep with him. And I see it isn't the thought of Richard that stops me—

as though my connection with him has become too tenuous, too frayed, for this to matter, and this shocks me. The fear is a deeper, more primeval thing—some superstitious sense of justice—that if I make love to Fergal I won't get Daisy back.

'Look,' he says, reading my mind, 'the bed's made up in the spare room.'

'Yes. That would be best probably.'

But when I get up, I go to him, reach out, moving my hands across his face, his head, like somebody blind, learning about him. He wraps himself around me. I press my mouth into his, closing my eyes.

In the little whitewashed spare room, under the People Tree bedspread, I think at first that I will be awake for ever. But something has been soothed in me, and I slip down rapidly into sleep. In my dream I am walking the cobbled streets of Prenzlauer Berg in the dappled afternoon, and I pass the greying block where the stucco is peeled away, revealing the naked brick, and I see the little girl high up on the balcony by the empty birdcage, the girl in the taffeta dress; and in my dream she seems to look like Daisy. I wave but she doesn't seem to see me; she is looking away. I try to call but no sound comes, and she turns and goes back into the darkness of the house, leaving me desolate.

C H A P T E R **40**

In the morning, Fergal wakes me with coffee.

Before I go to the case conference, I ring the number that he has, the doctor at Great Ormond Street. I speak to the doctor's secretary; I explain that we need a second opinion, half expecting that she will say this is impossible. But she makes a provisional appointment, as though my request is the most natural thing. All she will need, she says, is a letter from Daisy's GP.

Then I ring the Jennifer Norton Unit and ask to speak to Daisy. A different person comes to the phone, a woman. Terence is off till twelve, she tells me, and Daisy is eating her breakfast, she doesn't want to disturb her. I feel a little flare of rage, but there's nothing I can do. She agrees to give Daisy my love.

I drive to the hospital through the clear bright day. Heat lies across the car park in pools of glimmering haze.

A woman comes up to me in the entrance. She has baggy purple trousers and gentle eyes and riotous dark hair.

'Catriona?'

I nod.

'I'm Meera.' Her whole face creases as she smiles. 'I thought it must be you.'

She looks more like an infant teacher than a solicitor. I immediately like her.

'I guess we need to pitch straight in,' she says.

We sit in Outpatients' reception and she opens up her briefcase.

'OK,' she says. 'You'd better tell me.'

She listens mostly in silence, frowning a little, her dark eyes resting on me. She takes notes with a biro that's been comprehensively chewed. As I talk her frown deepens. When I've finished, she sits for a moment, biting the end of her pen.

'So today, at the conference, what would be a result for you?'

'I want to take Daisy home.'

'That's the thing that matters more than anything?'

'Yes.'

'You see,' she says, 'because of the wardship we won't

be able to undo it all at once, and they may well want to make Daisy the subject of a child protection plan.'

'What does that mean?'

'It's for children believed to be at risk. Really, if a professional has worries that a child is being neglected or abused, a child protection plan would be made pretty automatically. It means you'd have regular social work visits. I don't think we can avoid that—'

'But she isn't—'

'I know.' She puts her hand on my arm. 'Catriona, I know. But we need to focus on what we can achieve today.'

'OK. As long as I can take her home.'

'Catriona.' She looks at me, her head on one side. Her eyes are harder suddenly, penetrating. 'You've got to tell them exactly what's happened with you and Daisy—how you see it. I'll back you up, of course, but it's best if it comes from you. Can you do that?'

'Yes. I think so.'

'What you say will go in the conference notes, that's very important. It's your chance to tell your story—to have it written down. Don't worry about trying to say the right thing, or how you might be seen. You mustn't think you can help Daisy by being polite and quiet. You've got to speak out. D'you think you can do that?'

My mother is there in my mind, with all her lies and evasions, the discarded photograph, the things she wouldn't say. And I see how costly my own secrecy has been, the secrecy I learnt from her, all my attempts at concealment—the burnt letter, hiding my history. How my silences have not protected me, not protected Daisy.

'Yes. I think I can.'

I glance over her shoulder. I start. Richard is there, the distinctive outline of his back, his shoulders. My confidence seeps away. I'm shocked to see him; I never imagined him being here this morning. Yet of course he would have got the message from Lauren Burns, would know what was happening. He's walking away from me.

'Richard.'

He doesn't seem to hear.

I call his name again. People stare.

He turns, nods, comes to us. He doesn't seem surprised. It enters my mind that he knew already that I was here with Meera—that he saw as he came in and just walked on. I notice his shirt is crumpled.

'Where were you?' I say. 'I went back to the house, I couldn't find you. You'd just disappeared…'

'I might say the same of you,' he says drily. He looks quizzically at Meera. 'And this is…?'

I do the introductions, stumbling over the words, furtive, uncertain, as though I am guilty of some crime. He raises one eyebrow a little, but shakes Meera's hand with elaborate politeness.

Meera closes her briefcase.

'I guess it's time we got going,' she says, with a tentative smile. 'I know the way to the conference room. I'll show you.'

We walk there awkwardly, the three of us together, down a corridor that smells of antiseptic, Richard, who is always so good with strangers, talking lightly about the weather.

CHAPTER 41

It's one of those featureless hospital rooms, with neutral walls and grey acrylic carpet; it's chilly with air-conditioning. Dr Carey is there, looking flushed and anxious, and Jane Watson, in a black linen dress with a slit in the side of the skirt, and Dr McGuire, with his sleeves rolled up. He doesn't look at me. A man with earnest glasses comes and shakes my hand. He says he is Phil Hardy, and he will be chairing the meeting.

There's a table down the middle, and upright chairs with padded seats arranged around the table. I sit where there are two empty chairs together, and Meera sits beside me. Richard takes the remaining spare chair on the other side of the circle.

'We need to introduce ourselves,' says Phil. 'I imagine we'll all be happy with Christian names?'

There's a murmur of assent.

We go round the circle and people say who they are. Next to Phil there is a woman in a dress patterned with poppies who is an administrative assistant; she will be taking the notes. There are people who are new to me: a solicitor from the Civic Centre; a policewoman from the Child Protection Unit; a social worker with pulled-back hair and a practised expression of concern—she says her name is Lauren Burns and, turning to me, that she will be key worker on the case. So now it seems we are a case— Daisy and Richard and me. And there's a man with a sparse, sandy beard and perpetual slight frown, who says he is from the Jennifer Norton Unit. I study his face, try to read him. I want to press him with questions—How is she? Tell me, tell me everything. Did she eat any breakfast? Has she cried? But I know too well just how that would be seen.

It's Meera's turn. 'I'm Meera Williams, solicitor. I'm representing Catriona.'

'Not both parents—just Catriona?' says Phil Hardy.

She nods.

'OK,' he says. He glances round the circle. 'Right. Daisy Lydgate.'

People shuffle and settle and open their folders out on the table. Through the wide window behind him, there's a blue glare of sky. My heart pounds.

'Just to briefly summarise where we are now. I gather that a period of inpatient assessment in the Jennifer Norton Unit was recommended for Daisy, and that it was made clear to the parents that legal action might be taken if they refused to have Daisy assessed. I believe it was Catriona, not Richard, who objected to this course of action. That Richard was happy for Daisy to be admitted?'

Richard leans forward. 'That's correct,' he says. Even he seems nervous here: he's restless, shifting in his seat and smoothing back his hair.

'As most of you will be aware,' Phil Hardy goes on, 'Catriona then took Daisy out of the country. Richard was concerned for Daisy's safety and contacted Jane Watson. Jane immediately rang us. We had Daisy made a ward of court, which enabled us to bring her back to the UK. Daisy was then admitted to the Jennifer Norton Unit. Our purpose today is to establish a course of action for the future, and in particular to decide how far we consider Daisy to be at risk.' He turns to Dr Carey. 'I'd like to start with you, Geraldine—as the person whose involvement with the family goes back furthest.'

Dr Carey shuffles the papers in front of her. 'I've been with the practice for six months. According to the notes, in the past Daisy has attended surgery with the normal childhood illnesses.'

'Who usually brought her?' says Phil.

'Always her mother,' says Dr Carey. Nervous blotches flower across her neck. 'In January, Catriona brought Daisy complaining of a flu-like illness. This was the first time I'd met Daisy and her mother. I was worried about Daisy's weight, which was on the lowest percentile. I did suggest that Catriona might like some advice on appropriate diet—I felt she wasn't giving Daisy enough protein—but she refused to see our nutritionist.'

I'm cold, so cold: the little hairs stand up along my arms.

Dr Carey carries on. 'Catriona was also resistant to the idea that Daisy's illness might be psychological in origin.'

'Why did you think that yourself?' says Phil. 'That it might be psychological?'

'There wasn't any obvious pathology, and Daisy looked unhappy. As you will know, stress is a huge factor in the illnesses we see in the surgery. I did all the usual blood tests, and referred her to Graham McGuire.'

She looks up and aims a slightly obsequious smile in Dr McGuire's direction.

'Thank you,' says Phil. 'So, Graham, could you tell us about your involvement?'

Dr McGuire opens up the file on the table in front of him. 'I saw Daisy and her parents twice, in my paediatric outpatient clinic,' he says. 'The mother said Daisy was suffering from nausea, stomach pains and joint pains. I began by investigating physically. There were very few positive findings. Her blood tests were all normal apart from a rather high IgE, suggesting a possibility of allergy. A barium meal showed she had reflux. In spite of the complaint of joint pains, there were no arthritic changes at X-ray.' He leans forward as though confiding, his angular hands clasped together on top of Daisy's file. 'But

I did have great concerns about the mother's attitude. She seemed extremely overprotective towards her daughter, she had failed to comply with the treatment, and when I suggested there might be psychological reasons for Daisy's illness and recommended a psychiatric referral, the mother became quite belligerent, which I found worrying.'

To my surprise, Phil Hardy turns to me. 'Catriona, d'you want to respond?'

The room is suddenly vast: the edges of things seem sharp and far away.

'Yes, it's true I was angry.' I think what Meera said, I'm trying to speak boldly, but my voice sounds thin to me, like the voice of a child. 'I thought that Dr McGuire wasn't taking her illness seriously.'

But Dr McGuire moves on as though he hasn't heard.

'The mother's attitude and the shifting and elusive nature of Daisy's symptoms led me to believe that a diagnosis of MSBP or fabricated illness was one of the possibilities we should be considering here,' he says.

Meera raises her hand. 'If I could comment, Phil, at this point? What worries me is that a diagnosis with such serious implications was being suggested at this early stage.'

I see Phil nodding slightly.

'Could I just briefly ask you, Geraldine, as Daisy's GP,' Meera goes on, 'whether you at any point informed Catriona that she had a right to a second opinion on Daisy's illness?'

'Not as such,' says Dr Carey.

'So Catriona was unaware that that was her right?'

'I can't answer that,' says Dr Carey.

The woman in the flowered dress is writing all this down.

'Now, in spite of Catriona's reluctance,' says Phil, 'Daisy and her parents were in fact referred to Jane Watson. Jane, could you tell us what you found?'

Jane Watson nods. She's on the other side of the circle, but even from here I can smell her sandalwood scent. 'As you know, Graham and I work very closely together.' A brief, vivid smile in Dr McGuire's direction. 'I decided, in view of Graham's concerns, to work with the parents, without Daisy. I saw Catriona and Richard for three sessions. I found Richard quite responsive, but Catriona…' Her eyes that are green as leaves rest on my face for a moment and slide away. 'It's perhaps easiest if I read out some comments I made in my report.' She takes a sheet from her folder and glances down. Sunlight falls on the paper in front of her, so it looks white, blank, as though the words are erased. She coughs slightly. '"Mrs Lydgate is highly personable and appears co-operative and smiles frequently,"' she reads. '"However, I find her evasive and distanced from her feelings. Also, she has chosen to hide certain salient facts from me, about her childhood and background, and I find this secrecy highly worrying."'

'What facts were these?' says Phil.

'Most notably, the fact that at thirteen she was abandoned by her mother and spent the years from ages thirteen to sixteen in a local authority children's home, which is of course exactly the kind of childhood history that can lead to dysfunctions of parenting. Because of this evasiveness, I was forced to conclude that Graham was right to be worried about this family, and to take seriously the possibility of some maternal factor in Daisy's illness.'

Phil turns to me. 'Catriona, d'you have any comments?' he says.

I clear my throat. 'I read about Münchausen's in a book I bought.'

It sounds naïve. I think that people may laugh.

He nods and says, 'Go on.'

'It said parents who caused their children's illnesses had often themselves been in Care.' My mouth is dry; the words are hard to form. 'I was very frightened about what was going to happen to Daisy. I didn't want to tell Jane about The Poplars because I was worried what she might think if she knew.'

'Thank you,' says Phil. He turns back to Jane Watson. 'So, how did your sessions conclude?'

'In our final session, I told them my recommendation.'

'Which was a period of assessment in the Jennifer Norton?'

'Exactly,' says Jane Watson.

'I'd like to know how Daisy's parents reacted,' says Phil. 'Richard, we haven't heard from you on this.'

Richard clears his throat. Again that nervous gesture, smoothing back his hair.

'What Jane was saying made sense to me at the time.'

His voice is guarded, careful, but I note the past tense

and feel a surge of hope—that he has changed his mind, in spite of everything; that he is on my side.

'But you objected, Catriona?' says Phil.

'Yes,' I tell him. 'I thought it was all wrong for Daisy. I felt she'd be unhappy among strangers, especially as she's ill. It isn't what she needs. What Daisy needs is for someone to find out what's wrong.'

Phil turns to the man from the Jennifer Norton Unit. 'Finally, Paul, can you tell us about your observations of Daisy since she's been with you?'

'Obviously it's early days,' he says. His voice is tentative, full of a studied empathy; I remember such voices from childhood. 'She seems to display quite a lot of illness behaviour, especially around mealtimes. It's our policy in the unit to be quite brisk about such things...'

I feel a flicker of fear, about what they are doing to Daisy.

'We've noticed too,' he says, 'that she does seem quite distressed, but she's also rather inhibited and can't say why she's upset. And we're wondering why it's so hard for her to make her feelings known. How far this is to do with troubled family relationships—just what is going on here.'

There's silence for a moment.

I have Meera's words in my head. I make myself look round at them, at Dr McGuire, Jane Watson, Dr Carey: at their faces, still, intent, all looking straight at me. I speak into the silence, fighting for Daisy.

'I want you to tell me something.' My words fall into the stillness like pebbles into water, irrevocable. 'There's something I don't understand, that nobody ever explains. Exactly what do you think I've done to Daisy?'

The surprise in the room is like a tremor of air on my skin. I have said something that was not meant to be said.

Phil gestures towards Dr McGuire. 'Graham, perhaps you could answer that for us,' he says.

'A diagnosis of MSBP covers a number of different categories,' says Dr McGuire. He speaks to Phil; he never looks at me. 'For instance, there have been cases where parents have removed feeding tubes or put poison in their children's food or tried to suffocate their children.'

'But what you're describing is child abuse,' says Meera. 'And surely no one has ever suggested my client is guilty of any of those things?'

'If I could continue…' Dr McGuire goes on.

'I'd like you to answer Meera's question,' says Phil.

Dr McGuire is tapping a finger on the table. 'No one is suggesting at this stage that Mrs Lydgate has done anything like that. But there have also been cases where women have fed allergenic children with allergens, or have fabricated symptoms in order to put their children through unnecessary medical procedures.'

'So, can I be quite clear?' says Meera. 'Is this what you suspect Catriona of doing?'

'Something along those lines—that or emotional abuse. Those are our concerns,' he says.

Phil is frowning. 'I have to say,' he says, 'this all seems rather vague.'

'The fact remains,' says Dr McGuire, 'that when I first

saw Daisy, Mrs Lydgate's behaviour greatly concerned me, and I immediately wondered about some form of MSBP or fabricated illness.'

Something has shifted; I know this. It's there in the doubtful look on Phil's face, and in the way Dr McGuire is talking—rapid, over-emphatic.

'I'm aware this may seem a surprising diagnosis. But we know that these things happen; we have to be alert for them. And sometimes all you have is a hunch—a few clues. You have to listen to that. The life of a child may be at stake.' He speaks with passion; on his forehead there's a sheen of sweat. 'I am,' he says, 'always and absolutely on the side of the child. This is my duty—not to avoid uncomfortable facts, not to avoid the truth, however shocking or painful. Parents have all the power. Children need someone to be unequivocally on their side. And if there is a suspicion that a parent might be in any way harming a child or impairing a child's development, then my over-arching priority is to protect that child. That comes before everything.'

I turn to him. 'I know this. I know you have to take this into account—that terrible things happen, that there are cruel parents.' I take a deep breath. 'I spent three years in a children's home—how could I not know? But that has absolutely nothing to do with Daisy.'

He tries to interrupt. But Phil is looking at me; he's nodding slightly. This gives me strength; my voice is confident and clear.

'Daisy's ill, and all I have ever wanted is to get her well

again. But whatever I try, it's twisted and held against me. If I even bring a list of her symptoms to the clinic, that's proof that I'm overprotective, as though it's my worry about her that's actually making her ill. But I love my child, and everything I've done has been to try and make her well.'

When I've spoken, it's quiet, and fear floods me: that perhaps I have been too bold and destroyed everything.

'Catriona,' says Phil then. 'Perhaps you could tell us why you feel so sure that Daisy's illness has a physical origin?'

'I learnt in Berlin that my father had similar symptoms,' I tell him. 'That's made me still more certain—that whatever is wrong with her, it's something that's inherited.'

'Right,' says Phil. 'Well, that definitely sounds like something to pursue. Does anyone want to comment?'

'I've one thing to add,' says Meera. 'We've talked about the need to get a second opinion. I'd like to make clear that Catriona is now in a position to get that opinion.'

'Excellent,' says Phil. 'OK. I think it's time to tie all this up and decide where we go from here.'

My heart thuds. I try to read his face but his expression is opaque.

'Now, I have to say that in view of the concerns that have been expressed here, we have no choice but to make Daisy the subject of a child protection plan—at least till we're more certain where we stand.'

The cold is right inside me.

'But I also want to say,' he goes on, 'that from what we have heard today there is no clear evidence to suggest

Daisy is in danger in her mother's care—nothing that could possibly stand up in a court of law. And I don't think we have any grounds for keeping Daisy in the Jennifer Norton Unit against the express wishes of her mother. Obviously the judge will need to be informed, but unless the hospital is a designated place of safety under the conditions of wardship, which I don't think it is—' the solicitor from the Civic Centre nods '—I don't see any problem with discharging her. But I do need to check out with you, Richard, if you'd have any objection?'

Richard shakes his head.

'Right, then,' says Phil. 'We'll need to do a core assessment, and Lauren will visit weekly while that's being carried out. You should all get notes within forty-eight hours. And I'd like to reconvene in three weeks, by which time hopefully we'll have the second opinion. Are there any comments?'

Meera puts her hand on my wrist. 'Are you OK with that?'

I nod.

She turns to Phil. 'I think the social work visits are regrettable and unnecessary, but my client will accept them.'

Dr McGuire frowns. 'I'd like to put my reservations on record,' he says. 'Though of course I have no choice but to go along with the conference decision.'

Phil turns to me. 'How soon do you want to fetch Daisy?'

'Now,' I say. 'I want to fetch her now.'

He says he'll ring the unit straight away.

My eyes meet Richard's and he smiles and a warmth

of relief washes through me. And I think how everything is put right now, how it will all be healed: how Daisy is given back to us and she will be diagnosed and treated and we will all live together happily in the house that I love. I think how stupid I've been, to be so afraid, to feel it was all so fragile, that it could fall apart. My passion for Fergal shames me. I push it away from me, think how it was just a temporary thing, an aberration, mistaking friendship and transient attraction for something solid and real. It's my life with Richard I want: the life that plays out in front of me now, in all its vivid precision. I see us at the dining table, enjoying something lavish that I've cooked for Sunday lunch, Daisy eating greedily, healthily, all of us laughing at some story of Sinead's; or in the living room in the evening, just Richard and me together in a companionable silence, with a fire in our grate and our plum-coloured curtains drawn against the dark. All these things are there in the tumbling kaleidoscope of my imaginings, in the time it takes for him to make his way round the table towards me, weaving between the other people, who are gathering up their folders and putting on their jackets and who suddenly don't matter any more. It's this that I want, that I have always wanted. For Daisy to be well and all of us living together in our wide rooms full of sunlight and the smells of flowers and spices: a fortunate life, secure within the thickness of our walls.

CHAPTER 42

'Happy?' he says.

I nod. 'I'm going to get her.'

'Come and have coffee,' he says. 'She won't be ready straight away. Phil's got to ring them and everything. And there's sure to be paperwork to do at the other end.' He's talking rather rapidly. 'There's a machine in the corridor.'

He has his hand on my shoulder.

There's a drinks machine and a snack machine. He gets coffee for both of us. We watch silently as the liquid spatters into the plastic cups. The coffee is covered with bubbles that taste of water and a little indeterminate bitterness.

'I didn't have any breakfast.' I fumble in my bag for a coin.

'I've got plenty of change,' he says.

He buys me a Twix. I fold the paper down and take a bite. My hands are warm and the chocolate is sticky already.

He glances at me, then away. He's smoothing back his hair.

'There's something I have to tell you,' he says.

I stand there, the coffee in one hand, the melting Twix in the other. There's something about his voice, a tremor he can't control. This scares me.

'Not now, Richard. Surely it can wait.' I want to push all this away, not let it happen. 'Really, I need to go. Daisy needs me.'

'I want to tell you now,' he says.

And I know he is going to say what he has to say. I see the shadowed house, the murky water, the windmills turning in a shiver of wind.

He isn't looking at me. A nervous, mirthless smile flickers across his face. 'I mean, there's no good way of saying this, so I might as well get straight to the point— but I'm moving out,' he says.

I stare at him. He thinks I don't understand.

'I'm telling you I'm leaving you, Catriona.'

My heart lurches, my mouth dries up. Everything falls apart in front of me, our life together, the children, our house, our garden, our holidays and Christmases and all the hopes I had. I see all these losses passing dizzyingly before me.

'Are you all right?' he says.

I shake my head.

'You can't be surprised,' he says.

'No, I'm not surprised.'

But I put out a hand to steady myself. Now it's actually happening, it takes my breath away, this unravelling of all these intimate entanglements—so rapidly and completely, in a bland corridor, over a plastic cup of bitter coffee.

'I think it's for the best,' he says.

'Best for who?'

He doesn't reply. His silence enrages me.

'How can you do this? *Now?* When everything's so difficult? When all this is happening with Daisy?'

'We can't carry on,' he says. 'You know that.' Quite cool, as though he's recovered his composure, now he's told me. As though this is all fact—like a weather forecast or a tax statement. 'After the things you've done. I mean, how could I ever trust you? We can't possibly live together any more. I'd have thought that was blindingly obvious.'

I swallow hard. 'I know I shouldn't have taken her—I know that. But I couldn't bear her going to that place, I felt I didn't have a choice.' I'm fighting now, striving to pull us back from the brink. 'I'm sorry if I frightened you.'

'It's a bit late for that, isn't it?' he says.

I want to touch him—to put my hand on his, remind him that once he loved me, make him understand—but my hands are full with the coffee and Twix and I can't work out how to do it.

'Please, Richard—if you have to go… Surely it doesn't have to be now. Can't we just kind of stay together for a bit—now we've got Daisy back?' My voice is steadier now; it's all very rational, a business proposition. 'We can work together on this, we won't be pulling against each other anymore. We know what we're doing, I've found a doctor who could help her. Don't go now. We could lead separate lives if you want. But just to keep that safety for the children…'

He hears me out but he doesn't respond, except to shake his head.

'It's not the right time, Richard.'

I drop the Twix on the window sill, put my hand on his arm. He stiffens and pulls away. I see I've marked the sleeve of his suit with chocolate.

'I'll want Sinead, of course,' he says. 'Once we've worked everything out. But for the moment she'll have to stay with you.' He's looking into his coffee cup. 'There isn't room at Francine's.'

'Francine's?'

'You heard.'

'So…how long exactly?'

'We've been close for a while,' he says, as though this is the most routine thing in the world.

I hear a voice in my head, quite clearly: my mother's voice, nicotine-stained, full of self-justification, talking about my father and how he left her. 'I have to say he could have chosen better when he left… Well, she was there…conveniently to hand…' I feel a sense of overwhelming weariness.

He takes a little card from his pocket. It has her address, all ready for this moment, written in purple pen, in writing I don't recognise. That seems cruel to me, that he didn't take the time to do it himself, that it's written in her writing. I take the postcard, vaguely register an address in Twickenham. I put the card in my handbag.

'There's something I need to know,' I say. Slowly, struggling with it. 'Everything was fine till Daisy got ill. Wasn't it? I just want to know, to get clear about this in my head. It would be hard for anyone, what we've been through—hard for any couple to cope with. But we were all right till Daisy got ill. Weren't we?'

He doesn't reply.

The Jennifer Norton Unit is on an old site that's now largely disused. I drive round the perimeter road. There are separate blocks like big houses with patches of grass and empty car parks between them. Most of the blocks look Victorian; they are built of brick, now blackened, with cupolas and gables. When they were built, I guess the style of them looked Italianate, elegant—but now it inevitably suggests an asylum. Nothing much seems to happen here. I pass one or two outpatient clinics, and signs to an eye unit and to Adult Psychology. The chapel is boarded up. Some of the windows I pass have children's tissue-paper pictures still Sellotaped to the glass, but the windows open onto empty rooms.

I follow the signs to the Jennifer Norton, down a drive between ragged verges. It's another Victorian building, drab in spite of the coloured curtains at the upstairs windows, with peeling window frames and neglected ivies in wan pots by the door. To the side there is a play area, enclosed within wire-mesh fencing, with a park bench and some footballs and grass that hasn't been mown.

The door is locked. I ring the bell. The door is opened by a young woman with a label on her lapel that says Receptionist. She has very long purple fingernails with a pattern on.

I say I've come for Daisy. I have to sign in, and to give my car registration number. She indicates the chairs in the waiting area. I don't sit down.

'I want to see her now,' I say. 'There's been a case conference. I can take her home.'

'I'll get someone,' she says, a little wearily.

A charge nurse comes. He says he is Terence. He's fifty-ish, in a cardigan, smelling of oversweet aftershave.

'I'm Mrs Lydgate. I've come for Daisy.'

'Ah. Yes,' he says. 'We heard the conference decision.' He looks me up and down; he doesn't smile.

'I've come to take her home. I want to see her now.'

'I understand,' he says. 'I'll just get everything organised.'

I sit on one of the chairs. Silence falls over me like a blanket. I think how I hate all waiting rooms, their rubber plants, worn toys, goldfish, out-of-date copies of *Prima*, their thick muffling heat, the fear I feel in them. Through the open door beside the reception desk I can see a corridor, stairs to the dormitories, a plasterboard partition, a fire door. The silence is briefly broken by a sudden screaming shout from down the corridor, a high girl's voice, a fusillade of swearing. 'You fucking bitch, you fucking—' abruptly cut off as somebody shuts a door. The receptionist studies her fingernails intently. Silence falls again.

Panic grows in me, a fierce unreasoning panic that Daisy has disappeared. That she is lost or has run away, that they can't find her. I see her on that afternoon in the New Forest when she was two or three, running and running, my fear that she would be taken from me, that she might vanish in the brightness of the light.

I can't sit still. I go to the receptionist.

'Why is it taking so long?'

She looks at me pityingly.

'We do have a discharge procedure, you know,' she says. 'We have to go through the proper procedures. We can't cut the corners just because someone's in a hurry.'

I sit down again. I flick through a magazine, seeing nothing. Waiting there unprotesting is one of the hardest things that I have done.

There are footsteps. I turn. Daisy is there with the charge nurse in the cardigan.

I put out my arms, but it's not as I expected. She comes towards me, but her face is set. I put my arms around her; she turns her head away from me. I see the charge nurse watching this, as though he is noting it down.

I take her bag. 'Have you got everything, sweetheart?' It's just a meaningless question to get us out of here.

She nods.

'OK, young lady,' says the charge nurse to Daisy. He ruffles her hair. 'Well, let's just hope we're doing the right thing for you.' She doesn't say anything. 'Bye, then, Daisy. See you again, maybe.'

I take her hand and go.

We don't speak on the way back to the car. I can tell how tired she is; her hand is limp and cold.

As we drive out between the unkempt verges I look in the mirror. She's staring unseeing out of the window; her face is white, stiff.

'Sweetheart, I'm so happy to have you back.'

She makes a little noise in her throat.

'I've missed you so terribly,' I tell her.

I watch her in the mirror. She still has that stiff look, but she's turned towards me. Her eyes are fixed on my eyes in the mirror.

'Daisy, talk to me. I know you're cross…'

Her eyes blaze at me. 'Why did you let me go there, Mum?' Her face is fierce with anger. 'You shouldn't have let me go there. It was horrible.' The words tumbling out now. 'I didn't sleep at all. There was this girl who kept shouting and shouting—she wouldn't shut up. *And* they made me eat cornflakes. I felt so sick. You shouldn't have let them take me. You should have stopped them.'

It hurts.

I brake the car, there in the road, turn round to face her. I reach out my hands to her.

She resists, but only for a moment. Then she wrenches off her seat belt and starts to cry and falls into my arms.

CHAPTER 43

It's hot in the hospital, far too hot for sleep. My bed is by the window; I push the curtain aside and open the window a little, trying to be quiet, though Daisy, under her sheet with its pattern of red giraffes, shows little sign of waking. Her arm is flung out over the top of the sheet. You can see the canula in her wrist, through which some of her medicine is given. It was put in by a cheerful male nurse called Jason, who wore a Wall-E T-shirt under his white coat, and kept up an easy flow of talk right through the procedure. 'Look, it's a little man, this is his bed,' he said, tucking the cotton wool under the tap on the canula. It was suited, really, to a much younger child, but it distracted her; it did what was needed.

Our room looks over an inner courtyard of the hospital, which is full of the flues and pipes of the heating and air-conditioning system. As I push the window open the sound of it roars at me. I think the noise will wake her, but she doesn't stir. In the dim light from the corridor that comes through the curtained window in our door, you can make out the shapes of things in this little room, though the colour is taken from everything; it's shades of brown, like an old photograph. The ward is divided into these rooms, each with a high metal bed for the child and a fold-out bed for the parent. On one side of us there's an Afghani woman and her toddler, on the other an older man with a pallid teenage son. There's a television in our room, and labelled bins for different kinds of rubbish, and a basin with pink Hibiscrub, which has a wholesome smell and dries your skin. Down the corridor there is a kitchen, with snacks for parents, and some of the foods that children can have before a colonoscopy—jelly, juice, ice lollies. When we came here, the day before yesterday, Jason told me apologetically that they seemed to be clean out of lollies. You could get them, he said, from a newsagent's down the street. This surprised me, somehow, that the outside world was so near you could bring a lolly back without it melting. This place feels cloistered, apart—as though its walls are thick as the walls of castles, as though you'd have to cross a moat, a drawbridge, to come here.

* * *

Daisy turns in her bed but she doesn't open her eyes. She's still sedated by the drug she took for the investigation yesterday: it's meant to tranquillise you and help you forget what happened. I was worried they wouldn't be able to get it into her, but they're good at helping her with medicine here. They put the spoon at the back of her tongue and talk her through it with such patience. It takes an age but some of it stays down.

They let me go with her to the endoscopy suite. There were six of them in their blue surgical suits—several doctors, and Annie the nurse manager, and the consultant, a tall, quiet man with a shock of wild white hair. They sprayed Daisy's throat with an anaesthetic spray. The endoscopy tube had a fibre optic torch at the end, many-coloured and glittery. I was told to sit by the wall to start with. You can imagine that parents might find it too upsetting to watch the tube go down. I carefully didn't look at Daisy, just watched the television screen, the film of her digestive tract. It was the strangest thing, this journey through the body of my child. When they'd finished the endoscopy, the consultant said that was great, her stomach and oesophagus were completely normal, and did I want to sit closer and hold her hand for the second part, the colonoscopy. I moved my chair and I sat by Daisy's bed and stroked her hair. Daisy moaned and protested but you couldn't make out the words. Annie soothed her; the doctors talked together.

'I can't get into there.'

'No. Well, you're going backwards now…'

Afterwards, Annie came back with us and settled Daisy in bed. Daisy scarcely stirred.

'We did so well today,' said Annie, folding Daisy's sheet neatly under her chin. 'Well, I always say we, really it's them, of course, we don't have to go through it… She'll have a nice long sleep now—she'll be absolutely fine.'

Then Jason came, today in a Monsters, Inc. T-shirt, wheeling the blood-pressure machine. He fixed the machine to Daisy's arm and frowned at the display. The machine thought it was still attached to a printer, he said. I wasn't to worry if it asked me for more paper.

I sat in the armchair and wondered what to do now. My wrist was sore from stroking Daisy's head. I realised I hadn't eaten anything all morning, and I went to the hospital shop and got myself a sandwich and a magazine. I sat by Daisy's bed, but I didn't eat or read. I watched Daisy's face. Her lips were white and rough, like someone who has been acutely ill. As Annie had said, she slept for a long time.

The Afghani woman drifted in through our door, her toddler clutching at her. Her veil had silver fringes. We smiled at one another, feeling a kind of closeness although we couldn't talk together—sharing this thing, that we knew how it feels to have a child who is sick— and she touched Daisy's face with a gentle finger heavy with intricate rings.

Rain ran down the window, though you couldn't hear the sound of it. Every time the blood-pressure machine gave a reading it beeped and flashed a display that said it was out of paper. I could hear conversations from the corridor. Jason was greeting somebody. 'Hi, Carol! Not seen you for a while. Been having a career break?' A doctor who talked rather fast was getting frustrated with a parent who didn't understand. 'Now, how can I explain? What we want to do is to stop him developing. The medicine is to stop him developing so his height goes up...' Their voices seemed so far away.

I sat and watched the patterns the rain traced on the glass, and felt afraid. I kept thinking how they'd said they hadn't seen anything abnormal. And that was good, of course, that was a relief; and yet at the same time it was frightening—because what if they never discovered what was making Daisy ill? What if even here, with all their dazzling panoply of interventions, their torches that can see inside you, their drugs that make you forget, they couldn't find out what was wrong?

Around lunchtime, Daisy woke briefly.

'I dreamed I had the endoscopy,' she said. Her voice was hoarse.

'You did,' I said. 'You've had it.'

'Oh,' she said. She frowned. 'I can't have. It was a dream, Mum.'

'No, really. It's all over and done with. Isn't that great?'

She gave me a sceptical look, and went straight back to sleep.

It was late afternoon, and I'd just made myself a coffee in the kitchen down the corridor, when the consultant came. I felt flustered and awkward, not knowing how to handle this situation—whether to stand up and give him my armchair, whether to offer him coffee.

'Now, your little lady,' he said, propping himself against the end of Daisy's bed. He was wearing a faded sports jacket. He had Daisy's notes in his hand. 'As I said, her stomach and oesophagus seem fine. But the biopsies we took from her bowel do show she has a problem there. There are changes in the wall of the colon: she has inflammatory bowel disease, and there are also some of the changes you find in coeliac disease.'

'Oh,' I said. I put my coffee down, very carefully. All I felt at first was a sense of surprise.

'In this illness,' he said, 'the walls of the gut stop working properly, and become too permeable, so toxins get into the bloodstream and are carried round the body.'

He talked quite fast; I was struggling to understand.

'So—is that why she gets all these different symptoms?'

He glanced down at her notes. 'Yes,' he said, 'it would explain everything you've described.'

'You mean, the memory loss and the pains in her limbs and everything?'

'Yes,' he said. 'All those things. The treatment is a sulphur-based drug and she'll probably need to take it for quite some time—I'd suggest a year at the least…'

Something in my expression made him pause.

'Don't worry,' he said, 'these drugs have been around for ages. We know they're pretty safe.'

'It's not that,' I said. 'She finds it so hard to take medicines.'

'I'll give them to you in capsule form,' he said. 'You can split the capsule and mix the drug into her food.' He wrote me the prescription. 'You can get them from the hospital pharmacy.'

'Right.' It sounded so simple.

'Now, these problems are probably secondary to her allergies,' he said. 'The blood test showed she's a very allergic child. So you'll need to change her diet. I suggest that you exclude wheat and dairy products to start with, and if that doesn't do the trick, take her off soya as well. Allergies to soya are becoming very common—they seem to put it in everything these days. Our nutritionist will help you.'

I nodded.

'I'll see you in a month,' he said. 'D'you have anything to ask before I go?'

'Yes, I do,' I said. 'Where does the illness come from?'

He smiled. 'That's a pretty big question.'

'What I was wondering—could it be inherited?'

'Well, yes,' he said. 'There does seem to be a genetic link in this group of diseases. Has anyone in your family had a similar illness?'

'My father,' I said. 'D'you think there's a connection?'

'Very likely,' he said. He made a note in the file.

'That helps somehow,' I said. 'It makes it seem less random. I wish I'd known before...' And then, needing to explain, 'I never knew my father, you see, I only learned this recently.' I feel my skin go hot. 'I know that must seem odd, not to have known him…'

His eyes were on me; his gaze was warm, accepting.

'Whether or not you knew him,' he said, 'he's part of who you are. And what you pass on to your children.'

He closed the notes; he was about to leave.

And then I remembered what I should be saying.

'I don't know how to thank you…'

But he'd already gone.

I went straight to the pharmacy to collect Daisy's medicine. When I got back to our room, I opened the bottle. The capsules were an alarming sulphurous yellow. I pulled one apart over the basin and some of the powder fell and smeared the side of the basin with a startling yellow stain. I dipped my finger in the powder and stuck it in my mouth. It scarcely tasted of anything—just a faint musty bitterness, easily disguised. I glanced across at Daisy, the pools of shadow under her eyes, her open, strained mouth; and I saw her as she once was, flushed and vivid—as she might be again. Something inside me was singing.

I lie and stare into the sepia dark. Daisy's cards are arranged around the room, on every available surface, and here and there the light through the curtained window falls on them and glimmers. I can make out the shiny clown on Gina and Adrian's, and, on the card her class sent, the letters that spell Get Well stuck down in coloured foil. And there's one from Sinead that she drew herself with gel pen, showing a frog who's going into hospital. The frog has a suitcase and a bandage and a deliciously doleful expression. A familiar worry surges through me— worry about Sinead, and how she and Daisy will cope with living apart. For now, they're being positive: Sinead is teaching Daisy how to text her, and they're planning to talk on MSN every day, but I don't know how they'll react when it happens for real. On top of the television there's a black and white card from Fergal and Jamie, a photo of a cat looking rapaciously into a goldfish bowl, that made us smile when we opened it. The biggest glossiest one of all is from Richard. Richard for now is being guiltily helpful, striving to do all the things that a caring father should, however semi-detached his situation may seem. He hasn't told Gina yet that we're separating—I think he dreads that—and I am co-operating by keeping up the pretence that all is well when she phones, which in some weird way brings him and me a little closer, as though we have become co-conspirators. Richard brought us here, though later today, when we will need a lift home, he has a business conference, so Fergal will collect us. And on the way home, if Daisy is well enough, we're stopping at the petshop so she can choose her kitten.

Fergal's friend, the gallery owner, came to see me last week. His phone call panicked me: the house was in a muddle, Sinead was packing to go to Sara's and I was doing the washing ready for coming here. I worried what to wear, and whether he'd think my coffee cups too garish and my house too full of braid and flowered fabric. I didn't know how he'd expect me to show my pictures, so I simply spread them out on the dining-room table: the ones where the children are trapped and imprisoned in mazes of matted branches; and the latest ones, that I've done since coming back from Berlin. These are a little different. These children play, though it's like the play in nursery rhymes—sometimes grotesque or savage, and full of breakages and reversals. And there are toys and animals here: masks like the ones on our wall, and a cat playing the violin and a monkey on the drums, like my mother said she saw in that Berlin toy department. And I'm using colour again, acrylic paints with that sweet complicated smell that always makes me think of Miss Jenkins's lessons.

The gallery owner was called Mark Ewing. He had neatly pressed combats and close-cropped hair. I don't think he noticed my curtains and he didn't drink much of his coffee. He spent a long time looking at my drawings, and talking to me about what I liked to draw, and what other art I'd done, and whether I'd had any formal art education. I thought he was just softening me up, preparing me for the moment when he'd give me a thoughtful look, compassionate but pained, and say, To be honest, this isn't the kind of thing I'm interested in—but the best of luck for the future… But then he started to talk about money, about the price he would put on my drawings and whether I'd be happy with it. I couldn't believe we were having this conversation. The sums he talked about amazed me. 'I think we need to aim high,' he said. 'These are exceptional.' There was a brief moment of thrill, a rocket-burst of starry glitter that dazzled in my mind. But then the weight of doubt: I wanted to tell him—No, you're getting this wrong, these are just doodles I did, jottings from the inside of my head, you're taking them far too seriously. Honestly, I don't know what the hell I'm doing, I just sit down with a pencil and muddle through. No one will part with good money for my drawings. No one. I wanted to say all this, urgently, compulsively, but I remembered what Fergal keeps on saying, about how I do myself down, and I smiled and didn't say anything.

He talked about the catalogue. We could write something together, he said, about where your drawings come from. That all helps, he said. That would be good publicity. People like to know where you get your inspiration from; people like stories. Tell me, is there a story to go with these pictures? Yes, I told him. Yes. There is a story.

The heat has made my throat dry: I know I'll never sleep without a drink. I slip noiselessly out of bed and into the corridor. In the darkened room next door, the Afghani woman and her son are presumably still asleep. I pass the playroom, where the staff are sitting and quietly talking together; the ward notes are spread out on the table where, in the daytime, children play Monopoly. Their voices sounds significant in the night, hushed and profound, as though they are sharing a secret. They look up and smile as I pass, with a kind of intimacy, a recognition that we are the only ones who are awake here.

In the kitchen I don't need the light to see by: there's a reflected glow from the London streets in the sky. I get myself some juice and stand there for a moment, looking out at the apricot dark, thinking of all the people who are up now, like the nurses down the corridor: working, keeping things going. There's a thrill to cities at night, the way they never sleep, and the streets that are never entirely unpeopled, with all their dazzle and neon. Like on one of those postcards my mother sent from her last surprising home, showing Kurfürstendamm and Unter den Linden at night-time, with their extravagant lights and sharp dark shadows, and a wide bright sunset sky above the Reichstag.

Last week I had another letter from Berlin. But not in my mother's handwriting, so I knew what was in it before I opened it up. It was from Karl. She'd been rushed into hospital, he said; she died in her sleep, it was all very sudden. The funeral was on Thursday. If I wanted to come, he could pick me up at Tegel Airport. PS. She had told him about Daisy's illness, and he hoped she was feeling better. I wrote back straight away. I said I was sorry that I couldn't come, but I had to go into hospital with Daisy; I knew he would understand. I said that, as he probably knew, my mother and I hadn't always had a very good relationship, but I was glad I'd come to see her and that we had been reconciled. I added that I knew she was happy with him—that in many ways her life had been hard, but her years with him had been her happiest. Maybe this too, I thought as I wrote, like so much else in my life and my mother's, was a lie or an evasion, but on balance I thought there was something in it and I wanted to give him comfort.

I go back to our room. Daisy is stirring, saying something incomprehensible, with her eyes still closed. I stroke her back and she drifts down deeper into unconsciousness.

I get into bed and don't expect to sleep. I lie there a while, staring at the light reflecting on the ceiling. But the noise through the window soothes me, like the massive breathing of some great resting animal, and I go to sleep and dream.

This is the dream.

It's winter, in a wide white empty landscape, like a scene from a Russian epic. There are no people here or roads or houses, and it's high and far and bitter in the cold. The shadows lengthen and snow lies over everything, and yet more snow is falling on the wind. A woman walks alone through the empty land. Her head is bent against the driving sleet. And in the dream I see this is my mother. She's wearing a flimsy coat and lots of gilded bracelets and her gloves are pastel cotton with ruched wrists, and her boots have high slender heels, so she stumbles in the snowdrifts. I think how typical this is—that she goes on even this unguessable journey in such unsuitable shoes. Night presses in; the cold light thickens so she can scarcely see. She moves on through the bitter drizzle of sleet: there's somewhere she has to get to. The journey is long but she just keeps walking, one foot in front of the other.

At last she comes to a house set deep in a shadowed valley. The house is tall, substantial, built of stone, but looking shut-up, empty; nails have been driven into the shutters to seal them against the storm. In the dream I seem to feel her dread. It's a place to make you afraid, a place of desolation. She puts out a hand and pushes against the door. And it yields to her touch and she steps inside and it's not as she expected: she sees what she could not see from the other side of the door. For there is light and warmth here, the lamps are lit, a stove glows on the hearth, heat wraps itself around her. Someone was here before her; she is expected, welcomed. A pot of food is simmering on the hob; a good smell wafts towards her. The door in the front of the stove has been pulled open, to let the air flow in. Inside there's a red blaze of coals. She takes off her sodden gloves and flings them to the floor. The snowflakes melt, run off them. She kneels on the floor in front of the stove and holds out her hands to the blaze.

Read all about it...

MORE ABOUT THIS BOOK

MORE ABOUT THE AUTHOR

WE RECOMMEND

MIRA

Read all about it...

QUESTIONS FOR YOUR READING GROUP

1   How have Catriona's childhood experiences shaped the person she is now?

2   Did your attitude to Catriona change through the book? Were you suspicious of her?

3   How did you react to Catriona's own mother? Did you find it as hard to forgive her as Catriona does?

4   What was it about Richard that so attracted Catriona to him? What do you think would have happened to their relationship if Daisy hadn't been ill?

5   Catriona takes Daisy to a succession of doctors and these encounters invariably go wrong. How far is this Catriona's fault? Should she have behaved differently?

6   What does Catriona's art, and the way it changes in the course of the story, reveal about her?

7   Why is her time working at the nursery school so important to Catriona?

8   Do you think Catriona is wise to attempt to conceal her past from Jane Watson, the psychiatrist? What would you have done in her position?

9   How is Catriona affected by seeing her mother again? How far does this meeting free Catriona from her past?

Read all about it...

"...What if the doctor had accused me of actually making my daughter ill?..."

INSPIRATION

The story began when we took our daughter to our local hospital. She'd been ill for weeks – nauseous, not eating, sometimes unable to remember the words for things. The doctor took the history and then sent her to play in the waiting-room. "Is there anything else you want to tell me?" he said. I could sense what he wanted – for me to say that our marriage was in trouble or that she was being bullied. I said, "Really, there's nothing – I don't think it's psychological." "I think it is," he said. I protested. He said there were things that worried him – that I'd spoken for my daughter and sometimes I'd interrupted him. I felt a surge of rage. He remarked that I seemed to be getting angry and that just made him more sure he was right.

Months later, after our daughter's illness had been diagnosed and treated at Great Ormond Street Hospital, I thought back to that consultation. What if the doctor had gone one step further and accused me of actually making my daughter ill? I imagined how trapped you would feel, because everything you did could be seen as proof of your guilt. And what if this happened to a woman who had a dark, complicated past, a past she was desperate to keep hidden because it might be taken as further evidence against her? What if even those close to her started to suspect her? I knew this was a story I wanted to tell.

But a novel only really takes shape for me when I have the right setting for it. And one day I passed a house that I loved. It had seven steps up to the front door and stone dogs guarding the steps. I couldn't see round the back of the house, but I conjured up a little enclosed garden, with a rose bed and children playing on the lawn. Then I thought of the foxes that haunt these London gardens, scavenging in dustbins and generally behaving as though these ordered lawns and flowerbeds were theirs. This house and its garden with its flowers and wild foxes seemed perfect for the woman in my story.

A CLOSER LOOK AT MÜNCHAUSEN'S SYNDROME BY PROXY

Münchausen's Syndrome by Proxy is a diagnosis that covers a range of parental behaviour, from exaggerating or inventing symptoms, to falsifying the results of tests, to poisoning or otherwise injuring a child in order to induce illness. It was first described by paediatrician Roy Meadow. It's a highly controversial diagnosis and has been associated with some serious miscarriages of justice, where women have had their children taken away or have themselves been imprisoned after wrongfully being found guilty of harming or killing their children.

More information...

BBC News
http://news.bbc.co.uk/1/hi/health/medical_notes/3528517.stm

Mothers Against Münchausen Allegations:
www.msbp.com

Further reading about Münchausen's Syndrome by Proxy...

Hurting for Love by Herbert A Schreier and Judith A Libow

Trust Betrayed? edited Jan Horwath and Brian Lawson

Read all about it...

Read all about it...

AUTHOR BIOGRAPHY

© Nikki Gibbs

Margaret Leroy grew up in the New Forest and studied music at St Hilda's College, Oxford. She has worked as a music therapist, teacher and psychiatric social worker.

Her first book, *Miscarriage*, was published in 1987 and *Aristotle Sludge*, a story for children, was published in 1991. She then wrote two books about women and relationships – *Pleasure: The truth about female sexuality* and *Some Girls Do: Why women do and don't make the first move*. Both were serialised in the *Daily Express*.

For two years she wrote an agony aunt column for *Options* magazine and her articles and short stories have been published in the *Observer*, the *Sunday Express* and the *Mail on Sunday*.

Shas has writtien four novels. The first, *Trust*, was televised by ITV1 as *Loving You* and starred Douglas Henshall and Niamh Cusack, reaching an audience of eight million. She has appeared on numerous radio and TV programmes and her books have been translated into ten languages. Margaret is married, has two daughters and lives in Surrey.

Read all about it…

"…the moment
your baby falls
asleep, you
start writing…"

WHY I WRITE…

I wrote constantly as a child – rather fey
fantasies. But I was also into music and, from
about age twelve, my piano-playing became
all-consuming and I stopped writing till I was in
my early twenties. I started writing again when
I was studying Music Therapy. A session with
an autistic boy went badly wrong and I went
home, disconsolate, and started writing poems
to comfort myself. After that, I never stopped
writing again – though I never wrote any more
poems. But I only gave up my day job as a
psychiatric social worker after the birth of our
younger daughter. I found that writing while
looking after small children is difficult, but
not impossible, though you do have to be very
focused, so that the moment your baby falls
asleep, you start writing. That's a great discipline
– and perhaps the reason why women who
write while bringing up children never seem to
get writer's block.

"...the seed of a story can come from anywhere..."

Q&A ON WRITING

What do you love the most about being a writer?

The most pleasurable part comes some way into writing a book, when I've created a world that I can then re-enter every time I sit down to write – when I know what that world looks like, sounds like, smells like.

Where do you go for inspiration?

The seed of a story can come from anywhere – a news report, a television programme, something that happened to someone I know, something that happened to me. A sense of the place where the story is set will come very early in the process, often when the characters are still quite unformed, as happened with *The Perfect Mother*: once I saw a house that seemed exactly right for my heroine, the world of the story immediately felt more real.

What one piece of advice would you give to a writer wanting to start a career?

Keep notebooks. Make a note of anything that interests you – even a scrap of overheard conversation. That way you'll have a rich source of material to dip into again and again.

Which book do you wish you had written?

I'd love to have written Ursula Le Guin's Earthsea saga. Her sentences are so beautiful and it must be wonderful to create a whole new world and its landscapes, myths and magical creatures.

How did you feel when your first book was signed?

Thrilled and rather scared. Scared because I sold it on the basis of the outline – it was a self-help book, on miscarriage – and I still had to write the book!

Where do your characters come from and do they ever surprise you as you write?

I build my characters as I build my story and a particular story will seem to require a particular character. Catriona's life-story is in a way a fairytale – a rags to riches tale – as she moves from a wretched childhood with a neglectful mother to a fortunate adult life with the house and garden and children she has always dreamt of. But as in all fairytales there's a cost to achieving her heart's desire. Her world is actually quite fragile and that's in part because of the kind of person she is.

"... I'll build my main characters as I build my story..."

Do you have a favourite character that you've created and what is it you like about that character?

Aimee, Cat's friend in the children's home, is one of my favourite characters – even though she only appears quite briefly. She's rather wild and always full of hope and I love the way she fights against the limitations of her life and absolutely will not be kept down. I felt she wanted to come back, which is why at a crucial point in the story she reappears in Cat's dream.

What kind of research goes into the writing process?

To write Cat's story, I used my past experience as a social worker and I also read a lot of books – most memorably, the report of the inquiry into Pindown, a cruel method of disciplining children which was used in children's homes in Staffordshire in the 1980s. It's very disturbing to read. And I spent a magical couple of days in Berlin, wandering the streets of what used to be the East, choosing settings for my story.

Read all about it...

As a mother, how much has your own experience shaped your writing about parenthood?

Being a mother has shaped my writing tremendously – and especially so in this book. This is probably the most autobiographical of my novels – though Cat isn't me and Daisy isn't my daughter! And I also drew on my time working at a nursery school very like the one where Cat is employed. It was an enchanting place and I loved the idea of Cat spending time in that garden of children and in some way recovering her lost childhood.

"...being a mother has shaped my writing tremendously..."

A WRITER'S LIFE

Paper and pen or straight onto the computer?

I'm a very low-tech person – I use unlined paper and pencil. I don't like working directly onto the keyboard as I need to see my crossings-out.

PC or laptop?

Laptop.

Music or silence?

I crave silence when I'm writing. I hate hammers and electric drills, and I love my noise-reduction headphones.

Morning or night?

I'm absolutely a morning person. I keep the less creative stuff like typing for the afternoon.

"...I keep the less creative stuff... for the afternoon..."

Coffee or tea?

Very strong coffee in little green French-café cups.

Your guilty reading pleasure?

Re-reading *The Lord of the Rings*. It makes me feel guilty because I've read it so often I practically know it by heart.

The first book you loved?

Shadow the Sheepdog by Enid Blyton.

The last book you read?

The Other Hand by Chris Cleave.

A DAY IN THE LIFE

We live on the edge of town, near the Thames, and sometimes I'm woken by the lovely wild sound of geese flying over. I'm a great believer in breakfast – it's usually bacon and egg. Then I drive my younger daughter, Izzie, to school. My beloved Ford Escort is twenty years old now and I'm always listening out for new and ominous rattles. The traffic is horrible and I arrive back home with a slight sense of triumph that we've survived another rush hour.

I write in bed – which, I'm convinced, is good for creativity, because you're so much more relaxed than when you sit at a desk. Typically I'll be surrounded by a sprawl of paper. I don't mind a bit of untidiness around me – if things look too neat, it means there's nothing going on. My filing system is a pot of coloured paper-clips.

"…I write in bed – which, I'm convinced, is good for creativity…"

What form the writing takes will depend on the stage of the book that I've reached. I start with lots of brainstorming, then I'll put together quite a detailed plot: I can't just head off into my story without knowing where I'm going. Once I've sketched out the plot, I try to get the whole story down very quickly, scarcely looking back at all. Then I'll go through it lots of times, rewriting and developing. This is much the longest stage of writing a book for me and the part I really love. How well I work varies hugely and I try to have simpler tasks like research or typing lined up for those days when the writing doesn't flow. But if it's going well, I'm completely happy.

Lunch is fried rice and vegetables. I always cook the same thing: I'm hopeless at cooking, but my husband, thank goodness, is a brilliant cook, so we don't starve. While I eat, I read, something I can just dip into, maybe poetry; at the moment it might be Lavinia Greenlaw or Alice Oswald. Any work done after lunch is a bonus, and – perhaps because it's marked the end of my working day for so long – I tend to switch off around the time that school ends, even when no-one needs picking up.

At the end of the afternoon, I see to the practical stuff – shopping, e-mails, housework. Fortunately I'm short-sighted so I don't notice cobwebs. My inspiration for the practical side of life comes from J.K. Rowling, who was once asked how she managed to write while bringing up her daughter single-handed and said she just didn't do any housework for four years. My husband makes our evening meal and afterwards I'll probably watch television: after all that writing, I'm hungry for im-ages. I love television and there have been so many marvellously addictive series in the past few years – *Prison Break, Invasion, The Wire.* Recently Izzie and I have had a blissful time watching all seven seasons of *Buffy the Vampire Slayer.*

" ... My inspiration for the practical side of life comes from J.K. Rowling... "

MY TOP TEN BOOKS

A Wizard of Earthsea by Ursula Le Guin
I always go back to the Earthsea books when life gets difficult, there's something so healing about the slow, intricate rhythms of Ursula Le Guin's prose.

The Siege by Helen Dunmore
The siege of Leningrad, told from a female, domestic perspective. You really live this story when you read it – you feel the hunger and the cold.

The Mabinogion
Dream-like Welsh stories, written down in the Middle Ages, and full of strange transformations. I love the story of Blodeuedd, a beautiful girl who is conjured up from the flowers of the oak and the broom and the meadowsweet.

The English Patient by Michael Ondaatje
It's about a small group of people thrown together by war, worn down, somehow surviving. Ondaatje writes so lyrically about the desert and Renaissance angels and Tuscan gardens under rain.

The Pillow Book of Sei Shonagon
Musings and jottings and lots of lists from a court lady in tenth-century Japan. Her writing is intimate, sensuous and somehow very contemporary.

Rebecca by Daphne du Maurier
An iconic psychological thriller. I've read it lots of times, but at certain twists in the plot, my heart still goes racing off.

Housekeeping by Marilynne Robinson
It's the simplest story, about two girls and their elusive aunt, who reluctantly abandons her life as a drifter to bring them up. Perhaps the most wonderfully written book I've ever read.

Read all about it...

The Bloody Chamber by Angela Carter
Adult fairy tales – sexy, savage and gorgeous.

Jonathan Strange and Mr Norrell
by Susanna Clarke
This story of two wizards during the Napoleonic
Wars is my favourite new book of recent years. When
I got to the end – p. 782 – I went straight back to
the beginning and read it all again.

The Mahabharata by Jean-Claude Carrière
The script of the film directed by Peter Brook, based
on stories from the Indian epic. It's bloody but very
beautiful. As one of the characters says as he starts to
tell the story, "If you listen carefully, at the end you'll
be someone else."

Read all about it...

If you enjoyed *The Perfect Mother,* we know you'll love....

The No.1 Bestseller

MARGARET LEROY

The Drowning Girl

What if there was something deeply wrong with your child – and nobody believed you?

"She's my daughter, but in some weird way I feel she isn't really my child."

Young single mum Grace is drowning. Her little girl Sylvie is distant, troubled and prone to violent tantrums which the child psychiatrists blame on Grace. But Grace knows there's something more to what's happening to Sylvie. There has to be.

"This is a really special book. Sylvie's vulnerability is so powerfully drawn, so flesh-and-blood real, that you want to reach into the pages and protect her yourself."
—Louise Candlish

"One of those rare books you'll sit with till your bones ache."
—*Oprah Magazine*

Read all about it...

If you enjoyed *The Perfect Mother*, we know you'll love...

Coming in April 2010, the *New York Times* Top Five bestseller

The Weight of Silence by Heather Gudenkauf

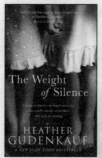

Callie is a gentle little girl who suffers from selective mutism, brought on by a tragedy she experienced as a toddler. Petra is Calli's best friend, her soul mate and her voice. When Calli and Petra disappear their families are bound by the mystery of what happened to their children. As support turns to suspicion, could the answers lie trapped in the silence of unspoken secrets?

The Bay at Midnight by Diane Chamberlain

Her family's cottage was a place of innocence for Julie Bauer – until her sister was murdered. It's been many years since that August night, but Julie's memories of Izzy's death still haunt her. Now someone from her past is asking questions about what really happened. About Julie's own complicity. About a devastating secret her mother kept from them all. About the person who went to prison for Izzy's murder – and the person who didn't.

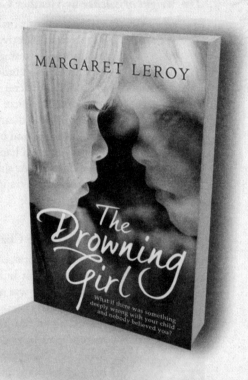